# THREADS
# THAT BIND

# THREADS
# THAT BIND

KIKA HATZOPOULOU

RAZORBILL

# RAZORBILL

An imprint of Penguin Random House LLC, New York

First published in the United States of America by Razorbill,
an imprint of Penguin Random House LLC, 2023

Copyright © 2023 by Kika Hatzopoulou

Visit us online at PenguinRandomHouse.com.

LIBRARY OF CONGRESS CATALOGING-IN-PUBLICATION DATA
Names: Hatzopoulou, Kika, author.
Title: Threads that bind / Kika Hatzopoulou.
Description: New York : Razorbill, 2023. | Audience: Ages 14 years and up. |
Summary: In a world where the children of the gods inherit their powers,
Io, a descendant of the Greek Fates, must solve a series of impossible murders
to save her sisters, her soulmate, and her city.
Identifiers: LCCN 2022051339 (print) | LCCN 2022051340 (ebook) |
ISBN 9780593528716 (hardcover) | ISBN 9780593528723 (epub)
Subjects: CYAC: Gods, Greek Fiction. | Private investigators—Fiction. |
Murder—Fiction. | Sisters—Fiction. | Fantasy. | Mystery and detective stories. |
LCGFT: Fantasy fiction. | Detective and mystery fiction.
Classification: LCC PZ7.I.H3865 Th 2023 (print) | LCC PZ7.I.H3865 (ebook) |
DDC [Fic]—dc23
LC record available at https://lccn.loc.gov/2022051339
LC ebook record available at https://lccn.loc.gov/2022051340

Printed in the United States of America

ISBN 9780593528716 (hardcover)

10 9 8 7 6 5 4 3 2 1

ISBN 9780593696064 (international edition)

10 9 8 7 6 5 4 3 2 1

BVG

Design by Alex Campbell | Text set in Centaur MT Pro

TO GEORGE AND MY FAMILY,
OURS ARE THE THREADS THAT BIND

## PART I

# ONE TO WEAVE

# SNAP

**THE STREETCAR SLICED** ahead inches above the tidewater. As it came to a stop before the station, the cables groaned with the weight of the overpacked carriage. Passengers twisted their heads to glower up at them. Just the other day, a cable had snapped over at Sage Street, emptying passengers into the malformed canal. Three had ended up in the hospital; the bay water was cruelly cold, even this close to summer.

The old lady in the back of the streetcar twirled her liver-spotted fingers over her chest, as if tying an invisible knot. She wasn't moira-born, held no true substance between her fingers but air. It was a common gesture, meant to ward off the youngest sister of the Moirae, the goddess of Fate who decides when a life-thread is to be cut.

*Knot it once,* the saying went, *and she will know you're still fighting.*

In the Silts, people added a second verse: *Knot it a thousand times, and she will still cut it.*

The old lady wasn't from the Silts. She wore a fur-lined coat, pristine and unpatched, and her gray hair was styled in upper-class fashion, braided and pinned at her nape. But her hairpins were missing the jade stones that should have decorated them, dull bronze shells left in their absence.

The cables squealed in farewell when the streetcar took off. The old lady waited for the passengers to clear the station, then started over the bridge, tugging a shopping cart behind her, its wheels echoing piercingly over every dent on the bridge. The streets were empty, yet she glanced at every shifting shadow and fleeting sound.

Her husband, who'd been twenty years older and enjoyed frightening his guileless wife, had told her something foul swam the flooded streets of the city of Alante at night. It hid in girls' shadows, he taunted, curled around their ankles, and never, ever let go. The woman had buried him a long time ago. She rarely thought about him nowadays but had begun to think of the foul monster daily. She could swear she felt it. A shackle around her ankle, dragging behind her.

How she wished to be moira-born, to feel the threads of life solid and whole in her fingers. She quickened her step, eager to be safe at home: nestled in blankets on her armchair, spirit-laced tea in hand, the latest episode of her favorite drama playing on the radio.

It must have already started; when she slipped into her apartment, she went straight for the radio, filling the room with the familiar voices of the cast, then began putting away her meager groceries—chamomile tea, a packet of cheese crackers, and a discounted jar of dried figs—when she suddenly sensed the impress of a body moving through air.

A hand clasped her mouth. The jar slipped from her fingers, clattering to the floor. She struggled to get free, kicking, elbowing, scratching blindly at her assailant. Her bun came undone, white wisps of hair floating across her vision, the heels of her boots became sticky with crushed figs. On the other side of the wall, a neighbor called her name in concern.

"Don't worry," they whispered in her ear—she couldn't tell if it was a person or a shadow-shrouded monster—"this is not the end."

If the woman had gotten her wish, if she had been moira-born, she would have felt them plucking her life-thread from the tangle of her other threads. She'd have watched them trace her life-thread up, where it stretched toward the ceiling, disappearing into the sky above. She'd have seen them take one of their own threads, stretching it between two fingers, silver and sharp as steel.

But the woman only heard:

*SNAP!*

And the thread was cut.

# CHAPTER 1

# FRAYING

IO STOOD AT the edge of the roof, trying to convince herself to take the first step.

She had explained it a thousand times: it wasn't heights she was afraid of, but rather . . . edges. She had no problem riding the trolley, she could tap-dance across terraces, but she would have to halt, take a few deep breaths, and mentally coax herself in order to cross a hanging bridge.

"Little idiot," her sister Thais would say when Io was younger. "You're moira-born. You can see the threads of Fate. Do you see your life-thread fraying anytime soon?"

Sharing a knowing look, Thais and their other sister, Ava, would then tackle Io to the ground. All three of them wrestled, limbs tangled and grins feral, until Io admitted defeat. Ava would draw Io's life-thread out and give it a couple of tugs. It stretched like a chain of silver, and shone just as bright.

"Look at that," Thais would chide. "Strong as ever."

"She likes being afraid," Ava would chuckle. "So that she has a reason to do nothing."

And young Io would whine every time, "I do *not!*"

How she hated to whine. It was their fault: they treated her like a child, so like a child she behaved. The girls' parents, before their deaths, had worked at the Neraida Plains out of the city, leaving their daughters to care for themselves from a young age. Thais, the oldest, took on the role of warden, cleaning and cooking and managing their money, while Ava, two years younger, busied herself with fun, inventing games to occupy their time and reading people's fortunes for a little extra cash. And so Io, the youngest, born six years after Ava, became the baby, looked after and teased. *One soul split in three bodies*, they whispered conspiratorially, heads huddled together in their shared bed.

Of course, that was years ago. Before Thais left town, before everything changed.

Io stepped carefully onto the bridge. It bounced under her weight, groaning with every step. Not really designed for humans, this bridge. It was a long, thin strip of metal built specifically for cats, to allow them a way to roam the city during the flooded high tides—the city's master plan to curb the growing population of rodents that carried diseases through the streets.

The problem with these cat bridges was that they had no railings. *Cats don't lose their balance*, the city officials declared. But that wasn't true; cats could slip and fall like any other creature—they just tended to land on their feet. Io thought the whole thing was counterintuitive; there was nothing to land on under the bridges, only murky tidewater, which, as already established, cats hate.

There should have been railings. There weren't. A statement that pretty much summed up the Sunken City of Alante, in Io's opinion. Needs were never met. People demanded, were denied, and learned to make do with what they had.

Io had no railings, but she had fear, lots of it. She wrapped it around her, clutched tight like a shield. Here's what her sisters never grasped: fear didn't numb you. It made you cautious, alert. Io was always, *always* alert. That was why she excelled at this job. She walked, with small, methodical steps, across the bridge, puffing her cheeks out in relief when she stood on solid ground again.

The roof hatch of the abandoned theater had been boarded up haphazardly; Io slipped through with ease. Mold and rot hit her nostrils as she followed the stairs down, a hand on the wall to guide her through the heavy darkness. Moonlight silvered the grand hall. The planks of the stage were bloated with humidity, and the rest of the theater, all two thousand seats, was completely submerged in water, leaving only dark impressions. She pulled her scarf over her nose and made her way around the gallery to the theater balconies, veering toward the middle one, which had collapsed years ago, bringing the wall down with it.

It was an ugly sight: wood and wires and cement hanging like the entrails of a gutted beast. But the view beyond it was nice. The ripped-out balcony of the Beak Street Theater was one of the few places in the Silts where you had an unobstructed view of all three moons. Pandia, the biggest and brightest; Nemea, traveling the bottom of the horizon; and Ersa, which rose and set in a matter of hours. Only Ersa was up now, bathing the world in her milky pink light. The dew-covered wallpaper glazed rosy, the water on the streets a soft cherry. It made the city, flooded to the brim with the night tide, almost beautiful. One day, Io would save enough for a camera and immortalize the otherworldly sight.

In the apartment building across from the theater, the light in the far-left window of the third floor flickered on. Io tore her gaze away from the moon and put her spectacles on. Sure enough, it was the very apartment she had been hired to watch. A figure moved inside— maybe two? She slid down and grounded her palms on the splintered wood of the balcony. *Before you slip into the Quilt, make sure you're safe,* Thais used to instruct. *We don't want you walking off a rooftop, do we?*

Io blinked and the Quilt appeared, a jumble of threads laid over the physical world. Only moira-born, descendants of the goddesses of Fate, could see the lines of silver that sprouted from every person, connecting them to the things they loved most in the world. Io focused on the apartment on the third floor. In the Quilt, she saw beyond brick and wood, straight to the two people in the apartment. Dozens of threads emerged from their bodies, linking them to the many different places, things, and people they loved. One of the brightest threads connected the two figures together, pulsing vividly, the kind of luster that consumed everything. *The singular brilliance of a love-thread*, in Ava's moonstruck words.

The singular tedium of a pain in the neck, more likely. A sigh escaped Io's lips. Why was it always cheating? Why couldn't it be a weird hobby or a late-night class for once, something that wouldn't crush her clients' souls? Io could picture it clearly: tomorrow, her client, Isidora Magnussen, would sit at the table farthest back in the café on Sage Street, her coat wrung like a dish towel in her hands, and Io would have to tell her, *Yes, your husband did go to the apartment he supposedly sold three weeks ago. Yes, he had company.* Then the hardest part would come: *Does he love her?* Any other private detective could shrug and say, *How would I know?*

But Io was different. Io was moira-born. It was why clients chose her; they didn't just want to know if their loved ones were cheating or gambling or drinking. They wanted to know the secrets that only the Quilt could reveal: if their spouses loved cheating and gambling and drinking more than they loved *them.*

And Io would have to tell her. *I'm sorry, Mrs. Magnussen. Their thread is so bright I couldn't stand to look at it for more than two seconds. It means your husband's in love with his mistress. It means I want to slip through a hole in the café floor and never come out.* That was what put a roof over Io's head and food on the plate: breaking people's hearts.

She watched the two figures a while longer, just to be sure. She made out no bodies in the Quilt, only the threads, but there was no mistaking it: the couple came together, silver interweaving in a slow embrace. Io's cheeks heated—she glanced away.

Something caught her attention. Close to the couple, on the third floor of the apartment building. It was a person, but also . . . not.

The un-person had only one thread. People loved in multitudes; they got attached to others, to places, to objects, to ideas. The average person's thread count was fifteen. Newborn infants had the fewest: their life-thread, a thread to their mother, and a thread to food—the last two usually one and the same. This person, however, standing in what must be the apartment building hallway, had a single thread. On its own, that was improbable, but not impossible.

What was impossible was that the thread was severed. It came out of the person's chest on one end, and the other just flopped limp to the floor, where it frayed into nothing. Threads *connected*—there was no such thing as a one-ended thread.

And worst of all, the severed thread was tilted at an unnatural angle, like the person was gripping it in both fists. Stretched tight and sharp, as though meant to cut someone else's threads. This single-threaded person, this impossibility, was a cutter. Io knew, because Io was a cutter, too.

The cutter was edging toward the lovers' apartment, their lone thread a raised weapon. Io's shoulders tensed. Her breath caught in her lungs.

*Little idiot*, her sister berated in Io's mind.

She breathed out and ran.

The apartment door had been left ajar.

Her heart pounded against her chest as she stepped inside. There was a long corridor with three open doors, all sheltering darkness. Io had dropped the Quilt to focus on getting to the building, but now she pulled it back up. In the second room down the corridor: the cutter and their single thread, gripped between their hands. A separate bundle of threads cowering in the corner.

Io could taste her terror in her mouth, sharp and sour. Her steps felt slow and lagging, as though she were underwater. Her fingers snatched up one of her own threads—it didn't matter which right now—and wrapped it around her index finger and thumb. Only a thread could cut another thread. If this person was armed, Io would be, too.

The apartment was carpeted, muffling the sounds of her footfalls. A mirror hung in the hallway with a narrow table beneath, full of little bottles of cosmetics. In the reflection, a woman stood in the middle of the living room, gray hair coming undone from a braided bun at her nape, waist jutting forward unnaturally. Her single thread tumbled from her fingers to the floor, its frayed end curling around her ankle like a pet snake.

Io couldn't comprehend what she was seeing. Up close, this thread had the brilliant luster of a life-thread, the most important of a person's threads, a connection to life itself. Normally, life-threads shot up into the sky, disappearing among the clouds. But this one flopped on the floor, unconnected, monstrous in its wrongness.

This woman should be dead.

Io noticed the body on the floor. She recognized him instantly—Mrs. Magnussen had shown her their wedding photos. He wore nothing but a pair of striped boxers, his neck bent unnaturally. Ersa painted his naked flesh in a lively pink, but it was a lie. No threads in the Quilt. The body was a corpse. Rattling breaths drew her attention farther into the room, where a woman in lingerie was hiding behind an armchair, sobbing quietly into her knees. It took Io a moment to place that white-blond hair: Mr. Magnussen's assistant. She had spotted them together this morning, having a smoke in the street outside their office. At the time, it had looked like innocent chitchat. Now it was evident she was his secret paramour.

The old woman with the abnormal thread stood still as a statue, surveying the room over her nose. In Ersa's moonlight, her silver hair seemed dipped in rosebuds. Io should go. She should backtrack to the front door, scream the whole building awake, find some way to get the old woman away from the assistant.

*Move*, she begged herself. She drew in a deep breath.

In the silence, her sharp inhale was a gunshot. The woman slanted her neck; their eyes locked in the mirror.

"There are crimes," the old woman said, removed as if in a trance, "that cannot go unpunished. I will rise from the ashes a daughter of flame."

And before Io could react, the old woman rushed at her, a whirlwind of white hair and sharp bones. Their bodies collided; Io fell on her back. The woman was on her, thrashing with no thought or reason, scratching at Io's face and chest. Io put her arms up and tried to kick the woman off her, striking the wall instead.

At the loud sound, the old woman stopped altogether and gazed down at Io. Or rather, at the thread between Io's thumb and index finger. "What a pretty thread. Little moira-born," she rasped. "I see you. I see your crimes, too."

Io had a second to think—*What crimes?*

To shudder—*Which crimes?*

To panic—*I have committed so many.*

Then the old woman was hammering her again with jagged fingernails. Pain stung Io's cheek and neck, jolting her out of her shock. She grabbed the first thing she saw, the woman's hair, and pulled. With a fiendish scream, the woman dropped away. In seconds, Io was up, running toward the open door. The woman launched after Io, bumping into the walls.

"Hide!" Io screamed over her shoulder at the crying assistant, hoping she would obey.

The moment she crossed the door, Io started shouting for help, glancing back at the maniacal creature coming after her. It *moved* like a creature, scurrying on all fours and lashing out with crooked fingers. And the thread, that terrible limp life-thread, was still in her hand, a weapon ready to strike.

"Help me, dammit," Io screamed, battering both fists on a door.

The knock cost her; in a flash, the woman had caught up. Her fingers latched on to Io's trouser leg. Io went down with a thud, landing hard on her palms and knees. She twisted and saw, in terror, that one of her threads was in the woman's right hand.

And then a door burst open, spilling light into the hall. A tall, dark-skinned man screamed at them in a foreign language—Kurkz?

The old woman over Io paused.

That was all Io needed. A pause. A moment. A breath.

She pulled her knee in and kicked the woman's jaw, hard. The creature flew back in an arc. Io scrambled away, putting distance between her and those insidious fingers. She straightened when her back hit the wall at the end of the corridor, cool air coming through the tall open window behind her.

Other residents emerged from their apartments. The Kurkz man was marching toward them. Io wanted to motion him to stay away, to call for help, but why wasn't her voice working—

Suddenly, the woman filled Io's sight, lunging for her, the severed life-thread a rope of silver in her left fist. Close, so close that Io felt wisps of hair on her face just before she stepped aside from the open window. The woman noticed it too late; she tried to stop, but momentum shoved her forward. Her legs smacked on the window ledge, her waist pitched forward, and she tipped, head over heels, out the window.

There was a distant splash as she hit the tidewater flooding the streets. Io's breath became shallow, as though her lungs were constricted to half their size. Her hands were numb, one holding the window frame, the other closed around the random thread of her own that she had grabbed to protect herself.

She didn't move when the Kurkz man shook her shoulders, when he leaned out the window and announced the woman was gone. She stood there, wheezing, and slowly, very slowly, the world came back into focus: the people emerging from their apartments, their robes and socks, their tousled hair, their languages.

She was still in the same spot, back to the wall, fists clenched, when she felt a vibration in her chest. One of her threads was pulsating; had the old woman harmed it? Io's body tensed, bubbling with panic—she had no energy left for another fight.

The thread stretched taut, leading straight down the corridor, into the chest of the young man who had just come running up the stairs. Broad shouldered and brown skinned, with brass knuckles on his right fist. He glanced the other way, then this way, and saw her. Io got the sense he recognized her, his eyebrows dipping low over his dark eyes.

"Where'd she go?" he asked.

Io jerked her chin out the window. He turned and left, taking her thread with him. Io had never seen him before, but she knew who he was all the same.

Her fate-thread.

The boy she was destined to love.

# CHAPTER II

# A WRAITH

**SOFT SNIFFLING SOUNDS** were coming from the apartment bathroom. Io leaned her forehead against the door, trying to cast out any thoughts about her fate-thread and the boy on the other end of it—now was *not* the time. She knocked once, softly.

"You can come out now," she said against the wood. "She's gone."

The lock screeched, the door inching open. The assistant's eyes were two wide circles of fear in the shadows of the room, framed by thin eyebrows and hair so blond it was almost white. Nina Panagou, Io remembered from her research, aged twenty-seven, Mr. Magnussen's assistant for the past eight years. Nina was slumped against the tiled wall, her cheeks streaked with makeup, the long shard of a mirror in her fist. Clever of her; she had smashed the sink mirror to create a makeshift weapon.

Io sat on her haunches at the doorframe, eye level with the woman. "Are you all right?"

"Is Jarl—" Nina's gaze flicked left, where the living room lay.

Io's jaw tightened. Certified deliverer of bad news, professional breaker of hearts. "I'm so sorry."

The woman's eyes watered, her voice growing high and nasal. "She just burst in, out of nowhere. Jarl told me to hide, and I . . ." She trailed off.

"Did you recognize her?" Io asked quietly. "Is she someone you or Jarl might know?"

Nina was shaking her head. "I didn't, but she kept talking like she knew Jarl. She kept saying that she could see crimes on him. That crimes demand punishment. What does that even mean?"

"I'm not sure," Io whispered. "Did she say the same thing to you?"

"No. She saw me, where I was hiding behind the armchair, but she said only, *I cannot punish you, child. Your crimes are not truly yours.* Then her attention turned on Jarl. Gods, *Jarl.*" The woman's shoulders rattled with sobs, head dropping into her palms. "She was standing across the room, but she was choking him. I'm not sure how—"

Guilt shot through Io's mind. She had little to offer the woman in terms of explanations. A secret rendezvous that had transformed into her beloved's death at the hands of a terrifying old woman. But Nina hadn't been a target—she had just been in the wrong place at the wrong time. Io's own body was still electrified with terror. She couldn't even begin to imagine what this woman must be going through right now.

"The police will be here soon," she told the woman. "Are you going to be all right with them? I can get you out before they arrive."

In the eyes of the police, there were few innocents in the Silts. All of them had taken up work for the gangs at one point or another, even if it was just bussing tables at their clubs or mopping the floors of their gambling dens. For people like Io and Nina, it was honest work, the kind that harmed no one and put food on the table. For the police, however, it was as good as a conviction. They would not treat you kindly, even if you had just witnessed your lover's murder and survived a rampaging killer.

"No, but please." The woman reached out, lacquered nails clipping around Io's wrist. Her skin was pinpricked all down her arm; she must be freezing. Io needed to fetch her clothes from the living room, perhaps also find a sheet to cover Jarl Magnussen's body.

She cupped Nina's hand with her own. "Don't worry. I'm not going anywhere. I'll be right here."

The officers called to the scene took everyone's deposition, sent Nina home with the backup, alerted the boat patrols to search the Silts for the old woman, then insisted on escorting Io home.

The building Io and Ava lived in used to be a tobacco factory; the officers wrinkled their noses against the lingering pungency while Io unlocked the door. It hit the chain and bounced back. Io knocked until Ava opened the door, her hair tousled, her eyes bloodshot. Whatever quip was firing up on Ava's smirking lips sputtered out when she saw the policemen over Io's shoulder.

They said they wanted to see Io's file on Isidora Magnussen's case, but Io knew better. They wanted to check her out. She was a cutter—that fact alone made her a possible threat. She could have ditched the whole scene before the police arrived, but what was the point? There were eyewitnesses who had seen her face. All the officers had to do was scour the public registry for the moira-born in the city and there her address would be. No privacy for other-born, thanks to the Kinship Treaty. Plus, she had wanted to make sure Nina would be taken care of.

Io sidestepped her sister and began shuffling through the desk beneath her lofted bed. Two long minutes passed, during which she was excruciatingly aware of the two officers studying their apartment, until she found the damn file and handed it over.

"Are you a moira-born, too?" the male officer asked Ava, his gaze inspecting every inch of their apartment.

"Uh-huh." Her sister was leaning against their kitchen island, green satin robe revealing long, curvy legs. She challenged him with a raised brow. "Need to see my papers, too?"

Part certificate of birth, part medical records, part court-evaluated mental health status, and almost entirely badge of shame, other-born papers stated the nature of their powers and their known relatives. Other-born always came in a package: in two or three or more siblings descended from sibling gods. Myths talked of the existence of other gods, too, but only twin, sister, or brother divinities bestowed their progenies with power. Some believed the power was too much for a single person to inherit, but Thais disagreed. *Multitude is power,* she used to say. *We are stronger together.*

Ignoring Ava, the man called across the room, "Anything interesting, captain?"

The female officer was thumbing through Io's notes on the Magnussen case, eyes half-closed, brows raised, as if she was doubtful of every word on the page. Io stood ramrod straight, trying to talk herself out of going ballistic on these officers. All she had to do was wait for this humiliation to end. It might take a long time, depending on how cruel the cops decided to be, but it *would* end. She kept meticulous files, and her other-born papers were squeaky clean. They had been sorted out before she was even born; her parents already had two daughters who could see the Quilt, which could only mean a third was on the way. The moira-born always came in three, like the Moirae, the goddesses of Fate, themselves.

The firstborn was the spinner, who could weave new threads. The second was the drawer; she could elongate or shorten a thread, intensifying or weakening the corresponding feeling. And the youngest was the cutter, able to cut whatever thread she desired, even life-threads.

Cutters were the dangerous ones. Cutters were the villains in radio dramas, and the first suspects in crime investigations. Cutters were escorted home to have their case files checked, even when they had their private investigator license, complete and up to date, on their person and a dozen eyewitnesses confirming their innocence.

But Io could wield patience like a weapon. Day-long stakeouts and hours skimming through public records? Her favorite part of the job, to be honest. Sliding her leather jacket off, she grabbed a piece of spinach cheese pie from the kitchen counter. The phyllo was divinely fresh and crunched loudly under her teeth. The male officer transferred his glare from Ava to her.

Her sister asked, "What exactly did you do, sister mine?"

Io shrugged. In her calmest, most measured tone, she said, "*I did nothing. I was hired to investigate a man that was murdered tonight by an old woman who then assaulted me and escaped. The officers want to see my notes on the case.*"

"They don't leave a stone unturned, do they? Our city's heroes," Ava said sweetly. Then, in alarm, "The old woman tried to kill you?"

"That's not even the worst part. Her life-thread was cut. It was hanging limp from her hand."

"That's impossible. She would be dead."

A shudder carved down Io's skin. "But she wasn't."

"A *wraith*."

That last comment had come from the female officer. She was Iyen, light-skinned with dark eyes and a muscled stature that filled her uniform to the brim. "That's what you called her in your state-ment, Miss Ora. *The silver-haired wraith.*"

Io didn't remember that. Then again, she didn't remember much after the woman had fallen out the window: only the rasping of her heart, the sting of her scratches, the assistant's cheeks stained with tears, the shock of seeing the boy on the other end of her fate-thread for the first time.

"Odd choice of words," said the male officer from the doorway. "Why *wraith*, cutter?"

"Sounds better than ghost," answered Ava, pulling her black curls over a shoulder to reveal the shaved side of her head. It was an intentional move, Io knew—a brass ear cuff covered the top of her ear, its characteristic muted color marking her as one of the Fortuna gang.

The cop's eyes widened; he whispered something to his partner. The woman made a grunt and tucked the Magnussen case file under her armpit. "I'm taking this with me. I suggest you don't leave town, Miss Ora. We might be in contact in the next few days."

They headed out without another word. Even the cops hesitated before Bianca Rossi, owner of the Fortuna and unchallenged mob queen of the Silts.

Ava closed the door behind them and eyed Io. "Are you all right?"

She nodded. The scratches throbbed and the back of her head was pounding, and *she had seen her fate-thread for the first time*—but she would be okay. Bolt the door and lock the windows, and this suffocating pressure on her chest would disappear. It always did. But no rest just yet. She made for the door.

"Where are you going?"

"The wife," Io explained, shouldering the familiar warmth of her worn jacket. It was her mom's; too small for Ava and not Thais's style, so Io had inherited it, a leftover presented as a gift. She didn't really mind; old, worn leather was one of her favorite smells. "I have to inform the wife before they paint me as the villain of the story."

Ava's face contracted with concern. "I'll come with you."

There was a knock on the door.

"What now," mumbled Io under her breath. She left the chain on as she opened the door.

In the sliver between wood, she saw *him*.

The boy from earlier tonight, the one she shared a fate-thread with.

Gods, did she have to think about *that*, too, right now?

He stood far from the door, as though to lessen the threat of his massive form. He had dark skin, rich brown eyes, and tight curls cropped close to his scalp. Brass knuckles hung from a loop on his belt. Io's eyes stuck on the weapon—the preferred choice of Fortuna gang members—and her breath lodged at the base of her neck. This was the mob queen's signature: the curved imprint of knuckles upon flesh.

"Edei?" Ava said from behind Io. "Edei Rhuna, what are you doing here?"

Concealed by the wood, Io mouthed to her sister, *What the absolute hell.* Io had managed, through no small inconvenience, to avoid the boy at the other end of her fate-thread for the better part of three years and Ava *knew* him? Was on a *first-name basis* with him? Outright treason, that's what this was.

Edei Rhuna nodded hello.

In a low voice and with a furtive glance, he told Io, "The boss wants to see you."

# CHAPTER III

# THE RIGHT THING TO DO

IO DIDN'T LIE often, but when she did, she committed thoroughly. Here was the lie she told herself, almost daily: she didn't care about the fate-thread.

Thais had noticed it first, when she was eighteen and Io was ten, barely a year after their parents' death. They were on the terrace of their old apartment building, lazing about in the first truly warm day after a fortnight of a relentless neo-monsoon. Early-spring pollen floated downwind from the gardens of District-on-the-Hill, making Io sneeze incessantly.

"That's odd," Thais had said, stretching one of Io's threads between her fingers. "This thread seems to lead off to somewhere unknown." She tugged it to show Io: like a beam of silver light, it arced across the roof and over the city, disappearing into the horizon. "It must be a fate-thread. How thrilling—my moira-born tutor said they're rarer than the triple moonset."

Io bounced on her feet, Thais's excitement sugaring her tongue. These were her favorite moments: Thais coaching her in the Quilt about what moira-born like them could do, Thais excited, Thais smiling.

"What's a fate-thread?" Io asked.

Thais leaned back on the slanted tiles. "Threads connect people to what they care about. A person you have met, an object you have used, a place you have been. You love it, deeply, and a thread is formed. But there are some rare threads that exist before the attachment is formed.

They lead to whoever or whatever you are destined to love, one day."

"Like your home-thread?"

Thais had a rare thread, too, which Mama always gushed about to anyone who'd listen: *Have you heard about my Thais's home-thread? That's true love, isn't it? It's dedication to our home, to all of Alante. One day, my baby girl is going to do great things for this city, just you wait.* The city was a part of Thais, a kernel of her soul.

"It's nothing like my home-thread." Thais dropped Io's thread. "I *earned* my home-thread. I prove my love for this city every day. What have you done to deserve this?"

And she marched away, leaving Io to feel, for some reason, ashamed.

But that initial exhilaration was hard to shake. A passion she was yet to meet. A love she was destined to feel. It soothed her, like waking up after a particularly convincing dream. As she grew, the fate-thread birthed a myriad of possibilities: she would discover a new craft, find an eager friend, a long-lost relative coming to pull them out of the quicksand drop to poverty. Or—and she blushed to think of this—someone to hold her and kiss her like they did in the radio dramas.

And one day when she was fifteen, Io's chest began . . . tingling. The fate-thread was moving. Every day, after school, she would climb to their roof and watch whatever lay on the other end of the thread edging toward her. She and her lovely unknown were celestial objects orbiting ever closer, destined for an inevitable collision.

He arrived the day before Winter's Feast.

Thais had sunk into their sofa, exhausted after a double shift, clothes stinking of fried food. She slumped a leg into Io's lap, over the homework she had been doing. "It's a boy. Your fate-thread."

Io kept her eyes on the notebook, swallowing her shock like a mouthful of bitter medicine. "How do you know?"

"I couldn't leave you pining on the roof every night—you'll catch your death. I followed your thread today. It leads to a boy."

Ava hooted over the pot of bean soup she was stirring. "A boy! Tell us everything."

Thais gave their sister a scornful look. "There's not much to tell. He's young, Io's age, or maybe a year older. He just arrived in the city, spent the entire morning at the immigration offices at the West Gate." Then she focused back on Io and her eyes softened. "I'm sorry, but—he was with someone, Io."

Io pressed her lips together, in her best attempt at a poker face. Her mind was a whirlwind that she couldn't comprehend. She didn't even know this boy—she shouldn't feel betrayed. And yet.

"So what?" said Ava.

"What do you mean 'so what,' you heathen?" scolded Thais. "How would you feel, if a girl came up to you and said you were destined to love her?"

"Depends on how cute she was."

Thais rolled her eyes.

"How cute is *he*?" Ava asked, wiggling her eyebrows.

Io had felt suddenly very small, and very lonely. "Ava, drop it."

"Oh, get over yourself, Io." Ava jabbed the ladle in Io's direction. "What if he is with someone? Doesn't he deserve to know that there's this thing between you, a fated thread? Maybe it's not even a thread of love; it doesn't have to be, you know. He could be your future best friend, or a cherished ally, or a faithful business partner, or your, like . . . art muse. You can't hide behind your fears forever; you have to find him and tell him."

"Let her be, Ava," Thais butted in. "Wouldn't it be cruel if someone approached your girlfriend and told her they were her fated soul mate?"

"Well." Ava pulled the corners of her lips down comically in an *eek* face.

Thais nodded, her mothering instincts sated. "Telling him is not the right thing to do."

The pressure around Io's rib cage loosened; there was a right thing to do. Of course there was, and of course Thais knew it.

"What should I do, then?" she asked, eager for a solution to this unwanted problem.

"Cut the thread. Set him free."

Her body rejected the idea instantaneously: her chest constricted, muscles tensing for a blow. She couldn't *cut* it. For five years, the fate-thread had been her anchor, a constant reminder that no matter how hard life became—her parents' death, their struggling finances, the sorrow she could see in her sisters' eyes—there was something waiting for her, a thread blazing silver against the horizon. One day, it would come, and one day, she would be happy. It was fate, impossible and otherworldly and utterly *hers*. No, she wouldn't cut it.

Thais read every thought, every feeling crossing Io's face. A scowl surfaced on her sister's brow. "It will be hard, but it's for the better, sister mine. You don't want to rob him of his choice, do you?"

Io said nothing.

After a while, Thais rose and went to wash. They ate bean soup. They discussed the latest mystery serial on the radio. In the months that followed, Io began to ignore the thread. It was especially hard now that the boy was so close; he had found a place in the Silts, Io had deduced, and Ava saw him frequently at the diner where she bussed tables. The fate-thread tugged at Io's chest; often, before she knew it, she would take a step in its direction. But in her ruthlessly honest way, Thais was right.

The boy had a choice, and right now he was choosing someone else. Io had to respect that.

But she, too, had a choice. Cut it or keep it. The threads of Fate were manifestations of what you loved, and in turn who you were. Io had to find out what her fate was, who she was destined to become. Its light shone brighter than all her other threads combined, an anchor and a beacon and a promise of better things to come. She chose to keep it.

She stopped mentioning it to her sisters entirely, fearing Thais might convince her to cut it, and dreading Ava might talk her into seeking the boy out. A year after the boy arrived in Alante, Thais left them; with her left Io's fear.

Sometimes, she caught Ava looking at her from the corner of her eye. Words bubbled on her sister's lips, ready to take shape.

Even now, almost three years later, Ava would blurt out, "I saw him today."

Io always remained silent.

"Don't you want to know who he is, what he does?"

"I don't care," Io always lied, hoping one day, it would be true.

# CHAPTER IV

# A THRONE GILDED WITH KNOCKED-OUT TEETH

**ONE DID NOT** deny the mob queen, or the messengers she sent to their doors. Those who had tried no longer had a tongue to deny her with. So Io made herself close the door behind her, ignoring whatever her sister was trying to mouth, and followed Edei Rhuna—a reminder of the right thing Io didn't do—out of the building. He was surprisingly polite, for one of Bianca Rossi's strongarms. He adjusted his faster stride to Io's. He kept the hanging bridge steady until she crossed. He glanced at her only when needed, to check she was keeping pace, which was good: too much eye contact, or none at all, was suspicious.

The thought needled her. There was nothing for her to be suspicious about. What was she watching him for? It took her seconds to realize: the fate-thread. She wondered if he knew about it, if it had anything to do with why he was in the apartment building across from the abandoned theater.

She stole glances, hyperaware of every little thing about him: The neckline of his wool sweater. A fading bruise on his jaw. His shoes, hard worker's boots that should have woken up the neighborhood but didn't. The smell of some kind of oil, shining on his tight curls. His nose, long and straight, and his full lips—

*Don't be weird, Io.*

But things had head-dived into weird and come up into uncanny the moment she saw him in that dark corridor, right after her near-death experience. Now she was walking by his side and knew his name and his job and his face, and *the whole world was tilting on its axis.*

He couldn't know, right? Ava and Thais would never have told him. There were a few other moira-born in the city who could detect their fate-thread, but Edei didn't seem like the type to pay preposterous amounts for a fortune teller's reading.

Should *she* tell him? Gods, the thought alone was too terrifying to examine. She'd see what this summons from the mob queen was about, and then she would decide.

They climbed to the North Walkway to find a line of passersby waiting. An outlier gang was tolling people to cross it, which could often turn violent. She made to retreat to find another path, but Edei slipped the brass knuckles onto his fist and rapped a beat onto the nearest streetlight. Four beats, pause, two beats, pause, three fast ones.

An answering rap came from down the block; within minutes, a Fortuna patrol came out of the alleyways, five of them armed with iron bars. The Fortuna gang acted like law enforcers in the Silts; cops rarely deigned to step foot in a place submerged in tide and filled with chimerini—the small, bloodthirsty animal hybrids that lurked in Alante's deep waters—unless, of course, they were running a raid. Bianca Rossi ruled the Silts, and she actually made a decent job of it: kept outliers from levying bridges, ran petty criminals out of the district, hunted down the most dangerous chimerini before they got hungry and preyed on people. She even supported worker unions.

The outlier gang took one look at them and bolted with whatever tolls they could grab. Edei steered Io to the newly liberated Walkway, where the Fortuna kids saluted him with brass knuckles to the brow.

Who exactly was he in the gang hierarchy? Every member of the Fortuna gang knew the knuckle raps, even Ava, who was only a singer at their club and didn't partake in any of the more unsanitary activities of the gang. But Edei Rhuna didn't just know the raps. He was high enough on the mob queen's retinue to earn a salute from the younger members.

The Fortuna Club came into view, two bouncers guarding its main entrance at the rooftop, bathed in the violet glow of the neon sign above their heads. The building was one of the trendiest places in the Silts, albeit a little tacky, in Io's opinion. The brick walls were hued black, the windows rimmed with gold paint, the glass tinted a shadowy gray. Electrical wires spilled like veins from its body to feed the chandeliers, mics, and dozens of gambling mechanisms inside. The two bridges connecting it to the rooftops across the street were retractable, a gaudy expense customary in wealthier districts that must have cost Bianca Rossi a fortune. Rumor was that after her rise to power during the Moonset Riots, an eight-day-long violent gang war twelve years ago that almost wiped out the Silts, she lived in constant fear of being attacked again.

The bouncers made to search Io—the Fortuna had a strict no-guns rule—but Edei nodded once and the two men stepped aside, holding the door open. Edei led her down carpeted corridors, piano music drifting up from the gambling pit on the ground floor. He knocked at a nondescript door but didn't wait for an answer before entering.

Bianca Rossi's office was as flamboyant as the rest of the club. Ornate black wood covered every wall and the ceiling, a superfluous extravagance given how fast the city's humidity would destroy it. A fluffy white carpet sat in the middle of the room, enveloped by heavy furniture: a sofa and two armchairs, a bar with rows upon rows of drinks, a desk inlaid with what looked like leviathan scales. A long window stood behind the desk.

The sun had begun its ascent, soaking the office in deep reds and setting Bianca Rossi's blond hair aflame. The mob queen of the Silts was in her early thirties, lean as a cat, with several skin discolorations on her neck and arms. Ersa's kisses, people called them—named for the largest of Alante's moons. Legend said that these lightened spots were the debris that fell from the sky the night the one moon split into three.

Bianca never wore anything but men's suits, tailored to cinch her waist and hug her long legs. Today, the suit was dark green velvet, the look completed by a lime silk tie around her neck. Ever since she started singing at the Fortuna a year ago, Ava came home every day with a new tale of how cool her boss was, but Io didn't buy it—Bianca Rossi ruled from a throne gilded with knocked-out teeth.

The mob queen sat back from her paperwork and spoke with a thick Silts accent, drawling every vowel. "Io Ora."

Io took the seat Bianca gestured at, noticing that Edei remained standing by the door. "Why am I here?" she asked, more sharply than she'd intended.

Bianca's face shone with mirth. "I do like you Ora sisters. Direct, verging on rude, yet never quite crossing it. Once, a customer was getting handsy with your sister—has she ever told you that story? I sent Edei here to help her, but by the time he reached her, Ava had already broken the man's nose against the table. And when I asked why she didn't just wait for help, you know what she said? *My mama taught me to take no prisoners.* Was that a lesson you took to heart, too, Io?"

It felt like buttering up, which meant it probably was. "Why am I here, Ms. Rossi?"

Bianca cocked her head to the left. It was an exaggerated movement, theatrical, and Io wondered at its purpose. To intimidate her? She didn't dare pull up the Quilt to look at Bianca's threads.

The woman would notice the unnatural glaze of silver reflected in Io's eyes. She would be reminded that Io was a cutter, sinister and unreliable. *Patience like a knife*, Io told herself. Patience always paid off.

"I am told you are a sleuth."

Io nodded, waiting. This wasn't why she had been escorted here at the crack of dawn.

"And that you were attacked last night by an unusual assailant."

This wasn't what she was here for, either.

"Luckily, we are not as useless as the city's officials." At Bianca's nod, the door behind them opened. "Look what Edei caught for you."

And there she was. The wraith.

Two gang members prodded her in with long brass bars, a red-headed boy and a dark-skinned girl in a close-fitting athletic outfit. The office filled immediately with the pungency of rot. The woman smelled and looked derelict: torn clothes hanging off her shoulders, shoes soaked with mud, wet hair stuck on her pasty skin.

Io's gaze came to rest on Edei, taking him in from head to toe. He wore a different wool sweater than when she first saw him earlier, and his boots left little wet imprints on the dark wood. Was that where he disappeared to right after the attack? Had he dived after the wraith? Their eyes connected—Io flushed and dragged hers back to the woman.

"What do you see, Miss Ora?" Bianca asked.

Up close, in the dazzling light of daybreak, the old woman's lips were deep purple, bags sagged under her yellowing eyes, veins inked her arms in blue, and flakes of dead skin dusted her clothes and hair. She looked like she was decomposing, a body with no life inside it, a dead woman walking.

Io went into the Quilt, hoping against hope that she had been wrong. That it had been a trick of the light. But there in the old woman's hand was the severed life-thread. Giving her a wide berth, Io circled her for a closer look. The unbound thread drooped to the white carpet, pooling by the wraith's feet. Io checked its color against her own bundle of threads, then Bianca's and Edei's. It was definitely a life-thread, made of the same lustrous silver that outshone every other thread in their chests.

"What is it?" asked Bianca.

"Her life-thread is cut," said Io. "Yet she is alive. I've never seen anything like it."

Bianca, surprisingly, didn't doubt her as Ava had. "Do you think that's why she killed that man? Did the loss of her life-thread drive her mad?"

*I don't know.* But that wasn't the answer Bianca was looking for, nor one Io allowed herself to give. Reasons, motives, resolutions, she excelled in those. People paid good money for her rational mind, her ability to see what linked people together, both the real threads of the Quilt and those of the metaphorical sense. The facts were: a dead man, a severed life-thread, a deathless murderess. Madness was *an* explanation.

But the woman had said, *There are crimes that cannot go unpunished.*

That was motive, however mystifying.

Io asked the old woman, "What crimes did you punish him for?"

The wraith didn't reply. Since she entered the office, she hadn't stopped staring at Bianca, with what could only be described as hunger.

Io stepped in front of the mob queen, blocking the wraith's view. "He hurt you," Io guessed. Half the art of sleuthing was in fishing up the truth. "You wanted revenge."

The wraith's attention switched, pressing like a dagger on Io's throat. "Revenge is for the wicked," the woman replied. "My purpose is justice. I am its servant, and it is mine."

Io's pulse spiked. She forced herself to stand still and collect her thoughts, then spoke to the room at large. "There have been other victims?"

"Oh, you *are* good, little sleuth." Bianca shoved her hands casually in her pockets. "She killed one of my men a few days ago. She managed to escape, but not before Edei gleaned the same bit of information you did: she wanted my man to repent. But this is not the first killer we've found lurking in the Silts, spewing the words of a lunatic. The first appeared two weeks ago. Another woman, as ragged as this one, strangled a border guard to death, right in front of his family."

"Our people told me," Edei said, "that she kept saying, *Your crimes demand punishment.*"

A shiver crawled down Io's spine. "Her hands, were they bent like this?" She indicated the wraith with her chin, whose pale fingers closed around the thread, invisible to anyone but the moira-born. "Was her appearance similar, the . . . skin?"

Edei nodded. "We found the first woman dead five days later—"

"Fools!" the wraith spat.

With a horrible smile, she inched forward. Edei and the girl surrounded her at once, brass bars pushing at her chest. The redhead fumbled at the back of his trousers and produced a gun. Io had never seen a revolver up close; it was big, with a wooden handle and a long nose. It caught the sunlight, the metal glistening bright orange.

"*Let them see your weapon*, they told me." The woman spoke in a hiss. "*Let them see what's coming for them*, they said. I'm neither crazy, nor dying. I am ascended."

Faster than lightning, the wraith whipped her severed thread in Io's direction, like a lasso. It sailed across the room; Io gasped and scrambled out of the way—but she was never its target.

It happened fast: the thread looped around Bianca Rossi's throat. The redheaded boy fired the gun, hitting the wraith's torso. Bianca fell on her knees, hands around her neck, gasping for air. Edei launched at the wraith, someone shouted, furniture toppled.

Io swiped at her chest for a thread. With practiced fingers, she grabbed one, skidded on her boots across the floor, and brought it inches from the wraith's severed life-thread.

"Stop!" she screamed.

Bianca Rossi was clutching at her neck, face turning scarlet.

"*Stop!*" Io warned again.

The wraith didn't—instead, she tossed Edei off her with inhuman strength and brought her severed thread down in an arc. Bianca dropped to her hands and knees.

Io didn't know if it would work, if the severed thread was in any way tying her to life, or to whatever form of existence this was, but there was no time to wonder—she brought her thread down like a blade.

Both threads snapped. Io's hand suddenly held nothing but air. On the floor, Bianca wheezed loudly, eyes bulging, crawling away till she hit her desk. The wraith, no longer held to life by that wisp of a life-thread, toppled lifeless to the white carpet.

Bianca spoke with a raspy voice. "Nico."

The redhead, gun still pointed at the wraith, came to attention. "Yes, boss?"

"Remind me of the Fortuna's rules." Bianca was sitting on the floor, elbows on her knees, breathing in and out in deep gasps. Her neck was bruising fast, her eyes bloodshot, but she was taking this surprisingly well.

Io, on the other hand, wasn't. Her hands trembled, her breaths came out shallow, and she couldn't look away from the blood spreading on the white carpet. *Close them, darling*, Thais said in her head. *If you can't bear to look, close your eyes.* Io did.

"No guns, no leeches, no paramours," she heard Nico reply. Leeches—the Silts name for cops.

"And why's that?"

"They're unreliable."

"What did you aim for, Nico?"

"Her head."

"What'd you hit?"

A pause. "Her chest."

"Chimdi was standing only a foot to the left." Coldly, Bianca added, "Patrol duty, two weeks, the Docks."

The upper class thought the Silts were the worst part of the city, but that was because they'd never been to the Docks. High tide swallowed them completely, special anchors letting the boats remain floating on the surface of the water. All sorts of other-worldly creatures were beached there in the morning. The stench was *unbelievable*.

"What's wrong with *you*, kid?" Bianca asked.

Silence followed.

Oh. Bianca was talking to *her*. Io forced her eyes open to find Bianca inspecting her. Chimdi, Nico, and the woman's body were gone, the door left ajar. Edei was rolling the white carpet, stained with the woman's filth and blood.

Io flexed her trembling fingers and said, "I—killed her."

"Isn't that what cutters do?"

Fury chased away some of Io's tremor. Bianca and her prejudice could go to hell. She opened her mouth—

Edei spoke up in a calm, nonchalant voice. "By necessity, not choice."

It was more or less what Io was going to say, then finish off with a nice *screw you*.

Edei placed the rolled carpet in the corridor and closed the door. "She was already going to die," he said without looking at Io. "Nico shot her. What you did saved Bianca's life. Probably all our lives."

Who was this boy? He wore the knuckles, gave orders to gang members, rolled a bloodied carpet as if putting away the dishes after dinner. But what he had said about cutters was . . . not what people usually thought of other-born.

Bianca spoke from the floor, where she still sat. "Well, little Ora, I think this settles it. Cancel the rest of your clients. I'm hiring you for the foreseeable future. You're going to work with Edei here to bring me answers about these gods-damned murders."

"I can't."

"Sure you can. I'll pay twice your price."

"It's not about the money." Io stepped away from the dark stain on the wood, away from her chaotic thoughts. "I work with scorned lovers and worried parents. I don't solve murders."

Bianca pulled her hair back from her Ersa-kissed cheeks. "These women are using threads to kill, and you're the only private eye in Alante who can see the Quilt. So, yeah, I think you're exactly the right person for the job. I can kill her. Kill the next one. But something tells me these women will keep coming."

Io glanced back at the door. She had a decision to make: refuse and take her chances with the mob queen's wrath, or accept and risk her damn life hunting down ghosts.

"I work alone." She probably sounded pathetic, but she didn't care. Her mind was full of panic, her body quivering with adrenaline. The thought of Edei—distracting her, confusing her, reminding her—while she chased murderous wraiths across Alante was too much to handle. She had kept their lives separate for three years, and she intended to continue. If she had to do this, she'd do it alone.

"Not anymore," Bianca answered, her voice full of steel. "You do this with Edei, or you find yourself another city to work in."

A threat: how all partnerships started in the Silts. Io's fingers were itching to grab a thread and slice Bianca's surety right off her face. If she let Bianca walk over her now, the mob queen wouldn't hesitate to do it again in the future. Io knew what mob kings and queens used cutters for.

"I'll do this for you," she told Bianca, "and this alone. None of your henchmen will come knocking on my door at dawn ever again."

On her left, Io thought she glimpsed Edei's shoulders tense. *This is just another job*, she told herself. She'd get it done, stay in Bianca's good graces, then go back to her normal life of adulterers and gamblers.

The mob queen of the Silts smiled a little, almost as if this haggling pleased her. "Deal. Ey, Edei?"

He gave a nod.

"She kept saying *they*. *They told me, they said*." Bianca propped her head against the desk and spoke the question on everyone's minds. "Who the hell is *they*?"

# CHAPTER V

# HALF A LIE

**A MOURNFUL VOICE** crooned about dreams and heartbreaks as Ava combed through Io's hair. Jetta Jamil, Ava's favorite songstress, was about to release a new album, and Ava had managed to score one of the first rare vinyls before it was even out. Io knew better than to ask how—her sister had a sketchy side even Io didn't fully know.

Ava had been waiting by the door when Io returned around midday, after visiting Isidora Magnussen. Ava had opened her mouth, but Io silenced her with a palm.

"Let me wash first," she had said.

Io's dark curls fell almost to her waist, which meant combing through them was a singular torture. When she had come out of the shower, Ava had held up the comb like an olive branch. Now, her head in Ava's lap, Io shivered at the sensation of the comb untangling her hair, roots to ends. Jetta Jamil sang of what the sun would taste like if she wasn't afraid to burn her tongue. The song was slow, and sleep draped on Io's lids.

"Aren't you going to ask?" Ava said into the silence.

Io's eyes fluttered open. This wasn't about the wraith or the visit to the Fortuna—this was about *him*. "Tell me."

"I tried telling you a hundred times, but you never wanted to know."

Io harrumphed; that was an excuse, and they both knew it.

"Thais had pointed him out to me when he first arrived in Alante, but I officially met him when Bianca hired me about a year ago. He's Sumazi, worked construction for a while, then Bianca poached him.

He's not on the front lines, I rarely ever see him at the club, but word is he does stealth work for her, spying, keeping tabs on rivals, tracking skirmishes on their turf. He's kind of Bianca's second, I guess. To be honest, the last couple of years, you've talked so little of the fate-thread, I thought you had decided to cut it." The comb paused. "Io, do you hate me? You insisted you didn't want to know, but should I have told you anyway? Are you angry?"

No, because what kind of irrational monster got angry at her sister for doing precisely what she asked? Still, it was a kind of lie by omission, which smarted. "I would have liked to be prepared," she replied. "Are you friends with him?"

"Gods no. I wouldn't befriend your fate-thread behind your back, Io. I'm not an actual villain. But he *is* nice. He could be a friend, you know, if you wanted."

"You just told me he does the mob queen's dirty work. How can he be nice?"

"I'm not sure how to explain it. In the Silts, you know how it is, there's so much danger, all the time. People are quick to choose violence. Especially Bianca's people. But Edei avoids violence if it can be avoided."

Io guessed she'd find out herself soon enough.

"Io . . ." Ava hesitated. "That woman, the wraith. You said her severed thread snapped when you cut it, so it must have tied her to life in some way. What if it wasn't entirely severed? What if it was just frayed, like that cormorant and those freaky triplets."

A long exhale escaped Io's lips. When Io was six and Ava twelve, a family with girl triplets had moved into the apartment next door. The five of them had formed a vagrant group that summer, spending endless hours on the roof garden, making fake flower potions and walking on their hands. Then one day, the triplets didn't show up. And the next day, and the next. On the fourth, Io and Ava found them on the rooftop across the street, in a circle above a cormorant with broken wings. Ava went haywire, screaming and batting at the triplets to leave the bird alone. For a short time in her youth, Ava had been one of the rare moira-born who could see the threads of animals. Later that same night, sobbing into Mama's arms, Ava had confessed that the cormorant's life-thread was fraying, but the triplets had kept it alive, drawing its death out for days. Within the week, Mama had rallied the neighbors—the family was evicted.

That was Io's first and only experience with the keres-born, who were descendants of the Keres, goddesses of violent deaths. The triplets had been unregistered, as keres-born often were, since their kind was less likely to be granted entry into the city-nations. Their treatment was unjust, but Io couldn't help the goose bumps on her arms every time she thought of that story, of what Ava might have seen.

"Maybe," she replied. "But that doesn't explain the things she kept saying about justice—it was eerie, Ava."

"I bet," Ava said with a shudder. Io listened to the brush running through her hair, that otherworldly echo coming from both outside and inside her own scalp. "Maybe they're a different kind of cutter?"

Moira-born powers stemmed from the ancient Moirae themselves, the goddesses of Fate. One to weave, one to draw, one to cut the threads of life. Legend said that the gods died out long before the old world Collapsed, the Moirae among them. But their powers survived in their descendants: whenever three children were birthed in their family line, they inherited their powers. Sisters, brothers, people outside the gender binary, it didn't matter—only the number remained unchanged: always three. The same was true of pretty much every other-born, the number of siblings dependent on the gods they came from. Their powers had been the same for centuries, documented in folk songs and history books and transnational art. It was why people didn't stone other-born to death anymore: their abilities had clear rules and strict limitations. A severed life-thread meant death. What did it mean if the rules were changing now?

"I could ask the Nine," Io ventured.

The Nine sisters, descendants of the Muses, held court at a massive mansion in the heart of the Artisti District. Their extraordinary knowledge of arts, science, and history made them an unofficial authority on all things other-born, but their services weren't free.

"No," said Ava. It was less suggestion and more command. "They're insidious creatures that serve only their own purpose."

Io didn't disagree. Two years as a private eye and many more running odd jobs with Thais, and Io had never dared go to the Nine, even in her direst need.

After a prolonged silence, Ava said, "It's always been weird to me, how easily you can sacrifice one of your own threads to cut someone else's."

Was it easy? Io had examined the question a hundred times in the past, unable to reach a conclusion. It was easy in that it was second nature, primeval almost: she reached out and just chose one, her fingers instinctively avoiding her most valued threads. It wasn't easy in that it cost her, both her own thread and her victim's. It didn't help that Io thought of them like that: *victims.*

"I don't enjoy it," she whispered. "It was either the wraith or Bianca."

Her sister paused and softly said, "I'm glad you chose Bianca. Which thread did you use to cut the wraith's? I can't tell. You have so many."

People averaged fifteen threads, the most common being threads to other people they cared about, places they loved, objects that bore some significance. For example, Rosa—Io's best friend and the only person who had patiently let Io count her threads—had seventeen: her life-thread, eleven threads leading to her family and friends, three to various spots in the city that were important to her, one to her typewriter, and one to her favorite pair of boots.

Io had thirty-seven—thirty-six now, she supposed, after losing one to cut the wraith's. She didn't mean for it to happen. Thais had said once that Io was a hoarder. If she loved something, even for a minute, like the fish noodles at the market stall or the teacher who'd smiled at her last week, she held on to that love with tooth and claw. Most threads frayed over time and distance, but never Io's. Her love was evergreen.

"Io. This thread leads to a frog," Thais had once chastised. "How can you love a frog?"

"He's a very nice green," six-year-old Io had replied.

Thais had laughed and kissed Io's head.

But to other moira-born, Io must look like a mess on the Quilt. Threads shooting in every direction, close and far, all of them strong and bright. No wonder Ava couldn't tell which one Io had used to cut the wraith's thread. She flopped over and studied her threads. Long minutes passed before Io finally said, "Monsieur Poire's éclairs."

"Ah, a true tragedy."

It was. Once a thread was cut, the connection, love—or in this case, enjoyment—you once felt was gone. Something . . . *meh* was left in its place. Éclairs were Io's favorite, and Monsieur Poire's were beyond divine. But when once Io's mouth had watered at the thought of them, now there was nothing special. The thread might grow back over time, but most likely it would not; such was the risk of cutting it.

Io sighed. "There must be better éclairs somewhere out there. I'll find them, one day."

Ava scoffed. "You and your *one days*. Gag."

A full-body chuckle escaped Io. She was so tired she felt drunk. Her sister's fingers moving through her hair had cast an irresistible sleeping spell to which Io was slowly surrendering.

Several minutes of half sleep passed. Then Ava's fingers stilled. "Do you want me to let the fate-thread out, weaken it? I mean, now that you'll be working with him? I can make it so you barely sense it. So that you don't feel . . . suffocated."

That was Ava's power: she could let out threads or draw them in, hence intensifying or lessening the feeling that accompanied them. Thais had tried to convince Ava to go freelance—did she know how much they could make from the brokenhearted? But Ava always refused. It wasn't her place to decide what or how much others loved, she said. Which Io found very noble, and very useless.

What would it be like if the fate-thread were weakened? If what bound her and Edei Rhuna wasn't a chain of destiny but a soft yarn of mere acquaintance? The thought made her panic. She spent her days dealing with the threads of cheating spouses and gamblers. Was it so wrong to have this one sweet thing to cherish, a fate larger than life, a destiny beyond the laws of nature?

"I don't feel suffocated," she replied. It was only half a lie.

Ava's fingers took up their ebb and flow. "One day, Io, you'll have to let go."

But Io was already drifting to sleep.

# CHAPTER VI

# CREATURE OF CURIOSITY

IO WOKE TO a room blotted in the purples and burgundies of the setting sun, her mind made up: the only way to get through this unscathed was to treat it like any other job.

No glancing at Edei Rhuna from the corner of her eye. No studying the way the muscles of his back moved as he walked. No sniffs of his sweaters. No flushing when he looked at her. She would act normal, and he wouldn't know a thing. They would get Bianca Rossi her answers, and life would return to how it had been. As simple as that.

But her body had a mind of its own. Her heart beat fast as she pulled on clean clothes—black trousers, gray sweater, and boots laced up to her calves—and styled her hair away from her face in one of her mom's old blue scarves. Her breath came in shots as she made her way across the roofs—the tide hadn't come in yet, but old habits died hard. And when she climbed onto the hanging bridge to the Fortuna, its metal planks echoing like a siren, her senses heightened to the point of light-headedness.

Edei leaned against the railing of the first floor, surveying the clients coming and going through the Fortuna's main hall. It was still early for the gamblers and drinkers, but the house's crew was there, setting up, cleaning, chatting over cups of coffee. Ava was probably somewhere in the back, warming up for the night's performance.

Io noticed how the lovely olive shade of his sweater accentuated his brown skin. How his legs were crossed at the ankles and his fingers tapped a rhythm on the railing. In the last dregs of sunlight shifting through the high windows, he looked like a painting, both faded and vibrant, ancient and timeless. *Rein it in, Io.* She needed to calm down. She pressed her palms against her cheeks, trying to cool them. Should she tap his shoulder? Say his name? She'd kept her distance for three years. Now even the little things felt too intimate.

He must have sensed her presence: he turned, nodding once in greeting. "Marhaban."

"Hello," she said back. Like any Silts resident, Io knew a little Sumazi, and a little Kurkz, and a little Rossk. The Silts were an amalgamation of cultures, and so were its people, one of the few things that actually made Io proud of her home.

Edei spoke in a low tone, his gaze steady on her. "I've got notes on the victims and a few witness accounts if you want to see them. But I've found little on the women. Only physical description and ethnicity."

Straight to the point, then. Disappointment twinged at her core, but she couldn't blame him. She'd made it quite clear earlier that she'd only taken this job to get rid of him. Gods, would she be the first person to ever get their destined lover to dislike them? A fate-thread of hate—Ava would get a good laugh out of that one.

"So, um," she asked, "did anyone recognize the body of the woman last night?"

The question was a test. The wraith had died inside the Fortuna Club, her thread sliced by a cutter. Bianca could dump the body at some gods-forsaken hole, and no one would blame her. Police officers were a nuisance in the Silts, more trouble than they were worth. But if Bianca was serious about this investigation, the police and their records were fundamentally necessary.

Edei shook his head. "Not yet. I'm told the leeches are looking into a few missing persons cases."

Io exhaled with relief. It was a complicated feeling, rooted in her own guilt. When they found out who the wraith was, she would pay the woman's family a visit. Offer her apology, for all the good it would do now.

"We can take a look at the public registry. If she was a cutter, she'll be on the other-born records. It'll have to wait for when the registry opens tomorrow, though." She paused, then added, "I'm sorry I arrived so late."

He gave a small shake of his head. "It was a long night."

"Let's go back to the apartment. We might spot something the police missed."

As they walked, Edei cataloged his findings. The first murder was two weeks ago at the Modiano Market. A Rossk chernobog-born was attacked in broad daylight while shopping with his family. One of the eyewitnesses was moira-born, a weaver, and thought the woman—younger, blond, but as ragged as last night's wraith—had a severed life-thread. Bianca and Edei hadn't believed that last part until Io confirmed it yesterday. The woman's body was found at the Docks five days later, too bloated to identify.

"A chernobog-born?" asked Io. The descendants of the Rossk god of darkness could create invisible walls that no one could cross; their twins, the belobog-born, could wield light as a shield. Io had never heard of a chernobog-born this far south; their powers worked better in the long nights of Rossk.

"He used to be a border guard. Rumor is his lifelong stash of bribes and payoffs led to early retirement and a life of luxury." Every city-nation was walled, and every wall had its cracks. "Bianca occasionally did business with him."

"How was he killed?"

Edei's voice hitched imperceptibly. "It's uncertain. There are strangulation marks around his neck, but witnesses report the death was fast, as though the woman snapped his neck. Same with the second murder."

He launched into the second murder: he had been in the Fortuna overseeing the delivery of a new shipment when he heard Minos scream. He ran outside, and the silver-haired wraith was circling Minos with her fingers all clawed up. Talking about justice and penance. Then her hand arced in the air, and Minos dropped dead. Edei went after her, but the tide was coming in, and she managed to escape through the streets.

"What did Minos do for Bianca?" Io asked.

" 'Protection' is the best word for it. Minos and his brother Grizz were in charge of securing Bianca's commodities. They're dioscuri-born."

Also known as Gemini, the Dioscuri were the twin gods Castor and Pollux, patrons of sailors and travelers. Their descendants, the dioscuri-born, were twins with the ability to track both the paths one had traveled and those one would travel. Much like moira-born, they used something akin to the Quilt, but instead of threads they saw pathways on the ground, alit in bronze. The eldest saw the paths taken in the past, the youngest the paths to be taken in the future.

Io had heard of Bianca Rossi's twins. The mob queen of the Silts had started in "acquisitions," otherwise known as smuggling. She procured and sold the kinds of things you couldn't get in an ordinary shop: medicine, machine parts, rare art, old-world remnants, even services. You wanted a pre-Collapse oak cabinet? Home remedies made from the bones of leviathans beached on the shores of coastal cities? For the right price, Bianca was your girl.

Her slow, meticulous rise to her throne of shattered jaws was owed partly to her own wits and partly to the twins. If her runners strayed on their way back with the acquisition, Grizz knew. If a buyer was about to run off with both the money and the goods, Minos knew. Bianca took care of the rest. After the Riots, she began investing her earnings in the Fortuna Club, hiring new members, opening new parlors. By the end, the little smuggler girl had taken over the Silts.

"What was the delivery you and Minos were overseeing?" asked Io. "Could the wraith have been involved?"

He glanced at her from the corner of his eye. "The wraith?"

Io shook herself at the memory of the flaky skin, the smell of decay. "I mean the woman last night."

He made a quiet grunt. "The shipment was spirits from our suppliers in Nanzy. None of it was harmed during the attack. She never so much as glanced at it. Her focus was solely on Minos."

"Did you get the impression he knew her? Or she him?"

"No. Grizz—his twin—was there, too. He said they'd never seen her before."

They turned onto the North Walkway. No outliers were tolling passersby today, but it was still early. Io watched the tide consume the paved streets below, a tongue of dark blue licking back and forth at the stones. The first tide bells began ringing across the city, but storefronts and ground entrances had already been boarded up. As the southernmost district, the Silts were first hit by the tide, which then traveled up through the rest of Alante. In an hour, the water would reach five feet. During neo-monsoon season, it was known to rise to fifteen.

"What of the victim last night?" Edei asked when the bells receded.

Io told him: she had been hired by Isidora Magnussen, who had recently begun suspecting her husband wasn't actually attending the grace-born support meetings he claimed to be at every week. His office specialized in investments—"cons" was the better word for it—Io had found out early in her investigation. She suspected Jarl influenced his clients to invest using his grace-born powers.

Yesterday, Io had arrived at Isidora's just as the officers were leaving. "I'm sorry," Io had started saying, "I tried to save him—"

She was silenced by the woman's bosom, against which she had been squished. "You poor girl," Isidora had sobbed. "You're too good for this wretched world."

Io most certainly was *not*, but the embrace was much appreciated.

Edei's gaze fixed on her as she spoke, still and focused. Self-consciousness took over Io's thoughts. Was she slouching? Did she have new pimples? Was her hair sticking out? Then she chastised herself. *You don't care, remember? This is just another case, a partner you have to work with.* It didn't matter what she looked like.

They reached the roof of the apartment building and started down the stairs. It was strange to see the place again: the taped-off door, the dark stains on the doorframe. The narrow corridor seemed far shorter than last night, when Io had been running for her life.

"A corrupt chernobog-born, a dioscuri-born smuggler, and a grace-born con man," Edei said. "The population of other-born in Alante is one in a hundred. It can't be a coincidence that the three men targeted were all other-born."

"Or how they were all killed: this unnatural strangulation," Io said. "The officers last night found similar markings around Jarl Magnussen's neck. It's easy to latch on to the wraith's appearance and disoriented musings and file this case under 'don't cross a woman.' But her last words were: *Let them see your weapon, they told me. Let them see what's coming for them, they said.* They said: there is someone behind this, guiding this woman, and we must assume the first one, too. Telling them what to do and say. Perhaps who to kill. It doesn't feel arbitrary to me. It feels like . . . dogma."

"What does that word mean, 'dogma'?" Edei asked. His accent was subtle, his Alantian perfect, but this was a word even native speakers might not fully understand.

"A belief system. Like the principles of a religion."

" 'I am ascended,' " he quoted.

She'd been thinking of that very line the wraith had said last night. Edei Rhuna went up a notch in her estimate of both him and his investigatory skills.

"Exactly!" she said, perhaps a little too cheerily.

His lips quirked in a soft smile as he leaned over to examine the lock on the door. It creaked open at the barest touch of his fingers. Inside, a man was standing in the living room, scrawling furiously in a notebook. A heavy camera was slung across his back. Edei's fingers immediately jumped to his brass knuckles, but Io pushed his forearm down.

"Xenophon Atreidis," she said, ducking under the police tape. "I should have guessed the vultures would be the first ones on the scene."

Xenophon glanced away from his notes just long enough to scan her and Edei up and down. He was a short man but built like a wardrobe: big and sturdy and unbendable. His face was a jump back in time; Io was suddenly sitting at a school desk, exchanging notes with her best friend, Rosa, while Xenophon was trying to get the teacher to notice their illicit activities. They were both older now but wore the same expressions on their faces as they had back then: Xenophon one of contempt, Io one of open dislike.

"I'm not the vulture here. It's your kind that's been lurking around this apartment the entire day." With his pen, Xenophon indicated out of the window, to the arched bridge connecting the roofs across the street.

A figure sat there, an old man hunched over the railing. The distance didn't dim the glazed-over expression on his face, or the specks of red swimming in his eyes. As silver reflected in Io's irises when she was in the Quilt, so did scarlet gleam in the eyes of a keres-born when they were using their powers. The old man must have been drawn here by the violent death of Jarl Magnussen.

Xenophon peered around her at Edei, standing by the entrance. "I didn't know you worked with the mob queen's lackeys now."

It was bait. Io didn't take it. She turned her back to the window and the keres-born and surveyed her old schoolmate. "What are you doing here?"

"The same thing you are, I suppose. I smelled a good scoop, and I came to investigate."

Glass vials and lipstick tubes were scattered along the corridor, and the air was scented with strong perfume. There was no hint of blood in the living room, but Io remembered where the body had lain, neck twisted, eyes unseeing. Where Nina had cowered behind the now overturned armchair. Edei began sorting through knick-knacks around the room, while she stepped closer to Xenophon, shamelessly trying to decipher the contents of his scribbles.

"What'd you find?" Io asked. She was not above snooping; beggars couldn't be choosy.

"You can read all about it in *The Truth of Alante* tomorrow."

Gods, this guy was asking for a good punch to the face. Six years of school, one more of running into him during jobs, and it was a miracle she hadn't obliged him yet. Quite frankly, it was owed to Rosa, who thought he wasn't even worth the effort to raise her fists.

"Another think piece on the dangers of unsupervised cutters?" she asked. "Have you ever considered how much trouble you're raising for folks who've never done anything wrong besides being born with a power you can't even begin to comprehend?"

"I don't raise trouble; I merely report on it." He folded his notebook into his coat and gave her a putrid smirk. "But no, I won't be writing about other-born at all. Much more important business here."

Involuntarily, Io scowled. The jab was directed at her, with the singular self-assurance of a man who knew more than you. What had Io missed and Xenophon caught? Oh. *Oh.*

"You don't think the women were other-born?" she guessed.

Xenophon looked very satisfied with himself. "You assumed they were. Who's prejudiced now, huh, Ora?"

"She had to be. She held the thread in her hand—I saw it with my own eyes."

"What if I told you that the police have found the women's names and are refusing to release them to the press?"

"There are hundreds of other-born in Alante; we'll find her tomorrow when the registry opens."

"Good luck with that," Xenophon said in singsong; Io had to physically keep her fingers from balling up. "The day after the chernobog-born's death, all other-born records were pulled from the public registry. Coincidence?"

"But that's illegal."

At the end of the month-long Kinship Treaty negotiations sixty years ago, the other-born delegation, led by the Agora of the horae-born, had conceded to a compromise: they would receive citizenship rights in all city-nations in exchange for several precautions, such as lower wages, special restrictions to rent and own property, as well as their private information made public. Their names, affiliations, and powers would be listed in public records for everyone to see. People had a right to protect themselves, authorities said. *Bullshit*, Thais always argued. *It's us that have had to protect ourselves from them.* But other-born were tired of being emigrants, seeking shelter from city to city, and so they accepted.

"No shit, detective," said Xenophon. "But as of a week ago, Alante is the first city under the Kinship Treaty that made other-born records private. Guess who confiscated them."

Io waited, eyes hard, jaw set. This had a bad smell all about it.

"Come on, Ora, don't ruin it," Xenophon whined. "Guess."

She truly hated the boy. And he *was* a boy, large as a boar, but more juvenile than a toddler. She would *not* indulge a child—

"The Initiative," Edei said, straightening from the dresser he had been going through.

"Ding, ding, ding." Xenophon mimicked ringing an invisible bell. "Edei Rhuna, is it? Witnesses say you were here yesterday. Got any comments for me?"

Edei ignored him, speaking to Io instead. "The Commissioner, Luc Saint-Yves. You've heard of his Initiative?"

Sure she had. Everyone in Alante had heard of the golden boy's brilliant idea. Barely thirty-five and yet he had been appointed Police Commissioner and swept the city off their feet, both the distrustful middle class and the snobbish elite of the Hill. This year, he was vying for City Mayor, the elections to be held in a few days. He was ahead in the polls mainly due to his Initiative for the New Order. In many ways, it was unoriginal: a task force that would capture and indict the city's most notorious other-born criminals. But the Initiative aimed to recruit solely other-born, when no other-born had ever been hired in the police force before. An impossible idea, yet Saint-Yves had proved determined, charming, and a little bit cocky, claiming he already had several "noble" other-born in his employ, led by none other than his moira-born girlfriend.

"Why would the Commissioner pull all other-born records?" Io asked.

The question was addressed to Edei, but it was Xenophon who answered. "Get it yet, Ora? This reeks of a good old conspiracy and *The Truth of Alante* is on its tail. And lucky me, I've got someone on the inside working on it."

The police were withholding the wraiths' names. As well as confiscating the public records that could identify them. Much to Io's chagrin, Xenophon was right: this had all the tells of a cover-up. The gears inside Io's head began grinding, thoughts tumbling over one another into an avalanche of an idea.

"So what we need," she said, pondering, "is probably sitting in a box somewhere in the police headquarters?"

A moment of silence, then a tight huff heaving Edei's chest. Was that a . . . laugh?

"First day on the job, and this is what you want to do?" he asked. "All right. Let's try it."

Io's breath caught in her lungs, like his laugh was a hook and she a starving fish. He couldn't possibly have guessed what she intended to propose; she hadn't even said it aloud! And if he had realized her absurd plan, why on earth was he agreeing?

"Really?" she asked.

"Really. It's mad enough that it might just work." He gestured at the door with a half bow, like an old-timey gentleman. "After you, boss."

With a jolt, Io realized: she had been misidentifying her body's reaction all day. For three years, she had done everything humanly possible to avoid him. Now she had an opportunity, however involuntary, to finally study him. To see what destiny had written for her, to see if she would choose it for herself. She was a creature of curiosity and he an exhilarating new mystery to solve.

She wasn't nervous. She was *excited*.

"Wait," Xenophon called as she walked around him to join Edei at the door. The knowing smirk was wiped from his face. "Whatever you're planning, I want in."

"Trust me," Io said in lieu of goodbye, "you don't."

This was the difference between a respected journalist with a source on the inside and two sleuths from the very bottom of the Silts: *they* had both the means and the guts to break into the police headquarters.

# CHAPTER VII

# OCCASIONALLY

CITY PLAZA WAS a giant complex of buildings at the base of District-on-the-Hill, where the courts, police headquarters, and City Council were housed around a magnificent fountain of the three Graces. The Charites, as was their original name, were depicted naked, embracing each other lovingly. They represented humanity's best qualities, hence their prominent place in the Plaza, which Io found both sexist and hypocritical. The former because more than two-thirds of government employees were male, the latter because they pretended to worship the goddesses when they treated their descendants, the grace-born, like harlots. But that was Alante for you: alabaster duplicity.

A wall topped with barbed wire surrounded the Plaza, with guards at each of the four gates. According to Io's intel, there were never fewer than thirty guards on duty at any given time. She and Edei stood on an arched bridge overlooking the Plaza, Edei's arms crossed over his chest. On someone else, it would have looked aggressive, even threatening, but Edei had a calm about him, a quiet resonance that made the gesture naturally contemplative.

He had been just as calm as he followed her silently through the Silts to gather the information they would need, which had not failed to impress Io, either.

"We're getting in through that," she said, pointing to a structure on their left.

The east wing of the police station had submitted to the tide's rot, like all buildings in Alante did sooner or later. Its western face had collapsed into the wall of the Plaza a month ago. Restorations were underway: scaffolding propped the rusty foundations up with stabilizing beams connected to the bank across the street. They could access one of the twelve-foot-long beams from the roof of the bank; if they crossed it without getting spotted, they would be over the wall and into the station within seconds.

"My client said the bank guards make their rounds on the roof every thirty minutes. We need to time it right and be fast. The door to the main structure is kept locked, but we can figure that out—I've got my tools with me." There was a reason picking a lock was such a private investigator cliché: it was a wholly necessary skill.

Edei didn't respond. His silence drilled into her certainty until it hit doubt. She glanced at him, trying to decipher his frown—he had so many of them, an endless collection of unknowable brow arrangements.

"Well?" she prompted.

"I just, um, can't believe we're doing this."

"You're the one that said let's try it!" Her voice went embarrassingly shrill.

"I did, didn't I? Gods." He rubbed his bottom lip absentmindedly with the end of his sleeve. His frown wasn't reservation, Io realized, but worry.

Which was perfectly understandable. "I can go in alone," she offered.

"No, no. We're partners. And it's a good plan. Only someone completely empty-headed would think of breaking into the police headquarters, which means they won't be expecting it—or watching for it."

His dark eyes fell on her, unyielding and relentless. Most people avoided such intense and prolonged eye contact—Io certainly did—

but not Edei. It seemed almost as if he employed it to his service, waiting for her to crack under the persistence of his inspection.

"I don't mean to offend you," he started, which immediately made every muscle in Io's body seize up in trepidation. Never trust a sentence prefaced by that phrase. "But how can you be sure your client told you the truth?"

"I'm sure," she said without missing a beat. "They owed me a favor."

The bank's cleaner, Roe, was a former client; they didn't have enough money to pay her at the time, so Io had settled for a favor in the future. Today, she had come to claim it, approaching Roe on their cigarette break an hour ago, while Edei waited outside.

"It just seems to me that risking jail time for abetting a break-in is a very dangerous favor to do for the girl you once hired to find if your lover scorned you or if your son loves to gamble," said Edei.

*I work with scorned lovers and worried parents*—those were her own words, back at the Fortuna. *Well.* Did he have to be smart, too? Why couldn't his perfect jawline and broad shoulders suffice? Why did he need to be intelligent and perceptive *and* unwilling to let go of the things that others ignored daily and happily? And why, *oh why*, did the fact that he had outsmarted her make Io blush even harder?

She considered her options: refuse to answer and lose his trust entirely; lie and risk getting caught; or tell him the truth. Io huffed a breath. The truth it would have to be, because by some inane sense of justice, she believed that guessing the nature of her secrets earned him an honest answer.

"Occasionally," she said, "I don't simply find out if your spouse is cheating or your kid is gambling. Occasionally, I *cut* the thread that ties them to their love of drinking or gambling."

She dropped his gaze. She knew it was wrong. But what was she to do when she kept seeing the same people fall into the same bad habits? When they dropped to their knees asking for help? She made a living breaking other people's hearts—she simply couldn't refuse when they begged her to put it back together.

"It's not like you think," she added, the words rushing out of her mouth. "Cutting someone's thread, I mean. I only ever cut threads of addiction and only if the addicts agree. Sometimes the cutting helps, takes off the fog and helps them focus again, keeps them from relapsing. Sometimes, the thread grows back. I'm not—"

She stopped. She was starting to sound apologetic, which she hated. Somewhere in the course of this conversation, she had tricked herself into feeling guilty, into fearing what Edei might think of her. But these were *her* choices, *her* threads she sacrificed to cut theirs, *her* consciousness stained. She had weighed it in her mind's scales and found helping them worthy of the cost. She refused to feel judged for that.

A finger tapped on her arm; she caught Edei's hand retreating to his pocket. The tenderness of the movement was enough to lull her into raising her eyes to his. "Listen," he said, "if it's any worth, I understand. There is violence in kindness, and kindness in violence."

Io took his soft words and cradled them against her chest. *Violence in kindness, and kindness in violence.* They felt intimate in more ways than she could count; her past was riddled with moments that proved their truth. The words didn't lessen the sense of wrongdoing, but she felt seen. Known.

She replied with a small nod. She veered toward the bank, saying, "Come on, then. Let's go be empty-headed."

Edei exhaled a laugh and followed, and they began zigzagging between shoppers. When they snuck into the nearest dark alley, Edei dragged down a flood-escape ladder. They climbed silently, one eye on the residents moving inside the buildings. They walked across ducts and overpasses until they stood on the roof of the bank, directly across from the police station.

Below, the final tide bells started ringing. The night tide had reached the Hill, seawater crawling up cobblestone streets like a horde of iridescent insects. The bells sounded less threatening in this part of town: the City Plaza was built on an elevated platform, and the surrounding wall kept most of the water out. Stores had automated shutters and sump pumps, and cafés and restaurants had already moved their tables onto balconies and rooftops. If you didn't glance down at the murky liquid harboring vicious chimerini, this scenery was close to idyllic. Swirly neon signs, strings of candle-lit lanterns, lush greenery spilling over rails, clean-shaven men in floral suits, and fur-clad women with large jade earrings dangling from their ears, sipping wine under the moonlight.

Io's lip curled with contempt, but if she was honest with herself, there was a part of her that longed for this kind of carefree opulence. A night off in the best bar in town, dancing and gossiping with Rosa—now wouldn't that be something?

She glanced at her watch. "We've got two minutes."

At the edge of the roof, Edei was testing the scaffolding beam with his foot—it bounced under his weight. Gods, it was less steady than a cat bridge. At least those were made of metal. He shuffled forward, arms outstretched for balance. After a few inches, he stopped, looked at her over his shoulder. "Are you all good? You're afraid of heights, right?"

Io's stomach somersaulted. "How do you know that?"

He shrugged, a minuscule movement so as not to disturb the beam. "Your sister makes fun of you a lot."

*My sister,* Io thought, *is going to die a slow, painful death.*

To Edei, she replied, "I'll be fine. Go."

In barely half a minute, he had crossed the beam and dived into the shadows of the scaffolding. The brass knuckles on his belt caught the light as he spun back to watch Io. Her panic was at once overwhelmingly present and far away. She stepped onto the wooden plank and began inching forward, keeping her eyes on the wood stretching ahead, its small fluctuations and infinitesimal creaks. It was always better when she didn't glance at what awaited her at the bottom should she fall.

The streetlights zapped, warning the arrival of electricity. If they switched on, Io would be exposed to all those high-class wine drinkers on the balconies below her, who would no doubt screech for the police. Io rushed forward, stepping onto the scaffolding a mere second before the lights flickered on. She grabbed the posts and waited until her heart stopped roaring in her ears. She should start looking for a desk job somewhere or wait tables at Amos's café. This was far too much excitement within the span of twenty-four hours.

When Io opened her eyes again, Edei was watching the bank guards dive back into the building after clearing the roof. They had timed it perfectly.

This next part was far less organized. Io and Edei moved with slow, exploratory steps across the planks of the scaffolding. His breath warmed her nape, and she could smell the sweet detergent of his clothes. *Do not*, she scolded herself, *be weird.*

Edei pointed to the illuminated outline of a door. The police station proper must be on the other side. She took out her tools and made quick work of the lock. Before opening it, she peeked at Edei over her shoulder.

"Hey," she said. "I have to pull up the Quilt to keep us away from the guards. Do you know how that works?"

"A tapestry of threads," he replied. "I hear they're silver."

"Um, they are." A well of surprises, this guy. Few people cared to know more about moira-born than the nonsense the media reported. "I can see the threads of every person in the building and know where they stand. But it will cost me: I won't be as aware of the real, physical world."

"What do you need me to do?" he asked.

"Guide me," she replied. Gods, she sounded like a complete creep.

"All right." He didn't wait—he stepped around her to take the lead, slid one hand into hers, and grabbed the knob with the other.

Io let the Quilt bloom around her. Threads blinded her momentarily, but her eyes adjusted fast. There were a dozen people in the police headquarters, far more than the lean night shift of five Roe had claimed. Blessedly, none of them stood behind this door, or on this entire floor.

"Go," she said.

His fingers tugged, Io's stomach jolted, the door swung open.

They were in.

# CHAPTER VIII

# RED

**THEY WORKED QUICKLY** through the eastern wing. Io kept watch on the Quilt, squeezing his hand every time she thought an officer might be climbing to their floor. Edei slowed or hurried them forward, pivoted Io to the side so she wouldn't trip over the things she couldn't see. His hand in hers made her hypersensitive, almost giddy. *I am touching him.* The thought buzzed like electricity through her wired veins.

"What are we looking for?" Edei whispered when they reached a corridor of offices. "Evidence room?"

"His office, I think. I would keep these files close if I were him, wouldn't you?"

She kept watch as he padded down the corridor, and soon she realized he was making a . . . sniffing sound before each door. Was he an actual greyhound? It was strange and endearing and caused a snort to burst out of her. "What *are* you doing?"

"He smokes," he explained, a murmur from the end of the corridor. "Cigars."

"The smell can't possibly linger that long."

"Come and see."

Io dropped the Quilt, relieved to return to the mundane world of colors and shadows, and joined him in front of the last door to the left. Sure enough, the acrid smell of smoke and ash lingered in the air. "Impressive."

Edei jammed his shoulder against the locked door. "Will they hear if I break it down?"

"You can break it down?" she asked, more than a little awed.

His eyes bulged, like he'd caught himself in a blunder. He said timidly, "Probably."

"Here." She handed him her lock-picking tools, assuming—correctly—that he knew how to work them. A minute of fiddling with the pins and tongs and the door swung open.

Light from the major moon, Pandia, squeezed in the room through a narrow window fit between half a dozen metal filing cabinets. A simple desk faced the door, paired with a high-back chair and little else: a vintage metal desk lamp and a framed photo of a couple silhouetted against a sky exploding with fireworks. A cigar lay half-smoked on a glass ashtray on the window ledge. The whole room reeked of it.

Edei stepped to the cabinets and read the labels aloud. "'Warrants, Arrests, Incidents, Cold Cases.' Gods, this will take forever."

"Start with whatever drawer is locked," Io said—and immediately held her breath, waiting for him to snap at her in response.

But Edei obeyed without so much as a backward glance.

She exhaled, wondering at the source of her trepidation. She had given him an order and expected him not to like it. What a silly reaction, that she should feel guilty of taking the lead on something she was clearly more skilled in. Guilt was an old habit, one she thought she had kicked. Gods, she was a bundle of anxiety tonight.

She pulled open the desk drawers, revealing piles of managerial documents: police budgets, patrol timetables, district crime reports, etc. The top drawer had a state-of-the-art, complex lock. Her tools were no match for it.

"Edei?" she whispered. "Some help?"

After examining the lock and drawer, Edei left the room and came back with a metal rod he'd found gods know where. He jammed it against the wood and heaved. The lock detached with a loud crack—Io raised a hand. They stood there, motionless and agitated, while she watched the Quilt for any movement. The officers on the ground floor didn't stir. It turned out to be worth it: Edei pulled out a hefty file marked SILTS STRANGLINGS.

She joined him by the window, where they lifted the papers to the moonlight. Police reports on the deaths of Konstantin Fyodorov, the chernobog-born; Bianca's employee Minos; and Jarl Magnussen; then a report titled *Emmeline Segal*. Two photos were attached to the report: a young, smiling girl posing in a feathered hat, and a bloated, white corpse laid on a metal table. The eyewitness had confirmed Emmeline was the wraith who killed the border guard, Fyodorov. The twenty-year-old had been a dancer in a dream palace on Lilac Row.

"Segal," Edei said. "I know the name. She used to work for the Miduchi gang."

The Miduchi were one of the lesser gangs of the Silts, a crew of young thieves specializing in breaking and entering. They never targeted the Silts, only the richer districts, which had earned them an unofficial go-ahead from the mob queen, so long as they "paid their dues."

"A gang squabble?"

"It's possible. Though Fyodorov was retired."

Io tapped at a file attached to the report: Emmeline's public registry entry. It was a long lineage of her known family and a conclusion at the bottom, underlined three times with blotched ink: *No known other-born affiliation*. "Emmeline is not recorded as a cutter. Could she have been unregistered?"

"I suppose the Miduchi could have an official on the payroll. Most gangs do."

Lots of other-born, especially those who society considered dangerous, tried to hide their powers. But even if they could get forged birth certificates that hid the existence of any siblings, it was hard to keep up the charade if you lived in a major city-nation like Alante: officials often employed the help of the muse-born to locate other-born who attempted to trespass into city-nations. *Stowaway lists* they were called. Muse-born like the Nine had an uncanny—and mystifying—ability to uncover the liars. It was easy enough to pay off someone in the public registry to disappear the file from the public records, but you couldn't just bribe your name off the Nine's lists. *Especially* if you were a cautioned-entry other-born, like cutters were.

"Look," whispered Edei. He was touching a photo of a face Io knew. Gaunt features, hollow cheeks, silver hair—the wraith from last night.

Io angled the paper to the moonlight. Her name was Drina Savva, aged eighty-one. She was the widow of a bankrupt merchant from the Artisti District who had been forced to move into the Silts fifteen years ago when the bank foreclosed on their house. The same phrase was underlined in her public registry file, too: *No known other-born affiliation.*

"It makes no sense." The records had to be wrong. Io's mind denied any other explanation on a fundamental level. Only moira-born could hold the threads of fate; it was a fact of life, as undeniable as the sun rising every morning and setting every evening.

They were silent for a few minutes as they skimmed through other papers in the file: coroner reports, witness transcripts, background checks on family members and neighbors of both the victims and the murderers.

"Wait," Edei said. "We've seen this name before."

He took the file from her, thumbed through the papers, and

pulled out two: a police testimony by Drina Savva's husband, claiming his wife had been assaulted with the intention of kidnapping, and the records of the orphanage where Emmeline Segal and her brothers were raised, stating the girl had been kidnapped when she was eight. Suspected but not convicted were two men: one Horace Lark and one Holland Lowe.

"I've heard of him. They're the same man—aliases of a crook called Horatio Long," Edei explained. "He has as many names as schemes."

"The attempted kidnappings are both dated the same day, twelve years ago."

Edei's mouth was scrunched up to the side. "He's known for setting up brutal fighting dens. Bianca banned him from her turf a few years ago, after he was accused of mistreating his fighters."

"Mistreating them how?"

"I've heard some strange stories. Supposedly, he uses nefarious methods to increase their stamina and aggression. Our neighbor used to wrestle way back when—he says Horatio's fighters were bloodthirsty, frenzied, like rabid dogs."

"Like the woman last night?" Io said. "So what, he tried to recruit Emmeline and Drina twelve years ago, failed, and now he's returned to finish the job? But then why would they be out in the city, murdering people and talking of justice, instead of fighting in his matches?"

"It's worth checking out."

"I suppose it's the only connection we have so far."

"You're in here, too." He had been skimming through the file and now handed her a witness report with her name typed in bold.

"That makes sense, the officers called to the scene escorted me home last night."

She read through her own deposition, then through reports

on investigations she had carried out for some of her more recent clients, a detailed account of her taxes, known addresses, and acquaintances. They'd been thorough. Attached to hers was a brief report on Ava, focusing mainly on her job at the Fortuna. And then: a file with a familiar name.

Thais Ora.

Io's heart started beating fast. She pulled the spotless white folder out slowly, almost unwillingly. A black-and-white photo was clipped on the first page. Her sister gazed back at the photographer with pure hatred, her dark brows cast close over her eyes, her lips pursed in a severe line. Io remembered the day the photo was taken. A new law had been passed, dictating the immediate renewal of other-born papers to include photos. Thais had joined the rallies against it, condemning the photos as an invasion of privacy.

Io leafed through the document. Born on Mint Street, in their parents' apartment, which Io and Ava couldn't afford when Thais left them. Received excellent grades in school, and even got into the Polytechnic School at the city-nation of Nanzy. Thais hadn't ended up going; her scholarship application was denied. Then a list of the various jobs she'd held over the years, ending with the private investigator office she had set up with Io, months before she left. The only thing of importance, circled in red by whoever had compiled the file, was her involvement with Thomas Mutton and his pyramid scheme, named obnoxiously For the Other. It was a bleak time in the Ora sisters' history that Io didn't like to reminisce about. At the end of the report was Thais's request to change her home address, signed almost three months ago. *Thais Ora. 64 Hanover Street.*

Io's mind blanked. She saw the letters, ink on paper, but the words didn't make sense. Hanover was one of the most famous streets in the wealthy walled community of District-on-the-Hill.

Thais was here. In the city. She'd been here for three months. And she hadn't visited or sent word. Why? The old shame came rushing back; Io's chest tightened with the revelation of Thais's return.

Edei's breath moved the soft hairs on her temple as he leaned over her shoulder. "Who's that?"

She pulled herself together. "My sister. She disappeared on us, two years ago."

"Mm-hmm. Ava says it was unexpected."

Why was Ava sharing so much with this boy? Gods, it didn't even matter right now. "If we couldn't still see the threads connecting us to her, we would have thought something had happened to her," she replied. The address on the page seemed to taunt her. "But she had packed her stuff and everything. Taken her passport and papers."

"She didn't tell you she was back in Alante?"

Io shook her head. Her thoughts had come undone, tumbling in her skull like marbles in a lottery machine. She could hear them echoing, an endless, erratic alarm. Thais had been back for *three months.*

Suddenly, boots clobbered down the corridor. They sounded close—too close. Blinking the Quilt into place, Io spotted four people in the corridor of their floor, more climbing the stairs after them. All were headed straight at them, without checking the other offices. Shit. How did they know exactly where they were?

The answer came to her instantly. An other-born. Saint-Yves truly had an other-born in his employ. Several, if his claims about the Initiative were to be believed.

Still, if Io had been paying attention, if Thais hadn't stolen away her very thoughts, she would have seen them coming up the stairs. She and Edei would have made it down the corridor, into the eastern wing, across the scaffolds to the bank. Now the way back was blocked, the whole station after them.

"We've got to move," Edei said. But instead of going for the door, he threw the window open. Ashtray and cigar tumbled over the ledge and shattered in the courtyard below. "Climb out. I'll follow."

"Out? Why out?" she stammered, but there was no time to argue.

The officers were banging at the door. As Edei shoved the desk in front of it, Io climbed over the window and stood at the foot-wide ledge. Three stories down, the marble steps of the police station glistened, hard and smooth as a chopping block. No tidewater to save her now; a fall meant death.

Edei appeared behind her, a hand on her waist urging her forward. They trundled awkwardly along the ledge, holding on to drainpipes and windows. The wall at her back was still warm from this morning's heat. Io's ragged breaths turned into silent sobs, and still she kept moving. No way out but through.

"Just a little further," Edei rasped.

Behind them, a ruckus. Faces popping out the window, telling them to stop or they'll shoot. A shadow climbing onto the ledge after them and others raising their guns. The sudden shock of bullets breaking the air, zapping past them.

"Shit, shit, shit," Io muttered, blinking furiously against the tears gathering in her eyes. She put one foot in front of the other. Up ahead, the building curved—they'd be safer there.

A bullet slit the air, far too close. A grunt escaped Edei. His body stumbled into Io's. She threw her arm out, flattening him to the wall. Several moments passed, Edei with his eyes closed, Io feeling his heartbeat under her palm.

At last, his eyes flickered open, focusing on her face. "Keep going."

But before she turned, she saw: red, on the wall behind him.

They rounded the corner to find the scaffolding right in front of them. Clever of Edei: they couldn't make it through the building, so he took them around it. With trembling fingers, Io pulled herself up on the planks. They scrambled through, objects plummeting, ricocheting on what sounded like every damn post of the scaffolds. Officers were moving above and below, behind them. They shouted and threatened; Io caught the glimmer of Pandia on their guns, but they couldn't shoot for fear of hitting one of their own.

An officer appeared before Io, his form pitch-black against the dark. She let out a strangled cry, and Edei was there, pushing her behind him and swinging a leg at the officer's ankles. The man crumpled with a shout and dropped out of sight. Edei reached back and took her hand, gripping her tighter as they reached the wooden beam leading to the bank. Io couldn't help it—she looked down at the gaping wound of darkness. It was a mistake. Panic grabbed her mind, allowing no room for reason. She pulled against Edei's grasp, but he dragged her, stumbling behind him, over the narrow wavering plank. Tears flowed freely down Io's cheeks. Gods, how she hated herself in moments like this, where fear was all she was. No reason, no strength, just mind-numbing, all-consuming fear.

She had to hold it together, for his sake. One misstep, one wrong move, and she would yank him down with her.

*Thump!* The beam beneath her feet vibrated hard. Halfway across, Edei and Io threw their arms out, barely managing to stay upright. Behind them, an officer was kicking at the plank, trying to dislodge it. Others were not far behind—when they arrived, dropping Edei and Io into the flooded street would be a certainty. Below, a patrol boat had spotted them and was quickly zooming in their direction.

The officer kicking the beam glanced up. Long face, brown skin, small, wide-set eyes, and black curls tucked neatly into her cap. Io recognized her; she recognized Io. Rosa Santos, an oneiroi-born, descended from the gods of sleep, Io's best friend, and—it turned out—a traitor. How could Rosa, born and raised in the Silts, work for the damned leeches?

All of a sudden, Io wasn't afraid. She was angry and a little bit feral.

"Go," she told Edei. She snatched her hand from his and called forth the Quilt. Threads flooded her vision, all those officers moving through the building, up the scaffolding, spilling into the Plaza's grounds. But she only needed Rosa's threads, dozens of them flowing in different directions. One was just close enough for Io to reach out and grab.

Rosa gasped at the touch.

Io moved fast: she brought one of her threads down on Rosa's.

Both threads split.

The other girl fell on her back, as though some unknowable force holding her up had abruptly disappeared. A cut thread felt akin to a breath stolen. Not to Io. She had gotten used to the sudden absence; being a cutter would do that to you. As Rosa clenched her chest and the other officers lowered her to the scaffolding, Io ran down the rest of the plank. The moment she was on the roof of the bank, Edei pushed the wood into the water below, stranding the officers on the other end.

Io and Edei rushed across bridges and rooftops for long, breathless minutes, until the officers' voices faded. Then Edei slowed, slumped into her. Io clenched her jaw and pulled his arm over her shoulders, feeling the warmth of his blood soaking her side.

# CHAPTER IX

# RECKLESS

**EDEI NEVER FAINTED.** He stumbled and fell and leaned so heavily onto Io she thought they might both crumple, but he never lost consciousness, perhaps because he knew they wouldn't make it if he did. He held on until they reached the Fortuna, entering through its side door, a repurposed flood-escape staircase, then sank to his knees on the dark wooden floor of the hall, taking Io with him.

The two guards on duty rushed to pick him up. With sharp orders that Io didn't fully hear, they carried him through a doorway to the right. Their footsteps and voices disappeared as soon as the door closed behind them. Io stayed on the floor. The blood on her hands had dried in ugly patches of brown. *My fault.* She tried to dislodge the thought with flimsy excuses—it had happened too fast, she had been too shocked, they had been too slow—but it wouldn't budge. The truth of it was that if she had been careful, it wouldn't have happened. And now Edei was shot. Edei was bleeding.

Io gritted her teeth. *Oh, don't wallow,* Thais would chastise during Io's moody preteen years. *Go find what you don't like and change it. You know you can change it, right, little idiot? Be better, make this world better.*

Be better. Fine. She wiped the blood on her pants and stood. The door opened to an employee-only staircase. Voices were coming from the floor below. This was a part of the club she'd never been in before, no doubt a private quarter for the gang's members. She took the stairs down and spotted an open door leading into a brightly lit room. The two Fortuna members Io had seen in Bianca's office last night held Edei's body on its side on a long table, while an older man examined the gun wound on his shoulder.

"Fetch Samiya," said the ginger, Nico.

The older man hurried out of the room, slipping past Io with barely a glance. Nico spotted her at the doorframe but said nothing, which Io took to mean she could stay. The windowless room was dressed in the same suffocating black wood as the rest of the Fortuna. It shimmered silver as Io pulled up the Quilt. They were all too damn close, threads tangled and bright—she couldn't make out a thing. She circled around to Edei's head. His eyes were closed, his lips pressed tight, but the vein on his throat pulsed steadily. Io focused on the threads shooting out of his chest. Carefully, she disentangled them: two led to people in this very room—Nico, the redhead, and Chimdi, the Anoch girl with the dark skin and shaved head who was pressing a towel on Edei's bullet wound. In between the jumble, Io found what she was looking for: his life-thread. With delicate fingers, she followed it up, where it disappeared through the ceiling to the sky beyond.

"Well?" snapped Chimdi.

"It's not frayed," Io replied quietly. "He'll be okay."

A voice boomed down the corridor. "Where are they?"

The door groaned on its hinges to reveal Bianca, her mauve satin shirt buttoned haphazardly on her midriff. Io flushed when she noticed the sharp juts of Bianca's collarbones and the amount of bare skin exposed below them. Her lips were tinted with blue, which was peculiar: either she had been drinking an exotic cocktail or had recently taken a sleeping potion.

"Did you call Samiya? Good. Tell her to get that bullet out of him and use whatever medicine she needs, no matter the cost. Ora, follow me."

Without waiting to see if she was obeyed, Bianca turned on her heel, leaving Io to trail after her. Brass knuckles hung like a lady's purse from Bianca's right hand. The stories of Bianca's punishments were notoriously gory. Enemies sliced open, traitors shot in the knee, bad customers found beaten within an inch of their lives. The streets whispered that she had slit the throat of her main rival—the mob king Hellas—during the Riots, ear to ear, ending his reign and establishing her own. Bianca Rossi traded in pain; Ava had once told Io that Bianca preferred the knuckles, not just because guns were inaccurate, but because knuckles could do double the damage.

Io had no doubt the knuckles Bianca carried were meant for her. The mob queen's every step took them farther away from the populated parts of the club, as though she didn't want any witnesses. Io began marking her surroundings in case she needed to make a run for it, and moved her fingers deftly to grab a thread and shove both hands in the pockets of her jacket.

The mob queen led her to one of the balconies overlooking the busy street below the club. A red clock was strung overhead, its sleek surface and thin fingers the remnants of the Fortuna's past life as a temple—or a whorehouse, depending on who you were asking. Its ticking filled the silence.

"How'd it happen?" Bianca said.

"We broke into City Plaza. We got caught."

"What were you looking for in the Plaza?"

"All other-born records have been pulled from the public registry by Saint-Yves. We needed to confirm the women's identities and find a possible connection."

"And did you?"

"Yes. Horatio Long. Edei knows him."

Bianca blew out her lips. "What does Long have to do with this?"

"We'll find out."

"I've been told he set up a fighting den again. I'll find out where."
A pause, then: "What else?"

"The women are not registered as cutters."

"So what? They were smuggled in. Not everyone is a Goody Two-shoes like you Ora sisters. What else?"

Io breathed out through her nose. She wasn't used to playing against an equal opponent. "Someone recognized me."

"Who?"

"An old friend."

If Rosa had revealed Io's identity, the police—perhaps even Saint-Yves himself—might be rifling through Io and Ava's tiny loft right this moment. Probably already issued a citywide *be on the lookout* on her.

"Do you need me to take care of it?" asked Bianca.

Fear stabbed deep into Io's belly. She could guess what *take care of it* meant for a mob queen: disappearing Rosa from the city, and any connection between the break-in and the Fortuna gang along with her. No matter Rosa's current affiliations, she had until recently been Io's closest friend, her only true confidante. Like hell would Io let Bianca Rossi get her hands on Rosa.

"I'll handle it," Io answered, hoping she sounded assertive.

For a few moments, they both gazed at the roof bar across the street. Someone was having a bachelor party; feather-plumed performers were dancing on the tables. The three moons had hidden behind clouds, shrouding the whole scene like a photo: gray and immovable.

Io felt on edge, as though at any moment she would have to fight for her life. She had expected anger, blame. This unruffled business talk was making her uneasy. The least she deserved was a stern scolding or a disapproving glare—Thais would have made her apologize ten times by now. Bianca had demanded no apology, which made Io all the more desperate to give it.

"I'm sorry," she declared. "It was my fault. I got distracted."

With slow movements, Bianca started gathering her blond locks into a high ponytail. Her neck came into view, spotted with the purple bruises from last night's squabble with the wraith and the discolored patches of Ersa's kisses. The pause elongated, and this eerie absence of response became the scariest thing Io had faced all night.

"Edei has been doing this job three years now," Bianca said, "and he's never been shot. He spends a couple of hours with you and comes back with a bullet in his back. Either you're reckless—"

"I'm not."

"—or you're making *him* reckless. Breaking into the Plaza isn't a two-man job."

Io kept her mouth shut.

"People warned me about you, Ora. Sometimes, they said, in your investigations, you cut what you find. But Edei insisted. *It's a dead end without her*, he claimed. Dead end or not, I don't like liabilities."

Io swallowed and took her hand out of her pocket. Invisible to Bianca, the thread was taut as a blade. She would use it if she had to. Liability was a polite word for "threat," and Io could easily guess how Bianca Rossi treated threats.

"Do you know of the term Roosters' Silence, cutter?"

Of course she did. A Roosters' Silence meant a silence agreed upon and obediently kept by a large group. The term had an element of the nonsensical, a silence impossible to achieve, like all the roosters agreeing not to crow at dawn. The most famous Roosters' Silence that Io knew of was the one kept after the Moonset Riots.

The Riots happened twelve years ago in Moonset month—a month every seven years when all three moons disappear from the night sky. No one knew exactly how the Riots started, only that one of the many gangs of the Silts went rogue, looting, beating, destroying whatever they could find. The police had no choice but to withdraw their presence; residents were left to fend for themselves, which escalated the infighting. The Order of the Furies—descendants of the Furies, law enforcement of the other-born population—was sent from the city-nation of Nanzy to mollify the situation, but the rogue gang prevailed, wiping out their entire force.

The few fury-born who survived the Riots succumbed to their wounds in the hospital. Two months later, the Agora made a public announcement: the Furies were no more. Complete extinction of the one force that could keep other-born in line—and the culprit was this insidious city, this harbor of violence, this scum of the world, Alante. Faced with the entire world's anger, the surviving gang leaders, headed by none other than the woman standing now in front of Io, convened and reached an agreement: no one would snitch and provide the identity of the rogue gang to the police. Their names would be lost to history. No retribution sought, no investigations and arrests, no new vendettas born. *No leeches, ever.* The Silts needed to rebuild.

And so they made a vow of Roosters' Silence.

"Yes, I know the term," said Io.

"Do you know what happens to those who break it?"

"Yes," Io whispered. Their larynx carved out of their throats, left to hang from their chin like a chicken's wattle.

"Everyone who works for me knows to keep the Silence. You want to break into the Plaza? Fine. You've got old friends in the police? Fine. But if you breathe even a word of me and mine to the leeches, consider yourself a crowing rooster. Do you get what I'm saying, cutter?"

Io's hand clenched into a fist.

The clock answered for her: *Tick-tock. Tick. Tock.*

# CHAPTER X

# A CAUTIONARY TALE

IO CALLED FORTH the Quilt the moment Bianca left the rooftop, leafing through her bundle of threads. They slipped through her fingers like gossamer hairs, the touch of each wholly distinctive. She knew upon contact what each thread led to: one reminded her of Ava's voice, the other of the taste of Amos's coffee, the next of her favorite mosaic in the Artisti District of a beach strewn with beckoning sirens.

And there—Rosa's smirk, the smell of her tobacco, the weight of her arm slung across Io's shoulders. The thread stretched eastward, which Io hadn't expected; it was neither the direction of the Plaza, nor of her and Ava's apartment. She threw back her shoulders and drew in a deep breath. Time for some more sleuthing.

Trolleys grunted past her as she took to the roofs, crossing the Silts at a swift pace. Every few minutes she double-checked the direction of Rosa's thread in the Quilt. Her steps slowed when she neared the giant apartment complex where Rosa and her extended family rented flats. How many times had she walked this same path, to drop Rosa off after school, or pick her up for a night of dancing?

She had met Rosa at school, a few blocks away. How exactly, neither of them remembered, though they often tried to coax it out of their brains.

"First day, seated next to each other?" Io would guess.

"Too corny." Rosa would shake her head. "Jumping rope during recess?"

"Too banal. What about the girls' bathroom, hiding from the prefect?"

"Bah. Too on the nose."

However it had happened, the point was that within a few weeks, they were two inseparable eight-year-old scoundrels devising insidious pranks on the teachers they didn't like. Throughout the years, they shared everything: homework, clothes, fears, secrets, and dreams. They loved playing make-believe as the Order of the Furies, which later turned into a plan to work together as an undefeatable duo of detective and prosecutor that would bring criminal other-born to their knees.

*And on weekends, we'll dance*, Rosa would say.

Io was there at Rosa's mom's funeral, three years ago now. Rosa was there during that horrible week two years ago that culminated in Thais leaving—more than there, Rosa was involved in a way that made Io skittish to think about. Then, about a year ago, at seventeen, they graduated. What used to be part-time jobs had to become full-time. Their paths began to diverge, but the girls refused to lose touch: they flirted with boys together, went out dancing together, tried to learn how to cook together.

The last time they had seen each other was with Ava at the dancing club Cellar, to celebrate the job Rosa had just gotten writing for the women's magazine *Miss-Matched*. But that must have been at least six months ago, maybe more? They had made plans a couple of times since then, but at the last moment, Io would just . . . succumb to the urge to cancel.

And now Rosa was a leech, and Io was working for the mob queen of the Silts. So much for dreams of justice. Gods, it sounded like a cautionary tale.

Her feet found their own way to the door of the apartment Rosa shared with her two cousins. The thread that bound them went straight through the door, where Io could see her friend moving through the small living room. Four other bundles of threads sat in various corners of the room. Her family? New friends?

Io could turn back and forget their meeting on that scaffolding tonight ever happened. That was the safest way to ensure Bianca, and all that mess with the wraiths, stayed well away from her friend. Perhaps Rosa wasn't even interested in seeing Io, in explaining things, after all this time they had spent apart. But the thread they shared was still there; their love for each other hadn't faded yet. Before she could talk herself out of it, Io knocked, two times fast, two times slow.

The door swung open in seconds, bathing the corridor with light. Rosa's face was still turned back, mid-laugh at something her friends had said. When her eyes finally registered Io, her smile faded, those high, joyous eyebrows collapsing into a frown. Her police jacket was undone, the sleeves rolled up to her biceps.

"Hey," Io said. "I just wanted to make sure—" *That you're safe. That I didn't hurt you.*

"Is it the food?" someone called from inside, an older, male voice.

Rosa startled, then quickly composed herself with a liquid "Don't be greedy, Marco. It's just my neighbor, the one I told you I babysit for?"

Casually, she leaned into the wood, blocking the space between door and frame with her body. She wasn't being cruel; she was trying to keep Io out of view from whoever was in the room. They must be her colleagues, then.

Io knew she didn't have a lot of time, if they were to keep this ruse going. "Are you all right?" she whispered.

"Yeah, yeah," Rosa said, her voice bored, almost blasé, appropriate for an overbearing neighbor. The apartment was small; her guests could probably hear her perfectly. "Listen, I can't babysit tomorrow—I'm working the night shift again."

Io played along. "Day after tomorrow?"

"Sounds good." Rosa's eyes bulged with exaggerated meaning. "I'll come to *you*."

Io nodded. Message received. They could talk at length the day after tomorrow.

The shadows behind Rosa's legs shifted, like someone had stood up from the couch. Io shuffled back from the door. Time to go before anyone unsavory spotted her.

Rosa called down the corridor, "Stay safe, all right?"

Worry clenched at Io's throat. That was easier said than done.

At dawn, when the last dregs of revelers left the Fortuna to stumble home, Ava found Io in the small parlor on the second floor of the club, three doors down from where Edei rested. She was in her golden dress with the plunging back, hair pinned over one shoulder as was the current trend. She patted Io's feet off the emerald-green love seat Io had fallen asleep on and slid down next to her.

"Hey," Io said, fingers working a crick in her neck.

"Here, your favorite." Ava presented her with a steaming cup of Amos's coffee. One of Io's thirty-five threads: the coffee shop in Parsley Square, two blocks away from the Fortuna. Amos Weinstein ran the place, a twenty-nine-year-old who'd traveled half the world as a lieutenant in the Iceberg Corps before settling in Alante and opening their coffee shop. They imported beans from four different city-nations and hand-ground them themself. Their soft dimples were the instigators of Io's first crush.

"I'm sorry we can't go home, Ava." Io pulled her sleeves over her palms to pick up the scalding hot paper cup.

Ava shrugged. "No worries. I can crash here; plenty of empty beds around."

Io didn't love the idea of leaving her sister within Bianca's reach, but if another wraith were to appear, the Fortuna Club was the safest place in the Silts.

"Look what else I've brought you." Ava produced two chocolate rugelach and proceeded to dip them in Io's cup and hand-feed them to her—Io chewed as fast as she could in a futile attempt to keep up with Ava's furious feeding.

She coughed, chuckled, coughed again. "Enough! I'm not a baby."

"Ehh, I could argue with that," Ava teased.

Of all her threads, besides the uncanny fate-thread, the one that connected her to Ava was the strongest. She was Io's favorite person in the world. Io already regretted the conversation ahead; she would have to hurt Ava, again.

Two years ago, when they woke to find Thais's drawers empty, all her stuff gone, her passport missing, Ava had been devastated. The police refused to investigate on the grounds that Thais left of her own free will, but Ava was persistent. She used their meager savings to follow Thais's thread through the perilous Wastelands between city-nations, arriving at last to the water town of Clyde twenty miles away. There she traced Thais's footsteps to an inn to find a note waiting for her with the innkeeper:

*Leave me alone. Haven't you done enough?*

Ava orbited back to Alante like a meteor scattering grief in its tail. She was inconsolable, and infuriated: What had they ever done to Thais? They were sisters, Fates, one soul in three bodies. She didn't understand what reason Thais could possibly have to desert them without a farewell, to forbid them from following.

Io could have offered plenty of reasons, but she had kept her mouth shut. That note was explanation enough: *Leave me alone.* Ava abandoned her search, but never her hope; every six months, she updated their address and contact information in the public registry. One day, Ava was certain, Thais would come back.

And now she had. Without a single word. Io could already imagine the astonished sadness in Ava's eyes. She would do anything—*anything*—to keep Ava from being hurt again. But she couldn't lie. Lies curdled love into something sour and noxious.

"Ava," she said. "Thais is back in Alante."

Io watched her sister's eyes fall, her shoulders stiffen. She knew at once what was going to follow: "I know," Ava replied.

The first thing Io felt, the strongest, was betrayal. All their lives, Thais was on one end, Io on the other, and Ava in the middle. Ava wasn't supposed to choose sides. She wasn't supposed to choose *Thais.* The coffee cup was suddenly too hot. Io placed it on the short table, sloshing some on the carpet in the process.

"You know?" Her voice came out a whisper.

Ava reached for Io's hands. "Sister mine, I'm so sorry! I wanted to tell you, but Thais made me promise I wouldn't. I remember how angry at you she was before she left, and how often you guys fought, and I didn't want . . . You are finally happy again. And she seems happy, too. I didn't want to ruin it, for either of you!"

Io's thoughts raced. "Thais is angry with me?"

"I mean . . ." Ava looked panicked, her thumbs running comforting circles on the backs of Io's hands. "I don't know if she's still angry, but she definitely was before she left. You guys thought I didn't notice any of it, because I was practicing for my Academia Aska audition, but I could hear you fighting all the time. I know she wanted you to keep working and you wanted to quit. I assume that's what you fought about . . ."

It was, in a way. When Io was fifteen, Thais fell in with a group of activists from the Artisti District. They had big ideas about how the economy would benefit from the inclusion of other-born in the upper ranks of society. Their leader was a blond charmer by the name of Thomas Mutton, who had no powers of his own and yet procured Thais jobs weaving new threads: a young mother struggling with postpartum depression, a failed artist trying to find his muse, a brokenhearted man looking to love again. Thais fancied herself a knight in shining armor, and the money wasn't so bad, either.

But then Thomas met Io. And he realized how much more money he could be making off a cutter. He started getting small jobs for Io, mainly with recovering addicts. Thais told her how wonderful it would be to help these people, how Io would be proving everyone who feared cutters wrong. *Cut*, they said, so Io cut. One day, Thomas proposed a different kind of job: one of the activists' rich parents wanted him to leave the poor boy from the Silts he'd fallen in love with. The money was enough to take care of rent for a year.

*Hell no,* Thais had said. *There are limits.*

*What limits? She's a cutter.*

So Thais left him that same day. They didn't need Thomas. They could do this on their own. Over the course of three weeks, Thais wove a thread between the rich parents and their son's boyfriend. Not a love-thread—that would be immoral—but a thread of timid fondness that could perhaps grow to affection in time. Io had never felt more in awe of her older sister.

But much as she tried, Thais was no charming socialite from Artisti. Thomas's friends refused to work with her. His rich acquaintances pretended they'd never met her. The Ora sisters turned away from Artisti, opened up a consultation office and sought clients in their own Silts, which would later evolve into what Io did now: private investigating. Business was good, yet Io saw her sister's despair growing by the day. No job paid enough, no noble deed satisfied enough. Thais wanted more, and Io couldn't give it to her.

Then Thais asked Io to sever a thread that . . . it simply wasn't right to cut. For the first time in their lives, Io told her sister *no*. For one long week, Thais locked herself in her room, playing her records, shutting Io out. On the seventh day, they woke to a silent apartment, a missing Thais, a room emptied of her valuables: her good coat, Mama's fancy boots, her savings, her papers.

"I'm not saying that's why she left," said Ava, pulling Io out of her memories.

"Kind of sounds like it."

Her sister gripped her tighter. "No, Io, that's not what I mean at all. Gods, I'm not good at this, okay? It just seemed to me that for a long time while you girls were working together, you were miserable. And she left that note, telling us to leave her alone . . . So she must have been miserable, too. Now you're happy. And she's happy. Maybe it's not so bad that she wants to stay away, huh?"

*She's my sister*, Io wanted to say. *She's not supposed to ostracize me to be happy.*

But she didn't want to argue with Ava on this. As children, whenever Io complained to Ava about Thais, her answer was always the same: Thais was teasing. That's what sisters do. She would turn up the music and drag Io into a dance, until they were both shaking with laughter. This was Ava's way: comfort, laughter, all in service of keeping the peace.

Io breathed in, then asked, "Is Thais weaving?"

What she meant was: Is she creating threads to endear herself to rich assholes who would otherwise ignore her? Like she had with her ex-boyfriend's stupid highbrow friends?

Ava's face hardened. "No, Io, she's not."

"She's living on Hanover Street. No other-born from the Silts can afford a place on the Hill."

Io could tell her sister wanted to say more, her cheeks red and puffy as if she was about to blow up, but she suddenly deflated. "Let's just leave Thais to her happiness, shall we? And get on with yours—Edei is awake."

Io's stomach lurched, Thais instantly forgotten. "How is he?"

"His left shoulder is stiff, but Samiya—she's horus-born, a healer—got the bullet out and mended him completely. She's saying the swelling should go down in a day or two. He's an ox, already trying to get back to business, but Bianca put him on mandatory bed rest. He's been asking for you."

Io lowered her chin to her chest, trying to keep the smile off her face. He was *asking for her*?

"Are you smitten? Is *this*"—Ava waved her hand at Io's face, which was no doubt the color of beetroot—"you finally acknowledging you're interested in your fate-thread? I *knew* there was a reason you never cut the thread!"

Io's whole body felt wrung like a dish towel, as though truth was being squeezed out of her drop by drop. "Where do they have him?"

"Upstairs. But don't go right now. Samiya is in there with him. The horus-born. His, um, girlfriend."

Oh. *That* was an unexpected sucker punch. But how had Io forgotten? The girlfriend was a subject she examined rarely, because it made her feel downright evil, but that didn't justify spending all of two minutes with Edei and speedily choosing to write off his girlfriend's existence from her mind!

She plastered nonchalance on her face. "Right. Yeah, I'll wait."

"Hey. Don't be like that." Ava flicked Io's nose. "You haven't done anything wrong."

"I haven't done anything right, either."

"Like what?"

"Cut the thread."

And here it would come: *We Ora sisters don't kiss other people's boyfriends*, like Thais had once said years ago. Io wanted to plug her fingers in her ears and sing *la-la-la-la* so that she wouldn't have to hear it again.

But instead, her sister made a long *pshew* sound. "Just because Thais said it doesn't mean it's right, Io. Just be careful. Bianca is . . . not possessive, exactly. But she values loyalty."

Bianca? Io hadn't expected to hear *that* name in this conversation. "What does this have to do with Bianca?"

"She doesn't like it that her infallible second-in-command broke the rules for you. No guns, no leeches, no paramours. They all follow these rules, strictly, even Bianca herself." Ava's mouth quirked down sourly. "They keep each other safe. Edei knows not to get the police involved. Gods, if the leeches know who we are, if Rosa said anything—"

"How do you know about Rosa?"

"Bianca mentioned that an old friend recognized you. I guessed it had to be Rosa, considering she's both your oldest and *only* friend."

"There's no need to be rude," Io grumbled, glaring at her sister's teasing smile. "I saw Rosa, spoke to her briefly last night—I don't think she snitched on us. Don't worry, all right? I'll fix this."

Ava patted Io's head like a dog. "I know you will, sister mine. Be better, right?"

Thais's old advice was salt rubbed in a still-open wound. Io didn't want to be better. She wanted to be *done*. She'd find this Horatio Long person, force a confession out of him, then deliver him to Bianca Rossi. She'd never have to step foot in the Fortuna again, or be threatened with a rooster's wattle, or feel the gentle severity of Edei's gaze, or wipe his blood off her fingers. She'd forget that one of her sisters didn't want to speak to her and the other kept secrets, that her best friend was now a turncoat. She'd forget about this whole damn thing.

"Be better," Io promised, but what she meant was *be over*.

The door flew open, and the ginger, Nico, entered, hopping on one leg while he pulled his boot onto the other. Io eyed the tall rain boots. They weren't city shoes.

"Bianca found Horatio Long?" Io guessed.

"It appears the old crook is running the chimerini fights," said Nico.

"Where?"

"The Docks."

Ava whistled. "Oh shit."

Oh shit, indeed.

# CHAPTER XI

# CHIMERINI

**THE DOCKS OF** Alante's port were long stretches of wood, parallel to each other, boats strapped haphazardly left and right. Each dock was supported by hundreds of spindly wooden pillars, dressed in thick sea moss. Some had half rotted, some had completely detached, but none were ever removed. People just added the new ones in between the carcasses. At night, the whole place was underwater, but now the Docks looked like particularly creepy, long-legged centipedes.

Io hated insects.

She was following Nico down the most derelict dock, trying to spot the missing planks and protruding nails through the heavy morning mist. The boy had talked the whole way, even when he ran out of breath or when all the morning commuters in the trolley stared at him. In the twenty minutes or so it'd taken them to get to the Docks, Io's spirits had lifted phenomenally; she now knew more than she ever thought possible about the lanky ginger.

He just turned nineteen, ten and a half months older than her, a Capricorn—thank the gods—born on the Neraida Plains north of the city. His parents had a farm, but with three sisters and four brothers, he wasn't really of any use there, so when he was sixteen and a half—precise numbers were important to this narrative, for some reason—he took the train to Alante and never looked back. His family wrote once a month, but he only sent back boxes of tobacco and candy. *The things I do for the gang are not exactly what makes parents proud*, he explained.

"So I have to sell these nectarines, you know, that I told you over-grew that spring?" he was saying now. "And I'm walking past this goat farm that's on the way to town. And there's a goat there, a baby, stuck in the fence, looking all sad and shit. I stop the cart and try to get it free, but the poor thing won't move. So I feed it nectarines and water, thinking at least she won't starve. And I make a whole detour and go up to the farmhouse and I say to the farmer's wife, 'There's a goat stuck—' And she interrupts me, right, and says, 'We know, we know. Her name's Milly. She can get out anytime she wants. She just likes the attention.'"

Io burst out laughing, the sound at odds with the gray, smelly horizon.

Exasperated, Nico went on. "So I tell my mom and she laughs, same as you, and you know what she tells me, the old devil? 'Ragged on by a goat, that's my Nico.'"

Which only made Io laugh harder.

He grinned at her. "What about you, hey?"

"I have never been ragged on by a goat."

"No, I mean, your folks. I know it's you and Ava in the Silts, but do you have other family?"

"We have an older sister, but she's . . . away. My parents were in the Neraida Plains during the Worker Strikes, when the dam flooded."

"Gods. That must have been hard."

It was and it wasn't. Io had already gotten used to their absence. Field work was dangerous, but it paid better. Most of the time, it was Thais putting her to bed, Ava cooking her dinner. She loved her parents from a distance, like one loves a celebrity, which Thais never failed to notice. *Mama likes hyacinths, not gardenias*, she'd say whenever Io brought home flowers she had picked with Rosa in the fenced gardens of the Artisti District. No caring daughter would forget that.

"We made do," Io told Nico. It was the best truth she could offer.

He nodded gravely. "I bet you did, boss. I was told to watch after you, but I think you'll be watching after me."

"Bah," Io said with a dismissive flick of her hand, "Ava is just being overprotective."

"Not Ava, boss. Edei. *She's got muscle on her,* he told me, *but you need to guard her back.*"

A blush crept onto her cheeks. She felt very, *very* close to death by mortification. She had always been fit—stalking suspects across the rooftops all night would do that to you—but she had never thought of her body as strong. Edei's attention to it made her suddenly self-conscious. Her pocketed pants felt too tight, her cropped sweater too revealing.

She couldn't process the comment, so she said, "This Horatio Long, what do we know about him? Edei said he's been accused of mistreating his fighters."

"Yeah, that's the rumor. It's why he was banned from the Silts and warned off using human fighters again. No respectable den will hire him, so he's started running his own chimerini fights, here at the Docks. He's an ex-sailor with a penchant for conjuring the most eccentric chimerini in the Timid Seas."

"Bianca banned him, right? Could he have reason to send a wraith to kill her?"

Nico visibly shuddered. "Don't call her that. Makes it sound like she's not human."

*She wasn't,* Io thought.

"I wouldn't know about that." Nico scratched the back of his head. He had freckles everywhere, including his fingers. "But the fights are hardly stable income; I'm told that on the side, he runs whatever errand is asked of him. You know what I mean?"

She did: Horatio was a mercenary, subject to whatever whim the rich folk of Alante had. A chill rose up Io's back that had nothing to do with the morning dew. Io's job wasn't exactly spotlessly clean, but at least it hadn't come to *that*.

*This city,* her mother had often said, *is going to try to steal the good out of you, Io. But you're not going to let it, are you?* As a child, Io had always promised she wouldn't. But then she had grown and had had to work and pay rent and bills and groceries, and she realized . . . All these people like her, the other-born and the immigrants and the lower-class who no one would hire, they didn't *let* the good get stolen from them, did they? It got nicked little by little, every time they were fired with no back pay, or their apartment application was denied for no reason, or they got looks of suspicion on the trolley. To assume they *let* it happen was to make them responsible for a system that was rotten long before they ever came along. But Mama had never been as poor as her daughters became after her death. And Mama wasn't other-born. She didn't fully understand.

The fact remained: this man would do anything for the right price. Whether by choice or not, he had become dangerous.

"Is he other-born?" she asked.

"Bianca doesn't believe so. He's not registered, and he's never shown signs of a power."

Like the silver glaze in Io's eyes, or the brass shimmer in a dioscuri-born's eyes.

"When we see him," she told Nico, "you don't rush him. Don't be aggressive in any way. I'm a rich girl from out of town, met you at the club, where you mentioned this is the best betting spot in the city. We get him talking about the Silts, about other-born. We've heard there's a woman walking the streets of Alante, her life-thread cut—is that true? He's more likely to answer if he thinks he can get money out of us, so we flash our coin every chance we get."

"Yes, boss," he piped chipperly.

"You do the talking—you're good at it."

Nico chuckled. "My sisters say that's all my mouth'll ever do. Talk, talk, talk, never kiss."

Io smiled. Nico was a pleasant—and very welcome—break from the frenzy of the last two days. Up ahead, several figures appeared through the mist, huddled together. Their voices carried down the dock, sharp and spiky. Most were middle-aged workers who had come straight here after last call at the district's clubs. They seemed to be gathered around a rectangular gap in the dock.

Nico placed his elbow on her shoulder and pretended to stumble, still drunk from the night's debauchery. "Hey, hey," he called, obnoxiously loudly. "Make room for my girl. She's just come in from Nanzy for the weekend. Daddy's given her a double allowance to spend."

Smirking approvingly at Nico, the men let them through to what must be the fighting pit. The dock had collapsed in on itself, exposing the supporting pillars and forming a makeshift fence around a rectangular area of mud. On each side, crabbing traps hung from pillars, covered by dark, wet cloths. Inside the traps, *things* hissed and rattled—these must be the fighters.

The proper word was "neo-hybrids," but the Silts called them chimerini—little chimeras. They had started coming out of the dark crevices of the world a few years after the Collapse, bodies mangled and mismatched, flashing rows upon rows of sharp teeth. Io's father used to fish rat-crabs on his days off, which their mom would bake to buttery perfection and sell at the farms as a side hustle.

Nico pretended to nuzzle her ear and cleverly whispered, "He's coming over."

The smell of rotting fish prefaced his arrival—Io twisted to find Horatio Long sidling next to her. He was around sixty, big and bulky, skin cross-stitched with wrinkles and nautical tattoos. Not much work for sailors nowadays; the seas grew rougher by the year, tidal waves upending boats into the dark waters.

His smile didn't reach his eyes. "The lady wants to bet? You're lucky—I got new ones today. Should be a real fight."

"How does it work?" Io asked, gesturing at the cages.

"You get a good look at our contestants, place your bet, then watch them fight. If your fighter wins, you get your money back, plus some interest."

"How much do people bet?" Io reached into her jacket. "Is fifteen notes all right?"

Nico, who was standing at her back, proceeded to theatrically choke. Fifteen notes was a ridiculous amount. Nico knew it, Horatio knew it, but daddy's girl from Nanzy didn't. "Let's start with three," Nico said carefully, "and see how it goes, yeah, love?"

Io scrunched her eyebrows in fake confusion. "Sure."

"Adam!" Horatio called out to a boy across the fighting pit. "Let's show these folks what they're paying for."

A roar of excitement filled the air. The fence in front of Io shook from the force of two dozen spectators beating it with their fists. The boy pulled a fragile-looking rope, and the cloths covering the cages fell away to reveal . . . There was no other word to describe them but "chimeras."

The first, on Io's right, was a cross between a hare and a crab. A furry snout caked with mud, long, twitching ears, four normal legs and four extra ones that sprouted from its spine and ended in curved, pointy pincers. Its crab legs shot through the bars, longer than Io had expected. The audience on that side of the fence jumped away, screaming ecstatically. The second, on the left, looked like a small crocodile but moved like a mouse, scurrying up and down the metal bars so fast Io's eyes couldn't follow. Its body was scaled and its tail spiked. But it was the last one, across from her, that inspired true terror: smaller than the others, with six spidery legs, a shiny, black shell, and three tails curving forward like a scorpion's. It sat in its cage with the unnatural stillness of a true predator.

"That one. Three notes on that one," Io said, the awe in her voice genuine. Careful to hide her wallet from Horatio, as though she had quite a large amount in there, she produced three notes and placed them in his palm.

"Good choice, pet," Horatio replied. To the crowd, he roared, "All bets are placed?"

Io and Nico must have been the last to arrive—the crowd shrieked in reply, stomping on the wood. Horatio nodded at the boy, and the bottom of the cages dropped open, spilling the malformed beasts into the muddy arena.

Io stepped a little closer, holding her breath. The hare immediately took the lead, dashing across the pit and pinching the crocodile's front leg. The latter retaliated by bringing its spiked tail down on the claw. It was sliced clean off; the hare screeched in pain and reared back. The crocodile lost no time—it launched into a fast series of strikes with its tail, sending the bleeding hare against the fenced pillars. It scrambled up one plank, but the boy was already there with a long stick, swiping it back to the pit. The hare fell right on the crocodile's back and stuck all pincers on its assailant's body. Turning around itself, the crocodile tried to get the other beast off, but every strike of its tail hit its own body as well. With a high-pitched wail, the crocodile flattened the hare between its body and the fence. The head of the hare squished, weird and liquidly.

The crocodile swiped its tail into the corpse twice more, then whirled on the large scorpion. The last creature hadn't moved from where the cage dropped it. It didn't even move now as the bleeding, frenzied crocodile rushed at it. The crowd around Io erupted in shouts as the two beasts collided. In a whirlwind of movement, Io caught sight of the scorpion-spider climbing on the crocodile's back. Its left tail struck once, lightning fast. The crocodile kept fighting for several moments, shaking its body to get the scorpion off, and then abruptly it slumped to the side and stopped breathing.

The crowd exploded—she couldn't tell if it was in anger or delight. Her heart battered against her rib cage. She smelled salt and fish and human sweat. She turned to Horatio, about to speak, but the fight wasn't over yet. The boy, Adam, produced a metal box and simply emptied its contents into the pit below. It was another scorpion-spider, bigger and paler than Io's victor. People went wild, jostling Io against Nico, against the fence, in their hurry to place their bets with Horatio Long.

The sailor wrote down bets and accepted money with a pleased smile on his face. The whole deal was done in minutes, during which the boy used the rod to keep the two scorpions away from each other. At Horatio's signal, the boy let go—the fight started anew.

Io made her eyes as wide as they could go. "Where do you find them, these . . . uh . . . fighters?"

"The night tide washes them out on the streets," Horatio replied, eyes on the fight. "Catching them isn't the hard part—keeping them locked up is. The hare did this just last night, when I was trying to feed it." He tapped an angry red welt on his forearm, then sneered at the hare's carcass. "Turns out it wasn't even worth the food."

"Aren't you scared, hunting them in the dark?" asked Io. "I heard wild, murderous women roam the streets, their life-threads severed."

Deliberately slowly, Horatio Long looked down his nose at her. "Where'd you hear that?"

"My aunt told me to stay off the streets at night because of these women."

"Is that right? You didn't take her advice, I see."

"Oh, she's not the scaredy kind, this one, boss," Nico chipped in jovially over her shoulder. "Quite the opposite. She's quite a fan of those horror books, by Melina Chokra, aren't ya, love?" Io nodded shyly—where was Nico going with this? "Ever since she heard the rumors, she's been obsessed. Been going on about them all day. *Let's find one, Nico. I wanna see one, Nico.* She wants to write a book about them. But hell if I know where to find one of them, so I brought her here instead to see the chimerini, boss."

Oh, Nico was good. Very good. She bit her lip and played along, mumbling, "I'm not *obsessed*, I just find it interesting. I've come all the way to Alante, the notorious Sunken City, and all I've done so far is attend dinner parties and afternoon teas with my aunt, getting introduced to every eligible person on the Hill."

"I ain't from the Hill, but my jawline makes up for it, don't you think?" Nico pretended to go in for a kiss, and Io shooed him away playfully.

Horatio Long had been watching them. His greed wasn't visible on the outside, but Io knew it was there—he kept glancing at the front pocket of her jacket, where she had stored her wallet. Abruptly, he leaned right into her ear and whispered, "How much? For information on the women?"

*Bull's-eye.*

"Seriously?" She made her voice tremble a little. "How much do you want?"

"How much have you got?"

"Thirty notes on me, but more at my aunt's place."

He moved away and gave her a hard, appraising look. "Follow me."

Nico started to move, but Horatio threw a palm out. "Not you, freeloader. You can wait for her right here."

Nico made to argue, but Io pulled him into a flirty embrace and secretly whispered, "Count to twenty, then follow us."

In a masterful performance, Nico leaned away with a naughty look in his eyes and said cheekily, "All right, girl. I can stay alone for a few minutes, I guess."

Horatio led her through the crowd and down the dock. The mist was thicker here—every couple of feet she craned her neck back toward the pit, like an inexperienced out-of-town girl would, but soon the fighting den was swallowed by the milky-white fog. They stopped in front of a small fishing boat. Now that the tide had pulled back, the boats were moored on their side on the muddy beach, like bloated whale carcasses. Horatio hopped on deck and used a hanging ladder to climb down to the mud.

Io glanced back at the pit. Gods damn it. Nico wouldn't know where to find her in the mist. She would have to make as much sound as she could. Hopefully, Nico would hear.

The sand was green and sticky, worms writhing here and there. Her boots sank deep, making a sickening *splotch* sound that made Io's lip curl up. Fish traps in all shapes and sizes were scattered unceremoniously around the boat, their metal bars rusted and draped with seaweed. One of them, covered with cloth, began to rattle as Io moved past them, trying to locate Horatio in the mist.

Where had he gone? Dread built up in her chest—she called forth the Quilt. The beachfront was eerily colorless, devoid of shimmering silver. One hand out to the trap on her right to orient herself, she turned in a circle, scanning across the mud for his life-thread.

Another life-thread peeked through the mist, coming around the fishing boat they had climbed down from. *Gods, let it be Nico.* Io fumbled for her spectacles: it was a singular thread, yes, the lustrous silver of a life-thread, but it was—

Severed. Dragging in the mud behind the figure walking on the beach.

The sight registered like a punch to the stomach.

It was a wraith, a *new* wraith, coming straight at her.

"Sir?" Io called out, voice choked with panic. "Sir, we need to go, right now."

The imprint of his body came from behind her; he *shouldn't* be behind her unless he had circled around her precisely to ambush her. She turned, too late. His hand reached for the air over her torso, fingers twirling as if unlocking an invisible door. The motion alone was enough to unnerve Io, but then she felt a terrifying jab in her chest, like being poked with a hot stick. Warmth slinked through her rib cage, welding like a shackle around her throat.

"Let's take a walk, little pet," Horatio said with a lopsided smile, "and see what's inside your wallet."

Io didn't want to.

Through the pressure in her chest, she thought, *Run. Run and don't look back.*

She thought, *He's grace-born. He's using the thrall. He's manipulating you.*

But she was under his spell now.

"Come on," he said, and Io came.

# CHAPTER XII

# PLAY THE PART

IO WAS A fool. She should have investigated Horatio Long before approaching him—that was her damn job! Unregistered graceborn could evade the authorities and stowaway lists better than most—their thrall came in handy—but the Silts were a cesspool of information, its residents packed so tight there was no room left for secrets. A neighbor would have spotted him doing strange gestures in the air, someone would have glimpsed a rose-gold glow in his irises. It would be a small thing, hardly noticeable if you weren't familiar with the ways grace-born powers worked, but it would have made Io suspicious and, thus, prepared.

Instead, she had trusted Bianca and her sources so that she could stay up all night in the Fortuna Club, checking the state of Edei's threads every few minutes. She had let Horatio come close, and now his grace-born hook was in her.

The offspring of the three Graces were gifted with a magnetic allure that slithered into the minds of their subjects and turned them to docile servants. Using a hook invisible to anyone else—something akin to Io's threads—they made their victim feel a heat in their chest, like being cradled in their mother's lap, snug and comfortable and utterly safe. If the grace-born said jump, their victim jumped.

"That's far enough. Your boyfriend should have lost us by now," Horatio said, pulling to a stop at the end of his maze of traps.

The beachfront stretched on all sides, rancid with seaweed and rotten wood. The mist clustered around them like an overbearing pet lapping about their legs. Io thought she spotted silver among the dock beams behind the fishing boat, but when her eyes returned, it was gone. The new wraith must have gotten closer by now.

"Give me your wallet," Horatio ordered.

Her fingers, the little traitors, hastened to take it out of her pocket.

*Breathe. Focus. What are your options?* She could fight against his will, steel her body against his commands, but it wouldn't do much good except to alert him that she knew what he was. His gait was assured, his smirk satisfied; Horatio thought she was easy prey. She could use that. Lull him into a sense of security, then run away as fast as she could. A grace-born's thrall wasn't limitless: all she needed were a dozen feet between them and she would be able to slip free of his hook.

*Play the part,* Io schooled herself. "So, what do you know about these women?"

"What my buddies at the police know: They look dead. They strangle with their threads. They're targeting the Silts." Horatio's head was bent over her wallet, counting notes.

"Is that all?" Io feigned nonchalance, stepping toward the closest fish trap. She gingerly lifted the canvas covering it, as though she were curious of its contents. Empty—she moved to the next one. Her back was to Horatio; she took a chance and glanced up and down the beachfront.

No silver in the Quilt. Where had the wraith gone?

Gods. Her heart thundered in her throat, in her temples, a drumming beat that threatened to overwhelm her. Her fingers trembled as she reached out for one of her threads, running a finger down its length like caressing a blade. She was not powerless, she reminded herself. She would get out of this, one way or another. A few more feet and she would be out of reach of his grace-born hook, then she would run back to the dock and to Nico and figure out some way to find the new wraith.

"I hear you used to run the best wrestling dens in Alante," she said.

"Sure did," Horatio said. She didn't dare look back at him but heard paper folding, then a *slosh* as he tossed her wallet to the mud. "Had the best fighters in any city-nation. I chose them based on skill, you know. They gotta be other-born. That's how they like it, my upper-class clientele. Wanna know why?"

She could feel his hook drawing tight at her chest. Just a couple of steps now, and she would break free. She glanced at him over her shoulder: his eyes were on her, a wolf assessing its prey, teeth glinting like fangs.

*Play the part.* "Why?" Io asked.

Horatio went on, "Because other-born fight dirty."

"Oh?"

"Do you fight dirty, pet?"

Then he lunged.

Thais started Io's education from the crib. *She's a cutter,* her older sister argued whenever their parents stated doubts. *Do you want her accidentally killing someone because she grabbed their life-thread from her stroller? She needs to know how dangerous she is, so she can keep herself safe.* Thais had taught Io exactly how to keep herself safe.

Adrenaline pumped through her, outweighing her fear. She didn't fight him but let his weight tumble them both to the ground. It startled him; momentum and mud slid his body off hers. Io rolled away, her hand shooting out and grabbing his life-thread above his head. He rose on one knee and she backed away, moving so fast mud flew everywhere. His grace-born hook was still in her chest—she could feel it—and soon, he would be lucid enough to use it against her.

She threw his thread between them in warning. "I've got your life thread," she shouted. "Don't move, don't speak."

The big man froze. They panted into the silence, neither of them moving.

"Take your hook off me, and I won't cut it."

"You're not a cutter."

"Oh, I am. But I can prove it if you'd like." She gave his life-thread a yank that made him stumble forward, relishing the fear that paled Horatio's horrible face. Her eyes must be shimmering deathful with silver.

"No, wait—*wait*. I'll let it go. I'm letting it go."

Heart pounding in her ears, Io watched as his fingers pinched something invisible from his neck and began uncoiling it, like a fisherman unspooling his line. She gritted her teeth against the horrible sensation of tugging and un-tugging inside her rib cage.

She had the upper hand now, might as well use it. "Where were you two nights ago? Where were you two weeks ago?"

He very well could be behind the wraith murders; a grace-born could order you to kill if they were physically in proximity. Maybe he had been hiding somewhere that night Jarl Magnussen was murdered.

"I was here," he answered. "I'm always in these damned docks, catching beasts, setting up fights, defending my turf. Let go of my thread, I'll let go of your hook."

"Do you know Minos Petropoulos, Jarl Magnussen, or Konstantin Fyodorov?"

"Sure I do. Everyone knows everyone in the Silts."

"Twelve years ago, you attempted to kidnap a girl named Emmeline Segal and an older woman named Drina Savva. Why?"

A moment's hesitation, a sharp intake of breath—that was all Io needed. Horatio knew precisely who these women were. He paused, the grace-born line still in his fist. "You know how many jobs I've had to take? Hundreds. I forget all of them the moment the coin is in my hand. Now let. Go."

Horatio stepped closer—Io stepped back.

"I think the cutter with the life-thread calls the shots," she warned.

With a sneer, he marched toward her. Io stumbled back. "By the look of her, I'd say *she* calls the shots here."

She? Who? *No*—

Something stinging cold wrapped around Io's neck, pulling her onto the ground. Mud got in her ears, muffling all sounds. A round, childlike face, spotted with acne scars and caked with cracked dirt, came into view—the new wraith. That vile man must have seen her approaching behind Io's back and pushed Io right into her reach.

Io just—*reacted*.

She knocked the heel of her hand against the girl's nose. The wraith flew back, blood spurting from her nose with a sick gurgling sound. Io pushed up, but the mud clung to her, her movements slow and heavy. Her hair was plastered on the right side of her face, making it hard to see, but she had kept the Quilt up. She spotted a bundle of threads in the mist, coming in from her left: Horatio. When he reached for her, she twisted and buried her knee in his stomach. He doubled over with a harrumph—there was her chance. Io scrambled away on all fours, stopping only when she bumped her back into a tall empty trap. She was far enough now; his hooks couldn't reach her. She was safe.

In front of her, Horatio gasped into the mud. "You little shit . . ."

Silver slashed through the mist. The wraith's severed life-thread wrapped around Horatio's throat. She followed, her body parting the mist, and came to stand above his kneeling form. She stretched her fist back, tightening the cord around his neck.

"There are crimes that cannot go unpunished," she rasped, her young, sweet voice at odds with her ragged appearance. "Hundreds of victims and you forget all of them, is that right? But I have never forgotten. I remember your face. I remember your thrall. I remember your threats."

"Please!" The word ripped through Horatio's lips like a prayer.

"You do remember us, don't you?" the wraith asked him. "What is my name?"

Horatio's legs kicked and fought, and the wraith loosened her hold on him enough so he could talk. "Raina!" he croaked. "Your name is Raina, and that older one was Emmeline, and that old lady was Ms. Savva! They asked me to kill you, they promised me riches and protection and a new identity in Nanzy, but when I caught you . . . You were kids, tiny and scared, and that lady was so skinny, so old! I was supposed to kill you, but I let you escape, didn't I? I could have pulled you back with my hooks, but I didn't!"

"You think you showed us mercy?" seethed Raina. "You think you did us a favor? What about the others you killed before us? It was no mercy; it was an apology. And it's not *enough*."

On his bottom, legs splayed like a toddler, Horatio looked nothing like a ruthless mercenary. His face was bright red, his eyes bloodshot, his voice trembling. "How do you know all this? Who ratted to you, huh? Was it those bitches? Whatever they promised you, they're lying, like they lied to me—"

"I did not need anyone's confession. I was *made* to know your crimes."

"Please," begged the grace-born, his voice strangled by the life-thread around his neck. "It was only business. Please."

"I don't deal in mercy," said the wraith. "I deliver justice."

Then, with her abnormal thread, she wrung his neck—*crack!*—the clean movement of a practiced predator. The sound of his spine snapping echoed down the misty beach. Io couldn't breathe, couldn't think.

Raina said, "I can see the taint of crime on you, too, sister."

Oh gods. Io bolted, bumping into fish traps, slipping on the mud, blinded by the tears and mud on her face. She heard a roar of anger, far closer than it should have been. The boat was just ahead, all she had to do was reach the ladder—

Fingers in her hair, yanking. Raina's leg connecting with her stomach, then pain. The world went white. She gasped for air. Distantly, she was aware of the wraith pushing a knee against her chest. Of her terrible thread reaching for Io's throat, silver flashing like a scythe.

"Justice always comes, sooner or later," Raina crooned.

And then there was the bang of a gun being fired. The weight shifted—and disappeared altogether. Io closed her eyes and tried to force air into her lungs. In, out. In. Out. Hands were helping her sit up. Someone cupped her cheeks. A muffled voice kept saying her name. Her eyes flew open. Edei was kneeling in the mud in front of her, Nico a few paces behind.

He was holding her, palms soft against her skin. He was talking. "I got you. I got you."

# PART II

# ONE TO DRAW

# CHAPTER XIII

# WE ORA SISTERS

**HE HAD FELT** the tug of the thread.

He didn't say as much, but Io *knew*.

He had already been on the way to the Docks, after hustling their location out of Ava, and he had sensed this strange pull in his chest. *A hunch*, he'd said, because unlike Io, he had no idea what bound them together. He had trailed it to the fighting den, stumbled onto a frantic Nico, then heard Horatio's screams and run to find Io gasping for air in the mud beneath the wraith's knee. Nico had shot in the air—thank the gods he still carried his revolver—and the wraith had scattered. Edei had sent Nico to alert Bianca about the new wraith and brought Io straight to his apartment. He hadn't given her the chance to refuse, practically dragging her to safety.

Now she sat on the floor of his living room, having washed in his shower, wearing his girlfriend's warm clothes while hers dried. On the short table in front of her sat a gorgeous tea set, steaming its sweet aroma in the room. *Koshary shai from Sumi*, he had said as he prepared it. *I added a few mint leaves.* On the countertop, his knife sliced back and forth rhythmically. He was making her dinner. Edei Rhuna, her fated thread, *was making her dinner.*

"Do you eat spicy food?" he asked over his shoulder.

"I eat everything," Io replied. She didn't like everything, but she ate it all the same. Knees tucked under her chin, fingers running through her wet hair, Io watched him chop and mix and grind things into the pan. He was favoring his right side. "How is your shoulder?"

"It's fine. Hurts, but I can take it."

The statement pretty much summed up their lives, didn't it? A hundred different things tumbled to the tip of her tongue. *You told Nico to watch after me. You came running to the Docks. You had a hunch, but it's not a hunch. We have a fate-thread,* she could say. *That's what you felt earlier.* But how obnoxious would it be to confess that, in the home he shared with his girlfriend, wearing her woolen kaftan? She already felt rotten that this thread existed, that it *still* existed even though she had known for years that the right thing to do was cut it.

Instead, she said, "I'm so sorry. It was my fault."

"Did you aim the gun and pull the trigger?" He leaned against the counter and raised his eyebrows at her. "Then it's not your fault."

Io almost sighed in awe. Gods, he was beautiful. Dark eyebrows, cheekbones that could slice your palm open, the shadow of stubble on his cheeks. He wore a soft shirt a little too loose around the neckline and no shoes. Seeing him in his socks felt intimate. Heat gathered in her cheeks.

For several minutes, neither of them spoke. Io studied his apartment: the multicolored rugs, the low table and plush pillows, the beaded curtain leading to what she assumed was their bedroom. The whole place was Sumazi in style, which was surprising. Imported furniture and fabrics were costly. They must have saved up for months to decorate it. It was worth it, though, a small pocket of home away from home.

On a shelf across from her, more than a dozen little bees were laid in a neat formation based on size. Some were made of glass, some of clay or stone. Most were painted in bright colors, but a couple were wooden carvings weathered by age.

From the stove, Edei followed her eyeline and explained, "When I was young, I thought honeybees were mythical creatures. Ra's maidens, carrying good fortune and growth, like lore says. Honeybees in Sumi are nearly extinct. I saw one in real life my first spring in Alante, and I almost fainted. I was convinced it was a warning from Ra that Osiris, his brother and the god of death, was coming to take me to Duat. Samiya choked laughing. She's been gifting me bees ever since."

Io imagined him fresh-faced and scarless, in soft linen clothes, unmarred by life in Alante. "Duat?" she asked.

"The realm of the dead in Sumazi lore. What Alantians call the underworld." He huffed and added, "My father would throw a fit if he heard me compare the two. But I think all our legends share the same roots. Your underworld has six rivers, ours has twelve regions. Your gate is guarded by Cerberus, ours is stalked by Apophis. And in both, the soul goes there to rest."

"There are similarities between other-born from different cultures across the world. The moira-born can see the threads of fate, like the norn-born from Jhorr. The asclepies-born control health, like the Sumazi horus-born," said Io.

"When we arrived in Alante, the lady at immigration insisted on listing Samiya as asclepies-born and not horus-born. Told us it'd help her land a job. *They do the same thing,* she said, *but Alantians like their own word better.*"

Io wanted to keep this conversation going but was unsure what the right questions were. Tentatively, she asked, "Why would your father throw a fit?"

He spoke in a whisper, bent over the kitchen counter. "He is against intermixing. Thinks cultures should keep themselves separate, that other-born should stay in their home city-nation. He believes the gods punish defectors by taking away their powers."

"Is he other-born?"

Edei replied bluntly, "No. He's a Separatist."

Sometime after the Kinship Treaty, when the civil rights of other-born were established, people started migrating across the city-nations in search of a better job and living conditions. At the same time, a wave of conservatism swept through the world: people like Edei's father who believed other-born should remain in their city-nation of origin to honor and serve the gods that gifted them with powers. It was called Other-Born Separatism.

"My father's beliefs," Edei went on, "are part of the reason we had to leave Sumi. His sect wanted Samiya to stop performing abortions. She refused."

"That's very brave."

"For a while, it was. But then her family started receiving death threats. Things escalated so badly that we were forced to leave Sumi and seek entry to another city-nation." Sadness swept over his features, shadowing his eyes. Then his lips curved in a soft smile. "At least my exile gave me the chance to experience little yellow legends buzzing all around me."

Io's heart melted a little bit at his lovely face, his lovely words, his smile that glimmered like starlight breaking through a raging night storm. She wanted to go to him, pinch his chin between her fingers and bring his lips down to meet hers—

The thought startled her. Not just the intimate nature of it, but the easiness with which it had arrived. Like it had been lodged in the conduits of her mind for a long time, and it had finally loosened free, a *plop* followed by a current of longing.

Edei cleared his throat and returned to the stove.

Io realized, too late, that she had been staring at him.

Heat bloomed on her cheeks; she pulled her damp hair over one shoulder, forming a curtain between them. *Get it together.* He had a girlfriend. Samiya wasn't here now, but there was evidence of her everywhere. The combs and beauty products in the bathroom. The delicate shoes by the door. A silver ring on the short table in front of Io. The encyclopedias and anatomy books, the bees on the shelf, the sweetness in Edei's voice when he spoke of her. Edei had followed her halfway across the world.

Gods, Io was making herself feel even worse. *Settle,* Thais always said when a bout of anxiety overwhelmed Io. *Name your feeling. Find the thought behind it, the reason. Breathe in through your nose, out through your mouth.* Io was feeling . . . embarrassment. Guilt—always guilt. And envy. Envy was the heart of it. Io rejected it viscerally. Jealousy was Thais's, not hers.

A few years ago, when Thais had first begun working for Thomas Mutton and his other-born scheme, the sisters had been doing well. For the first time since their parents' death, Thais seemed content. Thomas and his fancy friends treated her well, the money was good. She came home smelling of red wine and cigarettes and kissed the top of Io's head, or hummed songs as she cleaned. One day, she had taken Ava and Io on a day trip to the butterfly park just out of the city, like they used to do with their baba. The three of them had walked through the green, soft, multihued wings caressing their cheeks. When they returned home, Ava fell asleep facedown on the sofa, but Io stayed up. Thais's bliss was intoxicating.

"Sometimes," Io had whispered to her sister confessionally, "I like to dream he kisses me softly on the lips."

She had been fifteen, still in school—kissing was on her mind constantly.

"It isn't wrong to dream, as long as you don't act on it," Thais had replied in that hard tone she reserved only for Io. "We Ora sisters don't kiss other people's boyfriends."

The words were a slap on the face. Thais had taken all her innocent craving and perverted it into an accusation of immorality. She had a way with shame, her sister. If patience was Io's weapon, shaming was Thais's. She brandished it sparingly, but always made sure to cut deep. Right into Io's core, where the shame festered and infected her every thought.

Bitterness coated Io's tongue. Why did every memory of Thais have to go sour at the end? *64 Hanover Street.* She could march right up there and ask. She let herself imagine the scene: Thais appearing at the door, dressed in the latest fashion, one of those ridiculous pink cocktails in her hand. Her eyes would bulge at the sight of Io. *How did you find me?* she'd ask, and Io would say, *I broke into City Plaza with Edei Rhuna under orders from Bianca Rossi, mob queen of the Silts. What do you think about that? Are Ora sisters allowed to do* that?

But Io wasn't Thais. Her envy wasn't the noxious kind. Her heart just *craved*. The softness, the calm, the intimacy. To know what it's like to be loved.

Edei slipped a tray on the table. "You all right?"

Io smoothed the frown from her face. "I was just thinking."

He served her a plate of ful medames, fava beans with hard-boiled eggs and lemon slices on the side, topped with what smelled like paprika. It was a traditional Sumazi dish that Io loved because it was so close to her family's own Plains cuisine.

Settling on the floor across from her, Edei split the flatbread in two and offered her the bigger part. "About the wraiths?"

"About love, I guess," Io answered, surprising even herself with the truth.

His eyes came back to her, brows stitched close. "What about love?"

Io shrugged. Love was a dangerous wildland to explore with Edei, filled with poisonous vines and deadly predators. One wrong step, and your life was forfeit. "The complexity of it."

He made a sound for her to continue.

"I don't know," Io started, breaking the bread into pieces. "I feel like the world is shifting, and I can't decide what to do about it. I find myself constantly wishing family were always kind to you, that friendships stayed the same. I wish I could both defend myself against the wraiths and save them from whoever is using them. I wish—"

She almost said it. She was about to. *I wish you knew you were my fate-thread.*

"I wish," she amended, "that things weren't complicated."

He was silent for a time. "Can you uncomplicate them?"

Io huffed a tired breath and smiled. "I probably can."

By going up-Hill and facing Thais, by talking to Rosa, by figuring out a way to save the wraiths from dying, by telling Edei the truth and cutting the fate-thread. She could do all of those things; she *should* do them. Just . . . not right now. Her body ached, her nose sniffled, her stomach rumbled with hunger. She would stay in this quiet, soft moment with Edei just a little bit longer, and then she would grow up and face life. She promised.

"What are those?" she asked, indicating a row of small books next to the table.

"Fairy tales, folk songs, fables. It's kind of my hobby."

Her forlornness faded away at the soft smile on his lips, the spicy sweetness of the ful medames. They ate leisurely, because it was burning hot and because he started telling her where he had found each book, stories as strange and mythical as those inside the pages. He was particularly interested in similarities: how, for example, midsummer songs and festivities from all over the world celebrated death and rebirth in one way or another. His eyes shone, and he talked fast, going over narratives from faraway city-nations. In turn, Io told him about the local legends her parents came back with from the Neraida Plains, about nymphs and naiads. When they were done, Edei offered dessert: yogurt with sliced almonds and honey. They ended up shoulder to shoulder at the sink—she washed, he dried.

After a while, Edei spoke. "It's strange. That I only met you two days ago."

Her heartbeat thrummed in her throat. "How do you mean?"

"I feel like I've known you for a long time."

What could she possibly say that was neither the truth nor a lie? *Me, too* didn't begin to cover it.

He misinterpreted her silence and added quickly, "What I'm trying to say, I guess, is that we worked well together at the Plaza. Next time you want to follow a lead, wait for me. All right?"

"All right." She thought she might explode with giddiness. Was this what being with your crush felt like? Like your stomach had turned liquid, your heart fluttering in your chest? Why was she calling Edei her crush? Why was she thinking about kissing him? Had time reverted—was she fourteen again, crushing unrequitedly on Amos?

"Whenever you want," he said gently, turning off the tap, "you can fill me in on what I missed."

These few hours with him were swathed in the cozy shroud of dreams. She wanted to stay in this dreamscape a while longer, to savor his soft-spoken stories and tender movements. But she knew she couldn't.

"I think the new wraith, Raina, might have been lurking at the Docks, waiting for the right moment to attack Horatio when he was alone," she told Edei. "All these years ago, he had been hired to kill the wraiths—Emmeline, Drina, and Raina. He said someone promised him money and safe passage to Nanzy in exchange for their death. But he couldn't go through with it."

"That was twelve years ago?"

Io nodded.

"Why seek to punish him now?"

They were both leaning against the kitchen counter. Io's fingers were still wet; his were playing with the damp towel. She could see him working their new clues in his head, frown deep and contemplative.

"The new wraith said she was *made* to know the crimes of men," said Io.

"Other-born cannot be made."

"No, they cannot."

They looked at each other, their faces mirrors of doubt and alarm.

"If Horatio was promised passage to Nanzy . . . Do you know the kind of power that requires? City officials, the tycoons of the Neraida Plains, mob bosses across the city-nations—it could be any one of them."

"He said *those bitches*," Io intervened.

"What?"

"He asked the wraith if *those bitches* had ratted him out."

"So numerous women?"

"Powerful women."

Io let her mind wander beyond her fear. This morning, she was so eager to be done with all this that she risked her life, and Nico's, to deliver Bianca the murderer she had promised her. There were so many things she couldn't wrap her head around. So many things she didn't know. But she knew Alante. She knew the power players. She knew there was only one group of women powerful enough to guarantee passage to the Golden City of Nanzy and inspire the hatred of even the shadiest crook in the Silts.

It was time to stop pretending this was just any other case she'd worked.

Her gut roiled with dread. She was going to have to visit the Nine.

# CHAPTER XIV

# THE HOUSE OF NINE

**THE HISTORY BOOKS** were hazy on the details, but the consensus was that the gods had died long before the old world Collapsed.

Little was known about the time before the Collapse, but the remnants of the old world lay everywhere. Spiky metallic structures thousands of years old sticking out of deserts and lakes, paved roads in the middle of lush forests, found objects made of strange materials that might be art or technology or children's toys. And of course, the texts, written in languages old but recognizable, found on metal plaques and chipped marble.

Each historian and scientist seemed to have a different theory about what had brought on the Collapse, but they all agreed on its major turning point: the once singular moon split into three— Pandia, Nemea, and Ersa—causing the sea level to rise globally. Whole nations were swallowed by dark waters, and the few remaining coastal cities faced a tide that sank them half underwater every night.

At first, people took refuge at higher altitudes, waiting for the tide to settle. But despite every scientist's prediction, despite the very laws of nature, the shifting earth and sea never calmed. Instead came a never-ending circle of catastrophes: neo-monsoons and heat storms, chimerini coming out of the waters, leviathans breaking out of the ice farther up north, enormous and extremely hard to kill—and the appearance of other-born, more and more with every generation.

A new order rose from the chaos, in the form of other-born.

Horae-born who could alter the passage of time, muse-born who could see past and future in the arts, moira-born who could create and sever bonds. With the help of other-born, the Coastal Barrier was constructed, dams were built, icebergs were chased for the fresh water they could provide. Fertile valleys and terraced hills were formed; over-water trams and entire stilt towns were raised from the mud. The leviathans were hunted to extinction, the chimerini dissected and used for parts. Humanity started thriving again, conglomerating in city-nations, reestablishing trade and craft, electing new representatives.

But there was always a whisper in the air, a murmur shared when the candles were snuffed out: the Collapse was the gods' punishment. Humankind might be surviving at the moment, but the gods would always win in the end.

"I didn't take you for a doomsayer," Edei said, his voice teasing.

There was a newfound easiness between them today. They had eaten and washed dishes together, tended to their wounds, and marveled over bees and fairy tales, and it showed in the way their bodies had started moving to make room for each other. Shoulders touching as they rode the trolley, elbows brushing as they pushed through the crowd, feet falling into step as they crossed the arched bridges of the Artisti District. He made eye contact more often; she didn't look away the moment he did. And there was teasing.

Gods, Io felt euphorically drunk on teasing. She dared not want for the impossible, but perhaps when all this was over, they could be friends. She could swing by the Fortuna when Ava was done with her shift and the three of them, perhaps Nico, too, could go for a late-night crepe in Parsley Square. Casual and harmless.

"I'm not a doomsayer," she replied, unable to keep the smile from her lips. "I know the gods are long gone—otherwise, where have they been during all the chaos since the Collapse?"

"Vacationing undercover in the Artisti District?" Edei interjected, throwing a hand toward the House of Nine across the canal.

With a chuckle, Io continued, "But I think there's some truth in fearing them. In fearing any kind of all-powerful being, like the Nine claim to be."

They stepped onto Tarragon Bridge, one of Alante's most famous tourist attractions. It was an arched bridge made of old, yellowing stones. Along its body, several little shops were built: artists' galleries, jewelry shops, woodshops, and music stores. Outside the shops, street artists and musicians exhibited their creations on the cobblestone. Music flowed from every direction; Io tossed a couple of coins in a busking violinist's hat and moved along.

The House of Nine stood out among its peers, a beautiful redbrick mansion built on the currently dry West Canal situated at the heart of the district. Three stories high, with stained glass windows, a tall fence overflowing with vines, and over a dozen security guards walking the premises, the House wasn't something you could just walk by. Tourists and residents alike stopped to glance at the inscription over the intimidating dark iron gate: SING IN ME, MUSE, AND THROUGH ME TELL THE STORY.

The well-known phrase had been inspired by the muse-born's actual powers. Through the art their protégés produced, they could interpret truths about the past and future, about social conflicts, natural disasters, technological developments—even murders.

"The Nine are not immortal gods," Io said. "Muse-born are just extremely rare; it's uncommon for any family to have nine daughters, much less a family with undiluted muse-born lineage. But the Nine like to cultivate an air of mystique, of exclusivity. There's never more than one set of muse-born alive at once, and some people claim it would be impossible for it to happen. When one set begins to decline, a new set appears, always in Alante. The new set of sisters inherits their position and their House, and so, to the general population, it appears as though the Nine are unique. Reincarnations of their past selves. They even go by the names of the ancient Muses, rather than the names they were born with."

"Mysticism is good for business, I suppose," Edei murmured, surveying the iron gates. "Bianca says the Nine are running the most lucrative corporation in Alante. Every artist we passed by on that bridge claims one of the Nine as their muse and patron, dedicating their art to her, raising temples in her name, and more importantly, sending her a cut of their earnings."

Io's head rang with the echo of Horatio Long's last pleas: *Please. It was only business.* A bitter trepidation leaked into her. Horatio Long profited on the pain of his chimerini. The Nine traded in art and science, never giving without taking, never helping without being helped in return.

"My friend Chimdi used to be one of their protégés," Edei went on. "She does ceramics, these beautiful busts rendered with thorns and vines growing out of the face and neck. The Nine sought Chimdi out when she was only fifteen. Offered her a patronage in exchange for a cut of her profits. Chimdi says her art skyrocketed in a night, placements in famous galleries, orders coming in from every city-nation, more money than she could spend in a lifetime. But then her art started changing. Whenever she touched clay, her hands had a mind of their own, sculpting celebrities and public figures draped with flowers and petals instead of the things she wanted to create."

His gaze stayed on the House. "One of the people she was 'inspired' to sculpt was a politician from Jhorr who spewed a lot of anti-immigrant hate. Chimdi refused to sell to him. But her hands kept seeking to carve his shape. When she came to us, her fingers were scratched raw, nails torn and bleeding. She couldn't stop sculpting, even if she taped her fingers together."

"Gods," whispered Io.

"Hers was the very first case I worked as Bianca's second. I tried and tried, but there was little I could do against the Nine. The contract Chimdi signed was ironclad, and their influence over her was unbreakable. In the end, we had to pay for her freedom, with all of Chimdi's hard-earned money. She says she's fine with it, says it all worked out in the end, but I've always felt—" He paused, cleared his throat. "Like I failed her."

Io wasn't sure what to say. *I'm sorry* felt inadequate. She laid a hand on his arm; when his eyes dropped to hers, she said, "You didn't fail her if you tried."

In a voice that was barely a whisper, he said, "She hasn't sculpted since."

"We all heal in our own time." The statement sounded cliché even to her own ears, but it was the best comfort she could offer.

He squared his shoulders, jaw clenching as he looked back at the gates. A crowd of tourists and journalists was gathered outside the House, waiting for a glimpse of the reclusive Muses. Their every outing, even a mere walk around their garden, made the headlines, not just in Alante but across the city-nations.

"They never leave the House, you know. They used to, but not in recent years. Do you know how many times I've fantasized about dousing that place with gasoline and striking a match?" he said. "It makes me feel downright evil, but I think about it every day."

"I don't think it's evil," Io said carefully.

"No?" His voice was casual, but Io thought she sensed a true question behind it.

She shrugged, all too aware of his singular focus on her. "They hurt someone you love. They deserve to be in your revenge fantasies."

A huff escaped his nose, the twin to a laugh. "Just—" A pause, and a grinding of his jaw. "At the first sign of trouble, we're booking it out of there."

"Yes, boss," she said, then froze. *Boss.* It had just slipped out of her, but maybe she shouldn't be using it. Maybe it was a Fortuna thing, and Io was appropriating it?

But Edei was smiling. He started crossing the street, his eyes steadfast on the front doors of the House. "Hey, you're catching on fast."

Her cheeks warmed. "What does it mean?"

"*Boss?* We use it to show respect. I used to call my horse in Suma boss."

She snorted; this little irrelevant detail was perfectly endearing. "Always nice to be equated to a horse."

He glanced down at her, eyes wide with apprehension. "No, I didn't mean—" He halted at the sight of her grin. "You're joking."

"Unsuccessfully, from the looks of it."

"No, I'm not saying that—oh. You're doing it again."

"Hm. We're not great at this."

He nodded severely. "It does appear to be the only dissonance in our partnership."

"We'll figure it out, I'm sure."

"With hard work, we can conquer all things, even humor."

Io was truly beaming now. This was delightful; *he* was delightful.

"Halt!" The guard at the gate raised a palm. A collared shirt peeked beneath layers upon layers of armor: breastplate, arm plates, leg plates. Their material reflected the midafternoon sun in a strange, muted way. This wasn't metal; it was leviathan scales, scavenged from some felled beast, expensive stuff reserved for the military.

"Name?" said the woman.

"Io Ora."

The guard slipped into a small cubicle, speaking in whispers. From the corner of her eye, Io spotted one of the second-floor curtains fluttering back into place. Behind her, cameras snapped and tourists oohed. Moments passed, in which the guards sized Io and Edei up; then the gates buzzed.

Edei placed a hand on Io's back and leaned close. "Fifteen guards on the grounds, no doubt more inside. It's far more than they would normally need for protection. Something is scaring them."

Io nodded. He was right. "First sign of trouble," she repeated.

Edei replied with a thumb over his shoulder and a comical whistle. *We book it.*

Then they both turned back to the door, faces smoothing into scowls. Two more security women waited at the foyer, poised and soundless. As soon as Io's and Edei's boots thumped on the dark wooden floor, a voice called out from an arched entrance to their left: "Over here, children."

A shared glance of unease, and Io and Edei entered the high-ceilinged sitting room. The whole place was dressed in indigo, from the walls to the carpet to the cushions, as though a blueberry jam factory had exploded. Five sisters sat in different corners: a white-haired woman reading a newspaper on the velvet sofa; a plump, darker-skinned lady scribbling on a piece of paper at a small desk; a short-haired woman napping in an armchair; and two younger girls playing a card game on the plush cushions in front of the fireplace.

They all looked up when Io and Edei came in and fell utterly, impossibly still. It gave Io the chills.

"Ah, the cutter," said the youngest.

"The unseen blade," said the white-haired.

"The reaper of fates," said the one at the desk.

# CHAPTER XV

# AND THE WORLD ENDS

**EDEI SHIFTED ON** the thick Kurkz-style carpet, shoulders hunched with tension.

Io took in the room, the women, the diligence of it all. This was very obviously a show; she could spot the evidence plain around the room. The eldest Muse was reading a newspaper from four days ago—Io recognized the front page, with Commissioner Saint-Yves's face plastered on it. The woman at the desk seemed to be tracing and retracing the same lines on the page. The one pretending to sleep had damp water stains on her sleeves. And one of the girls playing cards was holding some facing out. They had hurried to take their places in this staged performance—but to what purpose?

Io remembered the curtain falling closed on the second floor. As if they'd been waiting for her and Edei. This demonstration was intended to mislead them somehow, or perhaps even intimidate them.

The eldest looked nothing like you'd expect of a Muse of the arts: her gray shirt was buttoned to the neck, her hair clipped back in a neat bun at the base of her skull, all around colorless and unfashionable. Against the deep purple background, she stood out like a mushroom in a rosebush.

It was she who spoke, in a firm, clear voice, over the ridge of her newspaper. "May we help you?"

Io said, "I'm looking for answers."

"From which one of us?" The woman extended a hand in turn to the hunched-over scribbler at the desk, the half-asleep lady on the sofa, the two girls by the fireplace. "Calliope, Muse of epic poetry? Erato, Muse of love poetry? Polyhymnia, Muse of hymns, or Urania, Muse of astronomy?"

Each greeted Io and Edei with a slight nod of their head. They looked alike, but also not. A long, hooked nose sat in the middle of their faces, and their brows rose in identical curves, but their hair, skin color, and body shape varied. Polyhymnia and Urania obviously shared both parents, their eyes uplifted and their skin light brown. Calliope was several years their elder, with dozens of freckles on her nose, and Erato was as short as a ten-year-old child.

"And yourself?" Io asked the sister who had spoken.

"Clio, Muse of history. The rest of our half sisters are occupied, I'm afraid. So, whose inspiration do you seek, daughter?"

"My partner and I are investigating a string of murders in the Silts," said Io. "Our latest lead has brought us to your doorstep. You need to answer some questions about Horatio Long and the women he claims you paid him to kill."

Clio only smiled, her teeth as neat and proper as the rest of her. *"Need we?"*

"I see no warrant," said Erato. "I see no badge."

"We owe you nothing," said Polyhymnia.

"If it's our help you need, you must earn it," said Erato.

"Not unlike your own business, hm?" Urania's eyes slipped to Edei, gauging his reaction. "Do you know what your partner does for a living, lovely?"

Io had the urge to march right up there and slap her in the face. This was a game to them—revealing things and watching how their guests reacted. If Edei hadn't known that Io sometimes cut her clients' threads, if—

But this was exactly what they wanted. To rile her up. Distract her. From what?

She scanned the room, a bloodhound out for prey. There, on the desk in the back, was the only dissonance in their charade. All the other sisters watched Edei, but Calliope, the Muse of epic poetry, sat perfectly still, pen poised absentmindedly over a piece of paper, her eyes intent on Io with interest, and something akin to . . . fear?

"Snip, snip, snip," Urania said, answering her own question and mimicking scissors with her fingers.

Io resisted the urge to roll her eyes. The curtain, the rehearsed show, Calliope's interest in her, not to mention whatever that detested "the cutter, unseen blade, reaper of fates" farce had been—it all meant the Nine wanted something from her. There was no point beating around the bush.

"What is your fee, then?" she asked.

"Our usual," said Erato.

"Art," said Urania.

"Inspired," said Polyhymnia.

"Created," said Clio.

Io felt foolish having to state the obvious. "I'm not an artist."

Polyhymnia leaned closer, elbows on her knees, like an overeager child. "Of course you are, silly! You all are. You've all got something that you are good at, something you make with the sweat on your brow and the blood in your veins. Something special, yours and yours alone. And we—*we* are the idea taking form, we are the inspiration striking, we are the talent showing through your fingers. We are the muse and you the maker."

There was a long hard silence.

Io twisted her eyes to share a look of *what the hell* with Edei.

He looked just as unimpressed. "I don't understand what you're saying."

Four heads turned to him, all except Calliope's. "Your partner has her threads, her precious silver Quilt," Clio began to explain. "We have something similar, though our power is more mediatory and less . . . aggressive. We have our protégés, our painters and sculptors and writers, our actors and musicians and dancers. They ask for inspiration, and we deliver through their eyes and ears and fingers. We gift them with ideas, thoughts, *secrets*. For what is art, what is inspiration, if not the artist's deepest, darkest secrets?"

That was a very pretentious way of looking at it. Art was no single thing, and art as suffering was a noxious, outdated concept. But Io guessed this kind of rhetoric fit perfectly into the facade of otherworldly mystery the Nine were selling.

"What is *my* art, then?" asked Io. "What do you want me to create for you?"

The Muses shared a glance, something silent passing among them. "You are a detective, are you not?" Clio asked in what could have passed for a motherly tone, if your mother was a viper. "You watch, you examine, you investigate. We want no more from you than that."

"An investigation?"

"A question, if you will."

"You want to ask me a question? That's it? Your protégés could do that for you."

"No, they can't, silly!" Polyhymnia giggled from the floor. "Haven't you been paying attention?"

"Your art is yours and yours alone," said Clio.

"This question can only be asked *by you*." This last line had come from the corner of the room, from Calliope, in a sweet, crooning voice. She was still watching Io like a hawk, her pen scraping cease-lessly over the paper, tracing the same lines over and over, ink laid so thick that the letters were bleeding into each other.

It was unnerving—Io took a step closer to Edei, and closer to the door. It all made sense now: their staged performance, the spooky way they spoke, the web they were trying to weave around her. Their powers had limits, just like any other-born's. They knew the answers and truths of the world, but only if the right person was asking the questions. And at the moment, the right person was Io, for some reason.

"Three questions you can ask," said Clio. "And the fourth one, we will choose."

"Five questions for me, one for you," Io bargained. "No vague prophecies, no double meanings."

Clio gave a curt nod of her head. "You may begin."

The first question was easy: the most obvious and urgent. "Did you order Horatio Long to kill the women named Raina, Drina Savva and Emmeline Segal twelve years ago?"

The Muses shot narrowed glances at each other, not calculating but inquisitive. As though trying to decide who should answer. Polyhymnia took the lead, saying, "Horatio Long was instructed to remove these women from Alante, in whatever way he saw fit."

"Instructed by you."

The women shuffled. "Yes."

*"Why?"*

A shared look again, laced with urgency. Clio raised a palm to her sisters and answered Io, "We had our reasons. The women were dangerous to this city."

"We agreed no vagueness," Io said harshly. "Try again."

Urania was the one to continue, speaking rapidly while her hands fluttered above the cards on the floor before her. *"Sing in me, Muse, and through me tell the story.* We saw this story unfold in maps of stars, in the chirp of songbirds, on the cracked paint of a half-finished portrait, but it was snippets, bits and pieces, nothing concrete, no beginning and no middle and no end. We made a story of the scraps and knew the women were dangerous. They had to *die* to stop the city from burning to the ground, and the children from wailing, and the streets from running red with blood."

Io and Edei shared a glance, each of them connecting the dots. On the same day, twelve years ago, Horatio Long kidnapped and attempted to kill Emmeline Segal, Drina Savva, and Raina—other women, too. The Nine had seen a tale in their artists' creations, one that demanded the women's deaths in order to save the city from *burning to the ground.*

Twelve years ago, the city had burned because of the Moonset Riots.

Hundreds fell victim to the turf war the anonymous rogue gang ignited, culminating in the loss of the entire Order of the Furies. If not for Bianca Rossi, the Riots would have annihilated the Silts. In a last hurrah, the young smuggler formed a passionate vanguard that hammered down on the aggressors on the eighth and final day of the carnage, essentially ending the Riots by sheer force of will. It took years for the Silts to rebuild.

But it still didn't make sense. If the Nine had gotten a premonition to sacrifice these women to end the Riots, and Horatio had let them escape, then how had the Riots ended? And if the Nine knew Horatio had betrayed them and let Drina and the young girls live, wouldn't they have punished him? They certainly had the means and, as it turned out, the vitriol. There was something the Muses weren't saying: altruism wasn't in their nature. They had ordered the women's deaths because they somehow served their purpose.

"You said you knew the women were dangerous," Edei said, startling Io out of her thoughts. "They're not recorded as other-born, and yet they can wield the threads of fate. They are inhumanly strong and resilient; they outlast their severed life-threads, but they rot from the inside out."

A moment of silence, then Clio said, "I don't hear a question."

"Are they—no." He paused, glanced at Io, reconsidered how to best phrase their question. "They said they were made. So, *what* are they?"

This time Polyhymnia answered, her eyes glazed over as though looking into the very fabric of the world. "They are daughters of the night, chosen for their honor, made to whip vengeance into the backs of the wicked."

Io waited for more. More didn't come. "That's not the clear answer you promised us, Muses."

"It's the answer to what you asked," Polyhymnia said. "It's what my powers provided. If you want a better answer, ask a better question."

Io rolled her eyes in exasperation. "If they were made, then *who* made them?"

She counted in her head: four questions asked, one of her own left, one to be dictated by the Nine.

"That *is* a better question," Erato said. Her clever eyes went from Io to Edei to her hands in her lap. "To which we don't know the answer. We have made our artists write and play and paint, but they become stumped. Whoever is turning these women into creatures knows how to hide from our powers. And before you snap again"— Erato raised a hand to Io's open mouth—"we will give you our best guess: laws can bend a little, but they cannot break. We are all the same, Muses and moira-born and grace-born."

"Descendants of the gods," whispered Io.

Erato nodded. "Whatever they may be, these women are of the gods."

"There is no god with powers like these."

The muse shrugged. "Even gods change."

The insinuation was world-shattering. Io said, "The gods are dead."

Silence filled the room. Five faces watched Io, full of devious glee.

Clio said, "Go on. Ask."

*Are the gods alive?*

Io wanted to, desperately. She was certain their powers would provide the answer, but the eagerness in the sisters' eyes felt wrong. Like they had been tossing her breadcrumb after breadcrumb, leading her to this unaskable question.

Instinct had never failed Io before. If this felt like a trap, it probably was. *Focus, Io. Think.* Four victims: a chernobog-born, a dioscuri-born, two grace-born—all shady characters. Two strange murderesses, now a third, who claimed to be made, to have been given purpose and instructions by *someone*. Who were dangerous enough during the Moonset Riots for the Nine to put a price on their heads—if the Muses were telling the truth. And now the gods. *The damned gods.* What was Io missing? There was a gap here. She knew the victims and the killers. She had seen the murder weapons herself, felt that vile thread around her own throat. She could guess at motive—

No. Here was the missing link. She could guess *the wraiths'* motive; they said it often enough after all. Vengeance. Justice. But what about that infamous "they"? Those who instructed the wraiths— who made them. Those powerful enough to hide themselves from the all-knowing Nine. This was the part that Io couldn't understand: Why create the wraiths? Why not take a gun or a knife or a set of knuckles and kill those who wronged you yourself?

Only one person would know the truth: Raina, the newest wraith. But first, Io would have to find her and save her, from both her bloodlust and the inevitable decay of her body.

"My final question," Io said. "How can I save her? The new wraith, Raina?"

An imperceptible frown, and Clio said, "*You* cannot save her."

Io caught the sadness in her tone. "Someone else can?" Io pried.

The corners of the Muse's lips rose into a satisfied smile. "Is that a sixth question, cutter?"

"The sixth question is ours to choose," said Polyhymnia.

"And yours to ask," said Urania.

Io rolled her eyes so hard she felt they would jump out of her skull. "Just tell me how to save her!"

A devious silence fell on the room, and the four sisters settled back, watching.

It was the fifth sister who spoke, from the desk in the back of the indigo room. She rose on trembling legs and circled around the room, holding out the paper she had been scribbling on like a knife. "Pay your fee and we will help you. We'll tell you exactly how to save her," hissed Calliope. "Here is our fee. Here is our question: What thread will you cut?"

"Ask us," said Clio.

"Ask: What thread will I cut?" said Erato.

"And then we'll know," said Polyhymnia.

"We'll know how you'll end the world," said Urania.

Io shuffled backward, away from Calliope, who was approaching with hunger in her snarl and bloodthirst in her eyes. She felt Edei's hand on her shoulder pivoting her behind him, a wall of muscle and fist between her and Calliope. The movement startled the Muse, and the paper slipped from her hands, fluttering to a stop by Io's boot.

It felt dangerous, this paper, life changing and earth-shattering. The disarrayed scribblings were letters, traced over and over again, letters bloated with ink, the poem of an erratic mind. Io squatted to pick it up.

> *The cutter*
> *the unseen blade*
> *the reaper of fates*
> *she watches silver like a sign*
> *she weeps silver like a mourning song*
> *she holds silver like a blade*
> *she cuts the thread*
> *and the world ends*

Her fingers were trembling. She was uncertain why—*they are just words,* the rational part of her kept saying—and yet her chest was tight, bound across with a thousand terrors. "What is this?" she whispered.

"This is our plague!" Clio spat. "This is our destruction. For weeks, our poets have been producing this poem—and *only* this poem. About how you will end the world."

"Hey," Edei ordered, deathly calm. "Step back."

Clio had stood up from the sofa and stalked to a mahogany cabinet between the two front windows. She threw the drawers open haphazardly and tossed paper after paper into the air. They scattered like leaves in an autumnal thunderstorm, a flurry of white around the room. Different lettering, different ink, and yet it was the same: *The cutter, the unseen blade . . .*

"Ask the question," ordered Clio, her eyes luminous.

Io was breathing hard now, unshed tears obstructing her view of the room. "H-how do you know it's about m-me?"

Clio let out a harsh laugh. At the other end of the room, the two young Muses stood up and disappeared through the second door. Io's chest rose and fell, fast and loud like a steam machine, and her insides felt like she was burning rough coal. The girls came back carrying armfuls of portraits, big and small, oil-painted or char-coaled, on canvas and parchment and paper, on cloth and wood.

"Ask the question!" Clio bellowed.

But Io couldn't focus on anything else: just Edei's back pressed against her palms, and the papers rustling around the room, and her face—her thick, angry eyebrows, her dark eyes, her curls bound back by a yellow scarf, her downturned mouth—on every portrait, every drawing, every doodle the Nine's artists had produced.

It was her face, her hand, her silver thread, and behind her, the world was burning.

# CHAPTER XVI

# SOMETHING SHARP AND SERRATED

"BACK THE HELL off," Edei snapped. Shielding her with his body, he retreated them toward the double doors.

The security guards attempted to block their path, but a squeak of alarm from the sitting room had them scrambling for the museborn. Over Edei's shoulder, through the blur of her wet eyes, Io glimpsed Calliope convulsing on the floor, her sisters leaning over her. Then Edei's hand clasped her own, gravel crunched under their boots, the gates screeched open against Edei's force, the street clamored around them. Newsies and tourists pelted them with questions, following on their heels down the pavement. Cameras clicked. Edei cupped Io's hand and pulled her up the busy Modiano Walkway running parallel to the trolley line, where the passing trains blessedly drowned out all other noises.

The Artisti District lay at the foot of the Hill and shared a small percentage of its grandiose views. From the elevated entrance to the domed Modiano Market, where the city's best fashion boutiques were housed, the city stretched like a lazy cat: the Minarets of Old sticking out like pointed ears, the long body of the red trolley line that connected the City Plaza to the natural history museum, the merry-go-round of the Newtown District spinning languidly like a tail. It was almost sunset, and bright rays of sunlight stole through the clouds, bathing Alante in gold.

Tension pulsed from Io's chest, a blood flow of acid. Keeping her breaths under control was a conscious effort. *Breathe in, breathe out.*

She made herself focus on this moment, here with Edei outside the Modiano Market, bathing in her senses: the trolley cars trotting by, the shoppers walking in and out of the market building, the sun licking her skin. The horrid smell of three-day-old trash stuffed in the bins outside the entrance. The sun playing hide-and-seek behind the clouds. She would not be consumed by panic. She had to stay in the here and now and calm the hell down.

The current of the crowd jostled them through the metal archways to the center of the domed marketplace, a labyrinth of winding paved streets, dotted with hundreds of shopfronts. They had no destination, but walking felt nice right now, so she kept going.

Edei kept glancing at her and eventually said, "Io, it was a trick. It's not real. They were telling you whatever they thought would get you to do their bidding. They were trying to manipulate you."

She had been tricked, that much was certain. Her ego could suffer the hit. What she *couldn't* fight was the rising dread of doubt. "What if it's not a trick?" she said. "What if they truly foresaw that . . . prophecy?"

Edei didn't immediately reply, forcing Io to glance at him. His muscles popped on his jaw, and his eyes revisited the crowd behind them, scanning their faces. Io wished he would contradict her, appease her, something! His silence was insufferable, yet more kindling to the raging thoughts in her mind.

The Nine had played their cards perfectly: they gave her a new mystery, one only they could solve, knowing she would not be able to resist it. *Ask us: What thread will I cut? And then we'll know. We'll know how you'll end the world.* What thread? What world? What end? She had come for answers, clarity, and instead she got a stupid poem recited by a thousand mouths, and a stupid picture of her stupid face drawn by a thousand hands. Eventually she would have to return to them, and they knew it. Perhaps that was why they had let her go.

She grabbed his elbow. "Maybe we should go back to them."

"Io, don't fall into their trap. They show you a cryptic poem and your face on a painting, and you're willing to give up everything else to run back to them?" he asked, a trace of irritation in his voice.

"It's my face, Edei. My hand that will *end the world.*"

"It's a story. A story *they* told you. It's not real."

"How can you be certain? They're the Nine."

"They're manipulative bullies."

The dome above their heads began to vibrate with the coming of another trolley. The Modiano station was located at the very peak of the domed market. The world filled with the trembling of metal and glass, the sounds proof of this city's delicate disposition: one wrong move, one earthquake or building collapse, and Alante would crash into a million pieces. Right now, Io was feeling just as delicate.

"Do you realize what they just told us? They confessed to putting a hit out on those women as if it was nothing more than tax fraud. They admitted it freely because they know we can't do anything about it. If we go to the leeches with this, or the newspapers, you know what the Nine will say? *We did it because of destiny. Because our artists foresaw that these women were dangerous, because it's our duty to protect this city.*" His voice rose to a sharp howl. "And no one will bat an eye. No human judge would ever dare indict them. The only ones that could— the Order of the Furies—are long dead. They will go unpunished even as they gloat that they ordered the death of innocent women!"

Edei's face was all eyebrows, two thick straight lines of fury over guarded eyes. His gaze darted from face to face as they shouldered through the crowd. "They have a hundred portraits of you burning the world down—the whole world, Io, not just the Silts. If they ordered the death of those girls because they believed them dangerous, what do you think they'd do with *you*? No matter what the answer to their precious question was, what they foresaw in your destiny, you think they'd let you leave that House alive? And you want to go back!"

Io dropped her eyes to her boots, the paved street beneath them, the seawater gathered in the crevices of the stones. The carcass of a squid-moth chimerini, squashed out of shape. She wasn't the target of his anger, and yet it pierced her skin, a bull's-eye hit.

He said, "The Nine have amassed all this knowledge, all this power. Three women were changed by gods know what, turned into murderous wraiths—and instead of telling you how to save them, these assholes harass you about some mystical prophecy. Bianca is right: the only way to deal with people like the Nine is a knife to the throat."

She startled. When had the conversation taken a turn to *a knife to the throat*? Her fury rose to meet his, and she snapped, "You know *I'm* people like the Nine, right?"

"That's not—" His scowl instantly mellowed. "You don't abuse your powers like they do."

"But I could. *She cuts the thread and the world ends*, remember?"

"They were trying to scare you."

"Well, they succeeded. And now I'm not just scared that this horrible future has been foretold for me; I'm scared that I'll wake up one day with *a knife at my throat*."

Edei halted in the stream of shoppers. "That's not what I meant."

"What did you mean, then?"

"That they're evil. People with amassed power and no one to put them in their place, like the Nine, and the leeches, even the City Council."

"And you think your precious Bianca isn't as evil as the rest of them?"

"She is necessary," he said with conviction. "We need her brand of evil, to survive. If it means we have to tolerate some wickedness, then so be it."

Something sharp and serrated sliced through Io. *A necessary evil.* She thought of Ava, palming the wetness from Io's cheeks after one of Thais's particularly snide remarks. *Forgive her, sister mine,* Ava kept saying. *She works all day to take care of us; her temper is bound to be taut.* So what? Io should have said. But she was young then; it didn't even occur to her that Ava could be wrong, that Thais's anger was undeserved. Now Io knew how to recognize a bully. Thais had been one. The Nine were one. So was Bianca, however necessary Edei might find her. Io was done making excuses for any of them.

"You might survive," Io told Edei, "but tolerating wickedness seems to me just a slow kind of death."

His eyes widened, his mouth opening to reply, but right then— thank the gods—a street vendor stepped between them, a particularly loud woman in a colorful headscarf who shoved pillowcases into Io's chest.

"Touch it, lady," the vendor said. "You won't lay your cheek on fabric softer than this."

"Very soft," Io agreed, running a hand over the pillowcases. Some of her wariness, her quiet fury, eased away from her.

Gods, she was tired. Getting angry, *staying* angry, was exhausting.

"Thank you, ma'am," Edei said to the woman. Glancing over his shoulder, he placed a hand on Io's back and mumbled, "Let's get some coffee."

They entered the souk, the food court of the market. The smells hit Io first: fish and seafood and spices, syrupy sweets and salepi brewed on makeshift fires. Then came the sounds, vendors calling out goods and haggling prices, ice dripping into the paved street, children stepping in front of them to offer cheese and fruit and candied nuts to taste. At a narrow coffee stall, Edei dropped a few coins into the vendor's palm for two cups of dark coffee, brewed Kurkz style. As they blew on it, Edei kept glancing at her. Glancing at the crowd. At her. A question was coming.

Dread pooled in Io's stomach. What if he asked the right question, the one Io had been fearing and hoping someone would ask for years? *Whose wickedness did you have to tolerate, Io?* Could she answer with the truth, about her family, about Thais?

But Edei asked, "Are you safe, Io?"

Safe? It took her by surprise. In all the imagined confessions, to Ava, to Rosa, to Amos, even to Thais, she had never pictured them asking this. Safety was a luxury Io had never had time to consider, like bubble baths or decorative plants. No one had asked her before. She hadn't even asked herself. Only Edei Rhuna had noticed the need to ask.

*Was* she safe?

The bully of her childhood had been gone for two years. The narrow-minded people who hated and scared her, she had learned to deal with. But there were still a few daggers that could slip through her armor: a woman rolled in a white carpet, dead by her hand. Five unnerving Muses, accusing her of a crime she hadn't yet committed. A boy calling her kind evil. She felt guilt: for killing Drina Savva, for not severing the fate-thread when she was supposed to. For not telling him. This was an abuse of power, too. Was she destiny's victim or another bully? She couldn't decide, couldn't choose one way or the other, and she hated that.

No, she wasn't safe, not from her shame.

But here, in this moment, with Edei, with his question, she . . . "I'm trying to be," she replied honestly. She downed her coffee in one gulp, scalding her insides.

He nodded, once and sharp. "I could help with that, if you'd like."

"Um—" She choked. "Yes. Thank you."

A knot inside Io became undone, its yarn unspooling, her careful loops coming loose. She didn't care about Edei Rhuna, she would treat him like any other case, she would cut the fate-thread and be done with it . . . Out and out came the yarn, all the lies and pretenses she had woven to protect herself. At the end, only wool was left, a single line. The truth: she *liked* him.

She said, "I'm not like the Nine."

"I know, Io, I *know*. It's just a stupid thing I said because I was angry—"

"No. Listen." Words whooshed out of her, a torrential confession. "I have a lot of power most humans don't. I didn't choose it, but it is mine, nonetheless. And you're right: there is no one to check that I'm doing the right thing with it. Which is why I need to tell you something."

*We share a fate-thread. You can choose what it means. You can choose to walk away, you can tell me to cut it, and I will. But I—*

*I like you.*

Edei's gaze did that thing where it skipped from one eye to the other, very fast, and she felt that he could read her every thought. Io wanted to squirm out of the spotlight like a wild animal, but she kept still.

"Wait," he whispered, his fingers threading around her wrist. "Io, do you trust me?"

Heart drumming, mind spinning, Io breathed, "Yes."

He placed an arm around her shoulders and leaned close to her ear. "Get ready."

For a moment—a silly, breathless moment—she thought he would kiss her.

But she noticed his eyes: beyond her, on the crowd. She noticed his arm: maneuvering her behind him. She noticed the fingers of his free hand: slipping into the knuckles.

Her hand was reaching for a thread before he even started moving. In one smooth whirl, he twisted her out of his way and plucked someone from the crowd by the collar. With thundering strides, he backed the man between the stalls and into a dark alley.

Io was left wheezing in the middle of the souk, getting hard looks from the passersby. Oh gods—they probably thought *she* was a leech, an undercover officer disappearing people from the streets. She scurried after Edei through the narrow alley stacked with old furniture.

She heard shuffling ahead and Edei's voice: "Who are you? Why are you following us?"

She thought of his scattered gaze, his backward glances—someone had been tailing them since they left the House of Nine. Io could make out their outlines now, Edei and a tall, lanky man backtracking fast toward a patch of light filtering through the dome overhead.

"What do you want? Who are you?" Edei shoved the man against a haphazard pile of porch chairs, his forearm across the man's throat.

He looked to be in his late thirties, with a neat, black goatee favored in the upper-class circles, light skin, and dark eyes. His modern, open-collar suit was tailored to his lean physique and cut from expensive marine-blue fabrics.

The Quilt lit up around her in a lattice of silver. One of the man's threads crossed the air close to her hip. She grabbed it, preparing to yank to add a little threat to Edei's interrogation. Her gaze lifted to their stalker's face, illuminated in the fading sunlight, and Io glimpsed his eyes—pitch-black, unnaturally so.

"Finally," said the man.

She stilled mid-stride, as though she were suddenly made of marble. A thought flew through her mind—*protect yourself*—but it soon fluttered away like a startled bird. Terror seized her. It was unlike anything she had felt before, an unfathomable fear, numbing her body from head to toe, rooting her to the spot. Sweat drenched her back; she was more than scared—she was consumed by a panic so monumental she was unable to form thoughts. The man's thread was still in her fingers, but she couldn't remember what she was supposed to do with it.

The same incapacitating horror must have ensnared Edei because his hand dropped from their stalker's throat like a stringless puppet's. The man stepped away from the chairs, walked to Io, and pulled the scarf from around her neck, then proceeded to meticulously brush the dust from his clothes. When he was satisfied his suit was clean, he surveyed the scene calmly: Io paralyzed in the alley, Edei frozen while facing the stacked furniture, breathing hard but otherwise unmoving.

He shoved his face in front of Edei's. "What was your business at the House of Nine?"

Edei shivered, but his lips remained firmly shut.

The stranger cocked his head for a moment, surprise in his lifted brows; then he switched his attention to Io. He took a single step toward her—the terror fell on her like a hammer. "Your turn, then, girl. What did the Nine tell you?"

She tried to form coherent thoughts through the chaos of nauseating fear. *He* was doing this. He was phobos-born, a descendant of Phobos and Deimos, the twin gods of terror and panic. He induced fear in his victims as long as he could ensnare them with his eyes, which reflected black like Io's reflected silver when she was in the Quilt.

"We talked about the Silts murders," Io gasped in answer.

"What about them?"

"The murderers had been targeted by the Nine during the Moonset Riots."

"Targeted how?"

"The Nine hired someone to kill them—"

"Don't lie."

His power washed over Io—her body convulsed. It wasn't pain, but the promise of it. She was standing on a bridge, a chasm of black beneath her feet, and the ground was shaking, her legs were weak, she was losing her balance. A pleading litany spilled from her mouth: "No, please, I'm telling the truth, the Nine's artists saw them in visions, please—"

At the end of the alley, Edei shifted, an infinitesimal twist of his head toward her. How did he find the strength to move, even a little, when all she could do was whimper?

"Do the Nine know what these women are?" The phobos-born slithered up to her. "Do they know who made them?"

Distantly, Io registered this was an oddly specific question. But in those black eyes, in her chest, there was only fear. Io knew trepidation: a hard look, lips pursed, the sharp scoff of disdain. It was coming and she couldn't escape, couldn't avoid it, and it would hurt her, hurt her, hurt her, words stabbing at her soft belly, carving away pounds of flesh.

Behind the phobos-born, Edei moved again. If she held the man's attention a while longer, Edei might be able to break out of his hold of terror.

"No," she whimpered. "They can't see who is behind them."

The man came so close she could smell his expensive cologne. He didn't wait for her to hesitate or elaborate—his power rained on her. Her body went rigid, her eyesight blurred, her heartbeat spiked to new levels.

"Please," she wailed. "Please, they don't know—"

The stranger spoke softly. "Stop lying."

Io screamed.

The phobos-born's fingers spasmed, readying for another strike, but Edei was already moving. A hesitant step at first, his hand reaching quietly for a broken-off piece of wood. Then, in a burst of speed, he had crossed the space between them and struck the wood hard on the side of the man's head. The phobos-born cried out, cursed, but didn't fall. He raised his eyes as though they were gun barrels—Edei was there in a moment, swinging the wood into the man's belly. The man doubled over, sucking in desperate breaths. He dropped to his knee, ramming Io against the furniture in the process. Edei grabbed her shoulders to steady her, and before either of them could react, the phobos-born bolted down the alley. A slew of curses, a spurt of movement, and Edei disappeared after him.

Io slipped to the damp ground, her bottom soaked immediately with gods knew what. Her heart galloped in her chest; her fingers ached, cemented into claws. There was silver between them.

The man's thread was still clasped in her first.

Edei reappeared at the mouth of the alley.

"I lost him. In the crowd. Are you—hurt?" he panted. Then he was touching her, fingers running over her torso, her neck, across her face. A sigh of relief slumped through him. "Gods, the way you were screaming, I thought . . . Gods."

*What did you think?* she wanted to ask. *Touch me again*, she wanted to plead. Her neck warmed with embarrassment at her own thoughts. "Who was he?" she mumbled.

"I first spotted him outside the House of Nine. He followed us into the Modiano and through the food souk, taking every turn we did, stopping when we did."

"He asked very specific questions."

"That he did."

The man was interested in what the Nine knew; the wraiths' connection to the Riots seemed to surprise him, but his focus was keen on their puppeteer. Why would he worry whether the Nine had figured out who had *made* the wraiths if he wasn't somehow involved in this?

Io asked, "How did you break out of his hold?"

Edei shrugged, dropping on his haunches before her. "There was a gang boss a few years back that was phobos-born. I had to— well, let's just say, I've dealt with their powers before. But you . . . It sounded like . . ." He composed himself. "I was worried."

She reached out and took hold of his arm, just above the wrist. The touch was small, light, but Io felt it like a firestorm. "I am safe, thanks to you. And we didn't lose him." She showed him her other hand, the clenched fist.

Edei looked at her like she had just sprouted a third ear right on the tip of her nose.

Io huffed a tired laugh. She really was a fool. Edei couldn't see the thread gripped between her fingers, the line of silver that would lead them straight to the man.

# CHAPTER XVII

# A DELIGHT

HER FINGERS THAT held the thread had started to cramp by the time backup arrived. Edei had sent word to Bianca about a potential other-born threat stalking the gang, via that strange knuckle-rap system the Fortuna gang had; in fifteen minutes, Nico and Chimdi were there.

Io studied the young woman, her gaze falling first on her fingers, long, calloused, ornamented not by clay but by the Fortuna knuckles. She was petite and lean, hair shorn so short Io could make out the curves of her scalp, a series of brass hoops on both ears. Her accent was Anoch, drawing out the vowels and tumbling over the *ps*.

"Bianca says do it properly this time," the girl told Edei instead of a greeting. "No screw-ups."

Edei gave a solemn nod, no hint that the threat rattled him.

The thread in Io's hand felt suddenly like a lifeline. Their visit at the House of Nine had confirmed the wraiths were once the target of the Nine, forewarned as dangerous by their artists. Whoever was guiding the wraiths' hands was clever enough to know how to hide from the all-knowing muse-born. There were other clues they could follow—such as tracking the wraith or looking into a possible link between the wraiths and their other victims, like there had been with Horatio—but the thread that now lay between Io's fingers called for more immediate attention.

The man had followed them from the House of Nine, assaulted them with his phobos-born powers, and appeared particularly interested in the possibility that the Nine might know who was behind the wraiths. Something connected him to these undying women, and Io intended to find out precisely what. She hadn't dropped the Quilt for a moment, in fear that the phobos-born's thread would slip out of her fingers.

A gray sky greeted them as they stepped out of the domed market. Io could already taste rain in the air. It was nearly summer, when neo-monsoons migrated from the south up to Alante, pelting the city with acid rain. They would need to find the man quickly and take cover somewhere inside, in case the weather turned ugly. Edei must have had the same thought, looking from the darkening sky to her.

Even with the Quilt casting the silver light of dozens of threads across her vision, Io recognized the tension in his face. "Where to?" he asked.

Io glanced at the thread. "East, to Newtown."

Newtown District was reconstructed a few years ago, its streets smoothed to accommodate automobiles. The frail constructions rack-rack-racketed on the uneven asphalt, honking at each other and pedestrians. They were mostly trucks carrying products, but there was also the odd private vehicle, its windows tinted, its drivers in shiny caps and elegant button-downs. Io's father had been in a private automobile once, an occasion he had narrated as though it had been the most marvelous fairy tale, complete with a beautiful princess and a fairy godmother. He had been crossing the street on Cardamom Avenue, not far from here, and the driver hadn't seen him. Nearly took his kneecap off. The owner of the car, a young lady clad in chimerini furs—the detail always made Io's mother roll her eyes—had been so distressed she insisted they drive him to the nearest hospital. Traffic was bad, and the ride took so long his knee had stopped hurting by the time they arrived. But as Baba watched the car take off, he vowed that one day, he'd get an automobile himself and take his girls on road trips in the countryside, and wouldn't that be lovely?

*And one day,* Mama had always replied, *I will get you girls chimerini furs, and we can all sit like princesses in the back while your baba drives us around.*

The memory brought a smile to Io's lips. Ava could make fun of her all she wanted, but the entire Ora family was obsessed with *one day,* with the adulation of *more.* Ava liked to appear as the grounded one, the come-what-may sister, but she hadn't escaped the Ora legacy, either: her aspiration wasn't just to be better off, like Thais or Io—she wanted to be the best. To sing the loveliest songs at the best clubs for the most adoring audiences. To dance surrounded by the most famous clubbers. To date the prettiest girl.

Io's attention was called back to the present. Nico sidled close to her, his threads spilling silver in her eyesight. She drew to a halt with a surprised "Careful!"

"Oops," said Nico. "Did I step on you?"

Edei came around on Io's other side, casually hooking her free hand into his elbow. To Nico, he said, "She's in the Quilt. It makes it hard to see the real world or discern your threads from the one in her hand. I suggest you tell your story from where you are now."

His tone was good-natured, his palm cupping Io's hand softly. Io remembered her admission—*she liked him*—and let the fuzzy warmth of his body seep into her, like a traveler coming in from the cold. If he wanted to help her, she'd let him. If he wanted to be sweet, she'd enjoy it. She had promised herself: no more guilt.

"How'd you know I was going to tell a story?" asked Nico.

"Is there anything else you do?" Chimdi chimed in.

"Do you see how they treat me, Io? If this is what friends are, I never want to meet my enemies."

"I've told you a dozen times: we're not friends," Chimdi commented.

"And what do you call the guys that you're always around, have drinks and share laughs with?"

"These particular guys? I call them Idiot One and Idiot Two."

Edei interrupted, very seriously, "Am I Idiot One or Two?"

"Two, of course." She quirked an eyebrow at Nico. "This one's idiocy vastly outshines yours."

Edei's laugh echoed down the busy street. A breathtaking sound; Io wished for a bottle so she could distill it. Open it on sleepless nights and lull herself to sweet dreams—gods. She really was a weirdo. She was Smitten, capital *S*, neon sign, symphonic orchestra playing in the background.

On her other side, Nico argued, "I am a *delight*."

"You are," Io piped in. "And don't listen to them. All three of you are connected by strong, bright threads. They love you, no matter what they claim."

Chimdi groaned. "That is a gross transgression of your powers, cutter. Where are the fury-born when you need them?"

"Let's not joke about the fury-born," Edei said.

The mood of the group sobered a bit. Edei was right: the extinction of the fury-born was one of the blackest pages in other-born history. When the Kinship Treaty was signed, humans required that other-born establish governing bodies. The horae-born, descendants of the goddesses of time, formed the Agora and became their leaders; smaller other-born compounds, like the muse-born, took charge of separate city-nations; and the fury-born, goddesses of divine punishment, formed the policing body, named the Order of the Furies.

The fury-born could see a bright orange latticework akin to the Quilt, which showed them a person's wrongdoings. A very useful and unique power when it came to other-born, whose unnatural skills made it particularly hard to prove and prosecute a crime. Io didn't really understand how it worked and probably never would, since the fury-born had died out completely.

For years before the Moonset Riots, there had been rumors that their bloodline was thinning, fewer of them born every year. Natural selection, some said. The hazard of trying to keep other-born in line, said others. And then the rogue gang had slaughtered them in the Moonset Riots. A few weeks later, one of the Agora had come on a globally transmitted radio news show to make the sad announcement: the last of the fury-born had died of their wounds, sustained in the Riots. There would be no more.

With forced cheer, Nico said, "I actually know a great story about a fury-born and a cockroach—"

"Dear gods, have mercy," Chimdi bemoaned.

"Fine! Just tell me what we're walking into, and I'll shut up!"

Edei replied, keeping his voice quiet. "A man followed us from the House of Nine. We believe he is involved with the wraiths, somehow. He's phobos-born." Both Nico and Chimdi stilled; they, too, must have crossed paths with the phobos-born gang boss that Edei had mentioned. "If he seizes you, remember that you feel fear every day and yet you keep going."

*"Feel your fear and keep going anyway. By Edei Rhuna."* Chimdi said it as though she was quoting from a great wordsmith. Nico chuckled.

Edei grumbled in irritation. "I only mean that the phobos-born creates feelings we're all familiar with. We've lived them, we've survived them, we can survive them again. In any case, avoid looking into his eyes—that's how he gets you."

*"Don't look fear in the eye,"* said Chimdi, *"by Edei*—hey!"

Edei had punched her on the shoulder. A laugh burst from Io's belly; Edei glanced at her, then grinned. Suddenly, in her hands, the thread stretched taut.

The man had stopped moving. Io followed his thread with her gaze, up a set of steps and into a tall building.

Nico whistled. "Gods-damn."

"The *Teatro?*" asked Chimdi. "Your bad guy is visiting the *Teatro?*"

The Teatro Blanco, as was its proper name, was a massive structure of white marble, ten tall columns supporting the roof, each decorated with figures of major deities. The Furies, depicted as ugly crones with serpentine hair; the Graces, young, beautiful, and naked; the Muses, each with their instrument; the Dioscuri, solemn and identical; the Fates, weaving their tapestry; the Erotes, seven winged brothers of love; the Horae, three sisters who controlled the passing of time, long-haired and holding hands; the Keres, the three dark sisters of death; the Oneiroi, three brothers of sleep and dreams; and the Asclepies, the four daughters of health and medicine.

Io was surprised the phobos-born was in there. The Teatro Blanco was one of the most expensive and exclusive opera houses in the whole world. It hosted established singers, renowned plays and musicals, and the occasional highbrow comedian or dancing act. To get tickets, people had to stand in line long before dawn, and sometimes even that wasn't enough.

Io recalled the man's tailored suit, the obsessive way he'd cleaned the dirt off it with her scarf. Perhaps he *was* rich. Other-born often couldn't hold a job because employers found them untrustworthy, but what if an other-born had been born into money? Io doubted they'd be treated the same way.

"How are we getting in?" Chimdi wanted to know.

Two bouncers flanked the entrance while a short, well-dressed lady checked tickets. Whatever today's spectacle was, it had attracted an unusual sort of audience: well-dressed and perfectly coiffed, but much younger than the usual Teatro-goer. University students, young professionals, no one over forty.

"Over here," Nico called. "I know the girl working the coatroom."

They followed him into a side door and down a heavy-carpeted corridor to the main foyer, where they waited in the shadows while Nico spoke with the coat-check girl. She patted his cheek fondly and slipped him a small object. Nico returned, his face as red as his hair, with a key to one of the vacant boxes.

"See?" he said, eyeing Chimdi, a thumb pointed at his own chest. "A *delight*."

It produced a chuckle from all three of them. They flowed up the staircase with the rest of the crowd, to the sixth floor, where they entered their box quickly, shutting the door to prying eyes. Io pulled on her spectacles and looked out at the Teatro. "Gods," she gasped.

There were six tiers of boxes surrounding the circular stage, each box dressed in red velvet with golden details, the walls decorated with floral patterns and satyr heads peering from the parapets. The entire ground floor formed the biggest stage Io had seen, right beneath an enormous chandelier with what looked like thousands of tiny little lamps in the shape of teardrops. Enchanted, Io dropped into a seat soft as a pillow. So *this* was what the upper class experienced—plush chairs and violins singing and chandeliers as bright as the sun. She thought of the abandoned Beak Street Theater at the Silts, of its collapsed side and misshapen balcony. Granted, she couldn't see the moons from the Teatro Blanco, but she didn't even care. This looked like a palace from a fairy tale.

"There he is," Edei said, pointing to the leftmost entrance to the stage, where the phobos-born stood with his hands in his pockets.

"Should we surround him?" asked Chimdi. "Catch him when the play starts?"

"No, let's wait. Watch who he speaks to."

A murmur swept over the crowd as the lights of the chandelier dimmed. In the faint glow, Io saw the phobos-born stepping aside as the door behind him opened. A man came in; the phobos-born whispered something into his ear; the other man nodded, planted a firm smile on his face, and climbed onto the stage. The Teatro Blanco erupted in applause as the spotlights came on, illuminating him in white.

Io clamped her mouth to stifle her gasp. She knew those high cheekbones, those thin lips, that shiny black hair and vibrant smile. It had been plastered on every major billboard in Alante for the past few months. The man that the phobos-born had just reported to was Luc Saint-Yves.

"Hello, ladies and gentlemen." Saint-Yves spun in a circle, arms out in welcome. "We are here today to introduce the Initiative for the New Order and all it has to offer you."

Another round of applause, Saint-Yves mouthing *thank you* throughout.

"First, let me introduce myself. Most of you know me as Alante's Police Commissioner or Mayoral candidate, and I don't doubt you've heard the rumors about my past. Yes, I do come from a rich family from Nanzy. Yes, I did join the Iceberg Corps against my family's wishes. And yes, I did come back with a horrible spinal injury and an addiction to opioid medicine. After a hard two years of rehabilitation, I enrolled in law school, graduated with honors, and, at age thirty-four, was appointed Commissioner of Alante. Many say being sent to the Sunken City was a test from my superiors, and I agree; this is the kind of city that can destroy you. It certainly destroyed the fury-born."

Deep in her seat, arms crossed over her chest, Io scowled. All those fancy Nanzy folks thought they knew Alante, but more often than not they knew the newsies' malformed version of it.

"In the year since I was appointed Commissioner, we have managed to shut down more than half of the city's chimerini betting fights, pleasure houses, dream palaces, and gambling dens. Dozens of outlier gangs have been disbanded. Our fine police officers and judges have managed to prosecute and win against factories breaking pollution laws, companies mistreating employees, notable city officials mismanaging city funds."

A pointed silence followed, a reference to something Io had missed. Hill politics rarely reached Silts ears. Who cared about upper-class riffraff when the Aeneas gang was tolling the Rosemary Bridge again? With the election in just a couple of days, rumor was that every mob boss in the Silts was throwing all the spare coin they had in supporting Saint-Yves's opponent, the conservative but more pliable current Mayor.

"For centuries," Saint-Yves continued, "we have trusted the other-born to police their own. The fury-born could spot crimes on your skin like dirt. They could extract a confession and deliver punishment with their mighty whips. Such were their powers. But the once-glorious Order of the Furies is no more. The Nine have become hermits, reclused in their precious House. There is no one to oversee the other-born criminals of Alante, and, boy, have they taken advantage." A series of numbers and graphs was projected on a white sheet behind him. "In the past decade, crime rates in most city-nations—but predominantly in Alante—have grown significantly. What's more worrisome, however, is the fact that indictment rates have acutely dropped. Only one in ten other-born is found guilty. To put it quite simply, we can't *prove* the other-born did it."

But that was just hypocritical bullshit. If only one in ten were found guilty, it was because only one in ten *was* guilty. Other-born were constantly accused of crimes they didn't commit, just because they had the *ability* to commit them.

"And here is where the Initiative comes in," the Commissioner went on. A new slide appeared, listing the Initiative's goals and methods in a neat diagram. "We need other-born to catch other-born. Let's imagine a simple scene: it's summer, the city's humidity is through the roof, and you have opened your window to let the breeze in. Through that window comes in an oneiroi-born with his brothers, putting you in a deep sleep before emptying your apartment of its valuables. You call the police, but what can they do? The best you can hope for is that the thieves make a mistake and get caught carrying one of your possessions.

"Now let's imagine this instead. The police assign the case to an other-born special unit. Two dioscuri-born, twins. They can look at your floors and carpets and see the paths of whoever was there during the night. Where they've been to, where they're going next. Within the day, the thieves will be caught and your valuables returned. But the Initiative would not stop there. These criminals would be delivered to special other-born prosecutors, which will be soon sanctioned by the Agora themselves, descendants of the Horae, goddesses of time, order, justice, and peace."

Saint-Yves stopped talking, as though letting his imagined scenario sink in. The crowd remained silent, a thousand people waiting for more. They liked this idea, liked *him*. This man, who claimed to have the support of the Agora, the highest form of government the other-born had. The same man who might have sent the phobos-born after Io and Edei.

Saint-Yves went on. "You might ask me: Luc, how do you know these other-born will tell you the truth? How can you be sure they're not in on the job themselves? Well, friends, my answer won't be easy to stomach. You must *believe*. You must *trust*. Our society has long been divided: those with the power of the gods, those with the power of money. But I believe—no, I *know* that other-born are not inherently corrupt or evil. They can be kind, smart, honorable individuals, who love their city and want to see it thrive."

Well, of course they could be! Why did Saint-Yves phrase it as if it was admirable that he actually saw other-born as human beings? Why did other-born need to prove their worth to the world by servicing a city that kept pushing them to the fringes whatever chance it got? Protecting the same people who created this screwed-up system, where other-born were a thing to fear? Io shook with fury. This was such propagandist bullshit, and the worst thing was these people were eating it all up!

"And I know, friends," Saint-Yves said, "because I have worked closely with other-born to form the proposal of my Initiative. Because . . ."

The crowd teetered with excitement.

"I am very much in love with one."

He threw one arm toward the side door; the spotlights swung to it.

"My dear friends," Saint-Yves said, "I would like you to meet my best friend, the love of my life—and as of last night, my *fiancée*—Thais Ora!"

# CHAPTER XVIII

# YOU, MOSTLY

IO EXPECTED SHOCK, anger, or sadness to register, but nothing came. Only a single thought, dragged sluggishly out of the depths of her mind: *Thais looks stunning.*

For most of their lives, Thais was a sylphid, slim and pale, all ribs and jutting cheekbones. Now her cheeks were full. Her skin vibrant and rosy. Her figure had curves in all the right places, and a little extra on the hips, like every Ora woman. Her silky brown hair framed her face beautifully, reaching just past her ears. She wore glittering eye shadow and a plum lipstick and a necklace with jade beads around her slender neck. Her high heels echoed across the stage, and her white skirt billowed gracefully with every step. She looked like you would imagine a girl of 64 Hanover Street. Smiley, sunny, shiny.

She placed her hand in Saint-Yves's and let him pull her to his side, where he pressed a kiss on her forehead. It was a tender moment, the kind you see on the cover of romance novels, and Io felt both embarrassed and hungry for more.

Then someone from the crowd heckled, "How'd he propose?"

On the stage, Thais gave Saint-Yves her famous lopsided smile. Io prepared herself for the shock of hearing her sister's voice after two whole years, after *Leave me alone. Haven't you done enough?*

"We were going over his notes for this very presentation, sitting on the floor of our living room, surrounded by empty boxes of Iyen food," she said sweetly. "And suddenly, he took my hand, and he said he couldn't have done this without me. That he never wanted to

do anything without me. And he gave me his grandmother's ring."
Thais extended her ringed finger to them—the crowd went nuts,
exploding with applause, whistles, and supportive crooning.

"My fiancée," Saint-Yves called over the ruckus, "is moira-born.
A weaver. She was the first volunteer to join our Initiative and to use
her powers to track the connections between other-born and their
victims. Tell them, darling, what made you decide to join us?"

"You, mostly." Thais laughed, and the crowd joined her. They
were loving this. They were *buying* this. But not Io. This wasn't Thais.
The Thais Io knew had walked away from Thomas Mutton without a second thought. She had sought to build an empire with her
own two hands, never sacrificing an ounce of who she was and what
she believed in. This impersonator with the trendy haircut and the
expensive necklace? With the dazzling fiancé who embodied everything Thais hated: rich boys who wanted to be the saviors of other-
born, privilege in all its putrid glory? This girl *couldn't* be Thais.

"Truly, though," Thais said. "The Initiative is necessary. It
should have been implemented years ago when the Order of the
Furies was wiped out. It will not only lower the crime rate in Alante,
but also remove some of the stigma around other-born. I was born
and raised in the Silts—"

The theater made a collective sound of disproval.

"*That.* Exactly that. I know what it's like to be looked down on. My
sisters and I were constantly mistreated: we were expected to work
for half the pay or cut corners to help our employers. People believe
other-born are corrupted and corruptive, but I know that couldn't
be further from the truth. What Luc suggests is a collaboration: we
other-born can be better and, in the process, make this city better."

*Be better, make this world better.* Gods, this part *did* sound like her.
Thais had always been an idealist. She truly believed that if you

worked hard enough, if you chose nobility and kindness over corruption, you could make a difference in this world. Better yourself and better the world—that had always been her mantra. But she couldn't have truly fallen for Saint-Yves, couldn't truly believe that he could solve injustice against other-born by simply making people *work together*. Thais wasn't that naive, was she?

When the applause died, Saint-Yves said, "Let me introduce everyone else on the team, our wonderful other-born volunteers and the police officers that will be consulting with us." He started listing names as people climbed onstage. Io didn't bother listening—she had eyes only for Thais, standing by Saint-Yves's side, smiling and prompting questions for him to ask the team. She looked so happy.

*It just seemed to me,* Ava had said, *that for a long time while you girls were working together, you were miserable . . . Now you're happy. And she's happy. Maybe it's not so bad that she wants to stay away, huh?* Did Ava know what—who—was making their sister happy? Was that why she hadn't told Io, because she knew Io would disapprove? Io couldn't help wondering whether that was why Thais didn't want Io to know she was back in the first place. Whether she had caused this, driven Thais away, right into the arms of Saint-Yves.

Io slumped in her chair, watching the scene unfold. There were more than twenty people onstage now, a mix of genders and races. And they all looked at Saint-Yves adoringly, chief among them Thais.

"Io," Edei whispered, leaning in, "is that your sister?"

"Yes."

"Did you know?" He sounded suspicious—she twisted to look at him. His brow was knitted, but he was examining *her*, not the people on the stage.

"I didn't. This is the first time I've seen her in two years, I swear."

He gave her a nod.

"Please, don't—"

"I won't tell Bianca," he promised. "You're really scared of her, aren't you?"

"Shouldn't I be?"

He looked solemnly at the crowd. "I suppose you should." They sat in silence for a moment. "Listen, I wanted to tell you earlier that, um. I think you're right. About tolerating violence being a violence in itself."

She hadn't quite said it that way, but his words were almost better. Deeper.

"And I wanted to say . . . that prophecy. It's bullshit. The Nine don't know you. Who you are, or what you'll do. Just because their protégés drew portraits of you, or wrote poems, it doesn't mean that it will come true. Only you can decide that."

Io had the urge to drop her face right into his shoulder, to feel his arms close around her. She wished to be enfolded in the cocoon of his tenderness, swathed in his soft voice, sheathed in his safety, like a knife pried from a clenched fist.

"That's the part I hate about powers like the Nine's," he went on, oblivious to the slow melting of her heart. "Discussing the future like it's something concrete, like our fates are inescapable, theirs to decipher like pages in a worn, weathered book. Destiny robs us of choice, and I can't live like that. I won't."

Io leaned her head back against the plush seat. Above her, the balcony was ceilinged in a pattern of anemones and waves. *Destiny robs us of choice.* There was no lie in his words, no anger or cruelty. For Edei this was a fact, trivial in its absoluteness. Yet for Io, it felt like a personal jab, every word picking at her scabbed wounds: destiny and choice—she was guilty of robbing him of both. She thought of his regret that he couldn't do more for Chimdi, his anger at the

Nine's manipulations, the sweet pep talk he had just given her. What would a tender, noble boy like Edei think of a fate-thread, binding him irrevocably to someone he barely knew, robbing him of choice?

He would hate it.

If she told him the truth, he would hate her, too.

"There's our guy," Nico said, interrupting her thoughts.

The phobos-born climbed onstage.

"Aris Lefteriou." Saint-Yves introduced him. His smile became more dazzling still, if that was even possible. "Head of my security and—should the Initiative move forward—head of security in all our divisions. A powerful phobos-born who served bravely with me in the Iceberg Corps and to whom I owe my life."

The crowd didn't applaud as warmly as before. All of them knew to fear the phobos-born, even when they were presented as the good guys.

"What do you want to do?" asked Nico.

What was there to do? Her sister was engaged to Saint-Yves, when she wouldn't even talk to Io. Her fiancé's head of security was the man who had terrorized her and Edei only half an hour ago.

"We can follow them," suggested Chimdi. "When the phobos-born is alone, we grab him and bring him to Bianca."

"Grab the phobos-born? It won't be so easy," argued Nico. "They're leaving. Decide fast, boss."

The lights came on. The crowd began rising from the chairs, heading for the exits.

Finally, Edei said, "We follow them."

Io made herself look away from Thais, made her legs trail the others, their footsteps muffled on the thick red carpet. People were coming out of the nearby boxes, talking to each other animatedly, but Edei led them through the employee entrance at the end of the corridor, where a winding staircase brought them to the ground floor. The door opened to a stage illuminated by a dozen spotlights. Empty. Saint-Yves and his team had disappeared.

Through the crowd, someone called, "Edei?"

Edei came to a sudden stop, forcing them all to pause. Io followed his gaze to a beautiful girl in a black high-collar dress highlighting her heart-shaped face and slender neck. Her arms were hooked through another girl's and a handsome boy's, the three of them waltzing down the corridor toward the exit. Self-consciously, the girl dropped her friends' arms and drifted in Edei's direction.

"Hey, Samiya," Nico said over Io's shoulder.

So this was Samiya—the doctor. The girlfriend. The source of half of Io's guilt. Io smoothed her face into casual neutrality.

Samiya flashed Nico and Chimdi a grin, then trained her eyes on where Io stood a step behind Edei. "Oh, hello! You must be the detective."

Gods, this was awkward. "Yes, um, yeah, hi," Io said unintelligently, hoping that the floor would open beneath her feet and swallow her whole.

"What are you all doing here?" Samiya asked.

A pressing silence ensued, while Edei inspected Samiya's male friend from head to toe. Edei looked . . . "uncomfortable" was the proper word, Io guessed. Something about the quirk of his lips and furtiveness of his gaze reminded her of a child called up to the chalkboard to solve an equation they hadn't studied for.

At long last, Edei replied, "We're looking into some things."

Which was excessively mysterious and rightly made Samiya roll her eyes.

"What are *you* doing here?" Chimdi interfered, her tone accusatory.

Some of the discomfiture edged out of Edei's face. "Leave her be," he warned.

At that same moment, Samiya's friends called her name. With an apologetic "See you later," she waved goodbye and sped to the exit.

Chimdi's arms were crossed. "I still don't get how you can be okay with this, Edei. She's attending his rallies now?"

He breathed out, long and slow, like these last few moments had been torturous. "She can do whatever she likes. I'm not the boss of her, and neither are you." He glanced down at Chimdi. "She's a clever girl. If she sees some value in the Initiative, then there must be some."

Io's first thought was, *She's not clever, she's gullible.* But that was mean, and Io hated mean. She didn't know the girl and, if she was being completely honest, didn't know the Initiative, either. Edei was obviously against it, yet he stepped back while his girlfriend made her own choices. If he trusted Samiya's instincts, then so would Io.

"Which way?" Edei asked.

No one answered.

"*Io.* Which way?"

Startled, she glanced at the thread in her fist. "Through that door."

Edei obeyed, holding the door open for them. The room they entered was a dressing area. Members of Saint-Yves's team were gathered in circles, chatting and taking their makeup off. The phobos-born wasn't among them—and neither was Thais or Saint-Yves.

"Excuse us," Nico said brightly. "Boss sent us down here for the good detergent—apparently the folks in box eighty-four left quite a mess behind."

The heads that had snapped up when they came in looked back down, disinterested. Still, Io had the sense to place her fist on her chest. If there was a moira-born among Saint-Yves's people, they wouldn't discern the stray thread from her many own. Edei crossed to another room, this one empty, and farther down to a door marked EMERGENCY EXIT.

Rain greeted them, sudden and cold against their cheeks. The neo-monsoon had arrived. A thin layer of water was forming on the cobblestones, soon to be joined by the tide. In a few minutes, the water would be up to their ankles; they had to get on the roofs. Others had the same idea, too. At the mouth of the alley, people ran by, holding umbrellas and raincoat hoods, on the way to the trolley or the bridges.

Something else caught Io's attention. One of her own threads was spinning directions fast—Thais's thread. Io ran to the mouth of the alley just in time to spot an automobile speed by, spraying twin arcs of water on the sidewalk. Saint-Yves sat in the back of the automobile, his lips stretched wide with laughter. And leaning into his side, a hand on his chest, was Thais. The thread connecting the sisters danced across Io's vision as the automobile took Thais up-Hill.

"Quickly," Edei said. "Chimdi, Nico, go after them."

The two friends rushed around the corner after the car. Io considered stopping them, telling them she would do it herself, but what if Thais noticed their shared thread? What if she realized her little sister, who she apparently hated now, was stalking her?

Edei said, "We should find the phobos-born . . ."

He trailed off. His gaze fell on something behind Io.

She had time to wonder, *What now?* Then she glimpsed it, over her shoulder.

A figure at the dead end of the ally, the glistening iron of a gun's barrel gripped in their fist.

# CHAPTER XIX

# THE NEO-MONSOON

**RAINDROPS TRICKLED DOWN** Edei's furrowed brow and hard-set mouth. His shoulders were tense, curled fists itching for a fight, eyes locked on the person holding the gun. Focused, angry, scared. He said, "Easy now."

Io's heart hammered frantically against her rib cage. She had outrun the wraith, tricked Horatio Long, slipped out of the phobos-born's grasp, but a gun? A nudge on the trigger and her brains would go *pop—splatter!*—on the cobblestones.

"Didn't I say," the figure said through clenched teeth, "the day *after* tomorrow?"

Io recognized the voice instantly. *"Rosa?* What are you— Are you going to shoot us?"

"Not anywhere vital, but I will settle for an arm or a leg."

The streetlight gleamed on the long barrel of the gun, like a flint struck in the darkness. Rosa stood in typical leech stance: legs apart, torso ramrod straight, both hands on the gun. She looked like she always did: tall and full-figured, with long legs that she never failed to accentuate, black hair pulled back in a low ponytail, with a severe middle part. Eyebrows plucked to perfect arches, freckles speckling her brown skin, a slash of dark plum on her lips. She wore civilian clothes, inconspicuous black khakis and a gray velvet jacket.

Io let the Quilt engulf her, fingers reaching for a thread. Rosa might have the entire Initiative on them in seconds, like how they'd been swarmed at the City Plaza. Io would make sure she and Edei escaped unscathed this time.

Rosa's eyes narrowed on Io's face, on the silver no doubt reflecting on her irises, and understanding dawned. "Oh, no, no. Don't even think about it, Io. Wasn't my poor grandma's thread enough?"

"Not Do-Lo," Io lamented earnestly.

Oh gods. This was worse than Io had thought. What she had cut the night of the break-in wasn't a harmless thread like her own love of eclairs, but a thread of familial love.

Dolores Santos was an exquisite old lady and even better grandma. Whenever Io swung by Rosa's before going out, Do-Lo—as her grandchildren playfully called her—would stuff her full of wonderfully spicy tapas and launch into delightfully ribald tales of her youth, making Rosa red with embarrassment and Io red with laughter.

Remorse weighed on Io's chest. Losing a thread was horrible—a sudden, inexplicable loss, as if a piece of your heart had been sliced off. Whatever intensity of love had formed the thread, it was gone. Given time, the thread might regrow, but right now, the love Rosa felt for her grandma had lost some of its depth and purity.

"Yes, Do-Lo. I visited her yesterday, and I only laughed at *one* of her jokes."

"Maybe she wasn't that funny?"

"My abuela is hilarious."

"She is," Io had to admit. "Are you going to put the gun down?"

"You tell me, Io. Don't I deserve a shot? Just a little one, for the justice of it?"

"Definitely."

A few feet to Io's left, Edei inhaled sharply.

"Excellent," said Rosa. "I'll let you choose: arm or leg?"

"Arm?" Io asked. She turned to Edei. "What do you think? Arm, right? It'll impede less with the investigation."

"I—I . . ." Edei stammered, eyes frantically switching between the two girls. "Perhaps we could consider neither?"

"Fair enough," Rosa agreed. In one smooth move, she loosened her grip on the gun and sheathed it in its holster under her jacket. With long strides, she led them back into the end of the alley, where the shadows swathed them from prying eyes. "Who knew a guy could be both cute *and* smart?"

Io glared at her friend.

Edei murmured, "Io, what is happening."

"Edei, meet my friend Rosa Santos. Rosa, this is Edei. You two met last night on that plank, but the time wasn't right for introductions, what with Rosa trying to drop us to our death and all that." Io could play the guilt game, too.

"This makes it twice now that I've caught you lurking where you shouldn't be," said Rosa.

"We're working on a case."

"A case that requires you to trespass into Saint-Yves's Initiative presentation and grab hold of the thread of his head of security? My, my, you've gone up in the world." Rosa wiggled her eyebrows. "The bad news is you were careless. Someone spotted you in the Teatro, and now Aris Lefteriou and his team are looking for you all over the building."

"How do you know?"

"How do you think? I'm part of his team, doofus."

Io was readying a magnificent comeback for her friend when voices rose at the mouth of the alley. The streetlight outlined three figures coming around the corner. Footsteps sharp on the cobblestones and then voices: "Where did they go?" "Check the back alley."

Rosa grabbed Io's elbow. "Quick! This way!"

With trained movements, she climbed on the trash can, jerked the flood-escape ladder of the neighboring building down, and started scaling. Io didn't hesitate, following her friend up the ladder, Edei close behind. They flattened their bodies on the second-floor landing, away from the reach of the streetlight, just as three men entered the alley. The man leading the team was dressed in a marine suit, his sleek goatee slightly askew. A dozen threads exploded from his chest, one of them running straight to Io's fist. Aris Lefteriou. The phobos-born.

"Keep going," Rosa whispered, ushering Edei ahead. She reached down the ladder and gripped Io's fist. "Io, you have to let go of his thread. The one on his left is moira-born. We've got seconds before they notice us up here. Tracking that thread goes both ways—how do you think they noticed you in the first place?"

Io *should* let go, before the moira-born noticed, before Aris forced his power on them. But this was the only tangible connection she had to solving the murders.

"Io." Rosa's voice was carved with wild panic. "Will you just trust me?"

Despite everything, because of everything, Io found that she could. She let go and ran.

The neo-monsoon was growing in force by the minute. The bridges became slick with water, the planks sticky with grime. Below, the rain bloated the tide to extreme levels; even the metal shutters used to protect the low-level entrances weren't enough to hold it back. Io could hear the gurgle of dozens of sump pumps working, drawing the water from the bottom levels of the buildings and throwing it out of higher windows.

Most Alantians had boarded up inside for the remainder of the night, for fear the rain was acid, and the few who were still out sprinted from cover to cover. But today, the rain was just rain. If it had been acid, Io and the others would be screaming in agony by now. They were all drenched to the bone, hair plastered on their cheeks, boots making disgusting squelching sounds. Io felt like the water had doubled her weight; lifting her legs and climbing across rooftops was twice as hard as it usually was.

"Are we going somewhere?" she shouted ahead to Rosa. "Or are we just running?"

"You tell me. Look back."

"You know I can't see that far without my spectacles."

"Where are your spectacles, then?"

Io hurried after her friend. "In my pocket. Do we really have the time for me to stop and put them on? Can't you just tell me what's behind us?"

"Where's the lesson in that?"

"*Rosa.*"

A sigh of exasperation from Edei and: "Three figures following us. One's the phobos-born."

"Don't enable her!" Rosa said.

"We'll never lose them up here," Io declared. "The moira-born will be tracking us in the Quilt. We need to go somewhere with lots of people, lots of threads."

"Already on it," Rosa called back.

The three of them kept going, parallel to Cardamom Avenue, which had by now turned fully into a canal. Rosa made them run across the Marjoram Bridge and take a sharp left when they met the Minarets of Old looming across the street. Rosa threw open a hatch leading into the building below.

"Be quiet," she commanded as they hurried down a dark winding staircase to the belly of the building. There were no sounds but the rain scratching on the windows and the low hum of a heater. No, not a heater . . . snoring. Every room down the corridor was filled with sleeping pods that the city provided for families whose apartments flooded during bad weather. Rosa had taken them into a homeless shelter.

"Here," she said, guiding them into the room farthest from the hatch. She indicated several empty beds on the bottom row, then jumped in the closest one and immediately shut the curtains.

Io and Edei mimicked her. Io's pod was wide enough to fit her comfortably even cross-legged. In the Quilt, she glimpsed Aris and the two other men climbing onto the roof of the building. Rosa's plan was brilliant: even if they got in the pod area, the moira-born would think they were just other guests. Up ahead, the hatch groaned open. Wet footsteps sounded on the staircase.

*Wet!* Gods, what if the men noticed the wet traces of their boots on the floor? Io stuck her head outside. Sure enough, their footprints gleamed on the linoleum floor of the corridor. Grabbing the blanket from her pod, she slipped out and furiously swiped at the wetness. She followed their prints out of the room to the corridor, breathing hard, one eye to the winding staircase. She could see the phobos-born's calves, his knees, his torso—

An arm came around her waist. Edei pulled her back into the pod room. They lunged into his pod, crawling in side by side. Edei dragged the curtain closed and covered them with the blanket in one smooth move.

A second later, a figure appeared in the doorway, silhouetted against the beige curtain. Io clapped a hand over her mouth. Edei's face was close; his rapid breath stroked her cheek; their bodies pressed tight against each other. In the darkness, she could only make out the silhouette of his face: the ridge of his nose, his heavy eyebrows.

"Are they here?" the phobos-born asked.

Io's breath staggered through her chest in a dry sob. Edei wrapped his arm around her shoulders, pulling her tight against his chest. His chin tucked over her head. His heart thundered beneath her cheek.

"Check all rooms," Aris Lefteriou said. "All pods."

Io squirmed, an infinitesimal, involuntary movement.

"Did you hear that?"

Edei pressed his mouth against her forehead, clasping her so tight that she couldn't move even if she wanted to. Io shut her eyes. She heard the curtain to their pod fly open. Edei breathed slowly—in, out, in, out. She focused on his breathing, on his fingers on her head, his lips on her forehead, the line of his body fitting into hers. *Don't open your eyes. Don't move.*

The curtain fell back. Her heart was beating fast, her breath raspy and hitched. She didn't dare move. Only listened. Footsteps, curtains dragged, a sleepy complaint. Then silence.

"It's only the displaced here, boss," one of the men said.

"In the other rooms, too," said the other man.

"Cori, stay here in case they hid somewhere," whispered Aris. He must have been standing right outside their pod because Io could hear him perfectly. "Jude, you're with me. We need to find them immediately. They were at the Nine. They know about the women."

"I recognized the big one, boss," the second man spoke again. "Edei Rhuna. He works at the Fortuna."

Io shifted back to look at Edei's face. Their eyes locked in the half-light. He did that thing again, his gaze shifting rapidly between her eyes. She had the urge to reach out and touch his thick eyelashes. Edei's lips moved. He mouthed something, but Io didn't catch it, only the feeling behind it. Calm, comfort, softness.

"Bianca Rossi's Fortuna?" said Aris. "Oh, Luc is going to love this. She'll be the next one he targets, for sure. Fyodorov, Petropoulos, Magnussen, Horatio Long . . . they're petty criminals compared to the mob queen of the Silts."

The victims—the phobos-born had just listed all of the murder victims.

Edei's eyes snapped to the outline of the man outside their pod. His fingers tensed where he was holding her shoulder.

*It's them,* Io realized. Saint-Yves was behind the wraiths.

# CHAPTER XX

# WHAT YOU HAD TO

**IO WOKE WITH** her forehead pressed against Edei's nape. For a moment, she lay there, feeling his body against hers. The heat. The softness. A dulcet sense of embarrassment. Then she extracted herself from him and noiselessly slipped out of the pod. It was just before dawn, pink light draping softly over curtains and metal pods. The boarders slumbered, gentle sleeping noises heightening the early-morning tranquility. The window at the end of the room was cracked open. Rosa leaned on the sill with an older woman, chatting in Rossk and blowing their cigarette smoke out to the flushed city sky.

When she saw Io approaching, the woman dropped her cigarette, inclined her head, and quickly left the room. "She's a Drifter," Rosa said, watching the woman recede. "You know how they are with cutters."

Drifters were nomadic travelers that journeyed the Wastelands from shelter to shelter. They were very superstitious about the moira-born. According to their lore, cutters in particular were believed to have had some nefarious part in the Collapse. Drifters didn't like to interact with them.

"So," said Rosa, eyeing Io wickedly. She offered Io her cup of coffee. The liquid was lukewarm and bitter, and Io handed it back after a single sip. "Did you sleep with a boy?"

"I slept *next* to a boy," Io answered quickly. Her lack of sexual experience was not something she cared to discuss before breakfast.

"Bah. Such a coward."

"Such a busybody."

Rosa snorted through her nose, puffing a cloud of smoke.

"Where's Saint-Yves's man?" asked Io.

With her cigarette, Rosa pointed to a man propped against the wall in the corridor, legs splayed before him, mouth open and drooling on his own shoulder. A casualty of Rosa's powers.

Rosa was oneiroi-born, descended from the gods of dreams; a single touch from her at a person's sleep cords and they dropped like a fly. Io had seen her do it many times: when men hassled them in bars, when Rosa needed her parents to sleep so they could sneak out. Rosa could see dream cords in the same way Io saw the Quilt. They looked like violin strings, she had explained once, and touching them sounded like music. The man would wake up in a few hours, thinking he had just fallen asleep on the job.

Io had spent most of last night tracking the man's movements on the Quilt. He had paced the length of the building, never straying far from the exits. Io thought he might be the moira-born, so she didn't dare make a run for it. Edei had fallen asleep first, and his deep breaths had eventually lullabied Io to sleep, too.

"Why didn't you wake us up sooner?"

Rosa shrugged. "I woke up half an hour ago, but you guys were getting it on—"

"We were *not*."

Chuckling, Rosa shook her head. "You make it too easy."

Io's answering smile was a tired, flickering thing. Her body was jittery from a sleep laced with terror and achy from her fight with Horatio and Raina yesterday—how was it only *yesterday!*—morning. She was hungry and thirsty and in desperate need of a bath. And she had just found out that the phobos-born who had assaulted them and hunted them down worked for Luc Saint-Yves, who had somehow been targeting the victims of the wraiths. Saint-Yves, the Commissioner and soon-to-be Mayor, and her sister's fiancé.

"What happened, Rosa? How did you end up working for Saint-Yves?"

Her friend took one last drag of her cigarette and put it out against the windowsill. There were dozens of similar marks there, some faded, others fresh. Beyond her, in the city, the dregs of last night's storm trickled down the streets to join the sea. "Do you want the short version or the long version?"

"Long?" Io ventured.

"Last time we saw each other, I had just gotten the job at *Miss-Matched*, right? It went well for a while: I wrote quizzes mostly, sometimes their health column. But I got bored. They shot down all my article ideas. So, when Xeno approached me about a month ago to go undercover for a big story, I couldn't say no."

"*Xeno?*"

Rosa sucked an awkward breath through her teeth. "Xenophon Atreidis."

"You're his undercover journalist? No wonder he looked so smug!"

"Don't start. He's amazing at his job; he brought political journalism into the Silts. He has a nose for good stories and great taste in girls, if I say so myself."

"Please tell me you didn't."

"I did."

"The guy bullied you all through school!"

The bona fide asshole had grown up across the street from Rosa. He would often follow the girls to school like a yapping dog, making fun of Io's oversized hand-me-downs, or trail after those stupid kids that sang little rhymes with Rosa's deadname during recess. Not defending herself and Rosa more was one of Io's deepest regrets. But back then, Io was the quiet kind that never caused trouble at school or at home. To be fair, she still considered herself quiet, but now she could put her enemies in their place with a swipe of her fingers and be done with it. As he grew older, Xenophon chose to make use of his pestering personality and became a reporter, writing for *The Truth of Alante*, which was known for its think pieces, well-thought-out interviews, and political exposés. It had always been Rosa's goal to write that sort of article, but for Xenophon Atreidis? It was like a butterfly willingly landing on a moth collector's table to get its wings plucked out.

"Only because he was secretly in love with me," Rosa said.

"That's bullshit."

"Absolute bullshit, but he's changed, and I enjoy his company and I want this job. And you're not my mom."

Io raised her palms in surrender.

"Anyway"—Rosa glared daggers at Io—"*The Truth* has already published a couple of my freelance articles, and Xeno thinks a big exposé like this will launch me into the scene and get me a permanent position. Investigative journalism, Io, just like I've always dreamed of."

Her voice dripped with longing. If she glanced in the Quilt, Io knew she'd find a thread shining brighter than the rest, connecting Rosa to her most prized possession: her typewriter. Xenophon's offer must have been impossible to refuse, honeyed by all those years of failed attempts, caramelized by a dream job offer . . .

"What was the job exactly?"

"Xeno has suspected Saint-Yves and his Initiative since he first heard of it; there's no transparency, especially regarding who's funding them. He claims to have the Agora's support, but there's no official statement from them. And besides, if the horae-born wanted to form a new judicial force, why involve someone non-powered like Saint-Yves? A month ago, the Commissioner's office started seeking *other-born protection* for a case. I got the job then and there."

"Other-born protection for a case—you mean the wraiths, don't you?" Io asked.

"Ew." Rosa's upper lip twisted. "Don't call them that. Yeah, the women with the severed life-threads. Saint-Yves took me on after the first attack, for extra protection against these raving murderers. So I worked as his bodyguard for two weeks—until I got posted at an Initiative meeting." Her gaze fell to a woman on the street below, walking two perfectly white dogs. "They are, surprisingly, a very nice group of people. The consulting officers are the rare honest kind, and the other-born truly want to save the city. I told Xeno I found nothing suspicious, that I actually *liked* the people there. He told me to keep looking. At the next meeting I worked security for, Thais walked in."

Io held her breath. Thais was a dangerous topic, especially with Rosa. Sharp as a blade, and just as swift: one word, one thought, and those carefully secreted memories would come spilling out, warm and sleek as blood. Their socked feet tiptoeing over creaking floorboards. Their hands cupped over their mouths under the covers, ears straining to hear. Io's cheeks sticky with tears, Rosa's jaw set hard as marble.

"What," Io said slowly, "did Thais say?"

"She was ecstatic to see me, asked about my sisters and cousins, told her friends she'd always known I would end up *protecting the people*. When I mentioned you and Ava, she changed the subject, but I didn't blame her, you know? She left you that note, *Leave me alone*, and all that drama."

Io's heart thumped a deafening tempo, like a drummer's beat before the earth-shattering crescendo of the show. "Up until two days ago, I didn't even know she was back. She asked Ava not to tell me. Ava thinks she's still upset about our argument."

"Yeah, she was very awkward when I mentioned you."

Io pressed her knuckles against her eyelids. The thought of Thais being angry still held power over her. Despite everything, all the secrets, Io had the urge to run all the way to Hanover Street, fall to her knees, and apologize.

"Then, four days ago," Rosa continued, "Xeno tells me he found out that Saint-Yves has pulled all the other-born records from the public registry. Which is odd, right? So I worked my charm on his first lieutenant—they're gorgeous, by the way, best ass you've ever seen on a person—"

"Rosa!" Io smacked her friend on the shoulder.

Rosa smacked her back. "Don't be a prude, Io. We all have asses and they're all gorgeous. Anyway, while I'm flirting with them, I manage to sneak a peek at the papers on their desk. A report from specialists affirming the murderers are *not* moira-born. And another document, marked for destruction." Rosa widened her eyes comically. "Your wraiths, Io, were volunteers in his Initiative."

"*No.*"

"They came to his meetings. Emmeline Segal, Drina Savva. And now he's trying to disappear the ledger that proves it. Suspicious, right?"

"Very. What happened next?"

"*You* happened next. You broke into City Plaza, for gods' sake. My job was to alert them to exactly that sort of thing, so when I saw strange dream cords on the third floor, I rang the alarm. When you were on that plank, I hadn't recognized you. If I'd known, I would have helped you escape."

"You almost dropped us to a watery grave."

"Well," Rosa deadpanned, "you cut my grandma's thread. I feel like the debt is paid."

Io grimaced, then reached for her friend's hand. "I haven't told you yet how sorry I am. Truly, Rosa, I was an idiot."

"Yeah. You were. But I'll find a way for you to make it up to me." Rosa smiled, genuinely, and a weight lifted from Io's chest.

"It might grow back, the thread."

"It better. But let me finish the story. After you broke in, Saint-Yves went ballistic. But he wasn't concerned about the public records; he was particularly obsessed with whether you had found the files of the *victims*. So, after probing Lieutenant Booty, I found out that Saint-Yves has prosecuted all four of them: Fyodorov, Petropoulos, Magnussen, Horatio Long. And all four cases were dismissed, never reaching the court."

The gears in Io's head started grinding. She half expected smoke to come out of her ears. Saint-Yves had built his career as a savior who put crooks behind bars. He'd shut down betting dens and dream palaces, locked up entire gangs. But some crooks were untouchable. Io already knew the Nine had promised Horatio Long protection from the law. What if the Muses, or some other high power, had stopped all of these cases from reaching the court?

"He couldn't get them through the proper channels," Io mused, "so he tried another way?"

"That's my angle."

"The wraiths seek justice—that part adds up. But there's another part that doesn't. There's a connection between the wraiths: during the Moonset Riots twelve years ago, the Nine hired Horatio Long to kill them. Because their artists prophesized the women were dangerous to the city somehow."

Rosa's brow furrowed over her eyes. "You went to the Nine?"

"The Nine believe the wraiths were indeed made. But they can't see who made them. Saint-Yves might have motive and opportunity, but he doesn't have the power to turn women into wraiths."

"If you pump enough hatred into a person's head, she will become anything."

"Even if that was possible, it's such a cruel thing to do," Io said. "You've met him, Rosa. Do you think he'd kill?"

Rosa considered for a few long moments. "I think he's fixated on his idea of a better Alante. We've known nobler people whose obsessions took over."

The silence that followed was pointed. Rosa meant Thais. Io's sister's ethics were made of iron and cast in gold. It was the source of their frequent fights and the reason she so often shamed Io for her behavior. But before she left, Thais's morals had faltered—catastrophically.

One of the sleepers yawned loudly, and others made soft waking sounds.

"What price did the Nine ask for?" Rosa asked quietly.

"Do you want the long version or the short version?"

"Short."

"They want to know how I will bring about the end of the world their artists have prophesized."

"That's a direct quote?"

A laugh escaped Io. "Unfortunately."

"One word for you, friend: char-la-tans."

Io laughed again, true relief blossoming in her chest. It was reassuring that both Edei and Rosa thought the idea of a prophecy was ridiculous. She scratched at the chipped paint of the windowsill. "I, um, have to tell you something."

"There's more? Gods, girl, I left you at boring and found you at spine-tingling."

After a bit of pouting, Io said, "Edei is my fate-thread."

Plastering a mischievous smile on her lips, Rosa knocked Io's shoulder with her own. "You sought him out at last! Good for you."

Io shushed her, dropping her voice extra low. "He doesn't know! Bianca Rossi ordered me to investigate the wraiths with him."

"Did Bianca order you to cuddle him to sleep?"

A snort escaped Io. "You're such a meddler."

"And you're such a chicken!"

A smile was blooming on Io's face. Small, tentative, but *there*.

Always sharp-eyed, Rosa noticed it. "Oh, baby girl, how bad is it? His-initials-in-your-diary bad or your-chest-feels-like-it's-about-to-explode bad?"

Io would not be answering that. This was real life, not a radio drama.

"You have been pining after him for years—"

"Well, it's a *fate-thread*! But I didn't even know who he was."

"And now that you do?"

Io shrugged. "He has a girlfriend."

"Does his girlfriend know Bianca ordered you to cuddle him to sleep?"

"Will you stop? It's not—" She paused and considered. "It's not right to force this fate on him."

Rosa's face scrunched up, like she was about to say something horrible. "You know, one day you'll need to grow the hell up and let other people decide for themselves if they like you or not."

There it was. The horrible thing.

Rosa had stabbed her right at the chip in her armor. The pain was twofold: first, because it reminded Io that she was a coward. It was safe to love people from afar, to dream of kisses but never seek them.

*We Ora sisters don't kiss other people's boyfriends*—no matter how much Io might have wanted to. And second, because it reverberated deep into Io's core to the numbing, inescapable fear that even if she did risk it all, if she did tell him about the fate-thread and how she felt, then the love would turn sour, soiled and corrupted, like Thais's love had. Thais: the first, the deepest, the most important of all of Io's unrequited love stories.

They came together: the fear and the longing. Io dreaded that her love was doomed to be rejected, or tricked, or manipulated. And at the same time, she wanted desperately to be loved.

She let her head drop on her friend's shoulder. The words spilled out of her mouth before she could shape them into a more modest form: "I'm trying. I swear, Rosa, I'm trying."

"Oh, baby," her friend said softly. Rosa's arms came around her, enveloping Io in her best friend's familiar scent. "I wish you wouldn't push me away. I've missed you, and *I know* you've missed me."

Io glanced up. "I'm not pushing you away. We just got busy."

But that wasn't true. Io remembered that time at the Cellar Club, where they had met up to celebrate Rosa's new job. She had spent the entire night watching Rosa dance with Ava under the neon lights. They had whispered to each other all night, probably about their joint crush on the waitress, but all Io could think was that Rosa would accidentally blab out the truth about that night Thais left. It had suddenly felt like danger, Rosa's presence in her life.

The sun rose over the outline of the city, its lazy light barely reaching them through the overcast sky. Rosa leaned away, looking down at Io. "We've always been busy. Sometimes I think you're embarrassed by what you asked me to do. By what we did to Thais."

Io's stomach jumped to her throat. *What you asked me to do. What we did to Thais.* Guilt was already pooling like acid in her stomach. She forced her dark thoughts back into the depths of her head. This was not the time and place to disintegrate.

"I'm not blaming you," Rosa said, caressing Io's arm comfortingly. "I'm trying to say the opposite: *you did what you had to.*"

"I know," said Io.

Rosa gave her a sad smile, a bandage coated with salt. "Do you?"

# CHAPTER XXI

# HIS GAZE WAS A WARNING

**THANK THE GODS,** Io didn't have to answer. A curtain rustled; Edei climbed out of the pod, pillow wrinkles across his cheek. They quickly filled him in on the new findings: the wraiths being Initiative pledges, the victims being Saint-Yves's failed cases, the murky funding of the Initiative. Then Rosa took off to report to City Plaza and make some excuse about her absence, patting the sleeping cop's head on the way out.

"We need to tell Bianca," Edei announced.

And off they went, back out to the streets, walking briskly against the morning chill. The Fortuna was dark and silent when they entered. The single guard posted on the side door jumped upright at the sight of Edei's grim expression and ran off to fetch Bianca.

In the guard's absence, Edei looked lost in the empty foyer. He fidgeted with the buttons of his overcoat, scrubbed at his growing stubble. He didn't look at Io, as if she were making him uncomfortable. Had she crossed a line by falling asleep next to him? His unease made *her* uneasy. Moments trickled by at a snail's pace. The room was too quiet, the walls too dark, her outfit too damp and stinky. She needed a bath and a change of clothes. Something to eat and a gallon of water. A painkiller would be nice, and ice on her bruises.

"Coffee?" Edei said.

"Yes, please."

He hesitated, as though about to speak again, but seemed to decide coffee was good enough. He led her down the corridor and into a small kitchen: stovetops, a kitchen island, four tall stools around it. There was even a fruit bowl on the counter. Much homelier than Io ever guessed the Fortuna could be.

"Sugar? Milk?" Edei was making modern-style coffee, lining up three cups on the kitchen counter, each with a small paper filter on it.

"A spoonful of sugar," Io replied. "No milk."

"Yes, boss." He paused, bent over a small pot, and looked at her from the corner of his eye. "I've thought of a good one. Comeback, I mean. About horses." His voice was undecipherable, somewhere between mischievous and nervous.

Either way, Io couldn't gods-damn wait. A running joke—it felt like a friendship milestone. "Let's hear it."

"You would say: *Always nice to be equated to a horse.* And I would say: *So you vote neigh on the horse, boss?*"

A stunned silence followed, long and unbroken. He grinned at the cups he was preparing, breathed a chuckle, peeked at her.

"It's . . . a pun," she said.

"What's wrong with a pun?"

"Nothing wrong. I just didn't, um, expect a pun."

He was properly laughing now, these strange full-hearted huffs through his nose, as though he was trying to keep it quiet. "It was bad?"

Io couldn't help the perplexed chuckle that bubbled through her chest. "Let's never joke again. It's clearly not meant for us."

"Never again," he agreed.

Doors banged somewhere farther into the club. Furious footsteps came their way. Edei, to her amazement, was still chuckling soundlessly. Io smacked his shoulder and thought, *This is surreal; I'm touching him, playfully, and joking, poorly.*

"Shush," she warned him.

The door flew open, and Bianca Rossi stalked inside in a flurry of silk, drama personified. She was clad in an ivory robe, her blond hair falling in smooth rivers over her shoulders. She looked shorter now that she was barefoot but still dominated the space. One hand keeping the robe together, she scanned Io up and down. Again, her lips were tinted blue.

"Well?" she asked.

*Do you know what happens to those who break the Roosters' Silence?* The threat lingered between them, an arrow nocked in a bow, a bullet placed in the chamber. The string would snap, the trigger pull; it was just a matter of time.

Behind Io, Edei replied somberly, "Luc Saint-Yves."

Bianca's face knotted into a smirk. It was small, untraceable for someone less observant than Io. But the mob queen's eyes lit, thoughts racing behind them, and her blue-hued lips stretched in satisfaction. "And how exactly did you reach that conclusion?"

"The victims are cases he failed to prosecute. The wraiths are volunteers in his Initiative. And his head of security was sent after us," answered Edei. "The Nine confirmed they hired Horatio to kill those women, claiming their artists foresaw they would be dangerous somehow, during the Moonset Riots."

"What do the Riots have to do with this?"

"We don't know that part yet. And we don't know how Saint-Yves is giving the wraiths those strange powers."

Edei placed one cup in front of Io and handed the other to Bianca. The blessed scent of coffee steamed up Io's nostrils, but she didn't reach for it. There was something wrong. She could sense it in the air, in the measured casualness of Edei's movements, in the predatory tone in Bianca's voice. Tension, the kind that made animals freeze deep in the woods and burrow into the undergrowth.

"Am I paying you to drink coffee then, cutter?" Bianca asked, heavy with sarcasm.

Carefully, Io said, "We need to investigate further. Track down the wraith, get her confession. Saint-Yves is our main suspect right now, but we'll need a stronger case if we want to bring him to court."

A pause, then: "A stronger case to bring him to court. Got it."

Bianca went to the counter, pouring a spoonful of sugar in her coffee. As she twirled the spoon, cling-cling-clinging it on the walls of the cup, Edei's eyes snapped to Io's. His gaze was a warning. Against what?

"Drink your coffee. Then Edei will fetch your money." Bianca talked with her back to Io, but her voice rang out in the small kitchen, precise and definite. "Your services are no longer required. The Fortuna gang doesn't get involved with leeches. Whatever you found on Saint-Yves stays between us. I will take care of the rest. Is that understood?"

On that last word, she turned, nailing Io with a foreboding look.

*This* was Edei's warning. *This* was the danger Io had sensed. She was expected to agree without hesitation. Take her money and leave Saint-Yves and his cops be. But she couldn't step away now; she was in too deep. Edei must have known. She saw the fear in his face as she opened her mouth to speak. "That's it?"

"That's it," Bianca repeated.

"This man might have caused the death of six people and have a new wraith under his command, and we're going to just let it go? Because you want to, what, protect your business from retaliation from the police?"

"My business was built on my blood and sweat. Damn right I'm not going to let some murderous rich boy or"—she waved a hand at Io—"some self-proclaimed defender of the weak ruin it. How did you think this was going to go down, little Ora? Let's say you get your evidence that Saint-Yves is behind the murders. What are you going to do with it? Take it to the City Council? Perhaps you thought you could go higher up to the Agora at Nanzy? Well, I've got news for you. These people are as one. They will cover for each other whatever the cost, because if one of them falls, the whole system falls. Who do you think invented Roosters' Silence to begin with?"

"There are other ways."

"Yeah? Like what? Sneak into his house at night, cut his life-thread, and be done with it? You would have done a good deed, but a moira-born killing Alante's shining hero? You would be hunted to your end of days. So would be Ava and anyone else you might care about. Or maybe you'll find what's precious to him and blackmail him to stop. That's a good plan, isn't it? No bloodshed, no officials involved. Try it. Go ahead. Try to prevail over the man who believes himself the savior of Alante."

Palms flat on the kitchen island, back straight and rigid, Io thought, *This is what cornered animals feel like.* Why they lash out with everything they have, killing themselves in the process. Because they can see no other way out. Well, Io didn't care anymore. She was going to go out with *style*.

"So what you're saying is you will do nothing," she snapped. "All that drivel about protecting the Silts, it was just talk?"

Bianca took a step closer. "This is *my* queendom, cutter. I take care of my own. I'll hire a hundred men if I have to. There won't be any more wraiths stalking my streets, no more bodies floating in the tide. But I'm not going against Saint-Yves. I'm smarter than that. And you should be, too."

It was bullshit, all of it. These were the excuses of a woman too scared to act. Io knew, because she had been that woman, many times before. It had been her life's motto: patience, resilience, intelligence. She had thought she could outsmart, outwait, and outrun everything life threw at her. But *this*? Women used, other-born dead, and the Police Commissioner somehow involved?

No, this didn't require patience or intelligence. It required the strength to stand up and *do* something, no matter the consequences.

"You call yourself mob queen of the Silts," Io said. "You promise to be protector and defender. You glory in pulling this district out of the Moonset Riots, but in the end, you know what I see, Bianca?" Io leaned over the counter and tipped Bianca's chin up. "A coward. You carved out this little place for yourself and you're so gods-damned proud of it, but I have news for you. This club, the whole of the Silts—you have it because they *let* you. A predator wanted someone to do his bidding, someone expendable. Where did he choose his pick? Here, at *your* queendom. From *your* people. If you think you're in control, you're just plain stupid."

Bianca snapped her chin out of Io's fingers and turned as if to gain momentum for a punch. Instead, her hand shot out in Edei's direction serpentine fast: her fingers snatched the brass knuckles from his belt. Dread quivered Io's legs into jelly.

In seconds, Edei was standing in front of Io, his broad shoulders a wall between her and the mob queen. One hand he opened palm up to Bianca as a peace offering, while the other reached behind his back for Io—his fingers found the edge of her sleeve and latched on. With unthreatening slowness, he began rotating Io toward the door, keeping himself between her and Bianca.

His touch, his sturdy presence before her, did nothing to shake Io out of her rage. If anything, it made her bolder; if he thought he needed to intervene, it meant he believed Io was as much a threat as the mob queen of the Silts.

Head held high, she leaned around Edei and barked at Bianca, "Drina Savva and those young girls he took from your queendom and used to do his bidding—where is *their* justice?"

Bianca growled, a throaty, animal sound. "Girl, haven't you heard? Justice in Alante died with the Furies twelve years ago." The mob queen of the Silts slipped the knuckles on and aimed a finger at Io. "Get the hell out of my sight, before you say something you'll regret."

Io wasn't scared. She knew she should be, because this was a powerful enemy she was making right now, but she couldn't find it in her to feel anything but pity for Bianca Rossi. She was the only person in Alante who could bring Saint-Yves down, and she wouldn't even try. If that wasn't pitiful, Io didn't know what was.

Edei's backtracking pushed her out into the corridor. "No need for threats," he said. "Io is leaving."

"Not without my sister, I'm not."

She fisted her hand and began bashing on the black wooden walls. "Ava!"

And again, louder, voice carrying through the silent club. *"Ava!"*

Down they went, in this peculiar, queued standoff: Io walking backward, screaming her sister's name, Edei in the middle, Bianca on the other side, approaching with a deathly gleam in her eyes and brass on her knuckles.

"AVA!"

The foyer opened up behind Io, a couple of gang members coming down the bifurcated staircase that led to the various rooms of the club. Ava appeared between them, hopping down the steps while pulling her boots on. She looked like she had been slapped awake, a mauve satin shirt buttoned up all wrong over her usual tight trousers. Wait a second—that mauve button-down, Io had seen it before. On Bianca Rossi, when Edei had been shot.

Her sister was sleeping with the mob queen of the Silts. *Dear gods.* That one would have to wait.

"We need to leave, Ava," Io said. "I'll explain on the way."

The less talk the better—they had to get out of here soon. She doubted Edei's wall of safety could keep Bianca's anger leashed for much longer. Io had pinched the mob queen's chin and given her a scolding. A giggle bubbled out of her. She was loaded with adrenaline. She felt powerful, bold, just as ballsy as she had claimed to be. She had called Bianca Rossi *plain stupid.*

"What is the matter with you?" Ava whisper-snapped, joining Io at the bottom of the staircase.

It was Edei who answered, over his shoulder. "You need to leave. Now."

Scowling, Ava grabbed Io's wrist. "Come on."

The Fortuna's entrance was right there, framed by two empty bouncer counters. Edei was pushing them toward it, putting more and more room between them and Bianca, who had come to stand at the bottom of the staircase, robe hanging open to reveal a toned midriff. She looked like a volcano about to erupt, all molten lava and sulfurous clouds.

Io had the urge to march right over and poke her in the stomach. Watch her go *boom.*

"Ava," Bianca said. "Where are you going?"

"Wherever this fool is going," Ava answered coolly, with a nudge of her head at Io.

"The fool can leave on her own." The woman's face was hard as iron. "Ava. Stay."

Io glanced at her sister, afraid of what she might see there. If Ava chose Bianca, Io didn't think she could let her sister go.

But Ava's chin rose defiantly. "I've told you this before, Bianca. You've got your rules, and I've got mine. Three sisters, but *one* soul. When my sisters need me, I go."

Something their mama used to say when she and Baba were getting ready to leave for the Neraida Plains, staring at their three daughters with narrowed eyes: *Three bodies, one soul. When your sisters need you, you go. No questions asked.*

The room was silent for a moment, then Bianca gave a nod, blond hair falling like a curtain as she turned on her heel and began climbing the staircase. Her goons stayed, but Edei paid them no heed as he guided Io and Ava to the doors.

"I tried to warn you," he whispered. "Bianca doesn't bend her rules, ever."

"I don't care," Io said. "If she won't do anything, *I* will."

He gave her a heavy look. "I thought you might say that. I'll be done by eight. I'll come get you—where will you be?"

"I'll ask Amos if they can take us in for the night."

"Good." He nodded. "We'll figure this out. Catch the wraith, collect proof on Saint-Yves, investigate the Initiative—whatever you want, I'm in."

Io thought she might explode. *I'm in.*

*"Feel your fear and keep going anyway?"* she teased, repeating Edei's adage.

"Don't." His head was bowed, hiding from the gang's gaze, but Io could see his mouth split into a grin. In a whisper, he said, "Do *not* make me laugh right now."

But she wanted to. She felt wild on defiance, high on rebellion— she wanted *more.*

"Just wait until eight," he said. "Yes?"

She made herself nod. "Yes."

With a furtive smile, he backed away. Ava was holding the door open, brows stitched together in suspicion. Outside, the sun hid behind a sheet of clouds, casting the city in tones of melancholy. The Fortuna's neighbors were coming back to life after the neo-monsoon: shopfronts dragged open, vendors sweeping residue seaweed off their stands. The hinges of the door groaned as it shut behind them, but all Io could hear was the steady beat of her boots on the cobblestones, the march of a soldier called to duty.

# CHAPTER XXII

# WAIT IT OUT

"SHOULD I BE worried, Ava?" Amos Weinstein asked over their shoulder as they threw open the door of the spare room in the small apartment over their coffee shop in Parsley Square. They leaned against the doorway and watched the Ora sisters unload their meager belongings on the floor. Io had kept watch on the Quilt while Ava went into their apartment and packed the few things they could take with them: underwear, clothes, shoes, legal documents, and the rare valuables left over from their parents. Ava insisted on bringing her favorite records.

She was hugging them to her chest now, refusing to put them down with the rest of their stuff. She surveyed the room with a mournful expression. Amos might be the reigning monarch of coffee and pastries in the Silts, but a sense of style they had not: no furnishings but a double bed, no carpet, no curtains on the window. Cardboard boxes everywhere, still packed, even though Amos had moved back to Alante years ago. One had toppled over, puking its forest-green insides on the wooden floor: Amos's old army uniforms, stars etched on the collars and shoulders—they had been a decorated first lieutenant during the Iceberg Wars.

Their question hung in the room, oppressively unanswered. Ava remained silent, as though the question wasn't directed at her. Io felt a twinge of irritation at her sister. When angry, Ava tended to shut down completely, in fear she would say something cruel. Which was fine, Io guessed, if it was just the two of them, but with Amos here, going out on such a limb to shelter them, it was downright rude.

Io gave Amos her best smile. "We're fine."

Ava made an imperceptible sound—a . . . *snort?*—and fell backward on the bed, the records squeezed tight. What the hell was *that* about?

"You don't look fine," Amos said. Io had always thought their voice was as smooth as their coffee. In the interludes between obsessing over what lay on the other end of her fate-thread, Io had developed a major crush on Amos. Even now, she found them breathtaking: blue eyes, wavy blond hair falling to their ears, lean, muscular arms from kneading all those pastries. And the dimples . . . Gods, they were irresistible. The only hiccup: Amos was eleven years older than her and never treated her like anything but a sister. And so over time, her crush had shriveled and died, and a friendship had risen from its ashes.

"We'll be fine," Io told them. "Thank you for your hospitality, Amos. I don't know how we'll ever repay you."

"You can start by eating something, then taking a nap. You look about to keel over, Io." They paused, appraised her with a comical frown on their face, then nodded decisively. "I'll bring up some matzo meat pie when I'm done with work."

They turned on their heel and stomped down the stairs to their café. Silence followed in their stead, broken only by the teetering clangs of porcelain in the café below. Io started pulling her things out of the duffel bag, stealing glances at her sister. There was definitely something up with her. Io blew air out of her nose, in silent protest. Whenever Ava got like this, Io had to prod and wedge and pry the answers out of her like a rotten tooth.

"All right," she said at last, circling around the bed to stand over Ava. "What's wrong?"

Ava sighed, the sound exaggerated and dramatic.

Io waited, in case she deigned to follow it up with actual *words*, but no luck. "Is it the apartment? I said I'm sorry a dozen times, but until I'm certain it's safe again, we can't stay there. A phobos-born is involved, Ava."

Ava's eyes slid from the ceiling to Io, hooded and tired. "I don't care about the apartment."

Okay, they were getting somewhere now. "Is it about Bianca?" Io had a whole list of questions to ask regarding Bianca, like *what do you even see in her* and *how hypocritical is it that she preaches no guns, no leeches, no paramours, then has a paramour herself*, but she wisely chose not to voice any of them, except: "Will she be angry with you?"

Ava propped herself on her elbows. The records remained balanced on her stomach, rising and falling with her breaths. "She'll come around eventually. Time heals all things, isn't that what Baba used to say?"

Baba used to say a lot of aphorisms, according to her sisters. Io didn't recall that; like many things in her life, her memories of her parents were secondhand, too: *Do you remember that time Baba took us . . . ? Do you remember when Mama . . . ?* Their father had been a clever fox of a man, but all Io could see of him when she closed her eyes was his sleeping form huddled on the sofa, and how she was not to disturb him under any circumstances.

"I guess," Io replied. "Do you think Bianca'll go after Thais?"

The bed groaned as Ava suddenly sat up, the records cascading to the floor. "Why would Bianca go after Thais?"

Shit. Io forgot she hadn't told Ava about the Teatro rally yet. She'd meant to, but the wraiths and the Nine and the phobos-born and Saint-Yves had taken precedence. She slid to her knees and began piling the scattered records, if only to avoid eye contact right now.

"Thais is engaged to Saint-Yves."

"What?"

Io placed the neat stack of records on the bed next to Ava's thighs. "She didn't mention it to you?"

"She just said she was staying with her boyfriend up on the Hill. She looked so happy, so in love. That was enough for me."

Ava was always like that: content with a little, stifled by too much. But occasionally her laissez-faire attitude backfired, and Ava would have to come face-to-face with hard truths. Io found it almost comical how so many of Ava's girlfriends had turned out to be something as bizarre as chimerini collectors or jazz haters, and Ava would only realize several months into the relationship.

Io leaned back until she found the wall. She removed her still-wet and mud-crusted boots and then crossed her legs. Her right side felt stiff and swollen; she should ask Amos for bandages and medicine. She began massaging the tender flesh between her ribs, pain and relief rocking through her in waves.

After a long time, Ava spoke again. "The Initiative is just the kind of equality moonshine Thais usually falls for. It wouldn't be the first time she got a little too caught up in 'the cause' and didn't see the truth of the people surrounding her."

The two sisters gazed at each other, the silence filled with shared memories: Malena Silnova, a sweet-talking artist who had hired Thais as a personal assistant, then convinced her to weave threads of loyalty between her and gallery owners; Thomas Mutton, a charming con man who set up a pyramid scheme around exploiting other-born powers for freelance jobs.

"She can't possibly know the truth about him," Ava said, "and those murders."

"I never said she did!" Gods, did Ava think that Io was an actual villain?

"You know," Ava continued, unfazed, "I've been thinking that's why she left two years ago. She signed up for another grand movement, was afraid we would try and stop her, so she snuck out. And when I kept following her thread, tracking her across the Wastelands, I was probably threatening to wreck her mission, and that's why she left that note."

*Leave me alone. Haven't you done enough?*

"Maybe it was Saint-Yves who convinced her to leave in the first place," Ava said raptly. "He used to visit Alante all the time when he was a prosecutor."

"Maybe," Io whispered, trying not to squirm.

Her instinct told her to bolt for the door, this conversation barking at her heels. She remembered the day Ava had come back to Alante, wearing one of those old-timey plastic raincoats, hued from top to bottom in orange. Dust clouds had stormed up from the south, and auburn rain coated the entire Neraida Plains. The note, however, was pristine white, folded neatly in Ava's bralette. *She's not coming back,* Ava had said before locking herself in her room for the rest of the week.

And Io . . . she had read Thais's note, and she had been *relieved.* How could she ever tell Ava that?

She cleared her throat. "Whatever is happening, we need to warn Thais. Edei won't tell Bianca who she is, but Nico and Chimdi heard her last name onstage, too. Eventually, they'll put two and two together."

The Ora legacy: a death mark.

Ava was shaking her head. "Bianca wouldn't go after my sister."

"She had no issue going after me," Io said through her clenched jaw.

"But ultimately, she let you go. Thais is from the Silts, and Bianca has spent her life protecting the Silts."

Io scoffed. "Doesn't look like it from where I'm standing. A series of women from the Silts are being turned into monsters and then slain—and she just told me to leave it be."

"Perhaps you should."

Io started. "You can't be serious."

"Finally, we have comfort. Finally, we are safe—more than safe. You have clients, I have shows, we have money and a place to live, we have the Fortuna's protection. Bianca is right. No court will indict Saint-Yves. They'll likely pin the whole thing on the closest other-born. That phobos-born you fought, or even Thais herself, Io! Are these women so important to you that you would risk us all for them?"

A sharp irritation skewered through Io, spiked with a thousand little prongs of injustice. It wasn't fair. Ava wasn't being fair. She phrased it like this was a choice Io was making, as if she was throwing their lives away because of some whim, some need to prove herself a hero. But in truth, Ava was making Io choose between her sisters and these poor, doomed souls. She called this a betrayal, when really it was a sacrifice, costing Io more than she ever thought she would give.

Io sucked on her bottom lip, trying to keep her tears inside. She didn't want to cry, she wanted to stay angry, because this was an infuriating argument, and just plain—wrong! Her chin trembled as she whispered, "Is our comfort so important that you'll let people keep dying for it?"

"Don't say it like that," Ava replied quickly. "I'm not letting anyone die."

"By asking me to step away, you are."

Ava's voice tendered. "I don't think you can save those women, Io."

"I probably can't. But I must at least *try*."

Ava was reaching for her, but Io could only see the blurred world of her tears. "Gods, Io, I didn't mean to upset you. I'm saying it all wrong. I just don't understand *why* you must save them. I can't understand why they're so important to you, why we don't just wait it out?"

Her sister's fingers brushed her wrist; Io immediately stood up, her side stabbing with pain, and walked straight out of the room. From the bed, Ava continued with gentle, apologetic words that Io didn't truly hear. The corridor was long, with several doors, and Io tried all of them before she found the bathroom and turned the tap on. All other clatter clouded into a singular sound: water spattering on the marble tiles of Amos's bath.

A wonderful steam had filled the room. Io stood in a towel before the sink mirror, freshly scrubbed and moisturized, feeling a million times better. Her fingers traced the red-and-purple blemishes that hugged her belly. The pain was minimal as long as she didn't reach up. She found a bottle of painkillers in the cabinet and swallowed two—that should do the trick.

When she was almost dry, she braved the door. Just an inch, but it was enough: she could hear Ava's music coming from the other side of the corridor, where Amos must have kept their record player. For a moment, she wondered if she should knock, talk it out with Ava, set everything right again. But what would she say? *You're being an asshole and asking impossible questions?*

In the spare bedroom, Io rifled through the bag, pulling on her violet, oversized knit sweater and stuffing it into the waist of her favorite black cargo pants, full of side pockets and belt loops. Her boots were still wet from last night's adventures. Those wouldn't do; she scanned the room. Gods, Ava would throw quite the fit when she realized, but there was no other choice. She pulled Ava's treasured leather booties on, winding the laces twice around her ankles.

Amos was sitting behind the counter when she climbed down to the café. The place had a couple of customers, talking softly over tea and pastries. As Io slid into her usual spot at the counter, the stool farthest from the door, Amos glanced up from the thick book they were reading and gave her a bright smile, all dimples. "Food?"

"Food," she agreed.

They came back with a tray of two enormous slices of the promised matzo meat pie and a steaming cup of chamomile tea. While Io ate, they narrated the plot of the gigantic fantasy book—a washed-up vagabond bands up with the last of the fury-born line to hunt down a resurrected leviathan—almost in its entirety, broken only by the occasional takeout customer. Only when her plate was clean, did they finally concede to taking the tray away.

"Amos," she asked. "When you were in the Iceberg Corps, did you ever meet Luc Saint-Yves?"

Amos chewed on the inside of their lip. "Only once, while our platoons were both in transit to the front. I was just a corporal back then, and he was a first lieutenant. Our platoons sailed together, trying to outrun the Jhorr and capture the *Lola*—that's what we called the iceberg. A hundred-megaton rank, it could irrigate the entire valley for years. I remember one night, just after we found out the Jhorr had taken the *Lola*, and that we would have to engage to take it from them, he kept the entire ship up with story upon story, joke upon joke."

The Iceberg Wars had begun when the world all but ran out

of drinkable water. Each city-nation on this continent—Alante, Nanzy, Rossk, Jhorr—sent forces up north, hunting the loose icebergs around the pole. Especially icebergs of higher ranks, such as the hundred-megaton *Lola*, which could provide some much-needed unpolluted water to their residents for years. The wars had lasted on and off for three decades, and even now, four years after the last bout, sightings of the odd iceberg floating in the ocean would set off the violence again. "Did you take it?" Io asked. "The *Lola?*"

A shadow played on Amos's face. "We did. We had three keres-born sisters in our service, as did every platoon. After weeks on the Jhorr's tail, we woke up to the sisters barking directions. Our captain sailed us straight to the slaughter: the *Lola* had capsized during the night, right into the Jhorr's biggest ship. The gals said they could see the death from miles away."

Io fidgeted at the thought of the keres-born and their creepy powers but kept it to herself. Amos talked about them with reverence; she didn't want to be rude, especially about the wars. "So you think he's a good guy," she asked, "Saint-Yves?"

Amos lifted their shoulders. "He was a good lieutenant to his soldiers."

A good lieutenant was also a good killer, though. Io didn't think he would hurt Thais—she was essential to his Initiative—but she was worried her sister might get caught in the crossfire of whatever Bianca Rossi was planning. *I'll take care of it*, the mob queen had said; Io held no illusions that Bianca's plans wouldn't involve violence.

She rubbed her temples, weighing her options. "Amos, do you have a Hill pass?"

They gave her a much-deserved appraising look. The Hill was a walled community, separated from the rest of Alante by a tide trench and heavy security. Entrance was allowed only to residents and their staff, including freelancers who carried special Hill passes.

"Yes," Amos replied hesitantly. "I sometimes deliver up there."

Io looked at her friend with big puppy eyes. "Can I borrow it?"

"Tell me what I'm getting into, first."

What, indeed? That was the million-note question. The gist of it was this: "Thais lives up there. I think she might be in danger."

# CHAPTER XXIII

# CREPES

**IO GOT OFF** at the Acropolis stop and stood ramrod straight as the guards checked Amos's pass. The Hill sprouted before her like a lush oasis in the middle of the driest desert. Green coated every surface: trees lining the streets, flowers spilling from every window-sill, climbing vines hanging on to balconies like clingy toddlers. The lazy smell of nature was overpowering, sweet and fresh and completely alien. Within seconds, Io began sneezing.

District-on-the-Hill had once been an archaeological site, home to a row of pre-Collapse columns and statues that people came from all over the world to visit. But when the tide began taking over the city below, turning houses and mansions into half-rotting carcasses, the elite decided to move into history. They built around the monuments, making sure to include a tide trench to separate them from the rest of the city. The ancient temple was still there, but it now served as a patio for the rich to rest on during their walks.

As soon as the guards handed back her pass, Io took off, climbing down the elevated trolley station and disappearing between the grand brownstones. They were neat, modern structures, two stories high, with dark red slate roofs, constructed from some anti-flood material that looked like it could outlast the end of the world.

She found Hanover Street easily, passed it, and turned on the next parallel street. Keeping a leisurely pace, a casual tourist on a walk, she slipped into the Quilt and checked every home on the street; few of the residents were in. Glancing up and down the pavement, she jumped over the fence of the closest empty house and circled around to its back garden, then into the garden of the house opposite— this one facing Hanover Street. The roofs would have been her preferred choice, but the Hill wasn't in danger of flooding overnight and stranding the residents in their houses, so there were no bridges connecting the buildings. Instead, Io reached the front porch of the empty house and plunged into one of the armchairs. She placed her spectacles on her nose. The porch railing was high enough that she wouldn't be visible unless someone stopped directly in front of the house. But through the railings, she had an unobstructed view of 64 Hanover Street.

Thais's house was perfectly white, with floral curtains waving through half-open windows. The porch was laden with flowerpots: petunias, zinnias, and rosebushes. It looked nothing like Thais's room in their old apartment, which was crowded by mismatched furniture. Then again, Io had no idea how her sister would decorate if they had money to afford it. Maybe she *was* a floral-curtain kind of girl and she'd just never had the opportunity to show it. *Opportunity.* Gods, Io hated it when she thought like that. Like they had lived in gloom and misery, thirsting for a chance to go someplace better, be someone better. Their life had been hard, but whose wasn't? And life could be hard and happy at the same time, couldn't it?

But Io was shrouding the past in the rosy mist of nostalgia. Thais had never been happy in their little apartment in the Silts. Her desire for *more* had its own thread, leading straight to the Hill. It was their parents' pride and joy: Thais's rare home-thread, bright and precious as a jewel. A home-thread connected you to the place you belonged, not your birthplace or home address neces- sarily, but a land that felt your own. Their daughter had a bright destiny ahead of her, their parents would say, and what a destiny it had turned out to be: the Hill, with all of its spotless marble, excessive green, and gilded safety.

Thais had sought opportunity like a wilting plant craning its stem toward sunlight: with Malena Silnova and her artist friends, and later Thomas Mutton and his freelance work. But things kept falling apart, and every time Thais returned to their little apartment in the Silts, defeated and unfulfilled, she looked at the place as if it was a jail. She had found her opportunity at last, and even though it had come in the shape of Saint-Yves, Io was glad for her sister. Perhaps she was established enough in these circles by now that losing Saint-Yves wouldn't cost her. Perhaps she could take over the Initiative and forge it into something truly honest and good.

But first Io had to tell her, a professional breaker of hearts. *Your fiancé is involved in the Silts murders. Bianca Rossi knows this and might come for him—and you. Our sister wanted me to stay out of it, to wait it out, but I came to tell you the truth.*

Wait it out. Gods, Ava could be annoying sometimes. Even as a child, Io remembered the sharp juxtaposition: Thais pacing the room, furious about one thing or another, and Ava on the sofa, calmly leafing through a book or listening to the latest radio drama. She would nod occasionally, or make a reaffirming sound, but Io knew she was only pretending to be listening to Thais's tirades. Ava had even told her once, in a whisper, "We'll just sit and wait till she gets it out of her system, all right? Then I'll make us all crepes." For the longest time, Io had obeyed. Then the rants began targeting *her.* And Ava still chose silence.

Io didn't want to think about this. She didn't want to be *hurt* by this. She and Ava had always had a wonderful relationship, which got even better after Thais left. So why was Io scratching at old wounds, and why was she finding scabs instead of healed skin? It was because of Ava's infernal questions: *Are these women so important to you that you would risk us all for them? Why must you save them? Why are they so important to you? Why don't we just wait it out?*

Because! she wanted to shout. *Because!* The wraiths were violent and murderous, but they were being manipulated. They were spewing someone else's venom. They were slaying someone else's targets. And they had been slowly and carefully coerced into thinking these were their own desires, their own beliefs. They had been made into villains, and they didn't even know it. If *Io* didn't fight for them, then who would?

*Settle, name your feelings*, came Thais's voice unbidden in her mind. Io closed her eyes and breathed until she could no longer hear the drum of her heartbeat in her ears. *In through the nose, out through the mouth.* How irrational it was that Thais was both the instigator and resolution to the mess in Io's head.

She leaned back and studied her sister's pretty new house.

The sun had traveled far into the west when Io finally decided to stand and stretch her muscles. Hours had passed, but she had seen none of Bianca's lackeys on Hanover Street. She would take up her vigil tomorrow, and the day after that, until she and Edei had gathered concrete evidence against Saint-Yves. Then she would return to this quaint, flowery house and whisk her sister away.

Her stomach grumbled. Maybe Edei would be hungry, too, when he came to pick her up. They could grab some food at Amos's and talk about their next steps. After all, whatever she wanted, he was in. The memory was a balm to Io's stress. Bianca had backed out, but Edei was right there, willing to help her take down Saint-Yves. Ava was safe at Amos's, and Thais was safe at 64 Hanover Street. Io would figure this out. She always did.

"Io?" said a voice. *Her* voice.

She turned to find her sister, elbows propped on the garden fence. She was in a beautiful floral dress with ruffled sleeves, and her hair was pulled back in a tiny ponytail on her nape. Her feet were bare and her cheeks delightfully rosy. She was smiling.

"Sister mine," Thais said, "why don't you come in?"

# CHAPTER XXIV

# THE SHAPE AND TIMBRE OF IT

"**I'VE GOT REVANI** cooling in the icebox. Just like Mama made it." Her sister waggled her eyebrows invitingly.

Io didn't remember what Mama's revani tasted like. Slowly, she managed, "How did you know I was here?"

"All those threads of yours—you shine like a beacon in the dark. I noticed you an hour ago. I thought Ava might have told you where I am, and you'd knock at any moment. But you never did, and Luc is running late and you know I hate eating alone." It all rushed out of her in a single gurgle of thoughts voiced aloud, and the way she talked was so familiar, so uniquely *Thais* that Io had to swallow a wave of emotion.

"I know," Io replied. Thais always did get very grumpy if Io and Ava didn't wait up to eat with her. And revani and coffee sounded amazing right now. And Thais was . . . here, smiling. It wouldn't hurt to go in, would it? "All right."

"Excellent!"

As Io approached, Thais leaned over the fence and unlocked the gate as though she'd done it a thousand times before. She probably had. The people in this house were probably her friends. They crossed the street and went past the rosebushes and petunias and zinnias, up the white porch, and through the door, which had been left ajar.

"Let me give you a tour." Thais started bouncing through the house. Io followed, keeping her distance. The living room was first, dressed in bright greens and soft yellows, the floral curtains waving in the soft breeze. On the mantelpiece above the fireplace was a case of the same cigars Io had seen at Saint-Yves's office. Next was the kitchen, which was salmon pink and cozy, like it had been taken out of a girl's dollhouse. The revani was in the tall icebox in the corner, but the scent of semolina and lemon lingered in the room, making Io's mouth water. Revani had been a rare treat in the Ora household, reserved for Winter's Feast or their parents' anniversary.

Thais took Io's hand and dragged her up the stairs, explaining how they had redecorated the bedroom and renovated the bathroom before moving in. Io's senses bubbled down to that point of contact between them: her fingers in Thais's, like when they were children, before everything changed.

They were in the guest room when Io burst out, "Are you angry with me?"

Thais paused in the middle of a sentence, something about the roof needing mending on this part of the house. She faced Io fully, with a serious frown. "Why would I be angry?"

Why? Thais used to scatter her anger like a queen throwing coins from her chariot. *Here, this is for you. Fall to your knees to grab it—aren't I generous?* And now she could find no reasons to be angry? An image of Rosa on that windowsill, puffing out smoke, came to Io's mind: *What we did to Thais.*

"You asked Ava not to tell me you were back," Io said.

Thais's bare toes stretched on the carpet. "I thought you were angry at *me*. I was harsh with you before I left. I didn't think you'd forgive me."

Was this . . . an apology? Io had never seen its like on Thais's lips; she could hardly recognize the shape and timbre of it. It resonated in the arcane hollows of her heart, and from its thrum, a tender hope was born. Things could go back, to the very beginning, when she and Thais and Ava were one soul sharing three bodies, one breath in three chests.

She said, her pardon as misshapen as Thais's apology, "It was a hard time."

"And now?" Thais's tone was expectant, pleading even.

*And now*—gods, how Io's heart melted. The two words were an olive branch, extended to mend the past and walk boldly into the future. "Now it's better," she replied breathlessly.

Her sister squeezed Io's fingers and pulled her down the stairs. Her voice was singsong, her face beaming. "Let's make ourselves some coffee, shall we?"

Coffee and revani, comfort and safety. Io imagined sitting down and just telling her sister *everything*: how she had finally met her fate-thread, and he was cute and funny and asked her to wait for him. How she had stood up to Bianca Rossi. How she had argued with Ava. How she had bargained with the Nine, at a terrible cost. Thais had always been good at calming her; perhaps, with Thais by her side, Io could be brave enough to actually think about that mystifying poem and what it might mean: *The cutter, the unseen blade, the reaper of fates.*

They entered the kitchen, filled with the sweet scent of syrup. Io wanted to savor every moment with this new, relaxed, cheerful version of her sister. She was tasked with brewing their coffee Kurkz style, grabbing it out of the fire just before it boiled over, while Thais arranged a large platter of fruits so brightly colorful they must have come straight from the Flying Orchards of the Neraida Plains. The two sisters fell into the easy rhythm of a shared past: carrying the trays to the back porch, arranging porcelain coffee cups and small crystal dishes for the spoon sweets on the patio table. Io was so entranced by the effortless way they had fallen back into their old selves that she only noticed the table when it was set. For six.

"I thought," she said carefully, "that we were having coffee alone."

"Oh, Io, don't be shy. We have a campaign meeting here in a few minutes, and I'm dying for you to meet Luc. You'll love him, Io—he's got Baba's sweetness and Mama's humor and Ava's taste in music and your razor-sharp wits. And have you seen his smile? Just wait, he's going to charm you off your feet."

Her sister's whole face beamed. A cold bitterness slithered around Io's heart, squeezing tighter and tighter. All their life, she had fought and sacrificed to make Thais happy, and here was Saint-Yves, a man she couldn't have met more than a couple of years ago, and he was making Thais beam with joy.

The very man who was the primary suspect in Io's investigation. Gods. She had to warn her sister. Protect her.

"I have to tell you something," she said. Immediately, her sister's smile dropped, the sharp intelligence called forth. "Did Ava tell you what I've been doing for a living these past two years?"

"You've grown our little business into quite the household name," Thais said proudly. "That's why I want you to meet him. His ideas, the Initiative—he seeks to do precisely what you have done with our detective business but on a larger scale, bringing the investigations to court."

Io shook her head. "Thais, listen to me. I was hired to investigate a series of murders in the Silts. Corrupt other-born have been turning up dead. The murderers are women who use their severed life-threads to kill, claiming to be sent by someone to deliver justice. I couldn't confirm if they're other-born because Saint-Yves pulled all other-born records from the public registry. The women signed up as volunteers for his Initiative. Their victims were people Saint-Yves tried to prosecute and failed. And yesterday, I overheard one of his men insinuate that Saint-Yves is behind it all."

Thais grew very still. Hands on the back of the porch bench, eyes nailed on Io.

"Luc wouldn't hurt a fly," she said with finality, as if that was that, and took off.

Io followed at her heels through the back door to the downstairs bathroom, where she stood at the doorframe, watching her sister wash her hands. "I know it's hard to believe, but all evidence points toward him. I have reason to believe Bianca Rossi might take matters into her own hands, which is why we need to go—"

"How is Bianca Rossi involved in this?"

"She's the one that hired me. She knows my suspicions."

"You made the mob queen of the Silts think my fiancé's the one killing her people?" Thais asked incredulously.

"Our *evidence* points to that. Please, just come with me. You'll be safe with me and Ava. I'll find the last wraith, get her to admit who is helping her, go to the authorities, and—"

Thais wiped her hands on the towel and looked at Io through the mirror. "I'm not leaving him. He's not who you think. It's not a publicity stunt or a grab for votes. He started putting this idea together after the Order of the Furies was wiped out. In their absence, the other-born community has fallen into chaos, Io. No one to keep them in check, to bring them to court. We need to establish a new Order that will be inclusive and transparent this time. Whatever these murders are, they're not related to him. I wouldn't be surprised if his opponents were creating the rumors to try and take him down before tomorrow's elections. I know it might look suspicious to people from the Silts, but he is truly trying to help."

"People from the Silts?" Io interrupted, trying to hide her irritation. Criticizing Thais never went well; you had to be careful with your tone of voice, cautious with your phrasing. *"You're* from the Silts, Thais."

"You know what I mean. The Silts believe the whole world is out to get them. Bianca Rossi in particular. They think every person in power—politicians, celebrities, the police—is corrupt."

It was true, people from the Silts loved to talk about how the world conspired against them, but they had good reason to. The Silts were made up of immigrants, other-born, the poorest of the poor. The rest of the city didn't look twice in their direction; in fact, after the Moonset Riots, the whole world blamed the Silts for the death of the Furies. The entire reason Io had a job was because the police never bothered with Silts affairs. Now a rich boy from Nanzy had a grand idea of uniting other-born and police, the poor and the rich. Damn right, the Silts wouldn't trust him. The world had burned to ashes because of men's good intentions.

"But Luc isn't like that," Thais continued. "For gods' sake, he turned his own parents in when he discovered they were keeping dozens of worker accidents in their factories quiet! In just eight months, he's arrested more criminals than his two predecessors combined."

"You sound like his voting leaflets."

"Well, that's because I write them," Thais snapped.

"Baby?" a voice called from the foyer.

Her sister craned her neck. "We're back here!"

A chill ran through Io's body, from her head to her toes. She heard the door close. Shoes taken off, coats hung on the rack. Voices chatting, coming closer down the corridor. Io glanced at Thais in alarm.

In a whisper, Thais said, "Stay. Give me a chance to prove it's not him."

"Thais?" Saint-Yves's charming voice called out. "Where are you?"

Grabbing Io's wrist, Thais pulled them out of the bathroom. "Coming!"

Four people lounged in the kitchen. Two women were discussing a file open on the table, a man was rummaging inside the icebox, and Saint-Yves was leaning over the kitchen counter, bringing a piece of revani to his mouth with his bare fingers.

When he spotted Io, he lowered the syrupy cake and said, "And who might that be?"

"Luc, meet my younger sister Io," Thais said brightly, swooping Io in front of her. "Io, this is my fiancé, Luc Saint-Yves. The girls are Marie and Hanne, our campaign managers. Oh, and that little mouse ravaging our icebox is our head of security, Aris Lefteriou."

The women waved a hello, but Io barely saw them. Her attention was on the man straightening from the icebox, two beers in his hand. Io recognized the lanky stature, the goatee, the pale skin and pristine clothes.

*Run*, Io thought. *Turn around and bolt.*

But Thais's hands were on her shoulders, nailing her to the spot.

# CHAPTER XXV

# AN ACUTE SENSE OF DISCOMFORT

IO INSTANTLY DROPPED her gaze to the floor. The salmon-pink tiles were so polished she could see her own reflection: curls frizzy from the humidity, bags under her eyes from lack of sleep. Perhaps he wouldn't recognize her. It had been dark in that alley at the Modiano, and darker still last night on the rooftops around the Teatro.

But the silence that followed was too long. His sharp "Hello there" was anything but inconspicuous. He knew exactly who she was. Shit. What should she do?

Saint-Yves was speaking. "I'm very excited to finally meet you. From Thais's stories, I can tell your input on crime-solving in Alante will be most invaluable. But I'll wait for coffee before I bludgeon you with questions."

"It's all set up outside!" Thais chirped. "You all go ahead and get comfortable. I'll cut up the revani and be out in a minute."

Saint-Yves was holding the door open. Marie and Hanne headed to the porch, and Aris Lefteriou joined them with slow, shuffling steps. Io's mind was on alert; her legs itched to make a run for the door.

"Actually, I should be going," Io started.

"Nonsense," Thais said, smiling at her fiancé. "You have time for a coffee."

"I really should—"

A hand nudged at her waist. "Stay," her sister whispered. "Ten minutes. That's all I ask. Go—I'll be out in a second."

All right. Io's mind began working. She would stay for ten minutes, pretend to need Thais's help to find the bathroom, then grab her sister and bolt out of here—before Aris Lefteriou could even realize what she was up to. She followed Saint-Yves onto the patio and took a seat at the far end of the long stone bench Lefteriou was sitting on, with Marie between them. That way she wasn't in his direct eyeline and thus not in danger of falling into his thrall of terror.

While Saint-Yves poured coffee and Hanne passed the tray of fruits around, the rest of the group carried on an inane conversation about the Mayoral campaign: meeting with sponsors, opening speakers, voter rallies, event security at tomorrow's elections. Io kept glancing back at the house; where the hell was Thais?

"So, Io." Saint-Yves smiled charmingly as he filled her cup with coffee. "Thais tells me you're the best private investigator in the Silts. It would be illuminating to hear the thoughts of someone as connected to the district as you are. What is your opinion of the Initiative?"

"It's ambitious," Io said, hoping that would be the end of the conversation.

The man laughed heartily. "Sure is. Do you think other-born from the Silts would join us?"

*I highly doubt it*, she thought, but she answered, "I wouldn't know."

"Thais believes that any other-born from the Silts who signed up would be seen as a turncoat. That it would cause internal unrest. Do you think she's right?"

He just wouldn't leave it alone, would he? Eyes on her empty plate, Io replied, "The Silts and the police don't work well together." Hadn't Saint-Yves heard of Roosters' Silence?

"But wouldn't a police force comprised of other-born be easier to trust? Despite what the newsies say, the Initiative isn't just another way to police other-born. Our ultimate goal is equality.

True social change, starting with the incorporation of other-born in law enforcement. We seek to establish a new, inclusive Order, yes, but it wouldn't be like the Order of the Furies. The fury-born were supposed to hold impartial trials of the other-born they arrested, but I'm told that, more and more before their end, their trials ended overwhelmingly in incarceration, despite evidence favoring the defense."

Io had heard those rumors, too, but they were all vague on the details. The death of the fury-born was so sudden and so tragic that no one wanted to taint their memory with the ugly bits. Perhaps, however, this was an opportunity to fish for a little information, before Thais got here and Io found an excuse to whisk her away.

"If it's true that the Agora is backing you," she said, watching closely for his reaction, "then more other-born might be willing to join."

Saint-Yves leisurely picked an apple slice to chew on, as if he expected the world to hold its breath for him. "The Agora is keen to see our dream succeed, yes," he said, a cryptic answer if Io ever heard one.

"Are you talking about business again, baby?" Thais scolded, appearing with an ornamented silver tray carrying neat squares of revani, topped with ice cream.

Oh, thank the gods. Thais was here, and Io could now get moving.

"Just getting to know your sister, love," he answered.

Io tried to catch her sister's eye, but Thais got busy with the revani, serving each plate laboriously. Hanne mentioned something about their engagement taking Alante by storm, dozens of articles, journalists calling for an interview. Grinning ear to ear, Thais carried the discussion to their wedding, planned for early fall in Nanzy.

Io stared at the revani on her little crystal dish, ice cream melting around its sides, and slowly worked her left hand under the table.

She kept her eyes on her dish; when she pulled up the Quilt, no one noticed the flash of silver in her eyes. Thread after thread she scanned, finding at last the one she sought.

With a quick flick of her fingers, she yanked the thread leading to Thais. Three short tugs, two long. The Ora sisters' call to arms.

Across the table, Thais paused with her spoon in her mouth, eyes glazed with a silver glow as she studied the Quilt around Io. Using nothing but her gaze, Io gestured at Aris Lefteriou and then at the exit. Such was the language of sisters: a whole conversation carried in looks.

But instead of finding an excuse to talk alone, which was Io's intended plan, Thais set her spoon down and faced the phobos-born. She spoke over the others like they were butter and she a heated knife—

"Why is my sister terrified of you, Aris?"

The table stilled, and Io's muscles tensed for flight. Thais Ora was more to the point than a sharpshooter. It was an admirable quality, one that Io lacked herself, but it made for uneasy conversations. Io didn't miss the embarrassed stare of the campaign managers or the concerned frown that descended on Saint-Yves's brow. Aris, for his part, shifted uncomfortably on the bench. Io couldn't see his full reaction because she didn't dare look into his face. But she heard alarm in his voice, or perhaps trepidation.

"Luc tasked me with watching the House of Nine," the phobos-born replied. "The Muses refused to meet with both the Commissioner and the Mayor, even after strict orders from the Agora to assist on the Silts murders—but they let a cutter and a gang member into their House, their first guests in months? I had to find out who they were and what the Nine told them, so I followed them. They realized and cornered me."

"Did you use your powers on them?" asked Thais, her tone dripping with danger.

"The thug would have roughed me up, if not worse! Am I not allowed to defend myself now?"

Thais leveled a finger at him. "You were stalking them—I'd say you deserved a good roughing-up. We are conduits of the divine, not gods ourselves. Other-born powers are ours to use, to control, and to limit. We will be harshly judged, and we, more than anyone else, do not want to be found lacking."

"Justice is the virtue of great souls," Hanne said gravely as if quoting someone. The campaign manager looked like ice cream coated in cherry syrup: her skin pale white, her long hair an artificial crimson color, cascading in waves over her naked shoulders.

Calmly, Saint-Yves added, "You could have explained the situation. Have you considered that Io might have *shared* her information if you had not terrified the shit out of her?"

"Apologize," Thais ordered the phobos-born. "And mean it."

Io felt as if the conversation didn't involve her at all. As if this was a performance and she a spectator, observing but never truly participating. And like in the theater, there was subtext beneath the layers of drama, delivered almost too fast to keep track of: The Nine had been refusing visitors, even after a mandate from the Agora. Lefteriou thought of Edei as a thug, which confirmed he must be a rare upper-class other-born. And finally, the Initiative was a damned cult. *Conduits of the divine, control and limit, justice and great souls*: this was some top-quality bullshit. Io had heard roughly the same drivel from Other-Born Separatists like Edei's father, or bougie assholes like Thomas Mutton and his For the Other scheme.

Io was peripherally aware of Lefteriou turning to her. She heard him say, "I am sorry. I overstepped, on both accounts."

There was a long pause, during which Io supposed she was expected to accept the apology, but she was too electrified by fear to respond.

Lefteriou grumbled, "See? She won't even look me in the eye. Doesn't matter how I behave. I'll always be a villain to them."

Next to her, Marie made a cooing sound, sad and understanding— it tore right through Io, charging her with energy. This man, who had stalked them through the Modiano, who had employed his terror to interrogate Io, who had chased them across rooftops, who was involved in a foul scheme that was making women into wraiths and using them to murder other-born—he thought *he* was the victim?

"Am I supposed to be 'them' in this scenario?" Io snapped. Adrenaline pumped through her chest; in a burst of courage, Io lifted her eyes to his. "I am a cutter. I'm paying an extra danger fee to live in my building. My private investigator license was rejected, twice, on the basis of *threatening abilities*. You have a job other-born can only dream of, you're drinking coffee with the future Mayor, and you're dressed in a suit the price of my rent. It's bad for all of us but this"—Io gestured at the porcelain cups, the well-dressed guests, the sweet-smelling patio—"is a layer of protection few other-born can claim. Take that into consideration the next time you demand the instant forgiveness of someone you assaulted in a dark alley."

In the silence that followed, Io could count her heartbeats. Time her breaths. A bug was buzzing somewhere close, and automobiles whizzed down Hanover Street. Aris had averted his gaze sometime mid-tantrum, but Io refused to look away. His shame was a tonic to her frayed nerves; she sopped it up like starved desert earth.

"*That*," said Saint-Yves, breaking the silence. "That right there. That's the perspective we need."

"Told you," Thais declared proudly.

"We need to address class issues if the Initiative is to be a success," Saint-Yves continued in the focused, pragmatic tone of a businessman. "And Thais was right: you're just the person to do it. A cutter from the Silts, a private investigator with a keen social mind."

"You could show them the necessity of reestablishing a policing body, the transparency and justice of a task force of other-born," Thais said, with a raised eyebrow.

"And," Saint-Yves added, giving Thais one of his spectacular teeth-out smiles, "we'd be happy to have you as our maid of honor. It's a good thing we're showing them true assimilation firsthand when we get married this fall."

Marie giggled. "I can't wait to be planning *that*."

Io's mouth was half-open, eyes flying between the five of them. They were smiling, laid-back, and warmly expectant. As if it was completely normal to apologize for assaulting her, lecture her about equality, offer her a job, and plan a wedding—all in the span of two minutes. And they were so *casual* about it, as though they couldn't imagine Io refusing. As though she was already one of them.

She squirmed in her seat, an acute sense of discomfort. It was the warped form of this conversation; she felt like she was being evaluated in some way. Like they had taken her very justified anger and twisted it to their advantage, to something they could *use* in their campaign. It was the familiarity of their beliefs: social equality, progress, morality. How many times had Io heard Thais orating about these very same ideals? It had seemed noble then, but now it just sounded naive.

*At the first sign of trouble*, she heard Edei's voice in her head. *Book it out of there.*

Edei, who would be getting off work soon. Edei, who would

be coming to find her. Edei, who had promised to solve this with her. Edei, the thought of whom made her feel like she could finally breathe again.

"It's getting late," she said after a moment, staring at her palms. "I should head home."

Her sister's fingers reached out across the table, jostling the cups and creasing the linen tablecloth. "Wait, Io, don't."

Io halted, forever unable to refuse Thais.

Thais turned to her fiancé. "Io has found evidence tying the Initiative to the Silts Stranglers. Their records were pulled from the public registry. They were our volunteers. The victims were cases you lost as prosecutor. My sister believes you are dangerous, Luc, and I refuse to let her go until you prove her wrong."

The silence that followed was terrifying. The weight of four pairs of eyes pressed on Io, their faces startled. She couldn't believe her sister had done that, but it was also so characteristically Thais, straightforward and unforgiving, no shit given, that it was peculiar it hadn't happened sooner.

Saint-Yves worked his chin with his hand. "We are aware of the women's connection to our Initiative. Aris is looking into it. So far, our belief is that someone is targeting these women precisely because they have worked with us. I made the conscious decision of pulling other-born records from the public registry knowing that these murders will incite violence against the other-born, cutters especially. The same goes for having prosecuted the victims in the past—I knew it would be misinterpreted. I have lost countless cases against members of the Silts gangs. If I sent out assassins to kill every single one of them, there would be carnage in the streets of Alante."

To Io's ears, this last part sounded like a show of power, and she didn't like it one bit.

"Bianca Rossi hired you, did she not?" Saint-Yves continued, addressing Io. "Did she ever tell you I tried to work with her? I'm not stupid; I know what she means to the Silts. The hero that ended the Moonset Riots." He said it with earnest admiration, which surprised Io. "I know that if I bring her down, I lose the Silts, and if I lose the Silts, I lose the other-born. So, about three months ago, I approached her and offered to legitimize her—give her official power over the district, a seat on my City Council, make her a founding member of the Initiative, as long as she follows our principles. You know what she replied? *Why be a councilor when you can be a queen?*

"I am not behind these murders," he stated firmly. "On the contrary, I am very much invested in solving them. So invested that I have in fact decided not to act against those who broke into my office the other day, who intruded on my rally, and who—I'm assuming—are currently trespassing on the Hill, because I believe they are essential to finding the truth about the murders."

He was threatening her. He really was threatening her.

If this had happened a week ago, Io would be cowed, looking for the fastest exit, disappearing before he could blink. This was the most powerful man in Alante, after all, and he had just made an open threat against her. But she had fought a wraith and won. She had withstood the terror of a phobos-born and the manipulations of the Nine. She had been chased and shot at and beaten into the mud. She had been bullied by the mob queen herself, and she had, surprisingly, stood her ground.

Because this mattered: the women, the victims, the mastermind behind it all.

Io looked Luc Saint-Yves straight in the eye and let the Quilt come up around her. She saw his form, emblazoned with silver lines.

A strong, bright thread of love connected him to Thais. Io had no true purpose in the Quilt, except this: to *intimidate*.

Right now, Saint-Yves was seeing the silver threads reflected in her irises. He was being reminded she was not weak or weaponless. She would not be threatened. She was a cutter. An unseen blade. A reaper of fates.

"That's enough of that, Io," snapped Thais.

The admonishment stung like an unexpected slap. Io dropped the Quilt and found the group—everyone but her sister—shrinking away from her. Aris was half-out of his seat.

"I don't care if you think he's innocent or not, Io," Thais said matter-of-factly. "Luc is a good man. Our whole team are good people. You can help our cause. The information the Nine gave you could be instrumental to stopping these murders. You can trust us with it, sister mine. Trust me."

Io's heartbeat spiked, but she made herself breathe. She wasn't a child anymore, scraping to indulge Thais's every whim. Some of Saint-Yves's explanations made a lot of sense, but Io's suspicions hadn't been appeased. Her visit to the House of Nine hadn't been just informative; it had shifted the very axis of her world. The Nine had hired Horatio to kill the women who were now becoming wraiths, and whoever was behind them knew enough about the muse-born to hide from their powers. Io's image stared back from dozens of portraits, a silver thread in her hand, and the world burning behind her. In her core, Io knew this was information she couldn't hand out to anyone, not until she understood it herself. Perhaps she could start trusting Thais again one day, but not today.

"I'm sorry," she said, proud that her voice came out steady. "I can't."

A flicker of emotion flashed in Thais's face, schooled almost immediately to blankness. "It's okay, Io," her sister said. "I understand."

"Thais!" Lefteriou snapped.

"No, Aris. My sister is the best at what she does. If she needs to figure this out on her own, then you bet your ass she will."

This time, there was no stopping the surge of emotion that flooded Io. Relief, so all-encompassing that it felt like she was exhaling for the first time in years. *Thank you*, she wanted to say. But her throat was choked; Io simply nodded.

"Right, Luc?" Thais pressed.

Saint-Yves reached for his fiancée's hand. "Right, of course. Consider our offer, Io. We would be honored to have you."

A smile burst like a firework on Thais's lips. She leaned and planted a tender kiss on her fiancé's cheek. A thought flashed into Io's head, nasty and malicious. She thought Saint-Yves might have charmed Thais with his lavish plans, but what if it was the opposite? Io could recall with clarity the sleepless nights Thais had spent locked in her room, secretly weaving threads into existence, fiber by fiber, to attach to one of Thomas Mutton's friends, or Milena Silnova's gallery connections, in order to endear herself to them. Once, Io had been naive and asked Thais about it; the ensuing outburst was monumental. An invasion of privacy, a betrayal—how could Io think such wicked things about her own sister? It hadn't mattered that Io was right, that Thais had been weaving those threads.

What if Thais was doing the same thing now? She seemed to have a hold over Saint-Yves—what if that wasn't just mutual love, but some thread Thais had woven precisely for this purpose?

Dread led Io into the Quilt. She focused on the space around Thais's chest. A weaver's sapling threads looked like the stems of a blossom or the roots of a tree: slowly reaching outward, seeking another body. But there were no untethered threads around Thais. She wasn't weaving. She was truly in love, truly invested in the Initiative and this marriage. Did that make Io feel a tiny bite of disappointment?

Something drew her attention—she spotted unusual movement in the Quilt, coming from the garden to their left. A streak of light beyond the fence, approaching fast—a lone thread, leading to nowhere. No, it wasn't possible. How had the wraith found her here?

She jumped upright, toppling the bench, Marie and the phobos-born with it. She screamed, "Watch out!"

But it was already too late.

Her eyes barely caught the wraith's motions. One moment Raina was jumping the fence like a great cat, the next she was on the patio, a hand around Saint-Yves's throat, pulling him to the ground with her.

Time slowed to snapped images: Saint-Yves gaped, breathless. Thais tackled the wraith. The three of them went rolling across the marble of the patio. Raina elbowed Thais in the chest and came up on top of Saint-Yves. Io jumped over the table, grabbed the wraith's severed thread—and yanked with all her might. The girl yelped, fell backward. Sprawled on the ground, Saint-Yves wheezed for air, an ugly, deathly sound.

The wraith lunged for Io. She was faster than wind, stronger than rock. Her first blow stole all the air from Io's lungs, her second rattled the teeth in her mouth. Io didn't remember falling, but suddenly, she was on her knees and the wraith was behind her and her arms had snaked around her neck.

"Io!"

Io heard her sister's cry of horror, then a loud crack. Porcelain shuttered everywhere as the kettle collided with the wraith's head. Thais launched herself at Raina, and they went tumbling, smacking on marble and wood, crushing porcelain bits beneath their bodies.

Io's sight cleared, her ringing head centered. The wraith's thread was still in her fist. Thais was on top of the wraith, trying to keep the wraith's hands from reaching her face, but she was losing the battle—the wraith was inhumanly strong.

"Stop," Io said—it came out weak and horse. "Raina, I can help you. I can *save* you."

Raina heaved and threw Thais off her and, with inhuman speed, clamped a knee against Thais's chest.

"End it!" Thais was screaming. "Io! End it!"

"Raina, wait," Io pleaded. "Step back. I can save you—"

"*Io!*" Thais screamed as the wraith's jagged fingernails edged toward her bare neck. *"Please—"*

It was the terror in Thais's voice that did it: Io sliced.

# CHAPTER XXVI

# BRASS GLEAMED

IO COVERED THE body with the linen tablecloth, its flowery pattern spotted with brown coffee stains. Porcelain crunched under her shoes. The entire revani tray lay upside down on the grass. Bees buzzed over the syrupy remnants. Beneath the cloth peeked the wraith's feet, caked with dried mud, and her left hand, veins swollen and purple.

Brass gleamed on the wraith's fingers. *Brass*—Io's mind seized on the object like a moth to flame: the wraith was carrying the Fortuna gang's brass knuckles, Bianca Rossi's infamous weapon. She glanced over her shoulder; everyone else was inside the house, tending to Saint-Yves. She slipped the knuckles off the girl's cold fingers.

"Io?" Thais called from the patio.

Startled, Io shoved the knuckles into the pocket of her cargo pants. If the Police Commissioner found them on the uncanny woman who had just tried to kill him, his eyes would set on the gang. On Bianca Rossi, yes, but also on Edei, Nico, Chimdi, even Ava. Alarms rang in Io's head: *danger, danger, danger.*

Her thoughts became detached. She had ended up at the same spot, with a body at her feet, a death of her doing, with a mystery unsolved, the people she loved in danger—and she couldn't comprehend *how*. She felt dizzy and confused, and her breaths struck like bullets, piercing the skin.

Thais appeared in her sight line, arms and legs nicked with tiny cuts. "Hey, hey." Her sister cupped her cheek. "Is it happening again?

bridge, baby. I'm right here on the other side. One foot in front of the other and you'll find me."

Io's lungs began laboring to draw breath. She was a child again, standing at the foot of a hanging bridge, frozen and wild with panic, and Thais was her favorite person in the world, the only one who could save her from her own fear. Her sisters would tease her first, but when that didn't work, Thais would lull her into crossing the bridge with the tender cadence of safety in her voice.

"I could have saved her, I could have stopped her," Io now wheezed through her constricting lungs. If she hadn't cut Raina's thread, she would have all the answers she so desperately needed.

"You tried," Thais said. "But she wouldn't listen. She would have killed me and Luc both. I can't tell you if you made the right choice—only you can do that—but I will tell you this: you are not evil, sister mine."

Io pressed her knuckles against her temples, to force back the tears gathering in her eyes. Her sister put an arm around her shoulders and tucked Io's head under her chin. Io knew it was a transient kind of comfort, for it would undo none of her crimes, but in that moment, Thais loved her and comforted her and didn't blame her. Io stepped onto the bridge and found her way home.

When the shadows on the lawn began to deepen, her sister pulled her up and guided her into the house. Saint-Yves sat in a kitchen chair while a medic bandaged the scratches and bruises around his neck. The women were gone, but Aris Lefteriou was speaking quietly to three officers, who soon exited by the patio door, no doubt to deal with the body.

In the silence that followed, Saint-Yves spoke in a hoarse, unhappy voice, his hard gaze landing on Io. "I suggest you get your priorities right, Io."

Thais whipped her head at him. "What are you talking about? She just saved your—"

"My love, do you think it is a coincidence this woman found her way onto the Hill—into our walled, secure community—on the day before the elections? After a month of senseless, frenetic murders, the Police Commissioner is found dead in his own house at the hands of an unidentifiable kind of other-born. All that we have fought for would be undone. The city, civilians, and other-born alike would revert to their old violence, and it would be the Moonset Riots all over again." With every word, his tone grew harder. "Whoever sent this assassin has been playing a very long game."

*Assassins*—was that what the wraiths were? Assassins sent to dispatch the Police Commissioner a day before he becomes Mayor, meaning to instigate another bout of violence. Gods, Io hated to say it, but it made sense.

Sent by whom, though?

The answer came to Io fast and obvious. She settled herself in that kitchen, hyperconscious of how her legs spread casually, how her shoulders hunched, how her hands sat in the pockets of her pants, touching the cold brass of Bianca Rossi's knuckles. *Compose yourself, show nothing, lest Thais realize the race of your heartbeat.* Her sister had always been too good at reading her.

But Thais was too busy bristling at her fiancé's quip, lip curled in that way of hers that showed she was about to go off. "Io will figure it out," she said assuredly. "And when she does, we will be the first people she tells."

Edei would be here any minute now. The café was empty, both of pastries and customers. Amos was reading their gigantic book and munching on a slice of raisin bread, while Io tried to put her thoughts in order, face propped on her fists, eyes gazing into space. Ava's soft music still crooned from above, but her threads were completely motionless—she must have fallen asleep—a relief, because Io really didn't feel like facing her right now. What would she say? *I think your girlfriend sent a wraith to assassinate our sister's fiancé?*

There was something indecipherable about these murders. The wraiths claimed to kill for justice, their hand guided by someone powerful enough to hide from the skills of the Nine. Io's first suspect, Horatio, had turned out to be another victim, punished for his involvement in the wraiths' abductions during the Riots. Her second suspect had been Saint-Yves, who concealed the wraiths' identities from the public and failed to prosecute the victims in the past. But he, too, could be ruled out: firstly, because he seemed loyal to the proper justice systems, secondly, because he had offered a partnership to Bianca Rossi, and thirdly—and most importantly—because the newest wraith had just attempted to kill him. The whole attack could be a ruse, but Io didn't think so. He had come too close to dying today; his fear had looked too genuine to have been staged.

And now Io's third suspect was . . . Gods, she couldn't even think it without a shiver of dread running down her spine. *Bianca Rossi.* The mob queen had hired Io to solve these murders and pulled the plug on the investigation the moment their suspicions turned to her most powerful enemy. A few hours later, a wraith was sent to kill Saint-Yves, carrying the Fortuna knuckles. What a victory it would be, if the mob queen exposed the Police Commissioner as the mastermind behind the Silts Stranglings, then quickly saved Alante from his evil.

But what Io couldn't figure out was the wraiths. The murderers were otherworldly, powerful in a way that didn't make sense, deemed dangerous by the Nine's artists during the Moonset Riots. Io still had no inkling as to who was making them into wraiths, or how. They were being used and manipulated and made into monsters— and no one seemed to care about this part except Io.

And the Moonset Riots. When Saint-Yves mentioned the carnage, it jump-started Io's mind, lightened all the secreted pathways of her thoughts. The Riots kept coming back, a call of fury echoing from the past. And the key players of these murders were connected some- how with the carnage twelve years ago: the wraiths and Horatio, the Nine and their mystic warnings, the brutal, nonsensical violence. The mob queen of the Silts.

She had to find out what had happened during the Riots. No more loose legends and half-told stories. She had a plan—she just hoped Edei meant it when he said, *Whatever you want, I'm in.*

The clock over Amos's head showed ten past eight. Io glanced at the front window of the café. No one passed by. He should be here by now.

"What exactly are we waiting for?" Amos said after some minutes.

"Edei Rhuna," she replied. "He's supposed to help me with a case, but he's late."

"Give him a few minutes. The weather's turning."

They stared out the café window. The wind had picked up, gathering litter off the street and twirling it in the air. Water had started trickling up the cobblestones from the direction of the sea. Amos would have to drag the shutters down soon to secure the café against the tide.

Eight fifteen now.

They quieted for a while, and Amos pushed the small bun of raisin bread they had been nibbling toward her. Io breathed in the sweet aroma. It reminded her of home; Mama would visit their neighbors for a coffee, steal raisins from their pantry, and bake the girls raisin bread with chamomile tea on rainy days. Said it chased away the winter flu. Io broke off a piece, glanced at the clock, chewed, glanced at the clock, swallowed, glanced at the clock.

Eight twenty.

"You are stressing me out!" Amos exclaimed. "If you need Edei Rhuna and he's not here, why don't you go find him?"

"What if," she whispered, ashamed of her self-pitying thoughts, "he's not here because he changed his mind and doesn't want to help me after all?"

"Io," Amos said, a goofy smile on their face. "That boy looks at you as if you're the sun. I very much doubt he is going to ditch you now that he's finally got you talking to him."

Io startled. "What? When have you seen him look at me?" They had never been in the same room with Amos, as far as she could remember.

Amos turned bright red and started fidgeting with the register. "I mean, um, a few times, when he comes in and you're here, too, he looks like he's about to talk to you, but then you take off before he has a chance to even cross the room. I thought that it's obvious, you know, that he has a thing for you."

Io held her breath. It very much was *not* obvious! She had sensed the fate-thread shining closer a couple of times while she'd been at Amos's, but she was a skilled deflector by then, lowering her head and quickly scramming away. It had never even crossed her mind his approach might have been *intentional*. Could Edei really "have a thing" for her? Or was it all in Amos's, a well-known daydreamer's, head?

"It *might* be a coincidence, and I *might* be too nosy for my own good," Amos was still blabbering. "I just think that if he promised you he'd be here, he would be, you know?"

Heat gathered on Io's cheeks. And then Amos's words registered. No matter what else he was to her, Edei *was* someone who kept his promises. Which meant something might be keeping him from meeting her. What if Bianca had found out he was disobeying her orders? That he was going to look for the very answers she wanted hidden? Alarm seized Io; in an instant, she was in the Quilt. The fate-thread was there, pulsing silver, incandescent in the low light of the café.

The clock ticked 8:25. Io stood so fast her head swam. Half-blind, she wound her scarf around her eyes and nose and threw the door open against the growing wind. The fate-thread was bright between her fingers, illuminating her way to him.

The tide rose around Io's feet, soaking the heels of Ava's lace-up boots. The wind was rough against her cheeks, slipping through the weave of her knit sweater. Io stood at the base of the steps to the grand building, cold, nervous, and very hesitant.

The Stitch-House, as the Silts so lovingly called it, was the district's medical center, a large building with its own electrical battery and clean water. Considering it was the only legitimate hospital in the Silts, this was, most likely, where Edei's girlfriend worked as a doctor. There might be no emergency at all, just Edei and his girlfriend stealing a moment between shifts.

Io didn't know if she could handle seeing them together. Sometime during the past couple of days, hope had begun to sprout in her chest.

All the little moments she had shared with him, the tenderness, the bad jokes, their bodies pressed together in a tiny sleeping pod. His intent eyes as he said, *Whatever you want, I'm in.* And now, Amos's revelation. Was it possible that Edei—she couldn't even think about it without squirming—actually *liked* her?

*Get yourself together, Io. He has a girlfriend.*

She shouldered past the workers lowering the tide shutters and followed Edei's thread to the second floor of the building. Knocked and steeled herself. She could do this, she thought, because you couldn't lose what was never yours.

Edei threw the door open, his brow furrowed, and instantly glanced down at his watch. "Shit, Io, I'm so sorry. I forgot. Things have been . . ."

Instead of explaining, he pushed the door open. Chimdi was sitting on the bed, her left arm raised to shoulder level as Samiya, in a white medic's frock and a matching cap, stitched a gash on her side. Nico was sitting on the floor, legs spread before him, his nose so swollen that his face looked deformed.

"What happened?" Io asked.

Edei pulled her inside by the elbow and shut the door behind her. "The leeches happened. Last night, they caught Chimdi and Nico following the Commissioner and arrested them on the spot. They've been in the holding cells at the City Plaza all day. They let them go an hour ago, but not before roughing them up."

"We couldn't tell Bianca," Chimdi said from the bed. "*No guns, no leeches, no paramours*—you know the drill. This would be my second strike and Nico's third. Who knows what new punishment she'd devise for us."

But that wasn't what was troubling Io. Only an hour ago, she had been having revani with the same people who did this to Nico and Chimdi. Was their interrogation what had kept Saint-Yves so late?

"Did Saint-Yves do this to you?" she asked.

"He asked us questions, which we didn't respond to, of course," said Nico. "But the leeches waited for him to leave before trying to beat the answers out of us."

"Unfortunately for us," Chimdi said, her tone flat, "we're not snitches."

"Hence the stitches," Nico added.

"What did they want to know?" asked Io.

"What do you think?" Chimdi answered, sucking air through her teeth as Samiya's needle went into her skin. "Why we were following Saint-Yves. What Bianca is planning. It's like they knew exactly who we were, exactly what we were after. His shit with the gang feels personal."

Samiya stared daggers at all of them, her arched brows knitted together. "You keep going on about his grand villainous plan," she said, with obvious sarcasm, "but I've met the man. He takes the time to meet all of the members of the Initiative. He's already helped my appeal for resident status move forward. He is no monster; I am sure of that."

"My nose would beg to differ," said Nico. "What are the next steps, Io? Edei already told us, and we want in on whatever you're planning. Let's bring this asshole down."

"I . . ." Io wet her dry lips. "My plan was to catch the new wraith, Raina. To interrogate her and figure out who has been guiding her hand. But I went to visit my eldest sister, Thais, today. I ended up having coffee with none other than Saint-Yves himself. The phobos-born, too. As I was leaving, the new wraith attacked Saint-Yves. I had to . . ."

She trailed off, closing her eyes against the image of Raina's body peeking through the floral tablecloth.

"Why would his own wraith attack him?" asked Chimdi.

All right, then. Moment of truth. "In the wraith's hand, I found *this*."

All four pairs of eyes in the room snapped to the brass knuckles Io produced from her pocket.

Edei's voice was razor-sharp. "What are you suggesting, Io?"

"I'm not suggesting anything. I'm just saying we need to look into the knuckles."

"No, we do not. If you found these knuckles on the wraith, it's because someone put them there. I handpick all the Fortuna hires myself. The people that carry these knuckles—I would trust them with my life. They're not involved with the wraiths."

"You didn't pick all of them," Io said. "*Someone* picked you."

His face closed. His shoulders hunched up. With a nudge of his head, he directed her to a smaller room off the side, a washing area for doctors and nurses. It smelled of ammonia and fresh linen and orderliness.

"You aren't seriously accusing Bianca, are you?" he asked quietly when the door was shut. "What reason does she have to send a wraith to kill Saint-Yves?"

"She dropped the investigation the moment we turned our suspicions to Saint-Yves, and a few hours later, a wraith attacks him in his home, wearing her knuckles. It's a statement of power for the whole world to see. It would be convenient if she pinned this all on Saint-Yves, wouldn't it?"

"Convenient for what? What would she be getting out of this?"

"Power. She's the mob queen, Edei."

He answered with a hard stare. "So what? You're a cutter. Did I ever accuse you of severing those threads?"

That was a low blow. "Don't compare us."

"Don't pretend you're not accusing her because you *want* her to be the villain."

"She *is* a villain! She hurt the mob king that ruled before her. She hurt the outlier gangs that opposed her. She threatened to hurt *me* just a few hours ago, simply because she didn't like what I had to say!" Her chest heaved up and down. "If there is a chance that she's behind these murders, don't we need to at least look into it?"

"She's not and we won't."

"What has she told you about the Riots?"

"Nothing. She doesn't like to talk about it."

"Have you ever wondered why?"

"It was the worst time of her life, Io, of everyone's life in the Silts!"

"But what exactly happened? I think the answer is at the heart of these murders. You asked me to trust you." She could hear her voice weakening, *pleading*, but she couldn't help it. "Now I'm asking you to trust *me*. I just need access to her room, and we can find out about her past, her connection to the victims—"

Edei's gaze was unforgivingly hard. "No."

Io felt the word like a physical blow. Her stomach tumbled. Her voice broke—"No?"

"You got it wrong. It's not her. She wouldn't do that." And without another word, he stormed out of the room, letting the door bang closed behind him.

# CHAPTER XXVII

# YOURS TO GIVE AND YOURS TO TAKE

**SHE WENT AFTER** him, but he was already out of the examination room. Chimdi and Nico followed swiftly, the latter casting Io an apologetic look. Io was left staring at the swinging door, faintly aware of Samiya's eyes boring into the back of her head.

She had been naive. *Of course* Edei would side with his boss. It was obvious he admired her, loved her even. He was loyal to the bone. And now he was marching straight to the Fortuna to tell Bianca of Io's suspicions. Whatever advantage Io had had was gone. And more than that, more than fear, anger, or disappointment, what she felt was heartbreak. She had hoped the promise of the fate-thread was finally coming to life. That Edei felt like he had always known her, and wrapped her in his arms, and told her he would help her no matter what. That he had been watching her as if she was the sun. Gods, she felt foolish.

"Your ribs are badly bruised," Samiya said from behind Io. "Let me heal you."

Io didn't have the strength to object. She obliged as Samiya led her to the table, lifted her sweater and undershirt, and brought the full ruin of Io's rib cage into view. The Sumazi girl's fingers gingerly traced her side. Samiya smelled like their apartment had, soft linen and black tea. Her skin was lighter than Edei's and spotted with black freckles, highlighting her uplifted eyes and heart-shaped lips.

Io tore her eyes away, not wanting to make the girl uncomfortable. "It doesn't feel as bad as it looks," she said.

When Samiya hit a particularly tender spot, Io couldn't help but inhale sharply. "This will hurt," Samiya said, "but don't lean away."

Io nodded. Samiya closed her eyes and began moving her fingers in slow rotations over Io's biggest bruise. A tingling sort of heat rose from deep inside Io's body, bringing relief as it bubbled to the surface. This was the power of a horus-born, descendants of the four sons of Horus, the Sumazi gods of the body and mummification: to mend the flesh, expedite healing—*SNAP!*

Io let out a gasp. Pain raked through her, making it hard to breathe. "Gods."

"I'm sorry. You had a fractured rib that I had to mend. Ice and anti-inflammatory meds twice a day will help with residual pain," Samiya said, patting Io's thigh. "Do you need a prescription?"

Io's lips wobbled as she tried to inhale and exhale slowly to chase the pain away. "Yes, please."

The medic leveled her with a studying look. "Has Edei told you the story of how he came to work for Bianca?"

"He hasn't."

Rummaging through a cupboard, Samiya produced a pill bottle. "When we first got to Alante, we had to take whatever job we could to make rent. I cared for an elderly couple, Edei worked in construction. One night, he came home badly beaten. The men he worked with weren't fond of Sumazi. Said we came here to take their jobs. If I wasn't horus-born, his knee might have never healed right. The next day, Edei went to the construction site and worked as if nothing happened. The big boss asked to see him."

"Uh-oh," Io whispered.

"That's what I thought, too. His boss asked why he didn't take a sledgehammer to his assaulters in return. Edei told her he wouldn't risk our tenuous entry permits to extract his revenge. He told her violence wasn't the answer. By the end of the day, every worker that had laid a hand on him was unemployed, and Edei was promoted. His new job was overseeing all construction in the Silts, making sure something like that never happened again."

Io looked at her palms. "The big boss was Bianca."

"Yes."

Io knew the stories. In the years since Bianca Rossi took over the Silts, the district was, if not lawful, at least more principled. The mob queen had established some semblance of order: she kept the outlier gangs from tolling the bridges, hunted every harasser out of the Silts, showed shop owners what happened when they paid immigrants half the wage they deserved. She made the Silts a little safer—but what was the point, when the biggest danger was Bianca herself?

"Edei realized early on that this line of work wasn't for him. He's tried to reform the Fortuna as best he can, but some things are beyond his control. Still, he stays with her, because she has the means to endorse his entry permit and, by extension, mine. He has sacrificed a lot to keep us safe in Alante." Samiya's face was lined with quiet fury. This, Io remembered, was the healer who had continued to help women with unwanted pregnancies even after her life was threatened. Who mended her boyfriend's bones after every fight. It was no wonder she and Edei were a good pair: tough and fearless. "It's bad for you native other-born, but it's worse for us."

Even when they filled the criteria and gathered the necessary fees, immigrant other-born were often turned away at the gates, left to fend for themselves in the Wastelands against the tide and the neo-monsoons. A resident's endorsement went a long way in a city as corrupt as Alante. It was more than enough reason for Edei to stay in Bianca's employ, or for Samiya to seek Saint-Yves's and the Initiative's help.

"What I'm trying to say," the girl concluded, "is that Bianca Rossi, however cruel, however cunning, has the loyalty of the Silts. Edei's loyalty, even mine. She is the only one who offers us the power to fight for justice in an unjust world. But, from what I understand, Edei has found another, kinder way to fight back—in your investigation, in you. Just be gentle with him. It's neither easy nor fast, reexamining your loyalties."

"I know."

And she did. She knew all about how hard it could be to reexamine your loyalties. To take the people you loved apart and decide if what was left was worth loving. Even now, two years later, she couldn't decide what she felt for Thais, her own sister, the woman who raised her. She was happy—she was *humbled*—that she was the reason Edei was rethinking his loyalties, that he thought of her as a kinder way to fight back. But the truth was she couldn't wait for him. She had already revealed too much. Now she had to race against the clock to get what she wanted out of Bianca.

"A couple of times now," Io said, "I have noticed Bianca's lips are tinted blue. Do you happen to know anything about that?"

Samiya frowned. "It sounds like a sleeping tonic."

"Aren't there proper pills for that?"

"Yes, but Lilac Row likes to use a serum diluted in cocktails. Mostly blue, sometimes red."

Lined with dream palaces, clubs, and gambling dens, Lilac Row was the center of the mob queen's turf, one long avenue ending in the Fortuna Club. She owned half the buildings and collected protection fees from the rest. The only places that served sleeping cocktails, however, were the dream palaces, where oneiroi-born could soothe you into a light, dreamless sleep. Just as Io had suspected.

"Why are you asking?" said Samiya.

Io slid off the table, giving the other girl a shy smile. "It's best that you don't know."

Samiya added in a hurry, "Be careful who you approach. None of the oneiroi-born will be willing to help."

"No worries," Io said. "I've got my own."

Io pulled the door open to find Edei sitting on the floor across from the examination room, back against the wall, elbows on his knees. His head snapped up when the door opened; he watched her approach. She stopped in front of him, unsure of what to do or say. Her heart thundered, squeezing the little air she had in her lungs. He was here, waiting for her.

Edei ran a hand over his head. "I'm sorry about what I said."

Io thought of his question at the Modiano Market yesterday— *Are you safe, Io?* Perhaps he knew exactly what to ask because he felt it, too. Was feeling it now: the danger of your loyalty, your love, being taken advantage of. The danger of loving someone who does cruel things. She stood before Edei, but what she saw looking down was herself.

*Be gentle*, Samiya had ordered, and so Io was as gentle as she could be.

"When my parents died," she told him, "Thais stepped in to raise us. She was only seventeen, and yet she started working two jobs to make rent, paid the bills, and made sure Ava and I did well in school. Whatever personal aspirations she had, she set them aside for us. And so, after some time, I think she wanted us to express our gratitude by accepting her word as law. To be smart and noble and independent. To remember our parents fondly. But mostly, she wanted us to ascend to better things. And when Ava and I—no, it was just me." Io took a deep breath. "It was always *just me*, maybe because I was the youngest, maybe for no reason at all. When I didn't behave the way she thought was appropriate, her reaction was cruel. She wouldn't talk to me for days. She would criticize everything I did, often infusing it with exaggerations or lies. And she would shame me, every chance she got. For the pot I didn't wash right, the school night I spent at Rosa's place, the moira-born skill I couldn't master."

Io knew his eyes were on her, but she didn't meet them. She couldn't handle whatever she saw in them right now, when she was this naked, this vulnerable. "When she liked her work and the money was good, she was an entirely different person, full of kisses and hugs and compliments. And I would forget about all the cruel things she had said when she was upset. I began to associate her moods with my happiness. If she came home tired and grumpy, I would stay in my room. If she smiled, my whole day would brighten up. When she asked me to cut the threads that tied an art gallery owner to some of his favored artists, I didn't hesitate. She said I would be giving her employer, a Rossk painter, the chance to succeed. When she suggested I take some of the jobs her boyfriend found for us, I saw nothing wrong with it. I was finally going to bring some money to the family. But her boyfriend crossed the line, and Thais got rid of him. We tried to continue the job ourselves, but we couldn't get clients. Thais sank into one of her dark moods again, and I thought I was to blame."

Io took a deep breath. This was the hard part. "Before that happened, we had enough money for Ava to take up singing lessons again. She had auditioned for a place at the Academia Aska in Rossk, and she got in with a fully funded scholarship. She was ecstatic. We dove right into planning: her trip, her apartment, how we would visit. Thais didn't say a word through any of it. That same night, she came into my room. *Cut it*, she said. *Cut Ava's thread to music.* I didn't know what to say. Did I want Ava to stay with us? Yes. Did I worry Rossk was too far if she ever needed help? Yes. But I could never cut her thread to music. It's the one thing that has always made Ava happy.

"So I told Thais no. For a week, she didn't speak to me. Didn't come out of her room. I had Rosa stay over every night that week, in fear that Thais would corner me and ask me again. On the seventh day, late at night, Rosa and I heard her pack up her things. Rifle through the drawers for her papers. I heard the door close behind her. I've never told Ava this before, but I was awake through all of it. I knew she was leaving us and I didn't stop her."

Finally, Io let her eyes drop to Edei. His gaze was soft, weightless on her skin. He had known, hadn't he? He had recognized this in her.

He said, "You were protecting Ava. There is no shame in that, Io."

But there was. A whole mountain of shame, of guilt, on Io's shoulders.

"Wait," she said. "That's not the whole truth."

She had made the choice to be honest about Thais's disappearance, for the first time in her life, and she had to carry it all the way to the end.

"The truth is I didn't just want to protect Ava. I wanted Thais *gone*. That week, day after day . . . I nibbled at Thais's home-thread, fraying it inch by inch. When it finally snapped, all the love that Thais felt for Alante, the reason she would never leave the city, disappeared. I asked Rosa to send her dreams of traveling so intense that she wouldn't be able to resist. When Thais packed up her things and left, it wasn't a surprise. I had wished it. I had planned it."

It was intentional, it was premeditated, it was slow and meticulous. It was malicious, *she* was malicious, and she knew it. She had thought telling Edei would be liberating, a burden lifted off her shoulders, a shared solace. But what she felt was sadness. Now that she had heard it spoken aloud, her story was one of unhappiness. She felt sad for herself, for Ava. For Thais, too.

"Io," Edei started—

"I saw her today," she went on, because she could feel that he was going to try to make her feel better and that maybe he was going to succeed, and she didn't deserve that. "With Saint-Yves. She was calm and kind and happy. And I just kept thinking, what if she just needed someone to fight for her? I didn't even try."

"It wasn't your responsibility to try. You were what? Sixteen? You were in pain, for years, and you chose to protect yourself." After a moment, Edei said, "Someone wise told me once that tolerating wickedness is just a slow kind of death."

A sound came out of Io's throat, half a sob, half a laugh. They were her words, reflected back to her. She looked at the ceiling. Gods, he was wonderful. If she went into the Quilt, she knew, the fate-thread would be pulsing bright as the moon of Pandia. She could reach out and tug it, and she could show him. *This is our fate-thread. This is how I feel.*

But the fear was all-consuming: she couldn't imagine any other reaction except betrayal and blame. She hadn't cut it, she had hidden it for too long, and worst of all, now she was fulfilling it. She was falling for him. She would asphyxiate him with what he hated: a destiny laid out for him, a choice made for him.

*Soon*, she thought. She would tell the truth, and lose him, after this mess was over.

"You really think it could be Bianca?" Edei asked.

"Yes." Tenderly, she added, "I think the people we love can be cruel. Our love doesn't absolve them. Nor should it."

"What kind of person are you," Edei whispered, "if you love someone who is cruel?"

It was a question Io had often asked herself. She opened her mouth, closed it. Tried again. "You're someone who loves. That's it. That's the only part that's yours to give and yours to take."

This was one of those lessons you had to speak to hear, wasn't it?

"You asked me to trust you," Edei said, massaging his palms. "I do trust you. For a minute back there, I forgot. I'm sorry."

Warmth suffused Io. She wanted to kneel before him and settle into his arms.

Instead, she extended her hand.

A smile flashed on his lips. His fingers slipped into hers. Io pulled him up.

# CHAPTER XXVIII

# BLACK WINGS WERE STITCHED

**THE GALE HAD** picked up, bridges grinding, shutters banging against the walls, awnings groaning in resistance. Lilac Row was as busy as ever, soaking the passersby in its eerie purple light. On each side of the street, dream palaces advertised their wares in large window displays, where you could peek in on the action: clients sleeping on silk-covered beds while scantily clad workers danced intricate numbers around them. The dances were a performance to attract customers, because the actual thing was quite boring; to cast you in a dream, the oneiroi-born just hovered their fingers over your head.

Io cleared her throat and advanced toward the dream palace Bianca frequented: a narrow brownstone with a sign in calligraphy that read **MISTER HYPNOS**. She held on to both railings to cross the hanging bridge, cursing the wind under her breath. A bouncer in a feathered crow mask held the door open for her at the rooftop entrance. Another man greeted her inside, this one with a dark gray lizard mask, and offered her a glass of champagne on a tray, which Io declined with a shake of her head. With a shrug, the man led her into a velvet-clad corridor that opened to a double stair-case, where an intricate chandelier hung at eye level. As they came to the top of the stairs, six pairs of eyes looked up at Io.

Two trios of oneiroi-born lay in the large foyer, draped on arm-chairs, sofas, and pillows. They would have presented themselves as siblings if a customer asked, but Io knew they likely weren't. Oneiroi-born in dream palaces often pretended to be siblings, to enhance the illusion. The six in Mister Hypnos wore bat masks in various shades of gray, as well as immaculate two-piece suits. Black wings were stitched on their backs, faithful to the lore: their ancestors, the gods of dreams, Oneiroi, were winged spirits.

Dream palaces had always made Io feel complicit, in some way. Some other-born, like the moira-born and keres-born, were demonized by the general public, and others, like the Agora of the horae-born or the Nine, were equated to deities. But oneiroi-born and grace-born were fetishized in the public media, always depicted as overtly sexual, or manipulative. In most dream palaces, oneiroi-born were obligated to work clad in nightdresses and robes.

"Come, come," said lizard face. "Meet Hypnos's children."

"Morpheus," a redhead said, feet propped on an armchair. "I use the pronouns they and them. Together, we will dream of the past, or the future."

Like many other-born, the oneiroi-born used the name of their ancestral god to classify their powers. Io had never heard people do the same with the names of the goddesses of Fate—Clotho, Lachesis, and Atropos—but then, moira-born powers were easy to describe in a single word: weaver, drawer, cutter.

"Phobetor, he and him," the younger man next to him said. "Together, we will dream of fears."

"Phantasos, he and him," said the boy sitting cross-legged on the sofa. "Together, we will dream of fantasies."

"And of course," said lizard face to Io, "if you prefer women . . ."

The other trio of oneiroi-born waved hello. Io blushed and looked away.

"I'd prefer the Morpheus," Io said, and to lizard face she whispered, "and a room in the back."

The man gave a nod and gestured for the redhead. The tall

oneiroi-born climbed the stairs in a languid, almost bored slither, then lizard face guided them to a door marked THREE. Well, that wouldn't do.

"Can I have that one?" Io asked, pointing to SEVEN. "It's my lucky number."

Lizard face shrugged again and held the door to room seven open for her and the Morpheus. "When would you like to be awoken, miss?"

"An hour," Io replied.

"So soon?"

"I have to get home," she answered, adding some shyness to her voice so that he would assume she had a sweetheart waiting for her at home. The door closed soundlessly, and Io focused on the room. Spacious and high-ceilinged, a double bed smack in the middle of it, a chair behind the pillow. It was all swathed in lilac silk: the curtains, the sheets, the robes by the mirror.

"Would you like one of our world-renowned cocktails first?"

A sleeping tonic like the cocktails of the dream palaces would knock her out for the next eight to ten hours. Io would absolutely *love* to, but she had to refuse. "No," she replied. "Your power will be enough. I'm only looking for a good nap."

"We have lots of options if you would like to step into something more comfortable," the Morpheus said, leading her to a rack of robes, nightgowns, and pajamas.

"Um," Io said ineloquently. "You choose for me."

They chose a sleeveless, liquid-soft nightgown in a shade of mauve with the shortest hemline Io had ever seen on a dress and left it and a robe behind a dressing curtain. While she took off her own, perfectly reasonable clothes, Io inwardly cursed herself for coming up with this plan. There must have been a dozen different ways to go about it that were less embarrassing than this.

When she came out, robe fastened tight around her waist, they asked, "How is it?"

"Fine," she lied. It was the softest thing her skin had ever touched. The carpet was so thick her toes got lost in it, and the bed, when she lay on it, was a small piece of heaven. She could see why people got addicted; this was a place where sleeping became a pleasure, not a necessity.

The Morpheus leaned over her, massaging her temples. "Any particular requests?"

Dear gods, that felt amazing. A blurred answer came out of her lips.

"A love story, an adventure, a dazzling success?" they prodded.

Her eyes drooped, lulled by the smooth circular movement of their fingers. "You choose," she whispered again.

"A love story, then," the oneiroi-born said and then—

*Clang!*

Io's eyes snapped open. Above her stood not the Morpheus, but Rosa, hands on her hips, lips twisted into a smirk. The poor Morpheus was facedown on the carpet, already snoring softly under Rosa's powers. Her friend said, "Am I interrupting, Io dear?"

"No." Io bolted upright.

"You got comfortable, I see," said Rosa, motioning to her nightgown. "Meanwhile, I was scaling walls and climbing balconies with that guy, who has the conversation skills of a stone wall."

From the balcony door, Edei gave a wave, head turned away. He was purposefully *not* looking at her, his cheeks a deep shade of red. Io glanced down at herself—her robe had slid open, revealing the tiny nightgown in all its glory. She was making him . . . *blush?* The thought was thrilling, but she tied the robe nonetheless and slipped on her cargo pants for good measure.

Rosa was studying the Morpheus at her feet. "Their name is Marino," she said, toying with the unconscious oneiroi-born's arm. "I went out with them a couple of times. Terrific kisser. Should go easy on the perfume, though."

"Did everything go as planned?" Io asked.

"Yes, boss," said Edei.

He was already on the balcony, and soon Io and Rosa joined him, climbing over the rail and jumping the short distance to the balcony on the left. Both rooms faced the back of the building, where the only attention they could draw was that of rats.

When Io had told Edei of her plans—employing Rosa's help to jump into Bianca's dreams—he hadn't even blinked. Instead, he had told her exactly which dream palace Bianca preferred, which room and which oneiroi-born, and how best to sneak into Mister Hypnos. Bianca used the oneiroi-born to sleep every night, even sending for their tonics when she was with Ava, which explained why her lips were tinted blue on every occasion Io had seen her in the early morning.

Wind lashing at her naked feet, Io climbed over into room eight. It was nearly identical to hers, except for the wheeled-in tray of wine and fruit. Bianca was sprawled on the bed, while her oneiroi-born and two bodyguards were out cold on a couch.

"So," Edei said. "How do we do this?"

"Lie down," Rosa ordered.

Not without some clumsiness, Io and Edei managed to squeeze next to Bianca, Edei in the middle, Io on his other side. He shifted so they could both share the pillow but otherwise didn't look much at her.

"I take it you've never done this before?" Rosa asked.

Edei shook his head no, staring straight up at the small chandelier.

"My parents wanted me to, because I had terrible night terrors as a child, but we could never afford it."

Rosa gave him a soft smile. "You know how the moira-born can see the threads that tie people together, right? Well, we oneiroi-born can do something similar. We can see these lines in a halo around your head, like a guitar's strings. If I pluck the right ones in the right order—kind of like playing a melody—I can help you fall asleep and guide you into the correct dream. And if I do it to all three of you simultaneously, you will all share the same dream."

"A symphony," Io piped up.

"Girl, please do not abuse my metaphors," said Rosa.

Edei interrupted them with a stressed "But how does that help us look into Bianca's part in the Riots?"

"I'm a Morpheus," said Rosa. "The dreams I make are of the past, or the future. I can give your mind a theme, say love, family, or *the Riots*, and then it will conjure the memory this feeling relates to. But the nature of the dreams depends entirely on you. Or, in this case, on Bianca. I have no control over it."

Io was watching Edei; she noticed the wave of fear that passed over his face. His night terrors must have been scarring. "You don't need to do this, Edei."

His face turned to her. "I need to see it with my own eyes. But . . . if things get bad, you'll get us out?"

Io wanted to grab his face and smooch him right on the lips. *Yes, I'll protect you, you precious, precious boy.*

"She can't," Rosa interfered in a blasé tone. "Only Bianca or I can do that."

"Well then," Io said. "If things get bad, wake us up however you can."

"Even a pinch to the butt?"

A chuckle burst out of Io. "Be serious," she said. "The guy's about to keel over."

"I'm not—" Edei started, then his eyes narrowed. "You're teasing."

Io smiled. "You caught on much faster this time."

Edei nodded proudly. "Progress," he said, and offered his palm.

Gods, his cuteness might actually kill her. She slapped his hand in congratulations. "Progress," she agreed.

"*Mm-hmm*," Rosa said, drawing out the word extra nasally. "Get comfortable, my little dreamers. We're going back to the birth of the mob queen herself. Remember, you promised me the first scoop. Whatever is in there, I'm publishing it first. I have to stay out of the dream to keep you asleep, so I'm expecting you to be my dutiful sources. I'm expecting detailed, descriptive language."

"All right, all right," mumbled Io. This was the last thing on their minds.

Her friend's tone changed. "Be careful. You'll be experiencing her memories. You might get the urge to alter things, but this is the past. It doesn't change. If you interfere, she might notice you. Cast you out of her mind. And all this climbing and breaking in will have been for naught."

Io's eyes were already heavy. Rosa was choreographing intricate routines with her hands over their heads, humming a rhythm under her breath. The sheets murmured as Edei's fingers searched for Io's, clasping her hand tight.

And then she was in the dream. People were screaming. Her eyes flew open. She saw a world painted in blood.

# CHAPTER XXIX

# RED RAIN

**THE SILTS WERE** red.

The streets, the walls, the roofs, every door and window: red. Heart pounding, Io walked to the mouth of the alley, where it opened to Lilac Row, recognizable by its wide sidewalks. The neon-colored dream palace signs were off and the shutters were down, no passersby on the street.

"Come on," said a voice behind her. Bianca Rossi, sporting dark-tinted glasses and far fewer scars, marched in Io's direction, about thirty teenagers following her. They carried iron bars on their shoulders and wore metal knuckles, but not the brass ones that would become the telltale of the Fortuna gang. These looked rusty and barbed, like discarded wires fitted into fists.

Io backed away with a panicked "Wait!"

But Bianca simply sidestepped her. "Are you coming, girl?"

The young mob queen of the Silts paused in the street, transfixed by a floating mass of red at eye level. It looked like a murmuration of a million ladybugs, lazily coursing down Lilac Row. Bianca's followers split around Io, a mix of anger and nerves stitched on their young faces. One of them stopped next to her, and Io knew without looking that it was Edei. They stood shoulder to shoulder, studying the flowing murmuration of red.

"What is that?" Edei whispered. "It looks like the *air* is red."

Forced to focus on the details of the eerie sight before her, Io realized he was right. The buildings weren't actually red, as she'd assumed a moment ago. Instead, there were little particles drifting in the air, infusing everything around her in a dark shade of scarlet.

Thunder rumbled above, and a vein of lightning cracked through the heavy clouds over Alante. Bianca and her gang looked unfazed; they marched on, rapping their knuckles and bars on whatever they could find, streetlights, closed storefronts, a trolley stopped dead between stations. Somewhere in the distance the tide bells were ringing every few minutes, the city's ominous warning to stay inside. It created a cacophony of storm and violence. No one noticed Edei and Io among the throng, invisible trespassers on the vivid memory. Edei pointed up ahead, where Bianca had stopped before a building.

"Come out, come out, wherever you are," Bianca sang up at the metal tide shutters that had been pulled over the front door. A machine groaned to life inside the building. The shutters lifted halfway, and a figure slipped out, fast and agile as a cat. Brown skin and gray curls, a widow dot between her eyes.

"Hello, Nalyssa," said Bianca with a smirk. "You know what I'm here for."

"You aren't getting him. He's under my protection."

"When did you decide to start taking in strays, Nalyssa? It certainly wasn't yesterday, or the day before that, when half the gangs in the Silts were banging on doors for help. How many dead bodies will I find on your safe haven's roof?"

The elder woman gritted her teeth. "We had to protect ourselves. Me and my people distill alcohol—we weren't prepared for warfare like you were."

"Warfare? Look at *my people's* faces." Bianca threw an arm around one of the youngest boys and pulled his head close to her own, almost in a headlock. He startled but amiably went along with it. "*Children.* The kids of the people that you and all these other cowards let die on your very roofs. The Silts are drenched in red, Nalyssa, and that blood is on your hands."

"I didn't kill them."

"You didn't save them, either." Bianca cocked her head in that predatory way. "I need him to end this. Consider this a loan. Whatever bargain you struck with him, I will pay you double to let me rent his services for a day."

"You aren't getting him, Bianca. Not unless you go through me first."

"Fine, then." And with an elegant swing of her iron bar, Bianca struck the woman once on the side of the head.

She went down like a rock. For a moment, the red particles around her bloomed, then began settling on her unconscious body, like the ashes of quiet embers. Bianca shouted up at the building, "There's no need for more bloodshed, people. Give him to me and I promise I won't rip this door to shreds and every one of you with it."

Thunder boomed overhead as if in answer: *Rip it, rip it, rip them.* It didn't take long for the people in the distillery to answer. Up came the shutters, and a man was pushed roughly through the narrow opening. He was hauled upright from the slick cobblestones by Bianca's people.

Io pulled on the Quilt—but nothing appeared. No threads of silver, no sources of light. This wasn't her dream. It was Bianca's, and it was through Bianca's eyes she was seeing this memory. Io couldn't alter or affect it in any way. Alarm shot through her veins. She had no control here, no way to get out if things got ugly.

And things were looking pretty ugly.

"Konstantin Fyodorov," Edei whispered, squinting at the man's round face and graying hair. The wraiths' first victim, a chernobog-born who worked as a border guard.

Bianca came close, pressing her iron bar to his chest. "Konstantin, dear, what took you so long? I require your assistance to end this."

"You don't need me," the man pleaded. "You and your people can manage it on your own."

"So thought all the other mob bosses that now lie dead on the roofs." Bianca tapped his jaw lightly with her knuckles. "No, if we're going to end this, we need your skills, Konstantin."

As a chernobog-born, a descendant of the Rossk twin gods of darkness and light, the man could set invisible borders around an area. Supposedly, if you attempted to cross a chernobog-born's border, your mind became hazy, your vision blurred, and a darkness enveloped you, leading you back into the marked area.

"Onward!" Bianca called like an unhinged maestro.

Her gang of teenagers obeyed, spilling down the street in the direction she had pointed, Fyodorov dragged between them. As they walked, Io began spotting evidence of the notorious carnage. Half-dried spots of blood on the streets and streetlights, abandoned pocketknives, bullet holes in the walls. On one of the arched bridges above, a body lay, limbs hanging into the void below.

Io whispered, "Has she ever told you about the Riots? Her part in them?"

Edei shook his head, never taking his eyes off Bianca. "Not once. She takes her vow of Roosters' Silence to the heart. But I've gathered bits and pieces. One of the gangs of the Silts began attacking the known outposts of their competitors; among the first targets was Bianca's smuggling business at the Modiano. Her people ran down the roofs of the Silts, screaming for help, but no one answered. It is said that the next morning, blood dripped from every roof and bridge. In the days that followed, the other gangs retaliated. An all-out turf war erupted, with dozens of casualties. The police tried to intervene early on, but after losing some of their people, they withdrew their forces.

"That's when the Order of the Furies was called in, but even the fury-born couldn't stop the carnage. The last three days of the Riots, no one dared come out of their apartments, even up on the Hill. They were sitting ducks, waiting for the rogue gang to attack every night. So Bianca gathered a few volunteers and went after the gang. By noon that same day, she was ruling the Silts."

Io gave a stiff nod, glancing at the heavily overcast sky. How close were they to noon? This was obviously the last, bloody morning Edei had described.

"Minos!" Bianca yelled to a man waiting on the corner of Parsley Square.

The older man, barely Io's height but built like a bull, approached Bianca. His graying brows were a strict line above his small eyes. A gun bulged at the inside pocket of his jacket.

Edei frowned. "That's Minos Petropoulos." The wraiths' second victim, a dioscuri-born.

"Have you tracked them?" Bianca asked.

"Yes, boss," Minos spat, unthreatened by the blood dripping from Bianca's iron bar. "A new battle has broken out at the school. Did you get the chernobog-born?"

Bianca's hand fluttered in Fyodorov's direction. "Is Jarl in place?"

First Fyodorov, then Minos, now Jarl Magnussen.

Minos nodded. "He's got the Mayor under his thrall. He made him issue an inter-district curfew a few minutes ago."

That explained the frequency of the warning bells. Slowly, Io was getting a grasp of Bianca's plan: Minos was needed to track the rogue gang's pathway. Konstantin Fyodorov, an unregistered chernobog-born, was likely needed to keep the rogue gang trapped at the spot where Bianca intended to make her last stand. Jarl, a grace-born, had enchanted the Mayor to keep people safe in their homes today. It was a clever plan, which Io had expected from the future mob queen, but also surprisingly protective of the innocent of the Silts.

"Minos, Fyodorov, Jarl," Edei said. "Three out of four victims, here in the Silts, twelve years ago, on the last day of the Moonset Riots."

Io felt her mind spinning faster and faster. "And we know Horatio was involved in the Riots, even if just tangentially, hired by the Nine to kill the wraiths when some of them were just children. They are all involved."

Bianca Rossi and her accomplices were at the epicenter, the fabricators of this end to the great carnage. But who was the bloodthirsty rogue gang they were banding up against? In all the recollections of the Riots that Io had heard, even in the history books, the rogue gang was a mystery, faceless and nameless. Roosters' Silence had the district in a choke hold; none of the thirty or so people here, none of the other gangs, had ever spoken of the rogue gang's identity. Even now, twelve years later, their names remained a secret.

Io could feel it in her veins: the knot of all the clues she had gathered was unspooling. She would finally know the beginning of the tale.

The mob climbed a flood-escape ladder to the roofs of Chamomile Avenue, heading toward the school. In front of her, Edei was silent, lips pursed, face ashen. Thunder rumbled in quick succession, and the sky seemed to crack open like an egg, rain pouring in thick droplets. In seconds, Io's hair was drenched, her spectacles a kaleidoscope of drops, the railing slippery beneath her fingers. They walked for a long time, passing through the various neighborhoods of the Silts. People would appear on flood-escape ladders or wait on bridges to join Bianca, knuckles and iron bars held tightly in their fists. But when they were almost at the school, Io noticed a change.

The rain was coming down red as blood. Scarlet was slathered on her, her jacket, her cheeks, her fingers.

"What is this?" she whispered, opening her palm to cup the red rain.

Edei's fingers reached back for her, pressing against her stomach. "Io, wait, don't look—"

His warning came too late. Io had already lifted her eyes—across a thick bridge stretched the rooftop of the school, the way paved with dead bodies. Dozens, more than she could possibly count, in various unnatural positions. One was so close Io could see the blood trickling from its unmoving lips.

And there they were, on the rooftop across the bridge: the rogue gang. Io couldn't decipher faces and forms through the heavy scarlet rain, only a great amalgamation of bodies lunging at each other, limbs wrestling, gunshots and screams. Some of them were fury-born, that much Io could discern by the leviathan-scale vests they wore. Some must have been the rogue gang, clothes cheap and torn, wielding guns in their hands.

Up ahead, Bianca tossed Fyodorov on the cement. "Put the area around the school on lockdown. I want a radius of a hundred feet. No one comes in, no one comes out."

The chernobog-born placed his palms on the wet roof, lower lip trembling. "It's done," he said after a minute. "No one will be able to cross my borders."

"Good." Bianca's blond hair was welded on her cheeks, the iron bar held loosely. She didn't look like a predator or a queen, but a young woman cowed by so much violence. Her chest heaved up and down as she tried to speak.

"When we join the fray," she called out to the sixty or so people around her, "we give it our all. We end this today, no matter what it costs. Yes?"

They answered in a determined chorus. "Yes, boss!"

Bianca turned her glassed gaze to the bridge. Someone had broken off from the battle ahead and was walking leisurely toward them. A middle-aged woman came to a stop at the middle of the bridge. Io wiped her spectacles with her sleeve, but still she could make out nothing but the woman's shape: disheveled hair, torn clothes, bare arms streaked with open wounds.

"Have you come to stop us, girl?" the woman crowed over the rainfall.

"You are trapped," Bianca yelled back. "Drop your weapons and surrender."

Weapons? The woman held none that Io could see. She said, "Or what?"

The question threw Bianca off; no answer came.

The rogue gang's leader began to walk, body bent at the waist. "You have done nothing wrong yet. But the moment you raise your iron bars against us, your fate is sealed. Turn around and leave, and you will all live another day."

Close to Io, a pair of sisters with white-blond hair glanced at each other, eyes wide. Others in Bianca's group were getting anxious, too. The younger sister took a step back, but Bianca raised a hand in her direction, palm up, still looking straight at the woman.

"For days," Bianca told the leader, "we have hoped your rage would stop. But it won't. Not unless we end this slaughter ourselves."

"Slaughter?" the leader said. "Oh, no, girl. This is your penance."

Bianca responded with a soft exhale.

Io knew what would follow. She had seen Bianca do it before: decide violence on the spot, without hesitation.

"Kill her," Bianca ordered. "Kill every last one of them."

# CHAPTER XXX

# DYING SOLDIERS

**THE YOUNG PEOPLE** around Io let out a unified war cry. They raised iron bars, gripped knives, unholstered guns, and ran across the roof. The great mass of Bianca's mob swept Io in their midst, bodies closing around her, screams of fury echoing in her ears. She was shorter than most of them; for a moment, she lost her bearings. Rage and violence pressed all around her, elbows and iron bars, the sharp stink of sweat and gunpowder.

Then an arm around her waist, pulling her into his side. Edei paved a way through the bodies for them, managing to tear away from the mob just as it reached the rogue gang leader on the bridge. The woman took out the first boy who attacked her with a sweep of her arm, but they were far too many for her—they overwhelmed her within seconds, the smaller ones sneaking past her while the bigger ones coordinated to take her down.

Three gunshots, the last one followed by a forlorn cry of pain.

Through the red hovering in midair, Io saw Bianca's group of teenagers cross the bridge in a gallop and collide with the rogue gang and the fury-born on the rooftop of the school. They became a sea of bodies, rising and falling in angry waves, iron bars frothing white with every crack of thunder above.

"You were right," said Edei. He and Io stood at the foot of the bridge, surveying the crush of limbs before them. She was still tucked close to his side, his arm clasped tight around her shoulder. "It all had to do with the Riots. The victims were all involved in the carnage under the Moonset. The wraiths are taking vengeance on them."

"But who is guiding the wraiths?"

"It could be any one of these people: one of Bianca's disgruntled allies or former rivals, a member of the unnamed rogue gang."

"It could be Bianca herself," Io whispered. "She doesn't like liabilities; she told me that a few days ago. What if she decided to make sure the survivors of today's carnage never broke Roosters' Silence, never revealed all that happened during the Riots?"

Edei's gaze flickered from fight to fight. "But why now? It has been twelve years. What's so special about now?"

The storm of red plumed over the eastern corner of the rooftop. Three bodies stripped away from the throng: a stout man back-tracking, hands on his neck; a woman in dark skin-tight clothes stalking after him; and—Bianca Rossi. The mob queen of the Silts raised a pistol to the back of the unsuspecting woman's head and fired. Blood and skull and brains spattered, and the woman toppled on the roof. Bianca went to the short man, who had collapsed against the side of the building, head lolling on his shoulder. She raised two fingers to the pulse at his neck and bowed her head in devastation when she found none.

"That's Hellas," said Edei. A deep frown carved into his features. "He's the mob king Bianca supposedly killed today and took over the Silts in his stead."

But it looked like Bianca had tried to save him.

Two white-blond heads caught Io's eye. It was the two sisters she had spotted earlier. The younger was hoisting the elder up by the armpits, dragging her toward the bridge, which was the only way to escape the battle on the roof. The elder was hurt, a deep gash on her forehead pouring blood across her face, her limbs heavy and weak.

"Isobel," the younger girl was crying. "Open your eyes—stay with me."

The blood flowed thick and dark red, and Isobel's eyes became unfocused.

"*Isobel!*"

The cry drew Bianca's attention. She straightened from Hellas's lifeless body, her gaze behind the dark glasses locking on the two sisters trying to make their escape. The mob queen marched with torrential fury to the sisters, leaned closer, and took Isobel's face between her hands.

"It's not time for you yet," she whispered. "You've got some fight left in you."

And as the younger sobbed and the elder bled, the red mist that lingered all around them suddenly moved, like a chest heaving or a pot boiling over, and began to swirl in the air toward Isobel's graying face. It stormed into her, through her lips and nostrils, through the corners of her eyes and the curve of her ears—and disappeared.

For a breath, nothing happened. Then the girl's eyes opened, sharp and focused, and she rose to her elbows.

"Isobel, stay down," said the youngest.

"I'm fine," Isobel replied. There was no slur in her voice, no slowness in her movements as she stood and grabbed a discarded metal pipe from the roof. "C'mon, Nina. We've got to end this."

*Nina.* The name sparked Io's memory. She studied the girl's face: the white-blond hair, the round eyes, the thin eyebrows. She had seen her before. Twelve years in the future, she would be Jarl Magnussen's assistant, the very same woman Io had saved from Drina Savva in that empty apartment. Nina was involved in the Riots, too, just like every person the wraiths had targeted, but . . . she was the only one the wraiths had *not* tried to kill. Why?

Nina glanced at Bianca, almost shamefully, and followed Isobel as she lunged into battle. Her sister looked more determined and violent than ever, and all the while, her forehead bled, staining her shirt crimson. In the Quilt, Io knew, the girl's life-thread would be fraying, minutes away from dying.

*Fraying.* The word came unbidden and stopped Io in her tracks.

A fraying thread. Like the wraiths. Like the thread of the cormorant those triplets had toyed with—

Gods. Oh gods.

*Bianca Rossi was keres-born.*

The peculiar red mist that clouded the Silts, that coalesced over the carnage on the school rooftop, that had slipped into Isobel's mouth—Io could see it because Bianca could. It was a material manifestation of Bianca's keres-born powers, like a moira-born's Quilt or a fury-born's whip.

The Keres appeared in the ancient epics that survived the Collapse of the old world as the spirits presiding over violent deaths. They flew over battlefields, swooping down to rip out the hearts of wounded soldiers and carry their souls to the underworld. The reclusive people of the north city-nation of Jhorr had a similar myth: the Valkyries, fabled female warriors. Their descendants were feared as much as cutters or the phobos-born, and they were almost always unregistered.

Bianca Rossi, mob queen of the Silts, was a keres-born hiding in plain sight. She had ended the Riots with the help of Fyodorov's borders, Minos's tracking, Jarl's thrall, and her own, dark violence. She had raised an army of teenagers to slaughter the rogue gang that was terrorizing the Silts. And when that army began to fail, she started making dying soldiers out of them.

She started making *wraiths.*

In horror, Io watched as the girl marched back into battle. Dying from the inside out. Like Emmeline Segal and Drina Savva and Raina.

She gripped Edei's sweater and pulled him back. The words tore from her lips like a blade through sinew: "Edei, Bianca is keres-born!"

Bianca's head snapped to where Io and Edei stood across the bridge. "Who are you?"

Palms raised, Edei said, "We're here to help. We joined you a few minutes ago."

The young mob queen removed her glasses—her eyes blazed scarlet. She had been wearing dark glasses that day to hide the keres-born powers mirrored in her irises.

"No you didn't. I know your faces." Her red gaze traveled to the rooftops around them, the fight breaking out on the bridge. "You're not supposed to be here."

*It's a dream*, Io thought in terror. *So wake up. Wake up, Io!*

But she had no control here. This was Bianca's world, and this was the day she ascended to the throne of the Silts. There was no one more powerful than her, here, now.

Bianca's hand twirled like she was mixing an invisible drink. Immediately, the red mist around them began shifting, slowly at first, then faster and faster in rhythm with Bianca's fingers. It engulfed Io and Edei in a cocoon of red, like they were standing in the eye of a hurricane. Through tears in the wall of red, Io caught a glimpse of Bianca Rossi crossing the bridge toward them.

"You dare invade my dreams? You dare force me into this wretched memory?" Bianca screamed from somewhere in front of them. "Who the hell do you think you are?"

She sounded close, too close—

A hand came out of the red mist and punched Io straight in the stomach. Io doubled over in pain, bile rising up her throat. She reached for the Quilt, the threads, *anything*, but her hands grasped only air. Bianca appeared through the wall of mist. Edei reached for Io—

"Don't move, Edei," snapped Bianca. He stopped midstep, eyes terrified. Lip curled, Bianca raked Edei up and down. "*Hire her,* you told me. *I can't solve this without her.* I knew *she* wasn't to be trusted, but you? I could never have believed I was nursing a viper in my own bosom."

"Is that all you have to say, *boss*?" His voice was dipped in sarcasm.

"What else would you like, Edei?" Bianca barked. "Eight days of slaughter, of sleepless nights by the door, listening to people shriek in pain. Eight days of fighting and losing, eight days of endless death. Someone had to take action, and no one was brave enough but me."

"Is that what you call sending injured fifteen-year-olds back to a fight they have no chance of surviving? Bravery?"

"I did what I had to."

*You did what you had to*, Rosa had said. It was the exact same excuse Io had used to justify sending Thais away.

"Tell me," Edei said, shoulders shaking with constrained rage. "Have you ever used your powers on us? When we go out, to deliver your punishments and defend your turf and risk our lives for you, did you ever force one of us to sacrifice their life for you?"

"Oh, darling," Bianca mocked. "I'm not to blame for your morals. My powers are not coercion—that's the grace-born. Isobel was already devoted to our cause. I just gave her another chance to prove it. Time, that's all I do. I buy them time."

For a moment, Edei was deathly silent. "That sounds like a *yes* to me, Bianca. Do you know how many of our people I've buried, Bianca? How many were your fault?"

Bianca's jaw flexed. "You and your cutter think you're so noble, knights in shining armor. You think you can go through life without compromising your high morals, but I've lived through the worst this city can throw at you, and let me tell you, Edei: sooner or later, you will need to cast off your morals and fight with your damned fists."

Then, with no warning whatsoever, Bianca tossed her hand at Edei, and the red mist swallowed him out of Io's sight.

"Edei!" Io screamed.

All around her, the blood picked up speed, hiding everything else from sight. And Io felt, in her chest, something *ripping*. Like a ship's sail against a gale or a page snatched from a book. Like a life-thread severing.

"I told you, little cutter," Bianca hissed, "what happens to crowing roosters."

Their larynxes torn out to hang like a chicken's wattle.

Desperately, Io swiped at Bianca with a fist, but the woman was faster. Bianca maneuvered her arms behind her back; the red plumed brighter, coming for Io's face. Io felt—Io knew—this was it. Bianca would force that blood-red wind inside her lungs and use her as a serrated knife. Was this how the wraiths had been made? Death poured in their chests, little by little, until they screamed for release? Their remnants manipulated like the strings of a puppet to do Bianca's bidding? Bianca's killing?

The particles sneaked into Io's nostrils, her mouth, her eyes.

A freezing cold, a hand on her cheek, a scream—Io was jerked awake.

The giant, round bed was drenched. Drops lingered on Io's skin and hair as she came upright, gasping for air. Her robe had opened, the wet nightgown sticking to her chest. Rosa was standing over the bed, a pitcher hanging empty in one hand.

The moment she noticed Io's eyes were open, she breathed a sigh of relief, dragged Io up, and backed them both against the wall. Her eyes bulged with fear.

Room number eight of the Mister Hypnos dream palace was in chaos. Officers were coming in, pointing their guns at Io and Rosa first, then at the struggling bodies on the bed. Three figures wrestled on the silk coverlets: Edei, Bianca, and . . . Aris Lefteriou.

Next to Io, her friend was shaking uncontrollably. "Rosa, are you all right?"

"He—gods." Rosa was trembling. "He barged in, forced me to put him in Bianca's dream. I don't know what you guys were seeing, but moments after he joined you, you all started convulsing, eyes rolling back. I couldn't wake you. I had to—"

She raised the pitcher. She had to jolt them awake with the freezing water.

"Lefteriou woke first and gave out some call. I guess the other cops must have been waiting in the corridor outside the room, because next thing I knew they were breaking down the door and—shit!"

Io glimpsed the shimmer of a gun raised to the ceiling. A shot followed, cracking through their skulls. Everyone in the room froze, Edei and Aris and Bianca in a tangled mess on the bed.

At the door stood Luc Saint-Yves, his arm still raised. A lit cigar hung from his mouth, curling smoke into the room.

The Police Commissioner's gaze slid to Io. "We had an inkling you might be planning something, dear sister-in-law, so we sent Aris to follow you. I hope you don't mind. It looks like we arrived just in time."

He leveled the gun at Bianca's head. "Arrest her."

The officers sprang into action, removing Edei and Aris Lefteriou from the bed and forcing Bianca's arms behind her back. She had stopped struggling the moment Saint-Yves burst through the door; she kept her chin up and her legs steady as the leeches led her out of the room. Io found herself wishing the woman would look at her, with defeat or remorse or even hatred.

But Bianca Rossi was a queen to her fall.

# PART III

## ONE TO CUT

# CHAPTER XXXI

# AN EXPOSÉ

**THE WORLD WAS** bouncing. Io forced her sleepy lids apart: on the pillow next to her lay Thais, head propped on her arm, still bobbing from having jumped on the bed. "Wake up, little idiot. It's past noon. Don't you want to be awake on the most glorious day Alante has ever seen?"

Io rolled to face the narrow window. All she saw was gray. "It's smoggy."

"This glory is not weather related. Look!" Thais waved newspapers and glossy magazines in front of Io's face and began reading the headlines. *"Rossi Revealed as Keres-Born: Details on Her Arrest. Mob Queen of the Silts? Luc Doesn't Think So. Liberator of the Silts Today, Mayor Tomorrow!* And here's the one by our very own, newly minted senior writer of *The Truth of Alante,* and my personal favorite: *The Keres-Born Conspiracy: An Exposé on Bianca Rossi's Part in the Moonset Riots.*"

A smile spread on Io's lips. Gods, she had forgotten how Thais's happiness felt. A firework of light and warmth ricocheting off everything around her. Io rubbed the sleep from her eyes. Amos's spare room was a disaster: Io's clothes shed by the door, towels and disinfectant on the carpet. Her side hurt as Io stretched, but the pain was simple fatigue, nothing like before Samiya fixed her bruised ribs. She pulled an unidentifiable sweater over her head and shuffled to the bathroom.

In the mirror, Thais's reflection lingered over her shoulder as Io brushed her teeth. Her smart suede coat and black leather boots were at odds with the mess of the apartment, like a racehorse in a pigsty. But her body was relaxed, leaning against the doorframe as if there was no place she'd rather be. "Amos made chocolate babka. And there's fresh coffee."

Io gave her sister a frothy toothpaste-filled smile through the mirror. At Thais's "Ew," she spat the toothpaste in the sink and rinsed, chuckling all the while. Such a squeamish baby, her sister.

Voices came from downstairs, but none of the jazzy music Amos usually put on. Io walked down the stairs with Thais to find the sitting area cloaked in darkness; the shutters were down, the lights off, and Ava, Amos, and Edei sat around a table lit by a single candle. Io glanced at the bolted door. It wasn't tide time yet—it had clearly been *day* when she glanced out the window upstairs. Sometimes, the city officials imposed a curfew on smog-heavy days, but then the warning bells would be going off every fifteen minutes. So what was going on?

Ava was sitting a little apart from the others, arms crossed over her chest, head leaning against the window. Misery emanated from her. Right. This detail got lost in the chaos of last night's revelations: Ava was sleeping with Bianca Rossi. *Stay,* Bianca had told Ava at the Fortuna. But Ava had chosen her sisters, one soul split in three bodies and all that. Io couldn't help the twinge of guilt she felt regarding Bianca's arrest; Ava must be devastated.

She slipped into an empty seat next to Edei, trying to catch Ava's eyes, but her sister appeared to be ignoring her. Gods, she couldn't really be angry at Io, could she?

"Hey," Edei said. His face split into a tired smile. He was wearing a black sweater and had puffy circles under his eyes, as though he had barely slept last night on Amos's couch, where he had crashed.

"Hey." Her heart did a little backflip in her chest. Her palms were legitimately sweating, like she was in a romance novel. She was all too aware that she had bedhead and her sweater was one of Amos's, gigantic and a fuzzy orange, also known as the least flattering color on earth.

"Coffee?" Without waiting for an answer, he poured her a cup from the kettle at the center of the table and placed a slice of babka on the saucer.

"So . . ." Thais said coyly, and, to Io's mortification, wiggled a finger between her and Edei. "When did *this* happen?"

Io wished the ground would open and swallow her. Or rather, she wished to be Rosa. One touch and *bam!* Thais would faint headfirst into the pastries. Another and *bam!* Edei's drooling on his shoulder. It'd make her escape so much less trouble.

She hastened to answer, "You've got the wrong idea, we're just working together, Edei has a girlfriend, Samiya, you might have met her at one of the Initiative meetups." It all came out in a breathless rush.

After a beat, Edei replied, sounding a little confused, "I don't have a girlfriend."

What? That was all Io could think. *What?*

"I mean, um," he continued, "Samiya used to be my girlfriend. But she's not anymore. For almost a year now."

The table was deathly silent.

Then, thankfully, Ava spoke from the window. "But you live together."

He squirmed, like the very act of speaking pained him. "Yeah, we decided it'd be a good temporary solution until Samiya gets her resident status. She's not allowed to lease a place on her own yet. She's been dating another doctor for a few months now. That was him, at the rally," he told Io, and she recalled how acutely uncomfortable he had been. "I thought people knew."

"People didn't know," Ava said.

"I'm so sorry," Thais said, hand over her heart. "You two make a good team, and, obviously, I misunderstood."

Dear gods, this was awkward. Io could sense everyone gazing at her: Thais and Ava, who knew about the fate-thread; Amos, who thought Edei liked her; Edei, who . . . was expecting some kind of answer from her?

She made herself nod. "No worries, Thais. We do make a good team."

Edei stuffed a pastry into his mouth. Ava glared daggers at Io, disapproval in her gaze. Thais reached for the kettle, and Amos brought their cup to their lips, their face tinted pink. Io felt embarrassed down to her very core, as though her insides were in knots and her skin was on fire.

"Why are the tide shutters down?" she asked into the silence.

Amos sighed heavily. "The general store down the street was looted a few hours ago. There are rumors outlier gangs are organizing a raid on Bianca's businesses. I had no affiliation with the mob queen, but I'm not taking any chances in this climate."

"The Fortuna has retrieved its bridges and fortified with weapons. They wouldn't let me in, but the rest of the gang are safe inside." Edei said this in a neutral tone, but the statement jarred Io. They hadn't let him in, because of his role in Bianca's arrest? But that was absurd—their boss was literally using her powers to make bloodthirsty warriors out of dying people.

"That's horrific," Thais said. "Haven't the police patrols been alerted?"

Ava let out a sardonic huff of air. "The police don't care about the Silts, Thais. You know that."

"Luc does," Thais countered. "He's been at the Plaza all night, setting up squads in key positions in the Silts, scouting candidates to take temporary control of the district, contacting other mob bosses to strike a deal. He anticipated a rough transition when the mob queen was exposed."

"Have you been gone so long you've forgotten who the mob queen is to the Silts?" Ava said. "A freaking hero. The transition won't be rough—it'll be catastrophic."

"She sent teenagers to their death to win the Riots." Thais arched her eyebrow. "Surely that changes things."

"In their eyes, she *saved* them from the carnage of the Riots, when even the fury-born couldn't," Ava said. "Whatever sacrifices she had to make are deemed necessary, not immoral."

*A necessary evil*, just like Edei had claimed.

"Ava's right," he said quietly now. "Even when I told Nico and Chimdi that Bianca has been using her keres-born powers on our members, they dismissed it. She's done good for so many that the story on the streets is that the up-Hill politician is exploiting Bianca to win the elections."

"Nonsense. Luc was perfectly willing to work with her before he knew about her part in the Riots," Thais said, her words short and clipped.

She was getting worked up, which was never a good sign. Over the years, Io had developed several ways to defuse this growing tension: change the subject, pay Thais a compliment, or just agree with whatever Thais was saying.

But this time, for some reason, Io didn't feel like defusing: she riffled through the newspapers on the table and said, "Wait. Why are we only talking about the Riots? Isn't the news reporting on her part in the Silts Stranglings? If people knew she had been killing her own people, turning innocent women into wraiths, they'd feel differently. Why hasn't Saint-Yves put the murders in the news?"

Thais settled back in her chair, crossing one impeccably shiny boot over another, and answered, "Because she hasn't confessed. She maintains her innocence. Luc says there isn't enough evidence to convict her—*yet*," Thais added when she saw Io's alarmed expression. "He will find it, Io. He will never let Bianca get away with it."

"Bianca didn't confess?"

"She has an alibi for the entire time the wraiths were active in the Silts," Ava said fiercely. "She is never alone—when she wasn't with the gang, she was with *me*."

Instinctually, Io turned to look at Edei. Found him gazing back at her. "It's true," he said. "I asked the rest of the gang."

"They could be covering for her—"

"*She didn't do this*," snapped Ava. "Ever since that woman attacked her in her office, she hasn't been able to sleep at night. She's been terrified."

Io and Edei held each other's gaze. Bianca had the power to turn the women into bloodthirsty wraiths. She had reason to want the victims dead—to guarantee their silence on the Riots. Except Horatio Long: she had no knowledge of his part in the Riots, as far as Io and Edei knew. And the second wraith, Drina Savva, had attempted to kill her. Edei was right: If she wanted her collaborators dead, why act now, twelve years later? And why turn the women into wraiths? Why *these* women in particular, who the Nine had claimed would be dangerous during the Riots?

Could they have made a mistake? Was Bianca innocent?

"What are you thinking?" asked Edei.

Distantly, she was aware of the others watching, but her focus was single-minded on Edei. They had started this journey together, following clue after clue, making connections, unearthing unimaginable truths. Where her thoughts lagged, his restarted, and vice versa.

They made for a better team than Io would have ever guessed, a perfect combination of instinct and contemplation, impulse and precision.

"Remember the younger sister, in Bianca's dream?" Io asked. "Nina?"

He nodded.

"I've met her before—five days ago."

His brow shaded, as he caught Io's meaning: *five days ago, when Drina Savva killed Jarl Magnussen.* "Should we follow up with her?" he asked.

"I think we must," Io whispered. "We've missed something."

Ava's chair scraped against the tiled floor, making all of them startle. Her sister was standing over them, her gaze hard. "You think," she said flatly, "that you've *missed* something? While Bianca rots in a cell?"

Silence reverberated in the café, smothering the breath out of Io's lungs.

"Or I could go to the Nine," Io offered, although she'd rather take the butter knife and stab her own eye. The image blazed in her mind: her own face, her own hand holding a thread, and the world burning behind her. She had cut a thread yesterday, Raina's. What if the prophesized end of the world was the unrest that had started with Bianca's arrest?

Edei hissed, "We're never going back to that House."

"What happened there?" Thais asked quietly.

"They were manipulating us from the moment we stepped inside," answered Edei. "They tried to pin some wild apocalyptic theory their artists produced on Io."

"What theory?" said Thais.

In reply, Io shook her head. How could she voice what she herself didn't know? "I can strike a deal with them, Edei. Give them what they want in exchange for having their artists conjure Bianca's past."

"If you give them what they want, Io," Edei said softly, "they will destroy you."

"Oh, sister mine." Thais's face melted in a soft, almost sad smile. She leaned over the table and cupped Io's cheek, then did the same to Ava's. "You would do anything for Ava, wouldn't you?"

What a strange thing to say—of course she would. One soul in three bodies, right? But it wasn't just about helping Ava and her girl-friend. It was about justice for these women who had been mutated and manipulated, who had died untimely deaths—two of them at Io's hand—who no one else seemed to care about.

Io massaged the back of her neck. Gods, she was tired. Days and days of nonstop gallivanting up and down Alante and all she had to show for it was a solution as leaky as a basement in the Silts.

"If we had a little more time at Mister Hypnos," she lamented, "we could have explored more of Bianca's past. When she created the wraiths and how. We would have our evidence."

"Yeah." Ava aggressively tapped the newspapers on the table with a finger. "Strange that Bianca was arrested the day before the elections, isn't it? Strange that it was publicized on election morn-ing, even though it's an ongoing investigation, right? Strange that it's ensured Saint-Yves a thirty-point margin in the exit polls. One would say it's almost convenient."

Thais ground her teeth. "Excuse me—*convenient*? What exactly are you insinuating, Ava?"

"Not insinuating. I'm stating the obvious. Her arrest has secured Saint-Yves's win. I hope it was worth the chaos that is about to ensue. Because this"—Ava flicked the shutters behind her, where Io could hear distant shouts and what sounded like gunshots—"is just the beginning, Thais."

Io's body tensed for an outburst, but all Thais gave Ava was a dismissing roll of the eyes. "I'm sorry your girlfriend's a murdering liar, Ava. And I'm sorry your home is inhabited by self-serving criminals who refuse to see the truth."

Ava's face dissolved in defeat. "You used to love Alante more fiercely than any of us."

Thais shrugged, the cold gesture of an ice statue. "That thread frayed a long time ago."

Io froze. Her mind conjured the memory of her own fingers over Thais's home-thread, snipping at it, little by little, every night, until it finally snapped. She felt Edei's gaze on her, then his arm lying softly on the back of her chair. It was a small comfort, that he knew, that he didn't blame her, but wasn't nearly enough. Gods, if Thais found out, if *Ava* found out what Io had done . . .

"I didn't think you were still naive enough to confuse love for loyalty, sister mine," Thais told Ava. "The two are nothing alike."

Ava's gaze dropped to the floor.

Io thought the old embers had died, but here was her fury again, an absolute inferno. "Don't talk to her like that," Io snapped. "Your fiancé found an opportunity and seized it with no thoughts spared for the consequences it would have on the Silts. Stop trying to hurt Ava because she disagrees with you."

Thais pursed her lips, that expression Io knew too well: the snarl of a big cat before it pounced. "Since when do you care about the Silts, Io? Aren't you the one that's made a career out of cutting their less wholesome threads like some almighty judge and executioner?"

Io should just drop it. If it had been two years ago, she would have. Bowed and conceded in this duel of words. But there was something about this interaction that felt imperative. She had to stay and talk and prove herself. She could see things clearly for the first time: Thais on top, Ava in the middle, Io on the bottom. But this wasn't how sisterhood was supposed to be.

"What has that got to do with how you talked to Ava?" Io asked, voice rising. Because that was the gist of it, wasn't it? Thais had tried to hurt both her and Ava by deflecting the conversation to their perceived flaws. "Or Bianca's arrest, for that matter? Isn't the issue here that you're defending an opportunist that leaked information to the news to get himself elected Mayor?"

In a cavalier fashion, Thais said, "All right then, Miss Brilliant Detective. If it's answers you want, far be it from me to stand in your way. Go check that loose end you think you've missed. Then you're welcome to take your findings to Luc, or even interrogate Bianca yourself if you like. Say your name at the City Plaza and they'll let you right in—the proper way this time, ey? I already petitioned for you to receive an official job offer from the Initiative. Let's see if you can get the results my *opportunist fiancé* couldn't."

Thais's punishments were always like that: subtle. Shaped as a surrender, dressed as assistance. In truth they were a challenge you would fail, again and again, until you learned to forfeit from the get-go. And that was your lesson: you were a coward.

But Io was done with shame—*done*. She stood up, in her frizzy hair and mismatched socks and the horrid orange sweater that fell almost to her knees. She felt like a hero from the epics, the wind against her hair, the sun glittering on her armor, tall and strong on her white horse atop the hill.

"You know what?" she said. "I think I will take you up on that."

Thais huffed through her nose like she was amused, and she *looked* amused, in a gentle, older-sisterly way. Her gaze was measuring Io up and down, as if she could read every grand thought of defiance in Io's mind.

"You do that," Thais said, not unkindly.

Io ignored her and turned to Edei. "Care to join me, partner?"

# CHAPTER XXXII

# YOUR PENANCE

**A HEAVY, ALMOST** liquid smog had gripped Alante in a choke hold. The city was curtailed to the cobblestones beneath Io's boots, the slithering bodies of streetlights and trolley support beams, the shadowed figures of passersby. The smog gobbled the sunlight and narrowed the roar of trolleys passing overhead. Io didn't mind the rain and the wind, didn't mind the horrid humidity of the summer, but she had always found this grayness downright asphyxiating. Before the dams were laid out in the surrounding plains, Alante was swathed in smog almost every single day, especially its lowest districts. Io didn't know how people had borne it.

"So, this woman from Bianca's dream, Nina," Edei asked, coming down the steps of the café. "You've met her before?"

"She was Jarl Magnussen's mistress—she was in the apartment when the wraith killed him. I thought she was in the wrong place at the wrong time, but the wraith talked to her. She told her—" Io paused, trying to remember the exact words. *"I cannot punish you. Your crimes are not truly yours."*

"Mm-hmm," Edei mumbled skeptically. "Nina also fought in the Riots, like the other victims. It feels like there's some connection that we're missing."

"Exactly," Io agreed. She had changed into one of Ava's cropped sweaters and her own dirty cargo pants, grabbed a scarf off the rack by the door, and wrapped it tight around her mouth and nose. It smelled strongly of cologne, which was just as well. She had no time for the killer of a headache that this kind of smoggy atmosphere could cause. "If I can recall correctly, Nina lives in the big complex on Chamomile Street."

They climbed the stairs to the North Walkway slowly, one step at a time, gripping the rail like old men, smog curling around their ankles. An outlier gang barely past childhood had boarded up the entrance to the Walkway with pieces of wood.

Edei unfolded to his full height and gestured at the kids with his brass-knuckled hand. His own scarf was wound tightly around his face; he looked like a bandit from a Wastelands adventure novel.

"Move," he ordered.

The kids hesitated only for a second, then scrambled to clear a path between the wood. As Io passed by, she could see the tolls they had already collected: coins, packets of cigarettes, a silk handkerchief.

"Shouldn't your gang be out here," Io asked, "safekeeping Bianca's queendom?"

"They're terrified. The Fortuna gang was supposed to be untouchable, and now our leader is locked in the Plaza."

"Will Nico and Chimdi be safe in the club?"

"That place is a fortress. But listen, Io. Ava is right. We need to find proof that Bianca orchestrated the Silts Stranglings. It's disgusting what she did to her fighters during the Riots, but to the general population, she ended the butchering of their friends and family. If we don't show them Bianca is evil, truly evil, they will try to save her. Break her out of the Plaza and get her safely out of Alante. And believe me when I tell you: they *will* succeed."

Io considered him. "They're already planning it, aren't they? That's why the gang locked themselves in the Fortuna."

"Yes."

They settled into silence, each lost in their own thoughts, and a few minutes later, the North Walkway came to an end in a downward arc. Under normal circumstances, the Walkway offered a brilliant view of the big apartment complex at Chamomile Street, a square building with a rare private courtyard in the middle of it. Right now, however, it was swallowed in smog, nothing but an eerie outline, like a castle out of a horror story.

"Panagou," Io said as Edei scanned the resident names by the double doors.

"Third floor, apartment six."

The door grumbled like an old man's death rattle when they pushed on it. They found a pile of furniture behind it; someone had tried to barricade it with whatever they could get their hands on. A stagnant silence followed them up the stairs to the third floor. No peep of living creatures, human or rodent, no garlic sizzling on the pan or babies fussing in their cribs. The Silts had truly holed up in their homes in terror.

When they reached apartment six, Edei knocked twice and stepped back, like he had when he appeared in Io's door a few nights ago.

Moments passed. Io slipped on her spectacles and called forth the Quilt. Light cast away the smog, illuming Alante in the silver threads of fate. There were around a hundred life-threads shooting up to the sky in the building, and a small bundle of threads in the apartment. Io stepped around Edei and knocked again.

"Hello?" she asked. "Is Nina here? I'm the private detective from the other night. I have some questions for her."

A voice came through the door, childish and uncertain. A young boy, Nina's son perhaps. "She went to get supplies." There was some shuffling behind the door, then a whispered "I'm not allowed to open the door when she's not here."

"Is it okay if we wait for her?" Io said gently. "We need to talk to her about something very important."

The boy hesitated. "I'm not opening the door."

"That's fine," she said with a smile. Nina had schooled him well. "We can wait out here."

His steps receded; Io joined Edei where he was leaning against the balustrade of the third floor. He gave her an appraising look.

"What?" Io said, feeling self-conscious.

"Are the glasses because of the Quilt?"

"Um, not really." She smoothed the scarf beneath the ridge of her spectacles. "I've been farsighted since I was a kid. The Quilt doesn't have side effects like that."

"What side effects *does* it have?"

"Well, when we were younger, my sisters and I had this competition where we tested who can see furthest on the Quilt. We were on it for hours, naming threads across the city. One time, we stopped, and I started bleeding from my ears, my nose, my eyes—"

"Your *eyes?*" he asked, sounding horrified.

"Yeah, it was terrible."

"So you almost stargazed to death?"

Io dropped the Quilt to stare at him. His lips were fighting a grin. Was he teasing? *He was.* "Not exactly."

He went on as if he hadn't heard her, with his infuriating smile and his infuriatingly mischievous tone. "*Young Cutter Meets Her End While Stargazing.* Now that's a gripping headline."

"There was no stargazing involved!"

"You should introduce yourself like that. Io Ora, private detective, extreme stargazing enthusiast."

"Will you stop?" She was glad for the scarf; her cheeks blazed. "It was serious."

"I mean, obviously." He pantomimed blood spouting from his eyes.

She shook her head, grinning like an idiot.

Edei crossed his arms over his chest, echoing her grin. "Admit it, boss. We're getting better. That was some solid joking."

Laughter broke out of her. "Yes, it was."

She settled next to him, their shoulders lined up. A moment passed, then another, and Io started relaxing against him, her side folding into his heat.

"What does it feel like?" he asked quietly. "Holding a thread?"

"Soft, but also strong. Like a metal wire wrapped in silk." She opened her palm to him. "Want me to try to show you? Some people that have diluted moira-born blood can feel the threads, sort of, but can't see or manipulate them."

"I doubt I have any moira-born blood," he said, but he had already placed his hand in her palm.

The Quilt blossomed around Io. She took his thumb and index finger and placed them right around the brightest, strongest thread she had: the fate-thread they shared. "Do you feel anything?" she asked, looking up at him.

Gods, he was beautiful. The diffuse light of the courtyard painted him in melancholy tones. His perfect, straight nose, the little nicks on his jaw and cheeks. His eyes were half-closed, his brow relaxed, his legs crossed at the ankles, body turned slightly to her. Her hip sloped into his side, her thigh pressing against his. He was so close she could smell him and see the stubble on his jaw and count the freckles on his nose. And his lips: full and rosy and—

Io lowered the scarf from her face. His eyes went to her lips. Heat seared her core.

He was here. For so long, she had yearned for him, for so long she had avoided him. Even when she had finally met him, she kept her distance and he kept his, avoiding touch. But now he was right here, by her side, his warmth snuggled into hers. It had to mean something, right?

Io needed to know if it did. If he felt the same way. She was filled to the brim with love, bursting with it. And these last few days, with wraiths and gods, with fate and death, with Edei, Io finally felt ready to ask to be loved in return. She wanted to feel the touch of his lips, to kiss him, if only just once.

And so she did.

She placed a palm on his chest; his breath warmed the air; she closed the distance between them. His mouth tenderly caught hers, and when he teased her lips open, their tongues twisted and danced. Her fingers traced his jawline, his ear, the short hairs on the back of his neck. His arm came around her waist, smoothing her body against his chest. She breathed in his scent and listened to his small sounds and tasted his mouth, and she thought she might become undone. She felt wild and calm at the same time, her heart raging, her stomach in tatters.

And then he shifted, back and—impossibly—away.

Her lips, desperate for more, grazed the stubble on his jaw.

"Io, stop," he said. He cupped her shoulders and gently pushed her back. "It's not right, like this. It's not real."

She didn't immediately understand. She studied his face, the flushed lips, the hard brow, the wide eyes. He looked alert, intent.

"I'm sorry," she said quickly, her words devoid of emotion. "I misunderstood."

She pushed away from the rail.

Edei followed her, trying to get a look at her face. "Wait, Io. Let me explain."

Her mind was spinning with embarrassment and longing, but

she gathered herself up. "It's okay. I get it. Let's forget this happened, all right?"

"No, let's talk about this."

Talk about what? He didn't want her. Her fate-thread, her destiny, her *one day*, didn't want her. Gods. Her embarrassment turned sour, a black bile of shame rising from the back of her throat. *Her own fate-thread didn't want her.* For years, she had evaded him and now she knew him and loved him and kissed him—and he didn't want her. She should have been content with their partnership, their friendship, because clearly that was all the thread was, but she had grown greedy. And now things would be awkward again and she would lose the one person aside from Ava and Rosa who actually cared for her and it was all her fault and this guilt would drown her, *drown her* one day—

Io stopped. She slipped her fingers beneath her spectacles and pressed on her eyelids. Where the hell had these thoughts come from?

She had nothing to feel guilty for. The fate-thread wasn't her doing. Avoiding him was the wisest thing she could have done to protect herself. And falling for him: there should have been no guilt about that, only joy. A great sense of familiarity enveloped her. She was doing it again. She was ripping herself at the seams and stuffing her body with shame. But it was never hers, was it?

*I earned my home-thread. I prove my love of this city every day. What have you done to deserve this?*

*We Ora sisters don't kiss other people's boyfriends.*

*The right thing to do is cut the thread. Set him free.*

It was Thais's shame, the Ora legacy, and Io had to denounce it.

She let her hands fall to her sides. Edei had come around to stand before her in the corridor, rubbing his thumb.

"Why?" she asked him. "It seemed—I thought you felt the same way."

His mouth opened, closed, opened again. "How do you know it's real, Io? That it's not a by-product of the fate-thread?"

Io felt her breath lodge like shrapnel halfway in her chest. "You know about the fate-thread?"

But of course he did. It all made sense now: The way he watched her, was aware of her. The blush on his cheeks when he said he felt like he had known her a long time. Amos's observation. The passion with which he had argued against destiny and the pretense of choice. He knew about the thread. And he hated it.

His voice was startlingly clear, hyperfocused. "On my birthday last year, right after my breakup, my friends took me to a moira-born for a reading, as a joke. She told me of the fate-thread, told me what it means. It stuck in my head, this idea that there is a person out there that I'm destined to love, so about a month later, I paid her to show me who was on the other side of the thread. You were at Amos's, sitting at the counter, drinking coffee."

"Why didn't you talk to me?"

He lowered his eyes to his fidgeting feet. "You're moira-born. You must have known for years that we shared a fate-thread, and yet you never sought me out. I thought there must have been a reason for that, and I decided to respect it."

He believed she had rejected him. Her silence had made him feel inadequate.

"No, Edei—I never sought you out because I knew you were with someone. It wasn't right to . . . interfere."

"But why didn't you tell me four days ago, when we started working together? Even just now, you kissed me"—his face flushed—"but did you plan on telling me?"

The answer was dual: *No*, she wouldn't have, because the words were impossible, life changing, and terrified her. And *yes*, eventually she would have, because she wanted him to know at last what she felt.

Honesty: a foreign concept to Io, riddled with expectations and judgment. But this was the one relationship in her life that wasn't fraught with lies and secrets. This was Edei, and he was clever and kind and horrible at jokes, and he wouldn't criticize her, would he?

"I thought," she whispered, "that you would blame me."

His brow thickened. "Why? The fate-thread is not your doing."

"No, but I—didn't cut it."

His brow spasmed, an expression of alarm. "Do you *want* to cut it?"

"Isn't that the right thing? To cut it? So that you can truly have a choice?"

She watched him closely, every movement of his eyes, every line on his brow. His face morphed into something serious, and mournful. "I won't lie; I have thought about it a lot. That there's this thing I can't control. This destiny that I can't shake. Because . . . how can I ever be certain? This thing between us, what we feel, how can we know it's real and not a fabrication of fate?"

He quieted but for the rapid rise and fall of his chest. He truly wanted her answer.

But if Io had one, it was lost in the chaos of their admissions: he felt something for her. She had made her confession, that she didn't tell him about the fate-thread, that she didn't cut it. And he didn't blame her. He questioned all the things she did: about fate and choice, love and uncertainty, but he didn't blame *her*.

Her heart was exploding with relief. It was out. It was over. She had chosen to take a leap of faith, claim her fate-thread, and kiss him. She chose to risk her heart; if her heart ended up broken, then so be it. She was free now. To love. To get hurt. To stitch herself back together. To love again, without guilt, and, one day, be loved in return.

Io said, "I wish I could give you the answer you want. I wish I could tell you that what I feel came first, and not the fate-thread— but I don't know for certain. What I can tell you, with absolute clarity, is this: if I had the choice, I would still choose you. We are a good team, you and I, and we could be so much more."

She closed her eyes and let her sorrow ascend, a balloon loosed from a child's hand.

"But if this is not your choice, I will cut the thread," Io continued. "I mean it, Edei. I will cut the thread, and I will be your friend instead. Maybe not straightaway, but eventually. I don't know. But I do know that I will be fine."

And she would be, wouldn't she? She had been surviving loss all her life: her parents, her childhood, Thais. It would hurt and she would mourn, but she had thought this was her penance, and instead it felt like . . . freedom.

*This is your penance.*

Her thoughts paused. Her heartbeat spiked, her mind numbed by the echo of the past speaking back to her.

*Slaughter?* the rogue gang leader had said on the bridge. *Oh, no, girl. This is your penance.*

These past few days tumbled into Io's head, line after line after line.

*I will rise from the ashes a daughter of flame.* Drina Savva's words.

*Revenge is for the wicked. My purpose is justice. I am its servant, and it is mine. I'm neither crazy, nor dying. I am ascended.* Drina Savva.

*I was* made *to know your crimes. I don't deal in mercy. I deliver justice. I can see the taint of crime on you, too, sister.* Raina.

*There are crimes that cannot go unpunished.* Emmeline Segal, Drina Savva, Raina.

*I cannot punish you. Your crimes are not truly yours.* Drina again.

And from the Nine: *They are daughters of the night, chosen for their honor, made to whip vengeance into the backs of wicked men.*

Shit.

Oh shit.

She had to find Nina—*now.* She pulled up the Quilt around her and approached Nina's apartment. The boy—her son—was standing behind the door, probably nervously watching them through the peephole. A dozen threads sprouted from his chest, and one of them was brighter, vibrating toward the direction of the exit. His mother, most likely, nearing the apartment building.

Io shot off in an instant, Edei dashing after her. "Io," he called, "what's wrong?"

She had a theory, and if she was right about it, *everything* was wrong.

They were barely down the first flight of stairs when Nina rounded the corner, carrying bags with groceries on both shoulders. Her white-blond hair was pulled up in a messy bun, and her cheeks looked gaunt, as though she hadn't eaten in days. A gun was stuffed down her waistband, and her hand shot to it when she saw them.

"Wait, wait." Io raised both palms. "We mean no harm."

"I remember you. That night when Jarl . . ." Nina looked around herself, at the narrow walls of the staircase, calculating her exit strategy. She had survived the Riots, Io reminded herself, and probably just had to fight other looters for that food she was carrying. Her defensiveness was justified. "Why the hell are you here?"

Io knew the woman needed gentleness and calm, but there was no room for that right now. "That night, you said the wraith told you, *I cannot punish you. Your crimes are not truly yours.* What did she mean?"

"How would I know? Leave me alone." Nina started up the stairs, shouldering between Io and Edei.

Io followed. "Have you committed many crimes?"

"What are you talking about?" the woman said over her shoulder.

"You have killed," Io pressed, feeling horrible for the dark memories she was bringing up for the poor woman. "In the Riots. But that was your only crime, yes?"

The woman paused on the staircase, her eyes snapping to Io's face, wisps of white-blond hair falling like streaming starlight around her face. "How do you know about the Riots?"

Io ignored the question—it was irrelevant right now, and it was costing her precious time. "Nina, this is important. In the Riots, who did you kill?"

The woman's lips pressed tight. "You know I can't tell you that."

Yes, right, Roosters' Silence. Bianca's entire battalion, who should be lauded as heroes, were instead sworn to secrecy and threatened with a horrible death if they ever spoke a word about the Riots. Why? Why bother to protect the rogue gang, who were either dead or runaways? Why bother—unless the truth was so horrible it would condemn the entire Silts.

"There was never a rogue gang, was there?" Io asked, high on adrenaline. "The day the Riots ended, there was a woman on the bridge, the rogue gang leader that tried to stop you from attacking. She said, *This is your penance.*"

Justice, vengeance, penance—again and again, Io had heard these words.

"It was the Furies," Io said breathlessly. "*She* was a Fury. The furyborn attacked the Silts for seven days—and on the eighth, Bianca Rossi ordered you to kill them all."

The woman answered only with silence.

"An entire line of other-born . . ." Io choked.

An entire line, dead. Not just a slaughter. A genocide.

Nina's voice came out a whisper. "You don't know what it was like. They were sent to put an end to some gang fight that had broken out in the Silts—turf wars were so common back then. But they went into this frenzy. They tracked every other-born involved in illegal work, and executed them on the spot, no trial, no conviction." Her eyes rose to Io's, hard and unapologetic. "We did what we had to. The Furies would have killed us all."

*We did what we had to.* There it was again. Violence in the name of survival.

Io glanced over her shoulder; Edei's mouth was agape, his fingers going white around the brass knuckles on his right hand. "One after another, all the other-born involved in the Riots were killed for their crimes," Io told him. "Fyodorov, Minos, Jarl, Horatio. *Only* the other-born, Edei. Not Nina, not Fyodorov's family, none of the nonpowered humans that assisted in the Riots. And they were all strangled by severed threads that the wraiths used like *whips*. The wraiths are taking vengeance for the genocide of their line, Edei."

His voice was small, barely a whisper. "The wraiths are fury-born."

Io nodded. That was her theory, now dreadfully confirmed.

"But, Io—they haven't *all* been punished." Edei paused and closed his eyes, as though to collect himself. *"Bianca."*

Not the puppeteer. A victim. Bianca Rossi was a victim.

# CHAPTER XXXIII

# GODS-DAMNED RECKONING

IO WAS PANICKING. Her every step carried the frenetic energy of a spinning top about to spiral out of control. It was dread alone that carried her across the Silts, past cat bridges and barricaded walkways to the Plaza gates.

The guards at the gates took one look at her papers and let her and Edei through. The Plaza was in a riot: policemen, city officials, and regular citizens had crowded the courtyard in front of the police headquarters, talking animatedly while waiting for the Mayoral election results. No one paid Io and Edei any mind as they crossed the courtyard toward the northern part of the Plaza, where the holding cells were housed.

There was only one guard in the single-floor building, legs propped on the desk while a long corridor of prison bars stretched behind her. A slim cigarette hung from her lips, the room smelling of a putrid mix of tobacco and bleach.

"We're here to see Bianca Rossi," Edei said in a hurry.

"Is that right?" said the woman, following it with a horrible sucking-on-her-teeth sound.

"Yes."

"And who are you, exactly?"

"We really don't have time for this," said Io. Her hand shot out like the head of a viper, fingers closing around one of the overseer's many threads.

She had meant to intimidate the annoying woman into letting

them through—the yank usually did the trick, as it produced a feeling akin to an electric shock in the chest—but it had an even better effect: the woman's eyes rolled back into her head, and she dropped cold on her desk with a loud thump.

"*Io!*" Edei chastised, rushing around the desk to examine the unconscious woman.

"There's no time!" Io snapped back, and grabbed the key ring by the ashtray.

Her footsteps echoed down the corridor. No life-threads shot up through the roof in the Quilt. The building was empty; Bianca must have been moved—

Io stopped before the bars to a tiny cell, barely long enough to fit the cot the mob queen was lying on. Bianca was curled on her side on a bare mattress, a holey blanket covering the same silken pajamas she had been wearing last night. Her blond hair was matted, sticking to her cheeks and neck like wet straw.

Edei had come up beside Io. He made to take the keys from her. Io placed a hand on his chest, halting him.

Hanging from the cot and pooling on the floor was a single silver thread, limp and lifeless. A severed life-thread, fashioned into a weapon. *The whip of a Fury*, Io's mind inserted unhelpfully.

The guilt was immediate. The severed thread, the bare feet, the raspy, chest-heaving breaths. If Io had been smarter, she would have pieced it together sooner. Whatever else she might have done, Bianca was this killer's target—*had been* a target from the very first time Io met her, when Drina Savva attacked her in her office. Io could have warned Saint-Yves, could have stood watch over this cell all day, could have caught the killer red-handed and saved Bianca from this terrible fate.

"Io?" Edei whispered.

"Her life-thread," Io got out through the lump in her throat, "is severed."

He sucked in a sharp breath. "How? Who could have done this to her in here?"

It was a futile question: a dozen officers had probably interrogated Bianca, and a dozen more had come in just to take a look at the fallen queen of the Silts. And anyway, if there was someone out there *making* these women into Furies, if they could hide from the Nine and had access to the City Plaza, who knew what else these monsters could do?

"Stay back," she instructed Edei.

Her eyes stayed on the slow rise and fall of Bianca's chest— was she asleep or faking it? Io slipped key after key into the lock, finding at last the one that fit. The hinges groaned as the door opened. She took a step inside. The mob queen hadn't moved. Io lowered onto her haunches and gingerly caught the severed thread lying on the stone floor. Watching Bianca's breaths, she started winding the thread—the *whip*—around her palm. Better to secure the weapon while she could.

When it was done, she leaned against the wall and looked at Edei. His hands were clasped behind his nape, his eyes brimming with wetness. "I can't . . ." He trailed off, voice thick with grief. "What are we going to do?"

Io wanted to scream—*I don't know!*—but she made herself close her eyes. Focus. In through the nose, out through the mouth. She could picture it already: an all-out war between the Silts and the leeches, to avenge their fallen queen. Saint-Yves caught in the crossfire, Thais, too. And Ava . . .

Gods, *Ava would be devastated*. And it would be Io's fault, *again*. A professional breaker of hearts, so ruthless she didn't even spare her own sister.

Unless she found a way to fix this. And there was a way, wasn't there? A way to save Bianca from a slow death.

"We're going to take her to the Nine."

The front door had been left half-open; even halfway across the police headquarters at the other end of the Plaza, Io heard a sudden burst of cheering and roaring applause. A chant began, quietly at first and growing louder, as the people in the courtyard celebrated. She wondered, momentarily, if Thais was among the crowd, bleary-eyed and ecstatic at the impossibility of her dreams coming true.

Saint-Yves had just won the elections.

Io heaved under Bianca's weight, her back and neck drenched with sweat.

They had woken Bianca as gently as they could, with soothing words and explanations of their plan to help her. It made no difference. The mob queen thrust like a frenzied leviathan, kicking, elbowing, and screaming nonsense at the top of her lungs. It took both Io and Edei to get her wrists bound and her mouth gagged.

"I hate this," Edei mumbled, looking miserably at his former boss, as they slipped through the abandoned northern gates—every police officer in the Plaza must be celebrating Saint-Yves's success at the police headquarters. "I should have helped the gang break her out of here. It's my fault."

"We'll fix it," Io answered through her silent sniffles.

She wasn't sure when she had started crying. She had been focused on putting one foot in front of the other, on holding the whip-thread securely, on keeping Bianca from escaping—when, suddenly, she felt the neckline of her sweater sticking to her neck, soaked by the constant flow of soundless tears down her cheeks. The world used to be ten blocks wide—her apartment, Amos's café, the rest of the Silts—and now it had bubbled in all directions: dark cities and fury-born, severed threads and sinister manipulators. She was terrified.

The House of Nine appeared through the smog like a beautiful mirage. There were no admirers gathered around it now, no paparazzi; they must all be covering the election. The security guards were having a cigarette, perched on the gate steps. Above them, the garden lights of the house were lit, a constellation of rectangle-shaped stars through the gray haze. A hare-serpent chimerini dashed by, paws pattering and tail slithering across the street.

Io stopped a safe distance away from the guards, who were pointedly ignoring her. Her voice came out like a croak in the deserted district. "Tell the Nine that Io Ora is here to see them. Tell them I'll do anything they ask."

A security woman with a swirly tattoo sleeve retreated to the small cubicle by the gates and spoke in hushed whispers to whatever device linked them to the main house. A few moments later, she beckoned for the three other security guards to fall around Io, Edei, and Bianca, and the seven of them started on an awkward procession to the mansion. A gravel path curved around the building and ended in a domed greenhouse overlooking the West Canal.

A dozen lamps bathed the greenhouse in white light, which reflected like snowfall on the indigo marble floor and indigo-and-gold furniture. Dark blue gossamer curtains embroidered with stars mushroomed in the soft breeze coming through the open panels. The Nine were positioned statuesquely around the room in their elegant gowns and gleaming brown skin, fuzzy chimerini furs draped on their necks and arms.

Calliope and Erato sipped champagne on one of the sofas. Polyhymnia and Urania, the younger ones, lounged on a settee, a plate of mini canapes on the orange fur between them. Four other women were sprawled around the room, in armchairs or on big pillows on the floor. They must be the Muses Io hadn't met: Euterpe, Muse of music; Thalia, Muse of comedy; Terpsichore, Muse of dance; and Melpomene, Muse of tragedy.

Clio was the only sister standing, arms on the back of one of the sofas. She was dressed exquisitely in a dark blue gown and golden jewelry that looked like it cost as much as an entire apartment at the Silts.

"Cutter," Clio said, inclining her head. "Have you come to pay your debt at last?"

The other Muses snickered, like they were all in on an inside joke. Edei took a step around the security guards, his face a hard mask.

"Stop playing," he told them. "This woman requires your help. Tell us how to save her and we will do whatever you ask."

The Muses slid to the edge of their seats, leaning to see around the security guards. Erato's champagne sloshed over the brim of her glass, but none of them cared. Clio's mouth stretched back over her teeth, showing all her gums. It was an ugly sight, like the snarl of a wild beast.

"Who is that?" Clio asked. "What have you brought to us, girl?"

Before Io could reply, Bianca began shaking.

Edei and Io shared a look of alarm, clasping the mob queen's arms tighter. Her shoulders were rolling with silent laughter, her head thrown back to face the gray sky. A haunting sound filled the greenhouse, the wild cackling of a demon, muffled by the makeshift gag Io had made from her scarf.

The security guards reached for the guns on their hips. The Nine craned their necks, even more riveted than before.

Clio spoke loudly to be heard over Bianca's laughter. "Who are you?"

The laughter snuffed out. Bianca leaned forward and spat the gag onto the Nine's pristine tiles. Her eyes reflected the orange of burning flames—but there was no fire in the room.

"I," she said through a curtain of greasy blond locks, "am your gods-damned reckoning."

Io instinctively tightened her fist around the severed thread. *I still have her,* she thought as her panic spiked. *I still hold the whip.*

But the mob queen didn't need a weapon—she was a weapon herself.

She yanked her arms free, landed a kick straight into Edei's chest, took Io's head between her hands, and kneed her hard in the face.

Io's vision went black, pain ricocheted through her skull, her ears pounded. For several moments—minutes? Hours?—she floated in a soundless, sightless void, unsure which way was up and which was down, nausea twisting her stomach, agony in her skull.

Then she could feel gravel beneath her cheek, smell grass and wet soil, hear muffled sounds: screams of fear, cries of pain, bullets flying, and the unmistakable thud of bodies hitting the floor. She tried to crawl to her elbows, but the world shifted sideways, and she rolled to her back, the gray sky above her coming in and out of focus.

*Get up,* she ordered herself. *Stand up, Io.*

A face appeared through the haze: brown skin, sharp cheekbones, dark eyes. His mouth was moving in the shape of words, his hands cupping her face. It hurt so much, a torrent of wet pain down her nose. She was distantly aware that this was Edei and that Bianca was loose and that she had to get up, but her stupid body wouldn't obey. She heaved herself to the side, gripped Edei's arms with all her might, and let him pull her upright.

Her head swam, shadows and lights dancing in front of her. She closed her eyes. Focused on the firm length of Edei's body against hers. Hip to rib cage to shoulder, one arm over his shoulders, his legs moving them away from the greenhouse. When she looked again, she could make out the grass under their feet, the individual green blades, the laces of her boots.

She pulled against Edei's grip; he came to a stop.

"No, Io," he breathed. "Don't look."

Her cheek throbbed violently and her left eye was already swelling up, but she craned her aching neck to look at the greenhouse.

It was a slaughter.

# CHAPTER XXXIV

# THE WHIP IS DEATH

**THREE SECURITY GUARDS** lay dead at the doors, guns glistening useless in their hands. There were other bodies strewn across the marble floor, their expensive furs discarded around them. Five of the Nine were dead: Erato, head slumped back on the couch, dress drenched in champagne. Young Polyhymnia, only feet away from the settee, and three of the Muses Io hadn't met in the middle of the carpet, as though they had tried to run. Their bodies were crooked, necklaces of bruises around their necks. The four remaining Muses were cowering behind furniture, too frantic to make an escape through the open panels of the greenhouse.

In the center of the greenhouse, Bianca was moving with impossible speed, her limbs so fast they were a blur. Where the other wraiths had been chaotic, Bianca was precise. As Io and Edei watched, Calliope made a run for the doors—the whip-thread soared through the air, pulling the Muse down by the ankle. Her face smacked against the marble. Bianca pulled the whip back and launched it again, wrapping it around Calliope's neck. For a few short moments, barely long enough for Io to realize what was happening, the Muse writhed. And then went completely still. *The whip is justice*, Io thought. *The whip is death.*

Clio, Urania, and a third muse-born Io hadn't met screamed as their sister slumped lifeless a few inches away from their faces, where they hid behind the bigger sofa. Shots split the air—there was a single security woman left alive in the greenhouse, firing bullet after bullet at Bianca. But again, the mob queen was uncannily fast: she dodged the first two shots and snapped the third straight out of the air with her whip.

"We need to go." Edei was panting by Io's side. His eyes studied her face with a pained expression. "We need to get you to Samiya."

The left side of Io's face was throbbing with pain. Blood poured down her nose, sticky on her lips, staining her sweater scarlet. Edei was leaning sideways, stepping on his right knee gingerly. What had happened to him while she was knocked out?

"*Please!*" the Muse of history croaked behind the sofa, tearing Io's attention from Edei. She was cradling Urania and the other young Muse in her arms, like a mother comforting a baby. "Spare the little ones. They were toddlers when the Riots happened. They are faultless."

Bianca cocked her head, meeting Clio's gaze through the reflection on the greenhouse windowpanes. "It's too late for mercy, don't you think, Clio?" she said. "Twelve years too late. *They'll kill us all,* you told me. *End this, end them.* So I did. I sent my kids to the slaughter, and I killed every last one of the Furies."

"Don't pretend innocence!" cried Clio. "You knew about the plan from the get-go. You and every influential other-born in the city agreed. We would let the next gang skirmish in the Silts escalate to a riot. We would ask for the help of the Order of the Furies, and when they arrived, we would use the riot to end their reign of terror."

Clio was overcome by raspy breaths. Io clenched her jaw, forcing herself to stay put, to listen.

"Someone had been influencing the fury-born for months," Clio went on. "They had been picking other-born leaders off one by one across the city-nations. There were hardly any of us left anymore.

You knew they had to be stopped. You agreed to play your part!"

"I did not agree to the death of hundreds of my people!"

"We didn't know how violent they would get!"

"I think you did," Bianca said smoothly. "And I think you decided it was a small price to pay for getting rid of your enemy. For twelve years, I have drowned my guilt. For twelve years, I have kept your Roosters' Silence. For what?"

Her hand rose, the whip-thread hanging like a carcass from her fingers.

"For *this*?" she continued with a sneer. "I wonder, did your protégés foretell this in their art, too? The mob queen of the Silts turned into a monster in her sleep, gagged and handcuffed by her second, brought to the mighty Nine to beg for their help?"

"The cutter is right: we *can* help you—"

"I don't want your help." Bianca's head turned, and Io got a glimpse of her eyes. They had a glassy quality, reflecting bright orange on her irises. Just like Io's reflected silver when she was using the Quilt. "I can see all your crimes with these new eyes, Clio. You're stained from head to toe, drenched in them. I cannot let you live anymore, not with crimes like these. You deserve no mercy, sister."

The whip split through the air. It wrapped around the leg of the sofa and sent it flying across the room, where it smacked right into the last security woman, knocking her down. Clio and the two Muses shrieked at the top of their voices, now exposed to Bianca's wrath.

Io trembled, right down to her core. Her legs were weak, her focus swimming. But she had to do something because she was the only one who *could*.

"I'll distract her and you get the Muses out," she whispered to Edei in a hurry. "Fetch the gang, Samiya, whoever else you can find."

His lips were pressed so tight they had gone white. His eyes glistened. He breathed out; it sounded like a sob. "I don't want to leave you."

Io dropped her head to his shoulder, knowing that if she let herself *feel* right now, she might yield. She might take his hand and run, let this world fall to collapse, if only to be safe with him.

"You must," she said.

His voice in her ear was strained yet gentle. "Yes, boss."

"Go."

They started moving at the same time. Edei dashed around the greenhouse to where the Muses cowered, while Io went for the gun in the hand of the security guard as noisily as she could, gravel flying beneath her boots. Bianca twisted at the sound, narrowed her eyes, and zapped her whip through the air. Io gasped in fear, fingers locking around the barrel of the gun. The whip-thread closed around her other arm. Bianca pulled; Io stumbled forward.

Behind Bianca, she could see Edei's dark shape moving, grabbing one of the younger Muses under the armpits and hauling her out.

Io raised the gun to the glass dome of the greenhouse. *Please, don't let me kill anyone by accident,* she thought—and fired.

Shards rained down on Io and Bianca both, a thousand tiny scratches at her arms and legs. Bianca's body cowed instinctually— that was all the opening Io needed. She grabbed the whip-thread from where it had wrapped around her left arm and began coiling it around her palm, like a fisherman pulling back his line. In the few seconds it took for Bianca to refocus, Io had it looped around her hand and tightened her fingers into a first for good measure.

"Don't," Io said through her heaving chest, "move."

The wraith—the keres-born—the Fury—let out a cry and lunged across the room at her.

Io allowed herself a split second to lock eyes with Edei. "Run!" she screamed.

And then Bianca's body crashed into hers. They smacked against one of the glass panes of the greenhouse. She felt the gossamer curtain caress her cheeks, felt Bianca's fist plow into her stomach. Shards crunched beneath her boots as she pivoted away from Bianca's second punch. Bending under the mob queen's outstretched arm, she circled away from Bianca, trying to keep her with her back to Edei, who had come back for the last muse-born, Clio.

The whip-thread was still in Io's left fist, smarting against her skin. The gun was gripped in her right. She could shoot her. They were so close the bullet was bound to hit its mark. But she hesitated—Bianca seemed more in control, more *herself*, than any other wraith before her.

Bianca's gaze was pure flame as she rounded on Io, reflecting the dancing orange of a burning fire. This was a fury-born's tell, Io realized. Bianca was in the world of Furies now, able to see . . . crimes?

"How ugly you look with these new eyes, cutter," the mob queen said. "How stained."

*Stained.* A few days ago—gods, a few hours ago—the accusation would have frozen Io to her core. Her shame would have taken over, those infinite seeds of guilt that Thais had planted and sowed for years. It was true: she had wronged and hurt and been hurt in return. But that didn't make her ugly or worthy of this noxious punishment. Things weren't really that uncomplicated. Black and white, crime and death, love and hatred. There were gradients, Io had realized. Endless shades of gray.

Heaving with pain, she breathed, "Stand down."

"Oh, you would like that, wouldn't you? Gallant Io saving the Nine from the murderous wraith. Now, that's a headline. But they'll never forget you're a cutter, girl. They might praise you, they might adore you, but they will always, always think, *She is danger. She is imbalance. She is death.* I was queen of the Silts, and all it took to turn them against me was a single word: keres-born. They starved me, they beat me, they interrogated me. They turned me into this *abomination* in my sleep."

"Who did?" Io pressed. "Who made you into this?"

"I wouldn't be here if I knew. I would be standing over them, watching the life leave their eyes. I woke up, and I was a bloodthirsty weapon. An unwilling servant of justice, condemned to an early death. Do you think I wanted this? Do you think I deserved this?"

She was right, of course. This world was a game rigged to make them lose: look at them now, fate and death tangled in a web of threads, and neither of them in control.

Io's jaw set, her thoughts cleared. "Prove them wrong, then."

Bianca didn't move.

"You are not like the other wraiths. Something is different this time. You can see crimes, yes, and you can use your life-thread like a whip. But your mind is your own, isn't it? You remember who you were before you were turned into this. You remember you were the *queen of the Silts.*"

And to Io's utter surprise, it worked. The bloodlust in Bianca's eyes snuffed out, the orange disappearing completely. She gazed at the carnage around them. One of the Muses lay facedown on the marble before her, neck bent in an unnatural position. Edei was gone, disappeared into the darkness with the surviving members of the Nine.

"You are a queen," Io went on. "And they took your queendom. They turned you into a monster. They manipulated you into killing your friends—"

"The Nine were never my friends."

"They were your allies once, weren't they? You . . ." Io trailed off, trying to put her thoughts in order. "You worked with them to end the line of the Furies. Because the fury-born were being influenced by someone and targeting powerful other-born across the city-nations."

"Alante would have been next" was all Bianca said.

"Who was influencing them?" Io asked, her heartbeat in her throat.

"We never found out. We only knew they were very powerful; they could hide from all of us."

Hide from the powers of the strongest other-born across the city-nations. Just like whoever was behind the wraiths could hide from the Nine's artists.

Something jostled in Io's mind. The masterminds behind the Order of the Furies and behind the wraiths were one and the same. Powerful puppeteers, who were guiding the fury-born's hand. Who, when their army was destroyed, sought a new weapon, a new Order to sow vengeance and deliver justice.

But it still didn't make sense. If whoever hid behind the wraiths had slipped into the Plaza, severed Bianca's threads, and turned her into a wraith, all so that they could use her as a weapon to slay the Nine, then why would they leave Bianca locked in a cell—

Oh gods.

They knew Io was the only person the Nine had let into their fortress in months. That Io was the only way into the House of Nine, the only way to take vengeance on the Muses for their part in the fury-born genocide.

They knew that Io would come for Bianca. That Io would find the mob queen threadless and try to save her by taking her to the Nine. They'd left Bianca locked in a cell because they *knew* Io.

They knew her better, perhaps, than anybody else.

Io took a breath that scraped down her lungs. "Do you want justice?"

With animal speed, Bianca moved in Io's direction. She stopped a few feet away, a finger raised straight in Io's face. "You know who did this to me?"

The greenhouse was empty now. Edei and the Muses were gone, hopefully somewhere safe, far away from here. Io and Bianca stood in a room of beautiful corpses.

Io exhaled shakily. "If it's justice you want, you need to do exactly what I tell you."

"And what is that?"

A terrifying calm had descended on Io. "You're going to help me get a confession out of them."

"So you *do* know," snarled Bianca. "Who did this to me."

Yes, Io knew. Of course she did.

It had been a trap, from the very beginning. A trap designed specifically for Io, relying on a single choice: that Io would find Bianca dying and choose to save her.

That Io, a professional breaker of hearts, with all her guilt and her shame, couldn't bear to hurt Ava again.

Thais's question echoed in the deathful night.

*You would do anything for Ava, wouldn't you?*

# CHAPTER XXXV

# ENDLESS SHADES OF GRAY

**IO SAT ALONE** in the middle of a room full of death, pulling on the thread. Three short tugs, two long: the Ora sisters' call to arms. Silver flowed through her fingers, casting a snowy iridescence against the furred bodies around her.

Nightfall had arrived in Alante like a drape tonight, the heavy smog swallowing all light. The glass doors were all unlocked, exposing every side of the greenhouse. Chill air kissed her cheeks and billowed the curtains. The hair on the dead women's heads stirred on the marble, like streams of ice water after the thaw. Bianca had disappeared to carry out the last of Io's commands. They had undressed and redressed the bodies in the room, arranged the chimerini furs just right.

Io's left eye had swollen shut, her heart beat in her ears, but her focus was razor-sharp. Her mind was clear for the first time since she took on this case. She felt no terror, no sadness, no guilt. There was only resolution: to find the single piece missing from the puzzle.

*We are all the same, Muses and moira-born and grace-born. Whatever they may be, these women are of the gods.*

*There is no god with powers like these.*

*Even gods change.*

*The gods are dead.*

*Go on. Ask.*

How had the wraiths been made?

Io gathered the thread slowly on her lap, like an old woman at a loom. She heard it first: footsteps on the gravel path, the whoosh of fine fabric, the jingle of jewelry. From the corner of her good eye, Io saw a slender figure approaching, in turn revealed and obscured by every wave of the tide of gossamer. She slipped between the curtains, sporting a turquoise dress with an embroidered neckline. Her eyes raked the room, taking in every detail: nine bodies in gowns and chimerini furs, no live threads in the Quilt.

Thais.

The sister who raised her, the sister who used her, the sister who had orchestrated everything.

Io had had time while she waited. She had gone over the details of the murders, of all the events of the last five days. She had been listing the clues that pointed to Thais over and over again, looking for a loophole, for exoneration. She had found none.

Thais had met the women who became the wraiths through the Initiative meetings. Thais had taken so long to prepare the revani, yesterday on the Hill, because she had called Raina to Hanover Street to attack Saint-Yves and steer suspicions away from him. That was why Raina had attacked them with her hands and not her whip-thread. Then Thais had guessed Io had a new suspect and sent Saint-Yves to Mister Hypnos, leading to Bianca's arrest. And just this morning, Thais had watched Io desperately try to comfort Ava and planted this idea in her mind: to visit the Plaza and interrogate Bianca herself. So that Io would find her threadless and bring her to the reclusive Nine to save her. Thais had led them here, to this blood-spotted graveyard.

But *why*?

What interest did Thais have in the Furies? How had she figured out how to turn women into wraiths? And who was behind her? Because there definitely was someone behind Thais. Her sister might be the strongest person Io knew, but she was not strong enough to hide from the Nine.

This truth, this confession, Io had to carve out from her sister's lips herself.

"What happened?" Thais whispered. "I came as fast as I could when I sensed your call for help. The gate was open, unguarded. Io, are these the Nine? Are they all . . . ?"

Io raised her face to the light of the chandelier.

"Your face!" Thais moved through the room like lightning, kneeling before Io, turning her face this way and that. "Who did this to you?"

Thais was looking around, brow furrowed. *She's worried Bianca is still close,* Io realized with a jolt.

Gritting her teeth, Io placed both hands on her sister's shoulders, as though going in for a hug, then slowly lowered them to the center of Thais's chest—and clenched her fists.

As fast as she could, before Thais could react, she jumped upright and backed away until she hit the sofa. Her fists were full of Thais's threads, every last one of them. A guarantee, because without the threads, a weaver was powerless. But it was also a secret plot. Io believed one of these threads would prove useful—she just didn't know which one.

Thais sat in a pool of silk, jade earrings swinging, her perfectly done-up face befuddled. "What are you doing?" Her irises glittered with the silver glow of the Quilt. "What happened here?"

"You became a conduit of the divine—that's how you phrased it, isn't it?"

*We are conduits of the divine, not gods ourselves. Other-born powers are ours to use, to control, and to limit. We will be harshly judged, and we, more than anyone else, do not want to be found lacking.* And then her friend had said, *Justice is the virtue of great souls.* Was this the justice Thais had been talking about?

Misapprehension struck her sister's lovely face, a picture so perfect it seemed painted by a master's hand. "You think . . . *I* did this?"

Io wasn't surprised. These were always the rules of the game: the Ora family toyed with the truth, twisting and turning it in unrecognizable shapes. It wasn't just Thais, no matter how much Io wanted to believe that. It was Mama with her expectations, it was, Baba with his love of bending the rules, it was Ava with her diplomatic choices. It was Io herself, with her secrets.

"Io, get yourself together," Thais said urgently, which Io felt was pure irony. She *was* together, more herself than she ever was. "*This* does not look good. The Nine dead and a cutter involved? We need to get ahead of it. Whatever happened, Luc can protect you. But we must go *now*. Do you know what will happen if they catch us here?"

Sure she did. She would lay out all her clues tying Thais to the wraiths, all her suspicions that Thais had orchestrated these murders. But it was Bianca's hand that had slain the Nine—the mob queen would be hunted across Alante. It didn't matter that they would have Edei's deposition, or the surviving Muses'. There was no concrete evidence that Thais was behind the wraiths, and, more than that, her sister was the Mayor's fiancée and the shining other-born spokeswoman for his ambitious Initiative. He would pull every string he had to pin this all on Bianca, on Io, on anyone else, because if he didn't, his career would collapse.

So Io had to play the game. She had to extract the truth, like a rotten fang from a hungry wolf's mouth. She had to get a confession from Thais's very lips that no court of law could ever ignore.

But first she had to buy some time for Bianca to carry out the last of her commands.

"Where did you go?" Io asked. "When you left?"

Thais turned to the open panels. "There's no time for this, Io—"

"Sure there is."

Her sister squirmed, attempting to take a step away. "You need to let go of my threads."

Otherwise, Thais wouldn't be able to move. Io was holding her life-thread in her fists; it was impossible to step away from it, like an invisible chain.

"Answer my questions," Io said, "and I'll let them go."

Thais exhaled deeply and dropped into an empty armchair. "Is this what you want? To hear my lowest points? To feel superior? I can do that for you, sister mine, even if I find it a bit cruel. After I left Alante, I spent months on the road, traveling through the Wastelands. I was denied entrance to several cities before I was told I'd have better luck at Nanzy, because of their factory indentures. You can't imagine the sight: a tall, impenetrable walled city and around it, floating slums stretching endlessly in every direction. There are thousands of people living in the slums, all working in the factories outside the city, trying to buy their way into Nanzy through yearly indentures. The working conditions—gods, I've never seen anything like it.

"Things are different in Nanzy. It's so much bigger than Alante, and it's the seat of the Agora. Protests and strikes have results in Nanzy. So, a little while after I arrived, I helped organize a walk-out. We got the heating system fixed, but I was sued for neglect by my supervisors. And that's how I met Luc. He was taking on pro bono cases for workers in the slums. During the months of the trial, he and I became close. We talked about equality, worker rights, other-born injustice. We came up with the idea that would later become the Initiative, and slowly found our investors. We began to fall in love.

"But his family didn't like it. He was the rising star of Nanzy, cavorting with an immigrant union worker that had nothing to her name except a long list of arrests. I was going to lose both the man I loved and the cause I believed in, and so I did the only thing I could think of: I hid all evidence of my moira-born status and made myself into a woman his upper-class friends would accept. He began rising in the ranks, with me by his side. We launched the Initiative.

"And then it all turned sour. His family exposed my other-born status to the press. Overnight, all the support we'd built was gone. When the Commissioner position opened in Alante, our investors urged Luc to accept. Lawless Alante was a prime testing field for the Initiative. But I wasn't going to make the same mistake twice: the moment I arrived here, I was open and honest about my moira-born powers. More and more other-born began coming to our meetings. Supporters appeared from every corner of Alante. When the Mayoral elections were announced, we realized it would be the perfect opportunity. Luc could do so much more as Mayor—and now he will. So, please, *please*, can we get out of here?"

"Not yet."

There was a lot to unpack here: the indenture, the trial, the relationship, the scheme. Io would have liked to doubt the story, but it sounded exactly like what one would script as the next chapter in Thais Ora's life. She had started with Malena Silnova and her "favors," and graduated to Thomas Mutton and his pyramid scheme. The pattern was always the same: Thais became enamored with some grand cause, and when the cause required her to betray her morals, she went along with it, ignoring the contradiction between her lofty speech and her actions.

No, the lie wasn't in the story but in the telling.

Thais had framed the whole thing as a love story. Two star-crossed lovers with shared dreams fighting against the rest of the world. It sounded like the presentation Io had watched in the Teatro, their romance marketed as a selling point. It felt like a deflection. So what was the heart of the story? What was Thais trying to hide?

Io stared at the threads in her palms, two dozen of them, coiling and serpentine. Some were dull, some brighter. Some were tingling against her skin, an indication that the people on the other end were nearing—good, that meant Bianca had done her job. Shifting her fingers minutely, Io spread the threads against her palms so that none was touching the other.

If one of them was triggered by what Thais was feeling right now, Io would know.

Her sister could lie, but the Quilt could not.

Io just had to figure out the right questions.

She had to be bold—bolder than Thais. That was the only way to shock her sister into revealing the truth.

"There's something I can't figure out," Io said. "You meet Luc, you create the Initiative, you get 'investors' and support from the Agora, you move to Alante to test it out—this all makes sense. You come to Alante with a secret agenda. You choose women from the Initiative meetups and turn them into wraiths. You send them to avenge the death of the Furies and pick off the culprits of the Riots one by one, leaving the Nine for last. But what is your goal, Thais? Justice? How is it justice to avenge death with more death?"

"Have you lost your mind? Do you hear yourself? Avenging the Furies? Killing the Nine? Turning women into wraiths? Who do you think I am?"

There it was—Io saw her opening. She aimed for her sister's softest parts: to offend, to infuriate.

"I think you're *no one*," Io spat. "I think you were caught in another snare, but this time there were no Ora sisters around to point out the truth. There is someone guiding you, someone powerful enough to hide from the Nine. Someone who revealed the genocide of the Furies to you and convinced you the right path was avenging them. In order to what? Create a new Order from the wraiths?"

"For gods' sake, Io! What genocide? What new Order? It's all in your head!"

Veins were bulging on her sister's neck. Io's heart was thrashing in her chest with a thunderous roar, but she didn't stop. She was close, so close. She could sense it.

"They told you that you are a conduit of the divine," she pressed. "You pick your first target from the Initiative meetings, a woman with access to the Silts. You cut her threads—somehow—and then weave this supernatural whip-thread. You send her to deliver the Furies' justice. But her life-thread is frayed. The first girl dies, but so what? You have a purpose. You pick another one, you turn her into a bloodthirsty monster, and when she does your killing, you are glad. You think you're making the world better. She dies, too, but who cares about that, right? There are plenty of girls in Alante—"

"*They weren't meant to die!*" Thais screamed.

Io held her breath.

Thais's chest rose and fell with rage, her eyes slits on her face. "They had fury-born blood, but diluted, not enough to give them power without intervention. I was told the transformation wouldn't kill them."

The wraiths came from *the line of Furies*. It clicked into place now, why Horatio Long had been sent to kill them. If the Moonset Riots had been an insidious scheme to end the line of Furies, then it made sense that the Nine's premonitions would render the women a threat, no matter how weak their lineage might be.

Her sister was still speaking. "I wove all their threads into one, into the thread that would become their whip, just as I was instructed. But their life-thread couldn't take the pressure—it started fraying. When Emmeline died, I cried for a week—"

"And yet you kept doing it!" Io pushed. "What about Drina? Raina? Bianca?"

"They told me I missed something! That the girls I chose didn't have enough fury-born blood, that I had to find stronger candidates! You don't deny them, Io. I've seen what happens to those who do. And I believed in the cause—I still do. The Nine, along with some of the world's most prominent other-born, conspired to kill the entire line of the Furies. So that they could be free to profit from their powers as they wanted. But we have to restore balance. To resurrect justice. We *have to*. If we don't, the world will die."

*The cutter, the unseen blade, the reaper of fates*, echoed the prophecy in Io's head.

*She cuts the thread and the world ends.*

"What about me?" Io's voice broke. "Did you ever stop to think what you were doing to *me*?"

"I—" Thais stammered. "Io, I had to. I'd been trying for months to coax them out of that wretched House, but they never leave. I fought to keep you out of it. To keep you safe. But in the end, it was the only way. And look, it worked. The Furies are avenged. Order is restored. Their line will begin anew now—that's what they promised me." A sob raked Thais's chest, and her arms came around her torso. "It was worth it in the end, if only for that."

*There is violence in kindness, and kindness in violence*, Edei had told Io once.

Dark blue gossamer bloomed with the wind. In the darkness behind Thais, between the curtains, Io could make out light in the Quilt. Silver against black. Motionless, silent, watching.

Listening to Thais's confession.

There was only one more thing Io needed to know.

"Who are you working for, Thais? Who told you how to turn them into fury-born? Who promised you that you were helping their line come to life again? Who are you so scared of? Who do you need to protect me from?"

"You know," Thais growled, venom in her voice. *"You know."*

"I want to hear you say it," Io whispered.

*The gods.* Io waited for Thais to speak it out loud. *The gods are alive.*

Io lowered her lashes and glanced at the threads spread across her palms. One was brighter, warmer than the rest. This was the thread that connected Thais to this cause, to this love of justice and equality, to one of her investors and manipulators. To one of the gods. Io carefully twirled her index finger, around and around, until the thread was wrapped tightly against her skin.

Thais's eyes shone with tears. "Is this why you brought me here, to torment me with this place of death? Let go of my threads, Io. We need to get out of here—"

"I think," a voice said from the darkness, "that we've heard enough."

Fear crossed Thais's face. She whirled around as four figures emerged from the dark garden. Bianca Rossi, a smirk on her lips, the dead thread lassoed in her fist. Rosa, frowning, camera in hand. Ava, her mouth covered by both hands, tears flowing. And Luc Saint-Yves, face broken with sorrow, aiming a gun straight at Thais's heart. The flash of the camera flooded the greenhouse with light, immortalizing Thais among the carnage she had caused.

Bianca gave Io a feral grin. "I figured a proper journalist would want to see this. In case our new Mayor got any ideas to bury this whole story," she said. "It so happened that your friend was covering the elections at the Plaza, and Ava was able to drag her along."

This had been Io's plan. Saint-Yves would never leave his victory party to come to the House of Nine, not unless he was urged by his fiancé's sister herself. Io had simply told Bianca to convince Ava to bring Saint-Yves here, on the pretense of an emergency concerning Thais, but the addition of Rosa was a smart play by the mob queen.

With frantic movements, almost hysterical, Thais looked at her audience. Her fiancé, her sister, a journalist, and her latest victim. Then her gaze twisted to the puddle of threads in Io's fists, where they had been safely stretched taut to ensure Thais didn't see them coming.

"You tricked me," Thais choked out.

Io nodded. Her mind toiled with opposing waves of victory and loss.

"Luc," Thais pleaded. "Let me explain. You'll understand everything, I promise. All I have ever done is to keep us safe. Didn't I tell you about Bianca? Didn't I warn you and protect you? Luc, please give me a chance—"

"Stop," Saint-Yves said. His eyes were wet, his hold on the gun shaking. "I trusted you. I loved you. What you did, no matter your reasons, goes against everything I believe in. I will see that you are judged fairly for your crimes, but whatever we shared, whatever dreams we had, it's over."

"Over?" Thais whispered.

Her head snapped to Io. Her face sobered. It was so sudden, so unexpected that Io felt like she had been kicked in the stomach. Thais reached for a marble ashtray from the table and launched it, hard, at Io's head.

Edei's lean figure slipped through one of the side panels. His arm grabbed Io by the waist and hauled her out of the trajectory of the ashtray, just in time. It hit the pane behind her instead, cracking the glass. In a fluid movement, Edei pushed Io behind him, and raised a knuckled fist to Thais.

"You okay?" he whispered over his shoulder to Io.

"Yes," Io breathed.

"I've used the knuckle raps," Edei said. "The gang is coming."

"Well, then," Thais said, her voice harsh. She looked about the room with frenetic energy, her gaze lurching from person to person. "If it's the truth you wanted, sister, then let's tell everyone the *whole* truth. Do you know how they approached me, Io? What they used to convince me of the need to resurrect the Order of the Furies and deliver justice? *You.* They knew exactly what you did to me. They told me you had your little oneiroi-born friend here visit me every night for a week with dreams of traveling. That you frayed my home-thread, little by little until it snapped. That you manipulated me. Exiled me to months of cold and hunger and terror. You accuse me of hurting you, but is there a worse manipulation than what you did to *me*? I knew if my own sister could do that, then the Order needed to be restored. Justice delivered."

"Io . . ." Ava whispered. "Tell me it isn't true. Tell me you didn't do that."

Io's eyes fluttered closed. Her guilt was a weight, dragging her into the dark. She kept reaching for the surface, breaking though for a single breath, and then a new current of shame would pull her under again. The blame was insurmountable.

It didn't matter that Thais had hurt her first, that Thais hurt her for years, tiny nicks at her heart. For two years, Io had tried to rationalize it, justify it, put it out of her mind. She did what she had to do. But these last few days, with Edei, with Rosa, with the threadless women and the dead Furies, had taught Io that the world existed in gradients, endless shades of gray.

*You're someone who loves,* she had told Edei in order to hear it herself. *That's the only part that's yours to give and yours to take.*

Io couldn't live in her shame any longer. Shame for hurting Thais. Shame for loving her still. She had to let go.

She opened her fingers and released Thais's threads.

Her eyes were shut. She heard Thais's sigh of relief.

"One soul in three bodies—that's what we've always been," Thais said softly. Here it would come: She would apologize. She would start to make amends. She would try to fix this. Be better, make the world better. That was Thais, even in her defeat. "When our sisters need us, we go. No questions asked. Right, Ava?"

Ava? What—no!

Io barely had time to open her eyes and catch a last glimpse of Ava, staring at Thais.

Ava nodded. "Three bodies, one soul," she repeated. "No questions asked."

Thais smiled. "The lights, sister mine."

It felt almost like a dream. Ava's arm shot out. It hit the light switch on the wall beside her. The greenhouse sank into darkness. Footsteps shuffled. Glass crunched beneath feet. Gunshots split the air.

# CHAPTER XXXVI

# OVER HIS HEART

**THE QUILT EXPLODED** around Io, dozens of bright lines. Two bundles of silver were racing through the garden at high speed, away from the greenhouse. Two more were in the room, frantically jerking around the glass panes. And one was on the floor, by her feet. *Please,* Io thought. *Please, please, please.* She knelt and fumbled with Edei's clothes. Wet—too wet.

A cry tore out of her, "Rosa, the lights!"

"I'm trying," came Rosa's frantic voice from the walls, and, in the next moment, the switch clicked and the greenhouse flooded with light. Saint-Yves was a shadow between the bushes, taking off after Io's sisters, a gun in his hand.

Edei was on his side, clutching his abdomen. His breaths were labored, and when he lifted his eyes to Io's, they were utterly terrified. He looked so young, a boy consumed by fear, curled in pain. Io eased him against the sofa, removed his fingers from the wound—it was too low, where all the precious organs were, and the blood was too thick, too dark.

"Shit, shit, shit," Rosa said. "Io, you're bleeding, too."

Was she? She didn't feel pain—only panic. Her pants were torn, revealing a gaping wound just above her knee. One of Saint-Yves's bullets must have grazed her. Stupid, stupid man, firing in the dark, in such close distance. She would survive, it was Edei who—

"In the gate shed, there's a radio," said Io. "Call for help."

Rosa lingered above them, watching the blood ooze.

Io covered the wound with her hands, trying to stanch the flow. "Rosa, go!"

Her friend startled and took off, stumbling over the bodies and objects on the floor.

"Is it bad?" Edei's voice was smaller than she had ever heard it. He didn't wait for her answer; he leaned back, closing his eyes, face morphed into an image of agony.

Io glanced over his head: his life-thread disappeared into the sky, but its light was lackluster. And its thread . . . gods, oh gods, his life-thread was fraying.

She shut her eyes. She needed to think. *Stay calm. Focus.* Patience like a knife, focus like a viper. He could be saved, even from a gun wound to the stomach, even from a fraying life-thread. She opened her eyes, looked at Edei's face, creased with fear.

"Samiya," she whispered. "Show me which thread is hers."

"Samiya?" he stuttered. His eyes were glazing, unable to focus on her.

It didn't matter. The question alone was enough. One of his threads sparked brighter than the rest. Io snapped it out of the air and yanked, hard and violently. But the moment she took the pressure off his stomach, Edei gurgled in pain. She put her hands back against the wound, threads and all.

"Io . . ." Edei's lips were pale. "Don't cry."

"I'm not," Io lied. She pressed on the wound with one of the discarded furs, feeling his pulse right there beneath her fingertips. He couldn't be dying before her eyes. She was a cutter. A moira-born. *She* was supposed to decide when someone died. Not a piece of metal. Not a pulsing heart. Not a fraying thread—

"No guns, no leeches, no paramours," said a voice.

Lounging on one of the armchairs, an unlit cigarette in her mouth, the threadless Bianca gazed down at Edei with pity. He used to be the mob queen's second, her most trusted ally. Until he betrayed her. Was she enjoying it now, Io wondered, watching him die?

"You should leave," Io hissed. "Find a place to hide."

Bianca flicked a silver lighter on, and the end of her cigarette blazed. She took a long puff and exhaled. "Why should I? Saint-Yves is Mayor and the Nine are dead. My girlfriend just abandoned me for the woman who condemned me to a slow death. I think I'm going to wait for my gang to arrive. Then we're all going to raze this place to the ground."

The poem came unbidden to Io's mind:

> she watches silver like a sign
> she weeps silver like a mourning song
> she holds silver like a blade
> she cuts the thread
> and the world ends

But she had cut no threads tonight. She had done the opposite: let go. This wasn't the foretold moment. This wasn't the end.

Bianca waggled her hand at Io, the cigarette caught between index and middle finger. "And you, girl, promised me justice. Unless I'm mistaken, you've still got a thread connecting you to your sisters. A thread that can lead you to them anytime you want. I'm sticking with you until you give me what I am owed."

Io pressed her lips together. "Help me, then. Use your keres-born powers. Keep Edei alive while I call Samiya here."

The mob queen's eyes fell on Edei. "What makes you think I still have my keres-born powers? I am a wraith now, remember?"

"*Try*," Io pleaded. She didn't know if it would work; she just hoped.

Bianca spat, "After everything you two have done to me?"

"Yes," Io hissed. "After everything we've done *for* you."

Another long puff of smoke filled the room. Bianca studied her in that feline way of hers, head cocked, eyes narrowed into slits. Then, suddenly, she sat forward, elbows on her knees, cigarette hanging from her mouth like a worker back from a long day in the fields. Her eyes went scarlet. Her fingers twirled.

Under Io's fingers, the blood flow slowed. Then stopped, almost entirely. What did it mean that Bianca could use both a Fury's whip and her own keres-born powers? She was a new kind of wraith, a new kind of other-born. Io wasted no time: she grabbed Samiya's thread and started pulling as fast as she could. Calling the horus-born to them. She looked up—Edei was watching her.

They sat like that for a long time, connected by their gaze. His head rolled from time to time, as if he could no longer keep it up. And still he looked at her, and still Io pulled, and still Bianca stalled his death. They waited, minute after long minute.

"You'll be fine," she whispered.

Edei nodded.

A moment passed.

"Will you?" he asked.

Would she be fine? She doubted that. Her sisters had betrayed her, each in their own way. Her destiny foretold the destruction of the world. She had promised vengeance to the lethal mob queen of the Silts.

But there was a thread wrapped around her index finger, tight as a ring of silver. The thread that she had schemed and sacrificed so much for: the thread that connected Thais to the gods.

Because that was the truth, the answer to this mystery. The Nine had hinted at it, the wraiths had played with it, Thais had all but confirmed it. Powerful beings, able to hide from the muse-born, influence the fury-born, and orchestrate the slaughter of the most powerful other-born in the world. They were gods. And Io now had a thread that would lead her right to them.

"How can you ask me that," she said, "when you're bleeding into my hands?"

His chest rumbled with a soft laugh, almost a sigh. "I didn't mean what I said, Io. I *do* care—"

"Stop. Don't talk like that. Like you won't have another chance."

"I might not."

"Please, just hang on—"

"They're here," Bianca interrupted. Her eyes were trained on the darkness surrounding the greenhouse.

The thread in Io's hand vibrated as Samiya came around the bushes of the garden, accompanied by Chimdi. Io loosed a sob of earth-shattering relief. Thick tears were rolling down her cheeks. Edei dragged her face back to him with his weak fingers.

"You need to go," he said.

Around them, people were shouting. Samiya in alarm, Chimdi in terror, Bianca barking orders. More gang members appeared through the bushes. But in all the chaos, Io could only see Edei, listen to Edei's soft voice.

"Wherever this thread leads to," he said, gesturing to the clenched fingers of her left hand. "Whatever you're planning—you need to go now. Before they put the city under lockdown."

Clever, clever boy. He noticed so much, said so little, cared so deeply.

Io shook her head. "No. I want to stay with you. I want to wait for you."

"Io, you need to go *now*," he breathed, eyes large and fearful. "And I promise, the moment I'm better, I'll come find you."

"How?" she asked, the word breaking into a sob. How would he ever find her in the endless Wastelands beyond these walls?

Tenderly, he took her hand and placed it, palm down, on his chest.

"I will follow this," he whispered, pressing their joined hands over his heart, over their fate-thread. "I'll always find you."

And then someone was pulling her back. Samiya was dropping to her knees by Edei's side. Chimdi was holding a hand over her mouth looking at all the dead bodies. A few gang members Io didn't recognize were clamoring around Bianca.

Io took a step back, then another. No one noticed when she disappeared into the night.

She had to make a tourniquet from a torn strip of her pants to stop the blood flow on her thigh. Pain electrified her with every step, but she would be fine. She had to keep going. Stop by Amos's first, for bandages and supplies, then find a way out before the police closed every entry gate in Alante.

The smog had settled over the city like a squatter, walkways and bridges disappearing halfway across. Music was drifting up from the direction of the Plaza, sirens wailing somewhere in the distance.

Minutes ticked by. She made slow progress: she had to switch between the real world and the Quilt every few seconds, to make sure she didn't step right off a bridge to the smoky abyss below. She would stop and check the fate-thread—still there. Stop and check Ava's thread—vibrating from a northern direction, likely headed for the north gate out of Alante, pursued by Saint-Yves and his police force.

Io halted. On the edge of the roof stood a thin strip of metal. A cat bridge, just what she needed right now.

"Scared, are we?" said a voice from behind her.

A lithe figure appeared through the smog, wearing silken pajamas, a severed life-thread trailing behind her. Bianca Rossi came to a stop a few feet away, eyeing Io up and down, feline stare settling on her clenched fist.

Bianca nodded at it. "What's in your hand?"

Io dragged herself out of the mouth of fear, pulled herself through the fangs of panic. Bianca thought she could intimidate her. But Io had uncovered the genocide of the Furies. She had solved the murders of four victims and three wraiths, the assassination of the Nine, she had let her sisters escape and left Edei behind, bleeding—all so that she could follow this thread and bring justice for these women. Bianca could terrorize her all she liked—Io refused to be cowed.

She looked at the thread between her fingers. It was silver, yes, but now that she could study it, Io thought she could discern gold among the silver. Strings as warm and bright as the sun, woven with those cold and sharp as the moon: the god's and her sister's.

"I believe," Io said coolly, "that it's your maker's thread. I believe it leads to the gods."

"There are crimes," Bianca said, "that cannot go unpunished."

Io restrained the urge to roll her eyes. *Furies.* "What do you want, Bianca?"

Already, the mob queen had secured her severed life-thread, her fury-born's whip, on her hip, like it had always been a part of her. Leisurely, she answered, "When I found Ava and she realized I was threadless, do you know what she told me?"

Io pressed her lips together. No, she didn't know. She felt like she didn't know her sister at all anymore.

"*Stick with Io*, she said. *She looks after wounded things*, she said." Bianca's chest rose and fell with easy breaths. "But I don't want your comfort, cutter. I want *my vengeance*. Can you give me that?"

Io thought of her in the indigo greenhouse, her eyes ablaze with the orange of wrath. None of the other wraiths had reflected orange in their eyes, the true show of a fury-born's powers. None of them had been keres-born and held on to those powers as well. Whatever Bianca Rossi had become, it was something new, something strange—perhaps something savable—but most of all, it was a weapon, whetted and slicked with poison.

The smog pressed close around them, curling around their ankles like a clingy pet. Bianca stood in the center of the roof, proud and rigid. The god's thread shone a path across the narrow plank, leading to an unseen future. And Io stood before the cat bridge, her heart racing.

"I'll make you a deal," Io said steadily. "Help me find the gods, and I will help you punish them. How does that sound?"

In a flurry of silk, Bianca stepped around Io and onto the bridge. Io gazed at the cat bridge stretching like a lifeline before her. On its other end, the god's thread was swallowed by the smog. She breathed out and took the first step.

"Come on, then," the mob queen said. "Let's bring down the gods."

# ACKNOWLEDGMENTS

It is a monumental, awe-inspiring thing to write your first acknowledgments for your debut book. It's sixteen years of writing, eight years of querying, two years of editing—how can I possibly bottle all these years of support and love down to a couple of pages?

Amanda Joy, you truly are the Great: greatest friend, greatest critique partner, greatest angst advocate. I wouldn't be the writer I am today without you. Anna Meriano and Laura Silverman, your support is felt keenly and deeply every day—long live Words and Thai. I can't wait for our next adventure together.

My deepest gratitude to Michaela Whatnall, my brilliant agent, my very own Fabergé egg. You feedback and support have been invaluable; without you I wouldn't be here today, writing this. Many thanks to Amy Elizabeth Bishop for her precious early feedback and for being our perfect matchmaker; to the amazing Lauren Abramo, Michael Bourret, Gracie Freeman Lifschutz, Andrew Dugan, and Nataly Grueder; and to my film agent, Stephen Moore.

Gretchen Durning, it has truly been a joy working with you. This book is so much stronger— and swoonier—because of you. I can't wait for our next journey, tackling its wild sequel into shape! A huge thank-you to my entire team at Razorbill and PenguinTeen: Misha Kydd, Krista Ahlberg, Brian Luster, Jayne Ziemba, Alex Campbell, Rebecca Aidlin, Lizzie Goodell, Christina Colangelo, Bri Lockhart, Felicity Vallence, Shannon Span, James Akinaka, and Kim Ryan. I'm ever in awe of Corey Brickley and Kristie Radwilowicz; thank you for gifting me such a jaw-dropping cover.

To my UK team at Penguin Random House UK: thank you for your warm welcome and enthusiasm, starting with my wonderful editor, Natalie Doherty, the excellent Michael Bedo and Chloe Parkinson, Bella Jones, Jamie Taylor, Alicia Ingram, Kat Baker, Toni Budden, Becki Wells, Rozzie Todd, Autumn Evans, Amy Wilkerson, Aimee Coghill, and Nekane Galdos.

To Marzena Currie, Amy Gordon, Kaye Baginsky, Lauren Vassallo, and Elena Pataki: your early enthusiasm for this story means the world to me. To my agent siblings and debut group friends: I am humbled to be by your side in this wild, publishing ride. To the lovely authors who blurbed *Threads*—I feel dumbfounded that my book will stand alongside yours in bookstores and libraries; thank you. To the early readers and reviewers: your messages and support are greatly cherished.

To Maria Foutzitzi: φίλη, thank you so much for being Io's first reader and for our silent summer hangouts, with our books and the sea at our feet. To my friends: you made one of the most stressful years of my life seem like a breeze; I'm forever thankful.

George, μπου, I wrote the first words of this story while we sat side by side on our old sofa. I edited it while you made dinner and three different kinds of dessert. You were in the other room when I chatted with my would-be agent for the first time. You were squealing with me right there on the dirty Central Line train when I got the offer email from my editor. You're an inextricable part of this journey; thank you for your love, your support, your humor, your inspiration, and your tiramisu. I'm so profoundly grateful to share my life with you.

To my wonderful family: Mom; Dad; Nikos; Argyris; Eleni; Alex; Eleftheria T.; Eleftheria V.; my amazing grandparents and my late grandpa Tasos; Sakis and Eirini, my very first allies; my Athenian family; my fantastic in-laws—I cannot adequately express my gratitude. I told you all I wanted to be a writer at age fifteen. I remember the scene very clearly. It was summer at the beach; the last book of my favorite series had come out and I was reading an interview by the author where she described how she spent her days: creating worlds for other people. You came out of the water and sat down next to me. I lowered the newspaper and told you this was what I wanted to do with my life: create worlds; become a writer. There was a short moment, a pause, where you probably considered all the rational reasons and the hard truths of life that could crush this dream in a second, but when you spoke, you only said: *All right, then. Let's figure out how we can help you become a writer.*

Mom, Dad, Argyri, look: I want to say *I did it*, but that wouldn't be true. These acknowledgments are proof of that. *We* did it. Thank you, thank you, thank you.